CAR WASH BLUES

A MAD MICK MURPHY MYSTERY

CAR WASH BLUES

MICHAEL HASKINS

FIVE STAR
A part of Gale, Cengage Learning

GALE
CENGAGE Learning·

Detroit • New York • San Francisco • New Haven, Conn • Waterville, Maine • London

GALE
CENGAGE Learning

LIBRARY OF CONGRESS CATALOGING-IN-PUBLICATION DATA

Haskins, Michael.
    Car wash blues : a Mick Murphy Key West mystery / Michael Haskins. — 1st ed.
       p. cm.
    ISBN 978-1-4328-2580-5 (hardcover) — ISBN 1-4328-2580-1 (hardcover) 1. Murder—Investigation—Fiction. 2. Drug dealers—Key West (Fla.)—Fiction. 3. Hurricane Frederic, 1979—Fiction. I. Title.
PS3608.A84C37 2012
813'.6—dc23   2012013197

First Edition. First Printing: August 2012
Published in conjunction with Tekno Books and Ed Gorman
Find us on Facebook–https://www.facebook.com/FiveStarCengage
Visit our Web site–http://www.gale.cengage.com/fivestar/
Contact Five Star™ Publishing at FiveStar@cengage.com

Printed in Mexico
1 2 3 4 5 6 7 16 15 14 13 12

DEDICATION

This book is for Seanan and Chela, Shane H., Seanise, Arianna, Alexa, Shane P., Patty, Howard, Alexis, Coco Joe, Celine and Alex—these are the most important people in my life.

Music has always played a role in my life. How a kid from Boston who can't carry a tune or play a musical instrument grew up liking country music has to do with good lyrics being poetry; lyrics are a novel cut down to its bare essentials. I believe that. Listen to Kristofferson, Waylon, Jerry Jeff, Hank Jr. and early Bob Dylan, and if your mind doesn't fill in the background of the song, you are not listening. Their lyrics have been there for me in the good times and bad and I owe them thanks for that.

ACKNOWLEDGMENTS

Thanks to the following for their help and support in my writing *Car Wash Blues:*

Jim Linder for his tireless efforts in helping me understand weapons and the difference between those that use them for violence and those that use them against violence; Jim's background knowledge of the drug cartels was priceless in my research. The men and women of the Key West Fire and Police departments for their willingness to answer my many questions, often taking their personal time to help me understand, especially Crime Scene Investigator Don Guevremont. The residents of Key West should be proud of these altruistic men and women. Bob Pearce for continuing to stand by me as a friend when it comes to living and sailing and for explaining the ins-and-outs of the sailing life; without him I'd be a landlubber. Bill Lane for his advertising expertise, and sharing it with me at lunch and a little more often with drinks and cigars; Shirrel Rhoads for his advice, criticism and support, which proved helpful.

Los Angeles Times reporters Ken Ellingwood, Tracy Wilkinson, Richard Morsoi (editor), and Sam Quinones, photographer Don Bartletti, and so many other staff reporters for the "Crisis in Mexico" series who have risked their lives to give us the truth; Mexico, it should be noted, is more dangerous for working journalists than the Middle East. And the editors of the *LA*

Acknowledgments

Times for continuing the delivery of what journalism used to be about.

I thank Roz and Marty at Tekno, as well as Tiffany and the gang at Five Star for publishing my three novels. Of course, the fine editing of Diane Piron-Gelman helped it all come together, and she never once asked how I could spell so many words wrong with a spell checker available.

CHAPTER 1

No good deed goes unpunished, the cliché says, and I am living proof of it.

My good deed was taking Tita Toledo's SUV to the car wash Friday afternoon because I had borrowed it to pick up a sail in Miami for my boat, *Fenian Bastard*. Little did I know when I slid my credit card into the computerized slot and chose the expensive, full-service wash that I would be the cause of unleashing unimaginable violence on the tranquil island of Key West.

A white Escalade waited ahead of me in the narrow building, getting its prewash soaking, when I pulled up to the entrance. I watched the robotic machinery move over the vehicle, wetting it in preparation for the next pass that would bring foamy soapsuds. The mechanized arms returned to the front of the vehicle and then moved again toward the rear, slowly squirting soap, covering the Escalade with suds.

Out by the gas pumps at the car wash exit, a black four-door SUV stopped and two men got out. They caught my eye when they walked into the narrow car wash holding Uzi pistols. You can hide the nine-millimeter pistol under a shirt, but in your hand the long, thirty-two-round magazine is an attention-grabber. While the car wash apparatus soaped the back of the Escalade, both men shot into its windshield, splintering the glass with spider-webbed holes. The noise from the automated machinery suppressed the Uzis' reports.

The Escalade's windows were tinted dark, so I had no way of knowing how many victims were inside. The machinery moved toward the front of the vehicle still spitting soap, and the sudsy white foam coated both shooters. They walked unconcerned to the sides of the vehicle, changed magazines and continued shooting.

I couldn't back up because of the car behind me. And that driver couldn't see into the car wash, so he wasn't panicking and trying to escape. I reached into the glove compartment and grabbed my Glock 26.

A small wall separated the car wash driveway from a side street. I opened the door and hoped to make it over the wall without being shot. I stepped out, and the shooter on the driver's side of the Escalade looked in my direction and yelled. The machinery's noise made it impossible for me to hear if he was yelling at the second shooter or at me.

I didn't really care; I wanted to get over the wall. I waved my hand, hoping the driver behind me would see the gun and realize something was wrong. The first shooter, covered in white suds like a small version of the marshmallow man in the original *Ghostbusters* movie, turned toward me and raised his Uzi.

The window on the door of Tita's SUV shattered. I pushed against the car wash wall to steady myself and shot back. The shooter fell against the Escalade, dropped the Uzi and slid down to the wet floor. The second gunman opened the Escalade's passenger door and shot some more. Then he backed out of the narrow space, shooting wildly toward me, his shots cracking Tita's windshield as the machinery began its wash cycle with long strips of absorbent material swaying over the vehicle, spreading the soap.

The black SUV started to move out. The second shooter jumped into the back seat. No one bothered to check on the man I had shot.

The rinse cycle washed the first shooter clean. I walked forward cautiously, not knowing his condition. When I approached, I saw that he was a Central American Indian. Years ago I was an active journalist covering the wars in Central America and had met many of these men. They were the descendants of the Aztec and Mayan people of that region, and fierce warriors. Most I had met were short, with raven-black hair, a hawk nose, eyes as black as coal and skin long ago burned a reddish clay color, just like the man I had shot.

I kicked the Uzi away and felt for a pulse in his neck. I knew there wouldn't be one because of the two holes in his chest. The car wash rinse had washed the blood and suds away so the man looked into oblivion with his hard black eyes, clean as he would ever be. Calloused hands seemed to push on the wet ground as if he were trying to stand.

I stared into the Escalade's shattered side window and saw a large Latin male lying across the bloody seat. There was no one else.

When I got back outside, the car that had been behind me was gone. I put the Glock back in Tita's SUV and called my friend Richard Dowley, the chief of police. "You ain't gonna believe this, Richard," I said, and heard him sigh.

I am Liam Murphy, and I picked up the moniker "Mad Mick Murphy" because of my Irish heritage and the crazy stunts I pulled at college in Boston. Today I am a semi-retired journalist living and sailing in Key West, Florida, and this was the beginning of my nightmare.

CHAPTER 2

The Key West police and fire stations are a block south of the car wash on North Roosevelt Boulevard, so it didn't take Richard long to lead a parade of cop cars, vans and two fire engines to where I waited, with sirens screeching and lights flashing. The ambulance garage is located two blocks in the other direction and an ambulance arrived as the vehicles filled the parking lot of the self-service gas station that housed the car wash.

The fire department is often the first responder to events in Key West and many of the firefighters are paramedics, but they were not necessary at the car wash.

Tita's SUV was a crime scene now, making it necessary for me to find another way to pick her up at the airport the next afternoon. Sherlock Corcoran, the crime scene investigator, led a small army of cops as they searched the car wash's wet pavement on their hands and knees for spent shells while others tried to locate bullet fragments inside the victim's vehicle and Tita's SUV. The recycled-water system may have sucked up shell casings and other evidence, so it would have to be dismantled, and that didn't make the proprietor happy. He would also have to turn over video surveillance tapes from the gas pumps. Sherlock bitched because the recycled-water system had also cleaned away blood evidence.

Detective Luis Morales, a macho Cuban with movie-star good looks, headed up the investigative team. Chief Richard Dowley sat on the low back wall with me as I told Luis what happened. Sherlock had already bagged my Glock.

"You don't know the shooter or the vic?" Luis asked, probably for the tenth time.

"Didn't know them when you got here, Luis, and I still don't know them."

Luis had rafted here from Cuba with his family when he was a child and has never returned to visit, though he has family there. His cousin Jorge Torres is a Havana police detective that I met on a trip to the forbidden island two years ago. We talked about it when I returned and I gave Luis a note from his cousin. He read the note and made it clear we would never discuss the topic again. He takes a lot of pleasure in helping Immigration and Custom Enforcement hassle boaters returning from Cuba. I am one of those sailors and we don't get along too well.

"And you had your Glock with you because . . ." His dark brown eyes stared as if they wanted to burn a hole in me while he waited for my reply with his bogus movie-star smile. He scratched above his ear, brushing at the gray hair beginning to appear at his temples.

"I have a concealed weapons permit," I said, knowing it wasn't what he wanted to hear.

"Half the people in the state have that permit, but I've never known you to carry." He continued to smile with a cold stare. "Why today?"

I turned to Richard, who shrugged his shoulders but said nothing. Richard is a big man, six-four, close to two hundred pounds, with a military haircut and hard gray-green eyes. He's in his mid-fifties and would rather be on the golf course than at a crime scene.

"Bob Lynds and I just came back from Miami." I knew it wouldn't satisfy him. "I picked up a sail for my boat and I don't go to the mainland without protection."

"You should buy a lotto ticket, Mick, it's your lucky day."

Luis' sarcasm was wasted on me. "There was no escaping this if you couldn't have defended yourself." He pointed toward the interior of the car wash and I knew he meant that it might have been me lying all wet and dead on the floor. "He has no identification, nothing in his pockets, but the vic did. We're checking him out."

"My guess is the shooter's Mexican or maybe Guatemalan."

That comment got his attention. "Why do you say that?" He turned pages in his notebook, searching for something he'd written earlier.

"The Central American Indians are tough, hard workers and loyal," I said. "And most of them are honest, but a few work for Mexican gangsters."

Luis turned his attention to Richard, looking for some response, before he came back to me. "And you know this how?"

Richard smiled but said nothing.

"Fifteen, twenty years ago I spent a lot of time in Central America." We had never discussed my past, but I knew Luis had checked into my background after our first encounter and that was before ICE was ICE. "I ran into some of these men working for the cartels as mercenaries. They were lethal."

"And you think the shooter is a descendant of the Mayans this far from Mexico, or are you profiling?" More of his wasted sarcasm.

I had called them Indians. His choice of words told me he knew more about the dead shooter than I probably did and he enjoyed wasting my time.

"Do you need me to come to the station?" I asked Richard as I checked my wristwatch. It was six and the late-afternoon sun reflected off the water at Garrison Bight across the boulevard. A soft breeze blew the pungent scent of low-tide saltwater, seaweed and fish across from Charter Boat Row where the crews were cleaning the day's catch for their paying customers. Traffic hummed along the boulevard, carrying tourists and locals in and out of Old Town, while the police and ambulance crew waited for the medical examiner.

"Are you done for now?" Richard stood and pushed his sunglasses higher on his broad nose.

Luis nodded and put his notebook away. "I'll need you to come in and sign a statement tomorrow. I should have some footage from the security cameras for you to look at, too." He walked away without waiting for an answer.

The police had to wait for the medical examiner to come from Grassy Key and that could take an hour or more before the bodies would be examined and removed.

"Don't say it." Richard raised his hands, palms out to stop me from complaining. "He's a good cop."

"Who'd pin this on me if he could see a way to do it."

"I don't believe that." He smiled. "Meet me at Harpoon Harry's for breakfast tomorrow and maybe I can save you a trip to the station."

"Eight?"

"Yeah. You going to the marina or do you need a ride somewhere?"

The *Fenian Bastard* was slipped across the street at the city marina.

"I'll walk. Any idea when I can get Tita's SUV or my Glock?"

"You think you need the Glock?" His tone carried suspicion in it.

Richard knew me well and had to be considering that I might know more than I'd admitted to Luis. Any other time, he'd probably have been right.

I smiled. "No. This was my being at the wrong place at the wrong time."

"Miami," he moaned. "The shooter is probably halfway back there."

"Better than him sticking around here. See you in the morning." I walked out the back of the car wash and crossed the boulevard toward the marina, having no idea about the violence that had been set in motion.

Chapter 3

Harpoon Harry's is on Caroline Street, a parking lot away from the city docks of Key West Harbor and an upscale, private marina. The popular eatery serves good portions of tasty food at reasonable prices and is a local favorite. Richard and I ate there regularly, though not necessarily together.

Richard sat at the end booth, his back to the wall with his *café con leche,* a mixture of espresso and steamed milk with sugar, and a copy of the *Key West Citizen* spread out on the table. I pushed past those waiting for a seat and sat down across from him.

Ron Leonard, the owner, brought my *con leche.* "You guys want your regular order?"

"Please, Ron," I said and Richard nodded as he finished reading.

"Thank you." Ron wrote the order as he walked away.

I tasted my *con leche* and added one more sugar. "Something interesting?"

Richard slid a manila envelope toward me as he folded the newspaper. "An editorial on what the city commission needs to do this hurricane season." He fixed his glasses on his nose and put the newspaper on the seat. "I'd like to see some of the editors stick around during a hurricane. Maybe help out with the aftermath and then let 'em write the damn editorial."

"You guys tell us to evacuate," I reminded him, "so don't criticize those that listen." I smiled as I took another sip of coffee, knowing most locals didn't evacuate.

The current hurricane season had been busy, with five named storms crossing the Atlantic already and the sixth, Hurricane Fred, approaching the Bahamas. Most locals in the Keys kept their TVs tuned to the Weather Channel, tracking the storm's movement and watching it grow in intensity. As Fred got closer, many would stop by the Grotto at St. Mary Star of the Sea and whisper a silent prayer that Key West would be spared a direct hit. So far the prayers seemed to be working, since four of the hurricanes tracked up the center of the Atlantic had died and one had hit the Carolina coast as a Category Two storm.

Sister Louis Gabriel had the Grotto built after the 1921 hurricane devastated Key West. "As long as the grotto stands, Key West will never again experience the full brunt of a hurricane," she is quoted as saying at its dedication on May 25, 1922. She is often misquoted as saying "devastating hurricane" in her talk, but it doesn't matter to the locals who believe in the power of the Grotto and whisper their silent prayers as they drive by the church when hurricanes approach the island. And that includes the atheists. This season the Florida Keys had escaped even a tropical storm, but with Fred the Lower Keys remained in the tracking cone.

I opened the envelope and pulled out a typed copy of the statement I had given to Detective Morales yesterday. Another loose sheet of paper came with it.

"No ID on the shooter." Richard sipped his coffee. "The vic is a Reynoldo Gilberto Santos from Miami."

"Big surprise there." I read the few lines on the loose sheet. It named Reynoldo's CPA firm, his address and his business partner's basic information. "Nothing here is familiar," I said and signed the written statement without reading it. "This is good?" I held up Luis' typed statement.

Richard pulled it from my hand. "Luis wrote it, so I am sure it's accurate."

Ron brought our breakfasts. Richard had a Denver omelet with a side of bacon and rye toast. I had two eggs over easy, home fries and wheat toast. Richard watched and shook his head in disapproval as I added salt, hot sauce and catsup to the food on my plate.

"The vic's name or his partner, this Feliciano, they don't ring any bells?" Richard handed me back my signed statement.

"Nothing, unless he's José Feliciano the flamenco guitar player." I scanned the two-page, single-spaced document I had signed.

"You know José Feliciano?" Richard began eating.

"Saw him on TV a few times." I handed back the document, mixed my eggs and home fries and began to eat. "Like I said yesterday, I was at the wrong place at the wrong time. I've got no dog in this fight."

"That's good to know." He raised his empty cup as Ron walked by.

"When can I get my Glock?" I ran a piece of toast through the egg yolk on my plate and ate it.

"You need it because you're going back to the mainland?" Richard stared at me as Ron brought him a new *con leche*.

"Nope, I just don't want you guys to lose it."

"Thanks for the confidence," he mumbled. "Sherlock took it to FDLE for testing, so maybe tomorrow or the next day."

FDLE, Florida Department of Law Enforcement, is the state's version of the FBI. Its technology far exceeds anything small Florida communities like Key West could ever afford, so it often assists local law enforcement in serious crime investigations. Murder in Key West is about as serious as it gets. Fortunately, violent deaths on the island are few and far between. We may only be a three-hour ride from Miami and South Florida, but Key West is a million miles away from the crime that plagues many Florida cities.

I finished my breakfast, not realizing that Key West was about to see the beginning of a horrific crime spree that would make hardened Miami cops cringe.

"Thanks for bringing the statement for me to sign." I left money on the table for the bill, my thank you to Richard as we got up to leave.

"If Luis has more questions, you still need to come in," he said. "He may want you to view the surveillance videos."

"Yeah," I answered without enthusiasm. "He can count on me."

Traffic moved slowly along Caroline Street. It had to be locals driving because we don't rush anywhere. The late-morning sun beat down from a blue sky and the temperature was in the 80s, with promises to go higher. September was off-season due to the heat and being peak hurricane season for the Keys but compared to mainland Florida, Key West had little humidity. The island is not a swamp like most of the state; Key West borders the Atlantic and Gulf of Mexico and more often than not has a daily breeze that keeps the humidity bearable even in the summer.

The parking-metered spots along Caroline were mostly empty and the city parking lot across from the restaurant had less than a dozen vehicles in it.

"What time does Tita get in?" Richard's glasses turned dark as soon as we stepped outside.

"Six o'clock." My glasses were supposed to go dark in the sun, too. "You'll have to deal with her about the car." I turned to see my reflection in the door window. My glasses were gradually getting darker.

"Hopefully she'll have it back on Monday." He looked around the street, checking those that walked by just like a cop. "Have her call me Monday morning."

I laughed. "I think she'll do that without my having to make her. Me, I'm the one that's gotta tell her it's been shot up." I was griping because she loved that SUV. "Where are you parked?"

He pointed toward the city parking lot. "You?"

"I rode my bike." I walked to the bike rack and bent down to unlock the chain on my bicycle when a long burst of gunfire exploded in the quiet morning, mixed with the sound of shattering glass. I fell to the ground. When I looked up, I saw a black SUV speeding away.

Richard sat against the restaurant wall, bleeding from his left shoulder. The French doors in the front of the restaurant had shattered from the gunshots and people inside had fallen to the floor or were trying to push their way out the side entrance. I ran to Richard, looking back over my shoulder, then pulled my cell open and punched 911.

"Where the hell did that come from?" Richard moaned as he reached out his right hand for me to help him up. He took a handkerchief from his back pocket and pressed it against his shoulder wound. Then he turned and walked slowly through the glass-door rubble back into the restaurant. Two people who had been paying their bill lay on the floor, amid shards from the glass display case. Liquor from broken bottles that had been on sale behind the register covered the floor, mixed with blood and panic.

CHAPTER 4

Richard ignored the panic in the room as people picked themselves up off the floor where they had ducked when the shooting started and rushed through the side exit. He knelt slowly to check the couple bleeding by the checkout register and shook his head with an angry expression ironed on his face when he couldn't find a pulse in either of them. He reached out and I helped him up. Broken dishes, food scraps and remnants of window glass that sparkled liked diamonds were scattered across the floor.

"You need to have that looked at," I said as we heard the first sirens. Outside, people began to gather on the side street, gawking at the scene.

"Let's see if anyone else is hurt." He ignored my concern and walked to the center of the empty restaurant as blood trickled down his arm.

A man in a gaudy Hawaiian shirt and pressed shorts stood over a woman wearing a colorful summer dress at the booth closest to the front window; her head rested on the table while he spoke calmly and stroked her auburn hair, removing pieces of glass from it. Blood and dishes with half-eaten food covered most of the table. Richard found a pulse in the woman's neck.

"Get a paramedic to her," he ordered and I assumed it was meant for me since the man was obviously in shock and unaware of us. Summer tourists.

The other booths were empty, half-eaten eggs and grits and

toast and unfinished cups of coffee spilled across the tabletops. Ron Leonard came out from the kitchen, his thin face expressionless. He stared at the disaster but said nothing understandable. He sat on a stool at the counter and mumbled to himself.

Richard leaned against another stool and nodded to Ron. "He was no marksman, he was shooting wild." Richard seemed to be thinking aloud and I figured it kept him from being concerned with his own condition. "Why?" He looked coldly at me. "Were you the target?" He turned and looked at the two bodies on the floor. "Or were they?"

We had both seen the black SUV and assumed it was the shooter from the car wash.

"Richard, I have no connection to the bodies at the car wash."

"Unless we can connect those two to the shooter," he looked at the bodies, "my guess is he thinks you can I.D. him." He tried to repress a moan but the pain showed on his face. "Why would he think that if you didn't know him?" He closed his eyes. "This can't be two different shooters."

"Over here," I yelled as Harry Sawyer, a firefighter-paramedic, came into the room.

He looked at the two bodies on the floor, then saw Richard and came to him.

"Not me," Richard yelled and pointed at the table, "the woman."

Craig Fraga, another firefighter-paramedic, came in and checked the two bodies, found no pulse and joined Harry, shaking his head as he passed Richard.

Two police cars stopped out front, their lights flashing. The officers ran in, saw their chief and stopped. An ambulance parked in the middle of the street; the man and woman that got out had been leaving the restaurant earlier when I had arrived. One of the police officers tried to find a pulse on the dead couple, stepping around the puddle of blood.

The paramedics from the ambulance rushed in carrying their medical bags. One checked the two bodies on the floor, moving the cop out of the way, while the other took over the care of the injured woman. The man with her muttered to himself as the medical team prepared to put her on a gurney. Harry Sawyer came to Richard, cut away his bloody sleeve and applied bandages. Satisfied the couple on the floor were dead, the other paramedic went to the table with the injured woman.

"You need to go to the hospital, Chief," Harry said, applying pressure to Richard's wound.

He grunted in pain. "Jesus, don't say that in front of Murphy. Now the asshole will think he's a doctor."

"Why's that?" Harry added another bandage in an attempt to slow the bleeding.

"He told me it needed to be looked at," Richard sighed, gritting his teeth.

Harry laughed. "Lucky guess. But he's right."

"What the hell happened, Chief?" Detective Luis Morales came out of nowhere and walked up next to Harry.

"Hell if I know." From where he sat on the stool, Richard looked at the destroyed front windows. "I came in for breakfast."

A second ambulance parked in the street and two paramedics ran into the restaurant. A cop waved them off the two bodies and pointed toward Richard. I recognized one of the paramedics as she headed over: a small woman, all of five-foot-four and involved with so many community events on the island that most everyone knew her. They called her Bunny; I doubt anyone knew why or what her real name was. She was cute in a pixie way with shoulder-length brown hair and pale blue eyes.

"Morning, Chief," Bunny said with a smile, holding her medical bag.

"Maybe it is for you, Bunny."

"He needs to take a ride," Harry said.

"You want a gurney?" Bunny knew Richard would argue.

"Give me a minute and I'll go with you," he said, surprising me. "Luis, the shooter was in a black SUV. I couldn't read the plate."

Bunny checked the bandage Harry had applied to Richard's shoulder.

"The guy from yesterday." Luis finished Richard's sentence.

"Be my guess," he winced, and both Richard and Luis looked at me. "Have Sherlock check the shell casings with those from the car wash." He pointed to the bodies on the floor. "And I.D. these two and see if there's any connection with Santos."

The first group of paramedics rolled the injured woman out and a cop helped her companion to the ambulance. One of the paramedics shook his head as he passed Richard.

"Jesus, help us." Richard placed his large hand on my shoulder. "Walk out with me." He stood carefully and we walked slowly out of Harpoon Harry's with his arm draped over me.

Bunny was right behind us. "My siren is better than yours," she said.

"Bunny, everything of yours is better than mine," Richard said between deep breaths and got into the ambulance. "Pick me up at the hospital, Mick."

The ambulance sped off, its siren wailing. I hadn't even heard the first ambulance leave.

"What are you into?" Luis said from beside me. His tone demanded an answer.

"I don't know what's going on, Luis." We stood in the middle of Caroline Street surrounded by police cars and a crowd that continued to grow. "I have no connection to the bodies at the car wash or this."

"But the shooter came back to get you." He huffed out the words, frustration carved on his face. "Why?"

"I don't have an answer." I felt as frustrated as he looked.

"You need to check out the two victims inside, see if they are connected to the Miami group. You can't focus on me."

"Get in," he ordered and opened the door to his unmarked police car.

CHAPTER 5

Luis surprised me and drove to the hospital on Stock Island. I thought we were going to the police station, but he drove past that and as we rode over Cow Key Channel Bridge I thought we were going to the jail.

It's a short drive off the main island to the jail and the local hospital, both on College Road. For most of the ride Luis remained quiet, his hands tightly holding the steering wheel. I suppose he would rather have had them around my throat. When he parked outside the emergency room, he turned to me.

"The Chief believes you," he said quietly. "I wanted to, but this shooting is too coincidental and now bystanders are dying." There was no Hollywood smile. He was angry about the shooting or at me or both. I wasn't sure. "I will find out what's going on, Mick, and if you're involved I'll crucify you." He opened the door and we got out. "You understand?" he said, looking over the car's roof at me. "Four people are murdered in less than twenty-four hours. Someone's gonna pay."

I followed him across the parking lot into the ER without saying a word. I had said all I could possibly think of to indicate the shooting had nothing to do with me, so I left him alone to stew in his own pot of anger. I understood it, but the longer he directed it toward me, the longer the perpetrator remained free.

He badged the first nurse he met and we were escorted into the ER. I've spent too much time in the white, sterile area with its small, curtained-off rooms and busy staff. Richard sat on a gurney hooked up to a heart-and-blood-pressure monitor and an IV, while a doctor attended his wound.

"My ride is here, doc," Richard said cheerfully.

There must have been some really good drugs in the IV.

"Leave the meter running, Chief," the young doctor said, "you're not getting out of here for awhile yet."

Richard laughed. "The Bobbsey Twins. You come together?"

"I need your car keys, Chief," Luis said, ignoring Richard's silliness.

"Murphy's gonna drive me home." He couldn't lose the cheerfulness or the smile. "Right, Mick?"

"He drove with me, so I'll have an officer drop your car off and then he can drive you home," Luis said quietly. He turned to me and whispered, "You take him home and not back to the station."

"Like he's going to listen to me."

"Just do it." Luis walked to Richard and took his keys. "You take it easy, Chief, and listen to the doctor."

"Sure," Richard said. "Doc, you know the Bobbsey Twins?"

"Never had the pleasure." He nodded to us and smiled. "He's going to be asleep shortly and I'd like to keep him for a few hours." He checked his wristwatch. "Come back around three."

Though Richard protested and threatened us, Luis and I walked out.

The ride back to Harpoon Harry's was as quiet as the ride to the hospital. Luis glanced at the police station as we rode by and I expected him to stop and leave me on my own, but he took me to the restaurant where police vehicles still blocked the street. The coroner's wagon was there, so the bodies hadn't been removed.

"Luis." It was my turn to say something as I got out of his car. "While you're trying to connect me to the shootings, the perps are getting away. And you know what? You don't know that the two victims aren't somehow connected and were the targets, and not me."

"There are people working on that." He closed the door and began to walk away. He stopped and turned to me. "My gut says you're involved."

I knew he was wrong. However, it turned out he was too damn right.

CHAPTER 6

I found Detective Donny Barroso with a couple of uniformed officers on the street and gave him the keys to Richard's car.

"Luis give you these?" He had seen Detective Morales and me together. He turned to look for his boss, but Luis was inside the restaurant.

"Yeah." I could tell from Donny's expression he wasn't happy with the responsibility. "I don't work for him, Donny. Give 'em back to him if you want."

"Shit, Mick, you know what that's going to be like?"

"You're not responsible for me, Donny."

"Try telling that to the Cuban dickhead," he joked, tossed the keys in the air and then caught them. "I'll ask him if I should maybe arrest you for trying to steal the Chief's car. That might make him happy."

"It will brighten his day. I'll be at Schooner's if you need to get me." I walked away.

"Have one for me," he yelled.

I raised my arm and waved it as my reply.

It's a two- or three-block walk from Harpoon Harry's to Schooner Wharf Bar, depending on if you cut through the city parking lot or walk on Caroline to William Street. The supermarket building with its mural took up most of the area behind the parking lot and the harbor. I walked down Caroline to William.

Schooner Wharf is a popular, funky seaside watering hole

made of gnarled wooden planks, open to the elements on three sides, and has a leaky tin roof that helps protect patrons from the rain and sun but little else. A P-rock patio fronts the covered stage and there are a few generously proportioned tables by the boardwalk shaded by thatched roofs, leaving smaller home-style picnic tables and chairs to fill up the rest of the open space. A small kitchen and restrooms are located across from the bar. It wasn't noon, but a cruise ship must have been in because most tables were occupied and many of the early-morning locals took refuge in the shadowy bar nursing their drinks.

I wanted a drink after the morning's shooting. The shootout at the car wash hadn't shaken me up because I knew I was just in the wrong place at the wrong time, but this morning's shooting was something else. I knew in my gut that the two dead people on the floor of the restaurant were not the intended victims, no matter how much I hoped they were.

As a journalist I've listened to my gut feelings and usually ended up with a good story. I thought about it on the ride to the hospital and back and couldn't see how I was connected to either shooting. I wasn't working on a story, I was vegetating in the tropics, yet I was growing concerned and that in itself worried me. A drink wasn't going to change my current concerns, but it wasn't going to make them worse, either.

Joshua Bonilla, a regular at the bar who always seemed to have money to spend and a fast boat or two, had an empty seat next to him. I sat down. "Josh, this seat taken?"

He looked up and smiled, showing stained, uneven teeth with a few missing on the bottom. His brown eyes were tired, and the usual cigarette dangled from his lips. "Saving it for you."

I ordered Josh another of whatever he was drinking—it looked like rum and Coke—and got a Kalik, a Bahamian beer, from Vickie the bartender.

"Thanks." He raised the new drink and clinked it against my

bottle. "I have been looking for you." He stared straight ahead. "You got a minute to talk?"

It wasn't like Josh to follow gossip, but I thought he wanted to know about the car wash shooting or what had just happened at Harpoon Harry's. The things I don't know could fill an arena.

"I've got a minute and then I need to run." I lied because I didn't want to be stuck with him.

He picked up both his drinks and moved to one of the small tables by the boardwalk and T-shirt booth, away from the crowded patio. It surprised me, but I followed him and sat down.

"What's up?" I squeezed a slice of lime into the neck of the Kalik and took a drink. It was cold and tasted too good for this early in the day. I realized how easy it would be to make it a morning ritual.

"You know Doug and Woodrow, right?" He looked over my shoulder and lit a new cigarette.

"Sure. I know Doug better than Woodrow."

Doug Bean was an old friend and the dockmaster at Conch Marina. We often sailed together. Woodrow Wentworth would not let anyone call him Woody because of a strip club in the Upper Keys and his belief that "Woody" was slang for an erection. He hung around the waterfront and worked as a boat mechanic when he needed money, which didn't seem to be too often.

None of these guys could be called clean-cut by any leap of the imagination, and anywhere else in the universe they'd stand out as suspicious, but not in Key West. Josh stood about five-eight, had long brown hair he wore in a ponytail and a few days' beard growth. He smoked too much, drank too much and wore shorts and T-shirts even in the winter months. His sneakers were threadbare. Doug was the oldest, maybe in his late sixties, yet he was on the go all the time. He'd climbed the mast on the

Fenian Bastard as if it had a stairway. He wore a hat to protect his thinning hair from the sun and his face was burned reddish-brown from his life on the water. He was also sane, which I couldn't say about Josh or Woodrow.

Woodrow smoked too much dope and drank too much, but he was a hell of an engine mechanic if you got him first thing in the morning when he'd only smoked his wake-up joint and drunk his first eye-opener beer. I have no tolerance for drugs, so I avoid him as much as I can on a two-by-four-mile island. He was just shy of six feet and dressed like Josh, but where Josh was quiet, Woodrow liked to hear himself talk. His sandy blond hair was long and often looked dirty.

"You hear about the oil executives staying on Harbor Key?" Josh drained his original drink without looking at me and exhaled smoke.

"Nope." I didn't want to get too deep into this conversation.

"You like the price of gas?"

"Nope."

"We got a plan." He looked up at me and smiled.

Doug I could see with a plan, but not Josh and Woodrow. "What is it?" I didn't want to ask, yet I knew he wouldn't let me go until I had heard him out.

His smile widened as he knocked the ash off the end of his cigarette. "We're gonna kidnap the fuckers."

CHAPTER 7

Josh's statement about kidnapping oil executives from their exclusive gathering didn't strike me as too unusual. With the booze and dope, Josh and Woodrow often schemed on outrageous ideas that were going to make them rich and famous, and by the second drink or toke they were off scheming on something else. You could say their memories, short or long term, and their follow-through on projects left a lot to be desired.

What did concern me was Josh's mention of Doug. I figured they'd run their idea by Doug while he was at the bar and he politely feigned interest. That's what I hoped.

"Kidnapping is a serious crime, Josh." I took a long pull on my beer. "Collecting the ransom is almost impossible without getting caught."

"Ah." He grinned and his drowsy eyes twinkled. "You see what the oil companies paid the Somali pirates?"

"Josh, that was for a tanker that costs millions and was full of crude oil." It surprised me that he knew about Somali pirates.

"What's more important—the ship and crude, or the heads of the companies?" He stared right at me as he spoke and his grin widened.

"Why are you telling me this?" I thought he'd ask me to join the plot, I'd refuse and be on my way. Wrong again.

"Doug said it's important that we get media coverage right

away. You can do that, right?" He took a drink waiting for my answer.

This kidnapping scheme was beginning to twist and turn in the wind and I wasn't sure where it was going.

"Josh, most kidnappers don't want news coverage." He was making me curious and curiosity is my catnip. "Why do you want it?"

"Will you do it?" He looked around suspiciously and moved in closer.

"Have you thought about the security these people have? Kidnapping and assassination are things they've thought about and prepared for." I kept my voice low because I didn't want some tourist overhearing us. I leaned in toward him. "Are you prepared to kill someone to do this?"

"That's the beauty of this, Mick." He leaned back, took a drink, lit a cigarette and laughed. "Doug has a guy in the kitchen who's gonna drug everyone and then we come in and take the two executives. No mess, no guns, no waking witnesses." His voice was rising.

I motioned him to lean forward again. "You think the security will be eating with them?"

"No, but they'll accept coffee and maybe a dessert." I'd never seen Josh smile like that. "Doug's thought this whole thing out." He stubbed out the cigarette in the ashtray.

Now I was getting concerned because he kept indicating the scheme was Doug's idea and Doug was sane, or so I had thought up until then.

"As unlikely as it is to work, let's say it does." I took a deep breath and a drink. "You're on a small island. How are you going to hide these guys without someone around here finding out where they are?" I wanted to add that too many people he knew on the island would turn in their own mother for the price of their next drink or half a kilo, but I didn't.

"They're not gonna be on the island." He sat back, finished his drink and lit another cigarette. "We're on a boat and heading into the Gulf."

"What about the ransom?"

"This isn't about us putting money in our pockets." He leaned back over the table. "This is about the fuckin' oil companies fuckin' the working stiffs of this country. This is about billion-dollar profits while the middle class shrinks and prepares to die. This is about . . ." He had lost his conspiratorial shyness and was in his bragging mode and talking too loudly.

"I get the point, Josh," I said to stop him. I was surprised he was able to express himself even though I figured the words were Doug's, and that worried me too. "Who gets the ransom if not you guys?"

"The beauty of this, Mick, I'm trying to tell you, is we don't get a ransom like kidnappers in the movies or like the fuckin' pirates." He inhaled deeply and crushed the stub of his cigarette in the ashtray. He lit another and moved in closer. "We make 'em lower the price of gasoline for everyone in the country and agree to keep their profits reasonable."

I doubted he had any idea of what reasonable was, especially on the price of gasoline or how the guarantee would work after the executives were released.

"Let me get us another round." He got up and walked to the bar.

I would have found all this humorous if it hadn't included Doug. I planned to walk to the marina and talk with him after the next beer. There was no way I could talk Josh out of this; he was delusional. I wanted to hear more so I could try to talk Doug out of it. I laughed to myself because I almost wished they were capable of pulling it off. Like most people who had to fill up a gas tank occasionally, it made me angry whenever the quarterly reports came out and the oil companies made billions off the shrinking working class.

"You keep strange company, Mick," Pauly Walworth said, and took the seat across from me.

"Pauly, nice to see you," I said as he sat down. "You know Josh?"

He smiled. "Better than you. I know him well enough to keep away. You gonna help with the kidnapping?"

"You know about it too?" I don't know why I was surprised. Most everyone at the bar would probably hear about it before happy hour and it wouldn't surprise me to hear Bill Becker or Bill Hoebee interviewing him on the radio Monday.

"Oh yeah," he sighed. "They wanted to use one of my boats."

"Why not one of Josh's boats?"

"Mine are better."

Pauly was another wharf rat, but he was quiet and professional in whatever business he had. Most everyone figured him for a smuggler. His shaggy strawberry-blond hair made him look younger than his fifty years. My red hair and beard were a lot darker than his and I was beginning to show a few gray hairs, but both our fair skins had burned copper long ago and any tourist would kill for the same. I have known him since moving to Key West and we even went on a few boat trips to the Dominican Republic and the Turks and Caicos Islands together.

"Jesus, you don't think they'll really try and do it, do you?" I finished my beer.

"Doug's idea," he reminded me, "and Doug's a follow-through guy. You tell me."

"I need to get a little more from Josh and then I'll talk to Doug."

"You and me, we could pull it off, but not Josh and Woodrow, not in a million years," he said. "Maybe we should talk to Doug together?"

"Pauly, I've got a lot on my plate right now."

"I'm only kidding, Mick," he said and got up as Josh came back with the drinks. "See me before you leave, I have something to show you."

"Don't disappear," I said as he lost himself in the crowd.

"Here." Josh put the drinks down and handed me a cigar. A new cigarette dangled from his lips. "So, can you get us press coverage?"

CHAPTER 8

The afternoon crowd of waterfront locals filled the four-sided bar, two deep in some places, as tourists clad in Key West T-shirts, shorts and sandals sat in the P-rock patio, drenched in sunlight and sweat, listening to the band while they drank cold beer and ate bar food, many trying to emulate the shabbily dressed locals' slang and attitude. They came in all ages and colors, sizes and shapes, and the more they drank, the more they schemed to move to Key West.

No one seemed concerned about Hurricane Fred and Monroe County hadn't issued hurricane advisories yet. The large flat-screen TV above the T-shirt shop aired the Weather Channel, but most ignored it. When the hurricane report came on, heads turned and watched.

Josh rehashed what he'd told me earlier and I promised I'd talk to Doug about a media blitz. I took my beer, excused myself as he lit a joint and found Pauly sitting by the magician's table on the other side of the bar.

"Scary," I said and sat down.

He smiled. "Anything Josh does is scary. Add Woodrow to the mix and it's frightening."

An orange tour trolley drove slowly down Lazy Way Lane, the narrow, one-way street behind Schooner Wharf Bar, and we were close enough to hear the conductor's magnified voice recite the history of the odd-looking watering hole to his passengers. Between the amplified live music, the thunderous chatter of drinkers and excited tourists strolling along the boardwalk, ambient noise forced us to sit close enough to knock heads while we spoke like conspirators.

Pauly excused himself and got us fresh beers from Vickie. He handed me a Kalik and motioned me to follow him, a cigarette dangling from his lips.

He stopped next to a green Mustang GT parked in the narrow spot next to the refrigerated trailer where the bar stored its beer kegs and spread his arms wide. "What do you think?" The cigarette fell as he spoke.

There were no Mustang ornaments on the hood, but I recognized the look. "Looks like someone's taken good care of it."

Pauly laughed. "You recognize it?" He placed his beer on the ground and walked around the car.

"Yeah, a late-sixties Mustang GT."

"Bullitt." His broad smile reminded me of a kid in a candy store, and any signs of the smuggler were hidden behind it. "The movie," he said to hasten me from my silence.

"Steve McQueen," I said.

"Yeah." He laughed. "This is one of five hundred replicas Ford Racing made."

I walked around the car. Except for the logo on the hubcaps, there was nothing to tell you what the car was. I recognized it, but I was sure there were some in the bar who wouldn't because of their age.

"Yours?" It wasn't really a question, but he answered.

"Oh, yeah. It's a replica of the '68 Mustang GT used in the movie," he said with pride. "With some improvements. The original Mustang would go zero-to-sixty in about seven seconds, this one will do it in four-point-eight."

"How fast will it go?"

"Speedometer reads 140." He smirked and opened the

driver's-side door. "But it'll do 165, according to the Internet. It's got a four-point-six liter, 315-horsepower engine." He sat inside, opened the passenger door and started the engine.

I can't tell you when I last saw the movie *Bullitt*, it had been years, yet when Pauly revved the engine the sound coming from the twin mufflers brought it all back. Well, not the whole movie, just the car chase in San Francisco. It's nine minutes where the actors don't speak because the action said it all, and it remains one of the all-time classics.

"How fast have you had it up to?" I left my beer on the ground and slid into the passenger seat.

"I've got it up to one hundred." He held the steering wheel with both hands.

"On the turnpike?" The car looked well cared for and had that new-car smell.

"Never been out of the Keys with it."

"Where'd you do a hundred?"

"Seven-Mile Bridge. Got to the top and there was no one in front of me and nothing headed toward me." He grinned. "Jesus, what a feelin'."

"I can only imagine." You need to remember I am a sailor and speed has nothing to do with it. It's all about mastering the wind and the sea, so people who have motorcycles to speed down US1, or classic Mustangs and other muscle cars, baffle me. I had to admit that this Mustang was a beauty. Speed was not something I was into. I am not in that much of a hurry because I know what waits at the end of the road. It waits for you and me and I ain't in any hurry to get there.

"Let's go for a ride." He closed the door.

"Can't." I looked at my wristwatch; it was almost time to pick up Tita at the airport. "I have to pick up Tita."

"What time?"

"She's on the four o'clock flight from Miami. You can drop

me at the marina; I need to get the Jeep."

At one-hundred-forty we'd get to Garrison Bight Marina before we left the bar, but I didn't say it.

"Shit, let's have another beer and I'll take you to pick her up." He shut the engine off and got out of the car. "I bet she'd like a ride in this."

"You don't have to do that." I got out of the car and picked up my beer. I hadn't seen Tita in almost a month and was looking forward to a quiet evening together.

"No problem, I'm glad to do it." He picked up his beer and walked back into the bar. "Does she know about her car?" I think he laughed, but by then he was in the bar and it was hard enough to hear yourself think in there.

Pauly got cold beers from Vickie and we took our seats at the magician's table. We clinked bottles as if in a toast—why, I don't know—and then I pushed the lime slice down.

"You know I don't pry into anyone's business." He moved closer so we could hear each other.

I didn't answer. He was probably going to ask about the car wash.

"What the hell happened this morning?" He took a long swallow of beer and lit a cigarette. "The Mexicans after you?"

"How'd you hear about this morning?" I was surprised because I didn't think anyone would be up to date on the shootings at Harpoon Harry's this early. Everyone would know something happened, but the police are tightlipped and the coconut telegraph takes a few hours to kick in.

"Friends in low places," he said. "Mick, having had dealings with some bad-ass Mexicans, I can tell you, you don't wanna fuck with 'em."

"Pauly, I haven't been to Mexico in almost fifteen years and don't know any Mexicans living in the Keys." I drank some beer. "I have no clue what's going on."

"We go back a long ways and I don't want to see you in a mess you can't get out of." His jokester's smile turned serious. "Mexican cartels make the Colombians look like pussies."

"I have friends in Tijuana and I know what's been happening."

"Jesus, TJ, they've been having gun battles down *Avenida Revolución* and around *el río*," he said, shaking his head. "It's turned into a ghost town."

"Yeah, I'm told I wouldn't recognize it any longer, no tourists and very little nightlife."

"We should get going," he said.

I left my unfinished beer on the table and followed him to the car, figuring his hurry was to get the Mustang on the road.

Pauly backed out slowly, avoiding tourists walking down Lazy Way Lane as if it were a sidewalk, scooters zooming between them like an old pinball game, and slow-moving cars. He turned left on Elizabeth Street and left again on Caroline Street, the street that singer-songwriter Jimmy Buffett made famous.

At the stop sign at Grinnell and Caroline, Pauly idled longer than necessary as he fooled with the rearview mirror. He turned right on Grinnell, stopped at the red light at Eaton and again toyed with the mirror. When the light turned green, he turned left and caught the light at White Street.

"Mick, you sleeping with someone's wife?" The A/C blew almost as cold as his question.

"What?"

"Two guys showed up at the bar while you were talking to Josh and they spent most of their time watching you," he said calmly. "They left when we did and now they're behind us."

"Don't tell me they're Latin."

"Okay, but when you see them you'll know anyway."

CHAPTER 9

Pauly kept the Mustang in third gear, its engine rumbling because its thirst wasn't being satisfied as we crossed White Street where Eaton turned into Palm Avenue. We stopped in traffic atop the Palm Avenue Bridge, with Garrison Bight city marina in front of us. The *Fenian Bastard* was in a slip to the left by the seawall and on the right side of the street were the fishing charters and party boats. The sky was bright blue with wisps of clouds slowly moving across it.

I wanted to turn and see what car was following us, but I knew better from my days in Mexico and Central America when my pal Norm Burke hung around with me because he was interested, as a government agent, in the same lowlifes and revolutionaries I was writing about. Norm and I never agree on much, yet we're honest with each other, even when we're lying, and that has resulted in our strange, long-term friendship.

"Still there?"

Is a question a question if you already know the answer?

"Two cars back." Pauly lit a cigarette, opened the windows and shut off the A/C. "Must be a rental."

"A Chrysler convertible?"

He laughed. "And the top's up."

"Pauly, don't go to the airport." I didn't see anything funny as I looked out over the tranquil bight and wished I were sailing with Tita and not where I was. "I don't need Tita involved in this."

Years ago in Tijuana, a group of us attempted to swindle a well-connected Mexican drug dealer out of millions with the idea he would follow us to California to get his money back, and once there the DEA could arrest him. I thought it would make a great story. The woman in my life, Melanie Florez, a CPA, was supposed to help from a distance; one thing led to another and she got too close. The dealer kidnapped Sully, an ex-cop and friend from Redondo Beach working with us, and we agreed to exchange the money for him. Hidden in the briefcase lining below layers of bills was a bomb ready to be set off when the case opened.

I opened the case and showed the money to the drug dealer's bodyguard, closed it, which set the bomb, and gave it to him. He took it and Sully was released from the car. None of us knew Mel was in the car, too. By the time Sully got close enough to let us know, the car had moved away. Within seconds it exploded, killing everyone inside.

I went mad at that precise moment.

Norm and my friend Alfonso Ruiz, a Mexican drug agent, helped me get back to Redondo Beach. Norm's concern and care brought a form of transitory sanity to my life and he sailed from L.A. to the Caribbean side of the Panama Canal with me. He left me there and a year later I sailed into Key West Harbor.

All these thoughts flashed through my mind as Pauly drove slowly because of the traffic and stopped at the light on North Roosevelt Boulevard. I couldn't let Tita get involved in this mess, especially since I wasn't sure what the mess was.

Pauly tossed his cigarette out the window. "What do you want to do?"

"I'm open to suggestions."

"We get on US1, we can outrun 'em." Pauly turned to me and smiled. "See how fast this baby can really go."

"All they have to do is wait at Cow Key Channel for us to return."

"But do they know that?" He turned left onto North Roosevelt. "Maybe they know Miami; they don't know the Keys. I think they're supposed to kidnap you, so they'll follow us."

"Why do you think that?" Things were getting strange.

"If it was a hit, they would've taken you out at the bar." He said it with little emotion, as if he was reading a baseball score.

Across the street, at the car wash where all this began less than twenty-four hours ago, a line of vehicles waited to be cleaned.

"I don't know what the hell's going on, Pauly," I sighed. "The shooting yesterday, Harpoon's this morning and now this. I don't see where I'm connected to any of it."

"No old debts in Mexico?" He drove along the crowded street, catching the light by the Winn-Dixie Plaza.

"Nothing," I lied, and wondered if someone from the cartel was trying to settle an old score for the briefcase bombing. From what Alfonso had told me, after the drug kingpin died, in-house fighting for control of the business had eliminated many of the old guard. So why now, after almost fifteen years, was someone out to get me?

Pauly moved into the left turn lane at the Triangle where US1 meets North and South Roosevelt Boulevards. He drove over Cow Key Channel Bridge.

"Do you have a plan?" We passed MacDonald Avenue, the main drag to Stock Island, and the last signal light until about twenty miles north at the Sugarloaf School and then we passed the blinking yellow light at Third Avenue.

"I think I can get far enough ahead to cut off at one of the communities along the way without being seen, maybe Bay Point because of the dip in the road, and they should continue north thinking they're following us." Pauly slowed down to light another cigarette. Warm air blew in from the opened windows. "Then we turn around and head back."

"That's a short-term solution," I said, lacking enthusiasm.

"We can kill 'em," he said seriously. "Mick, killing them is your only long-term solution. You know as well as I do, if the cartel is after you, you're in a shit-pot of trouble."

I closed my eyes. A hard, warm breeze blew through the window, and I could feel the Mustang pick up speed. This four-lane section of US1 had a speed limit of fifty-five mph; even with my eyes closed I knew we were breaking it.

"First things first, Pauly." I opened my eyes as we approached the Boca Chica Bridge. Sailboats and trawlers were slipped and anchored at the Navy's yacht basin on our right. The water was calm. "Let's lose them."

Pauly had the Mustang up to eighty when we drove off the bridge and sped past the exit for the Navy base. As we approached mile marker ten where the four-lane, fifty-five mph section of US1 turned into a two-lane forty-five mph road with businesses and homes to the left, Pauly slowed to sixty-five.

"They're staying two cars behind," he said without my having to ask about the tail. "When we get on Shark Key Bridge we'll take off." I could hear the excitement in his voice.

Traffic headed south toward Key West. The road north was open, so Pauly kept the Mustang at sixty-five. We passed the Shell station where Boca Chica Road met US1. Shark Key Estates was less than a quarter mile away on the left.

The blue-green waters of the Gulf of Mexico lay flat on our left and the deep blue waters of the Atlantic on the right hosted small and large mangrove islands. Pauly's foot hit the gas pedal hard and we were doing ninety a few seconds after getting on the bridge, the Mustang's engine purring. Hot air blew through the open windows, giving us a bad hair day. Pauly couldn't have seemed happier.

Concrete power poles sprouted out of the mangrove hedges along US1 on our right and blurred like fence posts. When I looked at the speedometer, the Mustang was doing ninety-five. Oncoming traffic looked like it was standing still and the mangroves and sea grape hedges blurred into green, yellow and orange abstracts.

"Son-of-a-bitch," Pauly griped. "They must have the pedal to the floor."

"How far behind us?" I fought the urge to turn and look.

"They're not catching up, but I hoped they'd fall further behind."

We were quickly coming to Bay Point, the area he had wanted to turn into, hide and let the Chrysler continue north, but even with the dip in the road at Blue Water Drive it didn't seem likely.

"Do we have a Plan B?" The large eye logo of Baby's Coffee at mile marker fifteen blurred as we passed and we missed both turns that would have taken us to Bay Point.

Up ahead at mile marker sixteen was the Sugarloaf Lodge and the skydiving airport on our left, Sugarloaf Drive on the right. The speed limit posted on the bridge we zoomed over was forty-five. We were still doing ninety-five and I could see the yellow blinking light by the lodge.

He laughed. "Yeah, of course, I always have a Plan B."

I couldn't see anything funny.

"Sheriff's substation at mile marker twenty-one." Pauly tried to light a cigarette, but the wind was too much for his lighter. "Cudjoe Gardens, maybe they'll think twice about stopping by a sheriff's station."

"Jesus, Pauly, these guys outgun the deputies," I said. "We gotta avoid involving them."

"Doin' ninety-five on US1 is not the way to avoid deputies." He tossed the unlit cigarette out the window.

CHAPTER 10

"Mick, the Bullitt did better in crash tests than the BMW."

We were doing ninety-five mph on US1 and passed a blurred Sugarloaf Lodge, the Sugarloaf Marina and a First State Bank branch alongside a volunteer fire station. Pauly must have thought the news would comfort me. It didn't.

Of course, at ninety-five a crash along the narrow road bordered on both sides with grassy slopes that ended at a wall of mangroves and water would have us flipping over a number of times and then we'd probably drown. A lot of good the airbags would be since they'd probably hold us in place as the Mustang sank. I wondered if the passenger side even had an airbag. I checked my seat belt again.

"Thanks, Pauly, that's good to know." A hot wind blew through the car and my sarcasm was lost in it. It reminded me of being on Pauly's Scarab and how hard it was to talk and breathe when he had the boat flying at eighty mph over the open water because of the wind it made.

He turned and smiled.

Ahead I could see the traffic light at Crane Boulevard by Sugarloaf School. The light was on weekday controls for the school buses, but cross traffic could turn the green to red with little notice at any time.

"He's still back there but not gaining." Pauly laughed and pushed the speed to a hundred mph as soon as we passed the light.

We flew past a blur on the left that I knew was Mangrove Mamma's Restaurant and didn't even see the mile marker twenty sign. The old-road bridge to the right and the people fishing off it melted into the blue-green of the Atlantic and the mangrove islands were only dots on the water. The right turn to Cudjoe Gardens and the sheriff's substation was a mile ahead.

Cudjoe Gardens is a well-to-do community of single-family homes, most of them on canals. A few of the side streets were horseshoe-shaped and I guessed that was what Pauly wanted. He could drive down one, come out behind the Chrysler, and head back to US1 hopefully without being noticed. Anyway, that was the short-term plan, I thought.

He downshifted to fourth gear and the Mustang began to slow. We were doing ninety, then eighty, finally seventy and he downshifted to third and we were doing sixty and then fifty-five. The right turn lane rushed toward us, the sheriff's substation sitting on the corner obvious from the roadway. Would it scare our tail?

Pauly must have used the brake because I felt the Mustang slow and then he downshifted into second and the car made a tire-screeching right-hand turn. My seat belt kept me from sliding against the door. I glanced out the large back window and saw two specks down the road.

"We can pull into the substation." Pauly shifted into third and the Mustang was doing sixty again.

I didn't say anything. I think my voice was still on US1.

The Mustang slowed and Pauly turned left on Sixth Street and pulled into the driveway of the second house on the left. He moved the car behind a wall of banana trees and stopped.

"Get the gun under your seat." He moved his seat back and reached under it, coming up with a revolver. "It's a .357," he said.

I found a rag that covered something and pulled it from under my seat.

"That's a .357 too." He checked the cylinder.

Inside the rag was a chrome revolver similar to the one Pauly held. It was heavier than the few .38 handguns I'd handled and the barrel was four inches, not three inches as I expected.

"I didn't know Ruger made a Magnum." I checked the cylinder. It held six bullets; it was a Ruger GP-100. "Four-inch barrel kind of takes it out of the snubnose category, doesn't it?"

He turned and looked out the back window. "You wouldn't want to shoot a .357 from a snubnose."

You could see where Sixth and Drost met from our hiding place.

"These aren't gonna do us much good in a shootout." I tucked the revolver into my waistband. "These guys probably have automatic weapons."

He smiled. "Shit, man, I don't want to shoot it out with them. We have serious trouble if they catch up to us on the road." He put his revolver on the dash. "If they try to come up alongside us, that's when we start shooting."

He didn't sound scared, but his tone carried concern and I was glad we hadn't stopped for Tita.

Me, I was at a loss for anything that made sense. I should've been shitting bricks because doing a hundred mph on US1 is suicidal and we'd just done that and we still had to get back to Key West.

"It's got a good kick?" I held the revolver again, using both hands.

"Oh yeah, think Dirty Harry." He laughed and took his revolver off the dash. "Ten minutes." He looked at his wristwatch. "They're gone or waiting at US1. Ready?"

"Ready to go back to Key West. Not ready for a shootout."

"Ready or not . . ." Pauly backed out from behind the banana trees and moved to the intersection. He looked both ways and smiled. "If they come up on your side, Mick, don't hesitate because if I have to shoot across you to get 'em, you could lose an ear or your hearing." He wasn't smiling now.

"Should I shoot the car or the driver?" I hoped I sounded confident.

"I'd shoot the driver, but whatever you decide by your second shot, I am flooring it because when that Chrysler loses control it's gonna get messy."

CHAPTER 11

Pauly drove the six blocks to US1 in second gear, scanning each cross street as we passed while nervously controlling the gas and clutch pedals, making the powerful engine rumble under the hood. I held onto the grip of the .357. Two cars turned onto Drost from the highway. Neither were Chryslers. He pulled in and stopped at the sheriff's substation on First Street.

"It's a long twenty miles to Key West." He gave me his roguish smirk. It said all there was to say about the chances we were taking because of what might be waiting for us. Unlike most in the Keys, Pauly understood these people and knew if we didn't beat them, we were dead.

A breeze crept through the open windows, carrying the summer heaviness of heat and the taste of saltwater. Tropical plants flourished and their mixture of sweet aromas filled the air. Going a hundred mph along US1 made the wind hard and hot, but parked it was gentle, humid and aromatic. People were having backyard barbecues and I breathed it all in.

"The way you're driving, it should be the shortest long twenty-mile ride ever." I gave him a grin.

"You going to be okay using that?" He pointed at the revolver on my lap.

"If it comes to it, I won't hesitate."

A long time ago I learned that there were those capable of cruelty beyond imagination and no laws or holy man would change them; there is one solution for those who thirst for cruelty and it's death, the final solution. Of course, the problem is there's always someone to replace them and often the cruelty becomes worse.

The men in the Chrysler would continue to kill without consequences until death took them and if I had to be the one firing that final shot, I could live with it.

Pauly nodded, letting me know he believed me, backed up the Mustang and stopped at the intersection of US1. Light traffic moved toward Key West. It was a little heavier going toward Big Pine, Key West's bedroom community, this late in the afternoon. The Mustang's engine rumbled as he pumped the gas pedal and kept the clutch in sync.

"Damn," Pauly yelled, and shot the Mustang into the southbound lane. "There's your guys." He kept the car a few lengths behind a silver Chrysler convertible with its top up as we drove at a steady fifty mph.

"Are you sure?" I couldn't see anything but the car.

"Positive," he said. "I watched them for almost an hour at Schooner, I know what they look like."

"What do we do now?"

"Plan B. See where they go and who their local support is."

"Jesus," I said and knew it came out tensely. "You think they've got local help?"

"I'd want someone locally." His hand moved nervously on the shift handle.

I hadn't thought of that. Of course, I hadn't thought any of this involved me. How could it? Where was the connection? It had to be about something other than what I'd witnessed at the car wash. Maybe it was payback for killing one of the shooters. They could've been family and honor was involved. I had the questions, but could only guess at the answers.

"I don't understand any of this shit, Pauly," I said. "Where's all this coming from?"

"First of all, it doesn't fuckin' matter at the moment." He checked the rearview mirror. "We gotta deal with the now and that's the two shits in front of us and the SUV behind us."

"I didn't mean for you to get involved . . ." I stopped and looked out the back window, something I knew better than to do.

"I had a feeling something was happening at Schooner." He adjusted the mirror and grinned. "That's why I came along."

"That can't be them." I turned back and tightened my seat belt. "No way they could've known we'd run off the rock."

The Chrysler picked up speed and Pauly pulled the Mustang to one car length behind it. I didn't have to look to know the SUV was keeping up.

"A little twist on the movie." He put an unlit cigarette in his mouth.

"What?"

"The movie *Bullitt* where Steve McQueen pulls a quick turn and shows up behind the car that was tailing him. I wonder what he would've done in this situation."

"What are we gonna do?" I moved around in my seat, lowering myself until I could see the SUV moving behind us in the outside mirror. Bullitt *my ass,* I thought.

Oncoming traffic passed and I saw three cars ahead of the Chrysler. We were coming up to the bridge before Shark Key.

"We got one good shot at this," he said, drumming his palms against the steering wheel. "They're gonna slow down at the bridge and the SUV will come up on my side." He stopped there, but I understood what he meant.

"We don't want that to happen, so as we approach the bridge I'm going to make it look like I want to pass and the Chrysler won't let me. Then the SUV will move up on your side to block us in and start shooting. Being on the bridge, we don't have an escape shoulder."

"Okay. I take out the driver."

"As soon as you see the front end of the SUV start shooting, put a bullet through the engine block. Then we go to Plan C." He grinned. "I'm gonna slow down and the SUV will pass us because they'll expect us to speed up and try to escape. Keep shooting until you're empty. The .357 can take out the engine and if we're lucky you'll get the driver too."

"Yeah," I said, losing the word in the wind. I wondered why he hadn't mentioned what the shooter in the SUV would be doing or what would happen if I shot out the engine.

One car going north passed just before the bridge. There was a gap in the oncoming traffic and Pauly moved to the left over the solid, double yellow line and began to pick up speed. As he'd said it would, the Chrysler began to straddle the double lines, cutting off our room to pass. Whatever hopes I had that the SUV behind us was only an SUV vanished.

Pauly picked up speed again, quickly moved to the right and tried to pass, riding close to the bridge's concrete wall. The Chrysler moved over to stop us. Pauly shot to the left lane, but the Chrysler followed just as quickly and Pauly bumped against its fender. The impact sent a shiver through the Mustang, but he kept control. The Chrysler's driver fought to control his own car.

"Here they come," Pauly yelled.

I lost my view from the side mirror because I sat up straight and gripped the revolver with both hands. I waited for the front of the SUV to appear. Without Pauly saying it, I knew the shooter would be behind the driver in the back seat and that I had a couple of shots before having to worry about him. I smiled because I figured that had to be Pauly's idea, make them come up on my side of the car so I could get the first shots off and he could control the Mustang. Of course, I hadn't been right about anything in the last couple of days.

The first thing I noticed was the insignia on the front of the SUV.

"Now," Pauly yelled, louder than the wind.

I turned, raised the .357 and shot twice into the side of the SUV, toward the engine block because the vehicle was a lot higher than the Mustang. Then the driver's window was there and I shot two more times. The first shot hit the door high; the second shattered the tinted window. The SUV crashed against the side of the Mustang, almost making me drop the gun. I heard shots coming from it, but didn't feel any hit the Mustang. I fired my last three rounds toward the opened back window as Pauly swerved the car to the right, forcing the SUV away. He slowed the Mustang down and we watched the SUV hit the bridge's wall like a pinball, then shoot back across the road and smash into the rear of the Chrysler as we came off the bridge.

The two vehicles slid out of control onto the dirt path to our left. The SUV had the most momentum; it spun and ended up in the mangrove bushes, just missing one of the tall palm trees, as the Chrysler twisted around and came to a stop in the mangroves at the water's edge.

"Quick-loader in the glove compartment," Pauly said as he stopped the Mustang at the entrance to the Shark Key compound.

I reloaded the .357. Pauly got out, his revolver held down by his side, and checked the damage on the passenger side of the Mustang. He laughed as I got out. My body shook, but I figured only on the inside, while the ringing in my ears blocked out everything else. I stuck the gun into my waistband.

"Damn." Pauly lit the cigarette he'd held in his lips throughout the chase. "Now this looks like Bullitt's GT."

The rear passenger side was dented from where the SUV had smashed against it and bullet holes peppered the side and trunk. The shooter had hit the car, but no place vital. Maybe he was trying for the back tire or gas tank as his last resort.

"Pauly, I'm sorry." It was all I could think to say. I should have thanked him for getting us through this alive.

"No sweat, Mick, I know a body shop guy that owes me. This is a Ford, the parts are replaceable." He tossed the cigarette butt to the ground and laughed. "Hey, we survived."

Cars were pulling over to see the accident.

"No one got out," he said. He got back in the Mustang, rolled up the windows and turned on the A/C. "Maybe they're all dead."

"Maybe the airbags got them?" I pulled my seat belt tight.

"Let's hope not." He pulled out onto US1. "Bullitt would be proud of your shooting." He drove the speed limit toward Key West.

Two sheriff's cruisers passed us, lights and sirens on.

"Steve McQueen couldn't have done a better job driving," I said. Bullitt, *my ass,* but I kept the thought to myself.

CHAPTER 12

Pauly drove to Garrison Bight Marina so I could get my Jeep. I needed to explain my current situation to Tita or at least try before she got so mad she wouldn't speak to me. Maybe she'd understand why I hadn't picked her up at the airport. No matter, I knew she'd be pissed about her SUV because she took care of it as if it were an appendage. Our relationship has always been rocky and this wasn't going to help smooth it out.

"Give me that." Pauly reached for the revolver. "If any of those assholes are dead, you don't want to be caught with it."

I gave it to him and he surprised me by handing me his .357. "You may need something because these pricks are relentless."

"Thank you." I got out of the banged-up Mustang feeling I hadn't said enough.

"Come by the house tomorrow morning." He lit a cigarette. "I have a better selection of handguns you can choose from." He revved the engine and the damaged green body of the Mustang vibrated while he ignored my attempt to thank him again. "It might be a good time for you to get off the rock, Mick." The banter was gone.

"I need to talk to Tita. None of this makes any sense, Pauly."

"Maybe we should fly to the D.R., take the Scarab over to the Bahamas and smuggle a few cases of beer. Sit on the beach and work on our tans."

One of my first adventures with Pauly was ten years ago in the Dominican Republic where he kept a sailboat and a thirty-six-foot Scarab with four 275-hp engines. At one point on that trip we were doing eighty mph across open water on our way to the Bahamas, a nice memory but a scary future.

"Remember the Bahamian customs agent?"

I laughed. "Oh, yeah."

The agent expected a bribe to avoid a customs check on the Scarab. Pauly refused to pay. In an attempt to intimidate the scrappy-looking American, the customs official had his agents remove all fifty cases of Dominican beer from the boat and place them on the dock for inspection. When there were no drugs found and a few bottles of beer had been broken, the agents walked away with Pauly protesting loudly that they needed to put the cases back. They never did.

Half a block down the road was a bar that paid Pauly fifteen hundred American for the beer and sent employees to pick up the cases. He swore back then that he did this a couple of times a month just to piss off the customs man.

"Let me sleep on it, Pauly, and thanks for the invite. And this." I put the revolver in my waistband, covering it with my shirt. "I'll see you tomorrow."

"I've gotta go to the body shop early, so call me first." The Mustang rumbled out of the marina with its powerful engine vibrating the dual mufflers.

I made a quick run down the dock to make sure the *Fenian Bastard* was secure. If they knew where I hung out for breakfast and where I drank, they probably knew where I lived. Or would know eventually.

My old, white Jeep has a sun-faded bikini top as a roof that helps keep the sun and rain off me. It's beat up but runs well and is the perfect ride for Key West. It gets moderate gas mileage by today's standards and it's a good four-wheel-drive vehicle to have during hurricane season, so it's a tradeoff I live with.

There was a parking spot a few houses up from Tita's, a rarity, so I took it. She lives in an old, faded yellow, one-story Conch house on Frances Street across from the Key West Cemetery. The front door was open and a mixture of Kristofferson and Waylon songs greeted me on the porch. I knocked on the screen door and waited.

The sun was ready to set and it reflected off the windows, washing them in a bright white light that filled Tita's living room with warmth. It was dinnertime and scents of barbecue swirled in the outdoor air.

"It's not locked," she yelled from somewhere inside.

"Tita, there's a good reason why I didn't meet you at the airport." I entered her house slowly.

"I wouldn't expect less from you, Mick." She stood in the doorway to the kitchen, holding a large wine glass.

All five-foot-five of her is made to break hearts. Shoulder length, midnight black hair circles her face and its Puerto Rican complexion, while emerald-green eyes sparkle and add brightness to her smile.

She leaned against the doorway and sipped from the glass. "Guess who I ran into in Miami."

I wanted to rush and hug her, pick her up and feel her warmth, smell her perfume. Instead, I stood in the living room, concerned about what had happened around me in the past twenty-four hours, and felt foolish with my reply. "Who?"

"Me." Padre Thomas Collins moved from behind Tita.

Padre Thomas is a Jesuit who walked away from his mission in Guatemala years ago because the angels he sees and talks to told him to. In time, he ended up in Key West. He still considers himself a priest and rumor has it he receives a stipend from the order.

I wasn't surprised to see him. I was shocked. A few months back, Padre Thomas saved my life. But in doing so he paid a heavy price with regard to his beliefs and vanished from Key

West. R.L. Beaumont, a corrupt city commissioner, had killed his partner in crime, a DEA agent named Reed Fitcher, and was about to kill me when Padre Thomas picked up my gun and shot him.

I'll never find the words to describe Padre Thomas' expression as he fired the gun, or afterward as he turned and walked away. His wrinkled face, etched with horror as he pulled the trigger, turned to disgust as he dropped the gun. I had seen that look of horror before in Central America, when parents identified a tortured body as that of their son or daughter.

He saved my life and most certainly his own, because after the commissioner had shot me, he would have killed Padre Thomas. None of that mattered, though, because Padre Thomas considered himself a Christian and he had broken a commandment.

"Surprised?" He held a bottle of Budweiser and sounded like his old self.

"Putting it mildly." I kissed Tita on the cheek and squeezed her hand.

Tita knew the whole story of that afternoon, though she and other friends didn't believe I hadn't shot the commissioner and the look in her eyes told me she understood what I was going through.

"Padre, we need to talk."

"Yes," he said. "I suppose we do."

"Dinner is about an hour away." Tita walked back into the kitchen. "Do you want a beer?"

"No." I sat on the couch and Padre Thomas sat across from me. "First, I want to thank you."

His smile faded and his eyes turned away from me. He took a drink of beer and said nothing.

"Where did you go?"

Minutes after firing the shot that saved my life, he had

vanished from the scene as sheriff's deputies and Key West Chief of Police Richard Dowley rushed into the old fish house. They saw the two bodies, my Glock on the floor and me. I told them how it all went down, but they didn't believe me because they couldn't find Padre Thomas and they had come through the fish house's door seconds after hearing the shot. The priest did not have time or an exit to escape, they told me.

"There are trap doors in the floor of the main room." Padre Thomas was still looking away. "Smugglers used them years ago and I hid under the building until the next day."

"Why didn't you come out when Richard got there? You had to hear them talking and know that they didn't believe me."

He sighed. "I had just killed a man."

"You saved my life, Padre, and your own."

"I killed a man, Mick, and I don't know if saving our lives justifies that." He stared at me, his blue eyes dull as his frown and beginning to tear.

"Why have you come back?"

"Your life is in danger and I've come to save you."

CHAPTER 13

I looked at Padre Thomas and wondered if he was capable of saving himself. A few months ago he was a happy-go-lucky Key West character pedaling his rusty bike around the island, helping people he never talked about, praying for all of us and talking to angels. Like many of the quirky characters that call the end of the road home, he would probably be in an asylum elsewhere but in Key West he was only average.

Now, though, he looked beaten down mentally as well as physically and in need of a good meal and sleep while he sipped his beer.

My current opinion of him had been colored by his sudden disappearance after shooting R.L. Beaumont and the information I'd received from government officials about his questionable past. I fought back the anger I felt and tried to stay focused by remembering he'd saved my life twice.

"Padre, we have a few things to talk about." I couldn't keep the harshness out of my voice.

"I understand you are mad." He avoided looking at me by staring out the window.

"It's not just the disappearing act, Padre. There's more."

He looked up and waited for me to continue.

"After the shooting fiasco was settled, Norm's government friend came to me with an amazing story." I wanted the beer Tita offered, but knew I was better off with a clear mind.

"Jim Ashe?" He mumbled the name of the Joint Inter-Agency

Task Force agent that had worked with us in locating the city commissioner and the Colombians.

"Yes. He ran a check on you. Any idea what he found?" It came out challenging.

Padre Thomas slowly shook his head.

"It seems a few years ago a Guatemalan truth commission archeology team unearthed a mass grave in the countryside and identified one of the bodies as that of Jesuit Thomas Collins from Ireland."

He stared at me with a confused expression. "Impossible."

"The accusation is that you're a fraud." I pointed at him and held back from screaming the words. "You stole the priest's identity and came here."

He didn't respond right away. "To what purpose?" He wasn't angry, only curious.

I hunched my shoulders. "I don't know. If it's not true, whose body was it? Has this all been a con?" I couldn't control my hostility. Was I mad at him or myself for being conned?

"Coco Joe recognized me," he said, of the Peace Corps volunteer who was also a government undercover agent hunting down a British mercenary that worked with the Colombians.

"You hadn't seen each other in years; maybe the time dulled his memory." I stood up and looked out the window because I wanted to grab him by his rail-thin shoulders and shake him like a snake. The sun had set, leaving the street in shadowy dimness. I realized Tita had turned the music down. I stared at the cemetery and looked for ghosts in the twilight. No ghosts and no angels.

"And you, Mick." Padre Thomas sat back and his gaze followed me across the room. "What do you believe? Have I come to take advantage of your troubles?"

"Explain to me, Padre, how a body in a mass grave held rosary beads and was identified as you?" I turned to face him.

"I wasn't the only priest in Guatemala," he said. "What else did they do to identify the body?"

"Shot in the face, so there's no chance of dental record checks, no flesh, just rotted pieces of the clerical collar and the rosary beads." The words came as an accusation.

He smiled and I wondered if it was the smile of relief for a successful con. "Then it comes down to what you believe."

"I want to believe you, Padre." I did, too. He had been there for me in the past, I couldn't see a con man's advantage to who he was and there wasn't money in it for him. "You know what Norm said?"

He shook his head.

"He thinks you're my guardian angel."

I could see the smile coming before it appeared on his face. "Too many people can see I am flesh and blood for me to be an angel."

"That's what I told him, but he asked if you weren't one, how could you see them?"

"I've answered that for Norm before." He pulled a package of Camels from his shirt pocket. "Can we go outside?"

Tita didn't allow smoking in her house. Now, I not only wished I had that beer but I could've used a cigar, too. I nodded and we walked to the front porch. He leaned against the railing, lit his cigarette and inhaled deeply.

"I went to Cuba to be with Captain Maybe." He finished the cigarette and flipped it into the front yard. "I couldn't sleep or eat afterward . . ." His sentence went unfinished, but I knew he was talking about shooting the commissioner. He lit another cigarette.

Captain Maybe is an old salt who lets Padre Thomas live in his William Street house and had set off to sail around the Caribbean. It was to be his final sail since he was dying of cancer.

"The old coot was breaths away from dying and all he was

concerned about was me." He blew smoke out his thin nose and looked toward the cemetery. "Like you, he only saw the positive side of my taking a life, how it saved you and me. I find that difficult to accept."

"You're changing the topic," I said, standing away from him.

"My Irish passport is old and it says I am Thomas Collins," he wheezed between drags on the Camel. "I have it in my bag." He tossed the butt into the yard. "I can get it for you. You can see the visas and dated old stamps, Mick."

"You're coming on a little strong," Tita said, standing behind the screen door. She sipped from her glass of wine and smiled. "Life is a lot more precious to Padre Thomas than it is to you. He needs time to sort through his beliefs and he has to make his own decision. As a friend, you should be offering support."

"What if he's lying and he's not who he says he is?"

"And you base that on what? One man's word? A man, I might point out, that you only knew briefly, while Padre Thomas has been your friend for years."

"I have my decisions to make, too." I felt foolish as I said it.

"Dinner will be on the table in fifteen minutes." Tita walked away and turned the music off.

"Padre . . ."

"Mick," Padre Thomas cut me off. "I wasn't aware of how angry you are. Sometimes there are things the angels don't tell me and other times they tell me things I wish they wouldn't." He played with his wrinkled package of Camels but didn't light one. "Two days ago I was in Cuba with Captain Maybe and saw images of you in trouble, and I knew I had to come back."

The porch light was off, so we stood in the shadows of dim light coming from the living room windows. A soft breeze blew the hot air around and the night did not bring a cooling with it. The aromas of Tita's *arroz con pollo* wafted through the screen door.

"Padre, the last twenty-four hours have been confusing and deadly." The subject had changed, maybe swallowed up in the darkness, and my anger began to dissipate. "Do you know what's happening?" For a change, there was excitement in my words.

CHAPTER 14

"Yes and no," Padre Thomas said as Tita called us in for dinner.

He put the package of Camels in his shirt pocket and walked to the kitchen. Songs from Jimmy Buffett's Margaritaville Radio replaced Kristofferson's and Waylon's music. It seemed Tita believed Buffett's island music went better with *arroz con pollo*. I couldn't argue.

"One or the other, Padre." We sat at the kitchen table and my words still had an edge to them even with a background of Buffett's live-and-be-happy music. "You know or you don't."

Tita had our plates filled with a steamy mixture of yellow rice, peas and chicken, along with tall glasses of beer. *Arroz con pollo* is the one dish she cooks that I would walk through fire for and she knew it. She pointed to a seat for me. The aroma filled the small kitchen and made me hungrier.

"Sam Adams," she said, telling me what my glass held, a good beer brewed in Boston—or at least it once was.

"Thank you." I added splashes of hot sauce to the food before I gulped a mouthful of beer. "How do you know I need help?"

Tita sat down and stared at Padre Thomas.

"I know something from your past is responsible for what has happened recently." He began to eat and his smile thanked Tita for the food. "I know bad people, dangerous people, hold you responsible for something."

"Are we talking about what happened yesterday and today?" I shoveled a large forkful of *arroz con pollo* into my mouth and savored the taste. "You're confusing me because you're being vague. Yesterday is my past and so is twenty years ago. In that time I've written about a few bad people."

Vagueness is a con man's tool and the fact wasn't lost on me. A good con man can tell a lot about a person by the way he or she dresses, their hairstyle and their perfume. Be vague with your answers and the mark will fill in the rest.

"What exactly happened?" Tita took small bites of her food.

While we ate, I told the story of what happened at the car wash. It allowed me to explain about her SUV and her reaction wasn't as bad as I'd expected, though her look assured me we would discuss it later. Then I told them what happened this morning at Harpoon Harry's. It seemed bad things were happening in a short span of time. When I was done, Tita's expression told me it frightened her. I hadn't mentioned the car chase along US1 and I waited to see if the angels had told Padre Thomas or if they were part of an elaborate con.

"And your past is responsible?" She sipped wine.

"I wouldn't know," I said with another mouthful of *arroz con pollo.* "My past takes in a lot, as the good Padre knows. Are we talking about my college days in Boston or the years I spent in L.A.?"

We both focused on Padre Thomas. He drank from his glass of beer without saying anything.

"How can you save me, Padre, if you don't know what you're saving me from?" I finished my beer.

"Once I told you something and you made me promise never to discuss it again." His voice was low and he looked nervous. "I am a man of my word."

Tita's gaze moved from Padre Thomas to me and her green-eyed, curious stare told me she was waiting for my answer. I became the center of interest and knew that the promise he made to me years ago had to do with Tijuana and Mel. Tita knew a lot about me, but she didn't know about Mel or the afternoon she died because of me. I wanted to keep it that way.

I had purposely put fathoms of water between Tijuana and me, but the incident seemed to break to the surface of my life at the most inconvenient times. I smiled and was thankful that as a journalist I had learned many things. One of the most useful was how to lie sincerely.

"Tijuana?" I said, hoping there was enough confidence in my voice to keep Tita from being suspicious.

Padre Thomas nodded.

"So it has something to do with the Mexican drug lord?"

"Not the dead one, but he could be considered responsible, because if he hadn't died this would not be happening." Padre Thomas spoke softly, keeping his eyes on me so he wouldn't have to look at Tita, but his words cut deep.

If the drug dealer hadn't died, Mel wouldn't have died, and that was something that haunted me every night.

I flashed back more than fifteen years to Tijuana and couldn't see any connection to the car wash shooting other than the co-incidence that the shooter could have been Mexican. *Mexico is a big country*, I thought.

"That's way in my past, Padre. I don't see any connection." I forced a smile because I knew that more often than not, the angels proved to be right. I couldn't see a link; even so, I decided not to rule it out.

Padre Thomas hunched his shoulders and finished his food. Tita smiled—it was her attorney smile that said we'd talk later.

"Why don't you want Padre Thomas to talk about Tijuana?" Tita asked as she picked up our empty plates. "Mexican girl-friends?"

"Bullfights." I took my empty glass to the sink. "I spent the summers at the bullrings in Tijuana, Matteotti's restaurant and along *el río*."

"I know that." She handed us cold bottles of beer. "I read your articles. I especially liked the one where you and your Mexican friend . . . what was his name?"

"Alfonso Ruiz."

"Yes, Alfonso. You and he would hit the clubs along *avenida de los héroes* looking for Salma Hayek." She smiled and her eyes twinkled as a tease. "And what would you have done if you found her?"

I laughed. "Never thought of that. I guess we were like dogs chasing a car. What would the dogs do if they caught the car?"

She laughed. "Stand there and bark." Then her question turned serious. "What does a drug lord have to do with your search for the Mexican movie star?"

"I was responsible for the death of a brutal man." I took a deep breath and prepared my lie. "What I did also resulted in an innocent person dying, and that's when I walked away and eventually came here. It's a long story."

It was the closest I'd come to telling anyone the truth about that day.

"I thought we had agreed that I was part of your life."

"We did."

"And this is a secret Padre Thomas can't discuss and you can't share?"

"For the time being."

Tita refilled her wine glass without smiling and sat down, giving Padre Thomas and me a deep evaluating frown. She was thinking like an attorney.

"So there was more to your life in Mexico than you wrote about in those articles I kept up with?" Tita sipped her wine and I could tell her smile was forced.

Padre Thomas squirmed in his seat, focusing on his damp bottle of beer.

"There are a few things in my life, Tita, that I am still trying to deal with," I said. "And, what happened in Tijuana is one of them."

"I can appreciate that," she said. "Working things out is different than keeping secrets, right? When you work out whatever it is, and you can deal with it or not, I will know, right?"

I nodded my agreement as Padre Thomas stood.

"I have to go," he said, leaving an almost full bottle of beer on the table. That was unlike him. "I think tomorrow I will go to the police and tell them what happened."

"Not a good idea, Padre."

"Why?"

"First, it's the sheriff, not the Key West cops. They've already issued their statement about the shootings to the media and they are not going to retract it. Let it go," I said, trying to keep my anger about what happened out of my voice. "Maybe one day we can sit down with Richard and tell him so he knows I wasn't lying."

He smiled sadly and avoided Tita's stare. "I need a ride home, I have luggage."

"Mick will drive you." Tita kissed him on the cheek. "I'm glad you are home safely, Padre. And come right back, Mick, we have things to talk about."

I grabbed the large suitcase by the door and wondered how Padre Thomas had managed to carry the bag from Cuba to Key West. "Do you need anything at the store?" I said before the screen door closed.

She smiled like someone who had figured out a way to get me to talk. "Just come right back."

CHAPTER 15

Padre Thomas was quiet on the short ride to his William Street home. Months ago I agreed to see that Captain Maybe's impressive library was sold after he died and the money sent to his daughters. We signed papers giving me that authority and he left the house for Padre Thomas to live in. The captain knew he would die somewhere else and he wanted everything in order before he set sail. I wondered if he intentionally sailed to Cuba or had become too weak to make it further. Single-handling a sailboat is a lot of work for a healthy person; it must have been straining for an old man dying of cancer.

"Do not go to the police tomorrow," I said, stressing *do not*, as Padre Thomas pulled his heavy suitcase from my Jeep. "Promise me." I hoped he understood.

"Okay, I promise," he grunted but couldn't pull off an attempted smile. "We can talk tomorrow?" He yanked the handle out of its hidden compartment and rolled the suitcase to the sidewalk. "Maybe I will know more then?"

He meant that he expected the angels to visit and tell him more. I hoped he was right because I needed to know what was going on, especially now that Tita was here. In the back of my mind the words *con game* kept popping up.

Tomorrow was Sunday, the day Tita and I made our rounds of the island's many watering holes, meeting old friends and catching up on the coconut telegraph's rumors. We usually began with breakfast at Harpoon Harry's, but that wasn't going to happen after what went down at the restaurant earlier. It might not even be open next Sunday.

"Get some rest, Padre, and we'll meet tomorrow afternoon."

"Be careful, Mick, something bad is coming for you." He turned and moved slowly into the dark walkway of the house.

I waited to see the lights go on inside and then drove away.

"Something bad is coming for you? That's what he said?" Tita looked into the large mirror on her bedroom bureau while brushing her hair. She wore one of my old Finnegan's Wake T-shirts, the one with a poem on the back that told what it meant to be Irish. It was a large T-shirt and didn't hide that she wore nothing underneath.

"Yeah." I stood in the doorway ogling her while I sipped from a glass of Jameson. "I think he may be losing it."

Tita had been in Boston for a month and I missed her in many ways, but right then I wanted to be holding her, making love, rumpling the sheets, not discussing Padre Thomas' predictions.

"His life is in turmoil," she said and continued brushing. I saw her stare at me in the mirror. "I can't imagine what killing someone has done to his psyche."

"And then losing Captain Maybe." I sat on the bed and continued to ogle.

"There's that, too." Tita stopped brushing her hair long enough to turn and look at me. "About tomorrow." The T-shirt never looked better. "I need to go to the office and meet Sue."

Sue Harrison is her law clerk and office manager. She took care of everything while Tita was in Boston.

"It can't wait until Monday?" I thought of our usual Sunday romp around the island.

"Monday I have clients." She sat down on the bed.

"I guess we can't have breakfast at Harpoon Harry's anyway."

"I'm meeting Sue at Banana Café at eight." She took hold of my hand and didn't invite me to join them.

"All business?" I said, while I wondered when she had made the arrangements.

"Yes." She squeezed my hand. "I'm concerned for you," she said softly.

"I was trying to get your SUV washed so it would be clean when you arrived."

"Mick . . ." She laughed, shaking her head. "The hell with my car, it's you I'm concerned about. I don't know why I'm going to admit this, but I believe Padre Thomas is special and that he sees what he says he sees."

"Angels?"

Tita let go of my hand. "Yes, angels." She stood up. "I wouldn't admit that to anyone else." She adjusted the photos and knickknacks on the bureau.

"I believe him, too," I said, "some of the time."

Tita turned and gave me a puzzled look. "Mick, believing he sees and talks to angels isn't something you can turn on and off to suit yourself. It's a do or don't."

"Okay, until he brings me something concrete I'm still up in the air." I was lying to myself. "I happened to be at the car wash when a hit went down. I had my gun in the glove compartment because I'd just come back from Miami. I shot one of the shooters and who knows, maybe it was a brother team, so the survivor searched for me and shot up Harpoon Harry's trying to kill me. Until someone can explain it differently, I don't see a conspiracy, just a revenge shooting."

"Will he keep trying to kill you?" She almost yelled the words.

Someone already had, but Tita didn't know that. "The smart money says he's gone."

"Why?" Her green eyes lost their twinkle and took on a hardness she used to break witnesses in depositions.

"There's at least one other person with him driving the black SUV and the longer they're here, the more chances there are of being caught. They're professionals. They do the job and leave; that's what makes them professionals."

"I hope you're right." She pulled the covers down and took off the T-shirt. "Coming to bed?"

CHAPTER 16

The noise of the shower running woke me around seven. The thought of Tita's soapy body excited me, but when I tried to open the bathroom door, it was locked. She never locked the door.

"Tita," I called out, loud enough to be heard over the water.

"Go back to bed," she responded. "I don't have time for two in the shower this morning."

I thought I heard her laugh.

"What time are you meeting Sue?" I slipped my cargo shorts on and sat on the bed.

The shower stopped.

"Did you say something?"

"Yeah. When are you meeting Sue?"

"Before eight. I overslept."

I heard her moving around. I yawned. "Me too, I guess."

Last night we'd made up for the month apart and I still wanted more of her.

"Call Bob and Burt," she said through the locked door. "They'll have to find a place to have breakfast."

"Yeah, my thought exactly," I lied.

Pauly would somehow get the Mustang into the repair shop on a Sunday morning and then meet me at his home on Key Haven. After listening to Padre Thomas, I'd feel safer with a weapon. I wasn't sure what his "something bad" would be, but so far it hadn't been too friendly. While I wasn't one hundred percent sure of the padre's intentions, I knew I'd be better off armed, and the revolver Pauly had loaned me wasn't my first choice. Maybe it was a good thing Tita wasn't going to be with me.

"How long do you expect to be?" I stood by the door.

"In the shower or with Sue?" She was toying with me and knew what I meant.

"What do you think?"

Tita opened the door. She was wrapped in a large towel. Her wet hair hung down and she smiled with a freshly scrubbed face that made her green eyes sparkle. Even without makeup, she was beautiful. She must have seen me examine the towel, because she pushed me away.

"Go take a cold shower."

"I can make coffee." I was really thinking how there were no tan lines hidden under the towel.

"I will drink too much coffee before the day is over." Tita started pulling clothes from a drawer. "Thank you for last night. Now take a shower before I leave."

Reluctantly I went into the bathroom and took a shower. I left the door open, but she ignored it. When I came out, she was dressed casually and raised her eyebrows at my nakedness.

She laughed. "I like this attention. Maybe I should go away more often."

"No way." I faked a cry as I took a clean T-shirt from the drawer she allowed me in the bureau. I slipped my shorts back on and brushed my shaggy hair.

I walked her to the door and she gave me a short kiss on the lips. "I'll call you this afternoon," she said.

"You're gonna be that long?" I'd hoped she planned to surprise me with a lunch call.

She sighed. "I have cases from before I left to catch up on. I also have to make decisions on representing new clients that came to the office in the last few weeks. It's time-consuming, Mick." She saw the disappointment on my face and gently mocked it. "You be a good boy, and I'll take you to dinner. Okay?"

"Okay." I said it with a playful pout.

"One of us needs a job," she said as she went out the door, reminding me I hadn't worked for a magazine or newspaper in months.

I stood there like a schoolboy with his first crush and watched her walk down Angela Street, a large satchel over her shoulder. Because of me, her SUV was in the police impound lot. She hadn't even mentioned it. When she was finally hidden by the city cemetery, I closed the door and called Bob Lynds.

Bob is a sailing buddy. I met him when I lived at a marina on Stock Island more than fifteen years ago. He lived on his sailboat a few spots from me and we soon became friends and did a lot of sailing together. I wouldn't want to make a long sail without him as part of the crew.

"I heard about Harpoon's," he drawled in his Oklahoma accent. "Where do you have in mind?"

"Camille's?" I suggested the restaurant on Simonton Street.

"Close to the Banana Café," Bob joked.

"I hadn't thought of that."

He laughed. "Tita thinks you're checking up on her, I wouldn't wanna be in your shoes."

"Choose someplace else."

"Goldman's Deli," he said.

"See you there." I looked at my wristwatch. It was almost eight. "Half an hour?"

"Works for me." He hung up.

I called Pauly's cell, hoping he was a morning person.

CHAPTER 17

Pauly was dropping the Mustang at his friend's repair shop when I called. He seemed anxious and said he'd call me right back. I was in the Jeep driving to Goldman's Deli when he did.

"Have you seen today's *Citizen*?"

The sky was a bright blue, cloudless and masking any threat of a hurricane. The morning was comfortable, very little humidity, but the day promised heat and more humidity as the sun rose.

"I haven't seen the paper," I said into my cell. "Should I?"

"Where you off to?"

"Goldman's. I'm meeting Bob for breakfast."

There was silence on the phone. Pauly had something to say but Bob didn't fit into the equation. Pauly was a private person and had survived this long by not trusting people, not even his friends.

"He's the best friend I've got in the Keys," I said.

"See you for breakfast." He hung up.

Goldman's Deli is in the Overseas Market, sharing the large center's parking lot with other businesses. Early on Sunday morning most of the shops were closed, which made parking easy for deli customers. I waited outside for Bob and Pauly because Goldman's won't seat you until everyone in the party is available.

"We waiting on someone?" Bob walked up from Winn-Dixie and checked the crowded deli.

81

"Pauly," I said. "He called as I was driving here."

We moved toward the Chinese restaurant's overhang to get out of the sun and saw Pauly driving his Harley-Davidson motorcycle in from North Roosevelt Boulevard. He parked at the closest empty spot to the deli and took a copy of the *Citizen* out of the Harley's saddlebag.

"I always thought of you as an Old Town sort of guy," he said with a grin and handed me the paper.

"My fault," Bob said, opening the deli's door. "I chose."

The waitress showed us to the last empty booth. Pauly and Bob sat facing me.

"Like the front page?" Pauly ordered three coffees.

I pulled the front section from the paper and opened it. A large color photo of Harpoon Harry's took up one-third of the page. The story was short on facts because the shooting was an ongoing investigation. Two people had been killed at the scene, one died at the hospital and the chief of police was treated and released.

"Look at page three," he said when I had finished reading.

A black-and-white photo of the SUV and a Chrysler convertible with a torn top still up and crashed into the mangroves was centered on the page. The headline of the story was *Shootout on US1*. The photo caption said two men in the SUV had died and the two in the Chrysler were arrested. This story was brief and to the point. Weapons were found in both vehicles, but the sheriff's office wouldn't speculate if any were used in the shooting. One witness told the reporter that both cars were speeding down US1 as if chasing each other. A short story because the sheriff wouldn't comment and a large photo to eat up space. Sunday had been a slow news day.

I folded the paper and looked at Pauly. It seemed I was responsible for killing two more shooters. My problems were growing. He made a throwing motion and I guessed it meant he had dumped the .357.

Bob unfolded the paper and read as our coffee arrived. He gave it back to me. The deli was noisy, but no one spoke at our table.

"Do you want me to leave?" Bob said between sips of his coffee. He looked at me. "Obviously you two have something to talk about."

Pauly ordered steak and eggs and we took his silence as approval for Bob to stay. Bob and I ordered steak and eggs, too. The waitress refilled our coffee cups and left.

"You involved in this?" Bob rested his hand on the folded newspaper.

"Yeah, kind of," I said. "I'll tell you the whole story later."

We didn't say much until after our breakfasts arrived.

Pauly finally broke the silence. "I think you should take a vacation, Mick. I'm going to the D.R. this afternoon. Join me."

"I can't leave Tita," I said between bites of steak. "She just got back."

"Bring her." Pauly attacked his steak. He didn't feel comfortable talking in front of Bob.

I noticed that Pauly wasn't smiling as he spoke or ate. He always smiled and looked like a kid caught at something he wasn't supposed to be doing.

"Pauly, what's wrong?" I stopped eating. "Anything you can say to me, you can say to Bob."

He chewed on a piece of steak, then added egg to it and chewed some more. When he was done he asked the waitress to freshen our coffees.

"Last night I made some calls to Mexico." He spoke softly and still didn't smile. "I asked a few questions about you." He stopped talking and drank coffee.

"I should be off the radar in Mexico." I sipped my coffee and picked at my breakfast. When Pauly didn't answer me, I went on. "I haven't been there in more than fifteen years."

"I got calls back early this morning," he said, and went back to eating. "There's a time difference, but I told 'em to call when they had something."

"And?" I asked while Pauly continued to eat.

"You're right about being off their radar," he said seriously. "But the car wash shooting put you back on."

"No way," I said, louder than I should have.

"Yeah, fuckin' way." Pauly frowned. "Mick, I got it from two sources and I called half a dozen. Most are keeping their distance and they all owe me."

"How? Who the hell did I shoot?" I lowered my voice, but my frustration was building.

"It ain't who you shot, it's who you didn't shoot."

"Doesn't make sense."

"All I know is, the TJ cartel is looking for some guys who took something that didn't belong to 'em. Drugs or money would be my guess. The shooter that got away at the car wash was an old-timer, a pro who recognized you."

"A Tijuana Indian recognizes me from fifteen years ago? Jesus! It ain't so."

"The victim at the car wash was part of a paper trail they were following and he led 'em to you."

"I don't even know him."

"The Mexicans don't know that."

"Have your contact tell them."

"These guys are never wrong, Mick. You know that." He finished his coffee. "You don't contradict them and live."

"There has to be a way to clear Mick," Bob said.

"Bob, with these guys it's kill or be killed," Pauly answered, keeping his voice low. "If they think you stole from 'em, you gotta die. They can't look weak."

"Why waste time chasing the wrong guy?" Bob wondered.

"Word is already out that Mick is involved." He signaled for another cup of coffee. "They don't undo things. It would make them look bad."

Bob stared at me. "What are you going to do?"

Pauly stared at me too, and finally smiled. "The D.R. will buy you time," he said. "They could lose interest, find who they're really looking for. Don't be a fool, Mick."

I finished my cup of coffee. It was cold. Bob and Pauly continued to stare at me, waiting for a reply.

"How do you run and hide from these people?" I took money and put it on the table, hoping it would get us the bill. "They have long memories and pockets as deep as some governments."

"But you can slow 'em down and hope for change." Pauly used a small piece of toast to wipe egg and hot sauce off his plate and ate it.

"I'd have to leave too much behind." I gave the waitress money without checking the bill.

"You know what to expect," Pauly said and held out his empty coffee cup when the waitress came back with change. She refilled all three cups. "So you might make a fight of it for awhile. But what about your friends?" He looked at Bob. "They can't find you, they'll go after Tita or Bob here."

"Mick can count on me," Bob said a little too quickly. "He can count on few others, too."

"Bob." Pauly held his hands up in surrender. "I didn't mean you wouldn't help."

"No," I added. "He meant you have no idea what these people are capable of."

"Exactly," Pauly said. "They'd take out all the patrons in here just to get Mick. The Taliban could take lessons from these guys and I think the cartels behead more victims than the Arabs do."

"I've followed the *L.A. Times* series 'Mexico in Crisis'," I said. "It's a terrifying story. The Arellano-Felix cartel in Tijuana is one of the most brutal even though most of the Arellano brothers are dead or in jail."

"The Mexican government is in a full-scale war with all the cartels," Pauly said. "And they ain't winning."

"So what do we do?" Bob finished his coffee. "There has to be something."

Pauly laughed. "Yeah. Kill 'em, kill 'em all."

CHAPTER 18

Outside the deli, the temperature had risen and the morning sun shone brightly in the robin-blue sky.

"What's Fred doing?" Bob asked, about the hurricane that was building in the Atlantic.

"Heading toward the Bahamas and then Puerto Rico," Pauly said. "Probably hit the D.R. afterward and then Cuba."

"And you're going there," I said. "If Fred hits the D.R. and then Cuba, the mountains should break it up and that will help the Keys, but the East Coast of Hispaniola can't escape it."

"I've weathered worse. The house is on stilts. The boats are what I worry about. My invite's still good." Pauly stopped at my Jeep. "Whatever you do, don't be foolish and stay here."

"Are you doing the rounds this afternoon?" Bob usually met Tita and me somewhere on our Sunday barhopping stroll.

"Naw," I said, realizing the barhopping was as much to be with Tita as anything. "Probably head to the Hog's Breath and listen to Ken and Cuba."

"Meet you there at noon." Bob nodded good-bye to us and walked to Winn-Dixie.

"Where's the revolver?" Pauly asked.

I unlocked the glove compartment, looked around to make sure no one was too close, took the short-barreled revolver out and gave it to him.

"I've got a Glock for you at the bike." He slid the revolver into his belt and walked to his Harley. "Here." Pauly took a taped, brown paper-wrapped package out of the saddlebag and handed it to me. "It's loaded and there's four extra magazines. If you need more than that, you shouldn't be where you're at."

"Thanks," I said and took the heavy package. "Pauly, how much faith do you put in what the Mexicans told you?"

"You ain't gonna like it," he said and hunched his shoulders.

"I appreciate honesty."

"They know you're here, so you gotta know they're coming and that's why I'm leaving. Mick, I like you and something sneaks up on you, you can count on me. But this, it's a no-win for you. You can fight 'em, but you'll lose and a lot of people are gonna die."

"I know it."

"You don't run, you're gonna have to fight 'em." Pauly frowned for the second time and shook his head. "You don't have the firepower," he said. "And I don't have the firepower to give you. These guys will take out your family and friends first, 'cause they want you alive. They want whatever they think you stole from them."

"I didn't steal anything." I said it in the deli, but I wanted him to believe me.

"It doesn't matter to me. I believe you, though only because I know you ain't that stupid. But in less than forty-eight hours it got around you were involved, and that means they wanted people to know. Think of it, you kill one of their shooters in Key West and in hours word is out in Mexico you were one of the thieves."

"Good news travels fast." My sarcasm went without comment.

"Yeah, well, I don't know the bosses anymore. Most of the ones I knew are dead, in jail or hiding. Younger, more brutal guys are fighting for control and whatever went down in Tijuana has to be settled so they don't look weak, and you came out on the wrong end of a shit mountain."

"Facts don't matter at this point."

"You got it." Pauly smiled. "Come to the D.R. with me, then sail around the Antilles and maybe in a year the current bosses will have been replaced. The Mexican government is after them, our DEA too. I don't think the new guys are smart enough to last."

"You believe that's my only chance?"

Pauly stared at me and gave me one of his devil-may-care smiles.

"Mick, if they were after me, I'd be over in Ireland where a Latin stands out and I'd have a new name and look. Your red hair doesn't help." He put his hand on my shoulder. "No one here, none of your friends or the cops, is capable of taking these guys on. You and your friends would hesitate to shoot in a crowd and that gives the bad guys the edge. They don't care who they kill as long as they get whoever they're after."

CHAPTER 19

Pauly had booked a seat on the last flight to Fort Lauderdale and said he'd call before leaving. His flight for the Dominican Republic was midmorning Monday. He also promised if he heard anything from his Mexican contacts, even while in the D.R., he'd get hold of me.

The news he gave about why the cartel was suddenly interested in me was surprising, to say the least. I wasn't involved in whatever theft concerned them, but as Pauly pointed out, it didn't matter. They would kill me for what I did fifteen years ago to their *jefe* and brag about it. This was a win-win for them; it would show no one could escape their vengeance.

Pauly was being smart. He would know some of the gunmen and if he wasn't with them, he was an easy target to eliminate. Money bought loyalty in the cartel, or maybe the promise of power bought it, but loyalty had little to do with friendships. So getting the hell out of Dodge was the smart move. It would have been the smart move for me, too.

Even if I had gone, Tita and my friends in Key West would not be safe. The cartels in Mexico and Colombia kill whole families to get to one man. Recently the Tijuana cartel lined a family up against a backyard wall in Ensenada and shot them all, women, children and old folks, while looking for someone that had cheated them. It was all about the message the killings sent. Most of these killings went unsolved. The Mexican government's fight against the drug traffickers had put kingpins in jail, deported them to the U.S., killed them, but there was no leadership vacuum. Underlings were quick to step in and in many instances the violence increased.

I hadn't been in Mexico in fifteen years; nevertheless, I'd followed the *L.A. Times* series since it began. Mexican friends have moved their families to the San Diego area to escape the increasing violence in Tijuana, while police officers from cities along the border have sought asylum in the U.S. I wouldn't recognize the city's nightlife now, a friend wrote me. When the sun went down, people stayed inside in safety. The Mexican people deserved better.

I drove by Sandy's sandwich shop on White Street, bought a large *café con leche* with four sugars and drove to the marina. If I were going to carry the Glock, I would need to dress to conceal it. I had the permit to carry a concealed weapon but I didn't want to advertise it. I unwrapped Pauly's package while I sat in the Jeep in the marina parking lot. I put the Glock in my pocket with my hand on it and the extra magazines in my other pockets and headed to the dock.

I walked slowly, checking every boat and empty slip as I headed toward the *Fenian Bastard.* Most everyone was inside with the A/C running. Colonel Mike McClure and Dania were outside watering plants and waved hello. Karen and Michael McAloon were on the deck of their sailboat, *Drifter,* with coffee and the *Citizen.* If they'd seen anyone suspicious around my boat, they would've said something. Masseuse Tycoon Tim was giving someone a morning massage on the sundeck of his floating home.

The *Fenian Bastard* rested in her slip near the end of the floating dock. The location offered a good view of anyone heading toward me from land or sea. Looking from the aft section, I had a view of most of the harbor and the cut that allowed access to the bight from the Gulf of Mexico. From the cockpit, I could watch the long dock and parking lot.

Stopping on the finger slip, I saw the hatchway was locked and nothing onboard seemed tampered with. I looked around, especially taking in the two boats across from my slip, and then climbed onboard, the Glock held tightly in my hand.

I unlocked the hatch and went below. Nothing looked out of place. My paranoia made me uncomfortable. However, I was beginning to believe Padre Thomas' prediction about something bad coming for me and I couldn't fight the tightness in my stomach whenever I thought of how this was going to affect my relationship with Tita. If I honestly thought running would make her safe, leaving her here or taking her with me, I'd do it quicker than you could find a cold beer in Key West. I knew she wouldn't be safe anywhere, not even with family in Boston.

This was my dilemma as I put on a clean pair of cargo shorts and a colorful, loose-fitting tropical shirt. I dug into my hidey-hole in the bilge and got the box that held my stash of money, documents, and extra magazines for my Glock. I took the money and magazines and put the box back.

I went through the cabins looking for any item that might have been moved. Nothing seemed out of place; not yet, anyway.

I locked up, giving the padlock an extra yank. It didn't prove anything, but it made me feel better knowing the lock held. It also kept me from thinking about Tita for a second or two. Her safety was more important to me than mine was.

CHAPTER 20

On Sunday bars and liquor stores in Key West do not open until noon. Just across Cow Key Channel Bridge on Stock Island, Bone Island Liquors opens early because it's outside the city limits and you can always find someone from Key West there. Most of us accept this antiquated blue law and eat breakfast without a taste of the hair-of-the-dog from Saturday night or an early-morning eye-opener one day a week. We all have our crosses to bear.

I found parking on the residential section of William Street and walked the half-mile to the Hog's Breath. Twenty-five cents for ten minutes in a parking meter in Old Town is robbery and most locals avoid meters as if they were hurricane magnets. Hell, even Jesse James was honest enough to use a gun when he robbed you, but the city does it by proxy.

By twelve-fifteen those sitting around the large outdoor bar at Schooner Wharf were on their second drink. I walked on by, waved at the bikini-clad young ladies washing down the Sebago and Fury catamarans for their afternoon snorkeling trips and walked onto Greene Street across from the old icehouse that now serves as Jimmy Buffett's recording studio. A crowd had gathered at the Conch Farm restaurant for lunch and to hear Joel Nelson; at Sloppy Joe's, which was full of Hemingway *aficionados,* I turned onto Duval Street and walked into the Hog from the busy parking lot.

Barry Cuda's upright piano was already on the stage. He

pushed it from one gig to another, which probably makes Key West the only place on earth you can catch a piano player single-handedly pushing his piano through traffic. Ken Fradley didn't get that kind of credit for toting his horn around. The duo, billed as Ken and Cuda, weren't on stage yet.

Bob nursed a beer at the far end of the outdoor bar, away from the stage and the internet cameras the tourists loved to wave into, usually with a drink in hand as friends, fellow workers and family watched on a computer screen back home. They were glad to be here, so why not rub it in the faces of those not enjoying Paradise.

"Damn, you know Steve closed the cigar shop?" Bob said as a greeting.

"Yeah." I handed him one of my cigars. "You need a cutter?"

Steve had owned the cigar shop around the corner, but when his rent almost doubled he called it quits. His landlord raised rents for all his tenants even with the declining economy.

Penn State Brian, the bartender, brought me a *Negra Modelo* as Bob and I cut and lit our cigars. There was no talk as we sipped beer and smoked. Noontime had brought mostly tourists to the bar and if looks told the story, they were nursing hangovers. Mark was behind the Raw Bar waiting while no one ordered oysters. Inside, the air-conditioned restaurant was busy. Art tendered inside and Penn State Andy was getting ready to work with Brian outside. Penn State graduates were welcomed at the Hog and you probably needed a degree from that college to be bartender there.

"That asshole can really piss me off," Bob blurted out.

I knew he meant Pauly.

"He knows the situation," I answered between sips. "And everything he said is true." I blew thick cigar smoke into the air.

He turned to me, a concerned look on his face. "You think they'll try to kill you?"

"No." I forced a smile. "They'll go after my friends first. They want me alive, for a little while anyway." I was unable to keep the smile. "Pauly is right about these guys and what they're capable of." I tried not to sound anxious. If I let myself, I'd be scared for Tita, then my friends and finally myself.

I wasn't ignoring the situation. Subconsciously I was working on it and knew I needed to talk to Richard Dowley if he was out of the hospital as the paper reported.

"You know what really pisses me off?" There was an uncharacteristic hint of anger in his voice.

"Besides Pauly and hurricanes?" I kidded him.

"Hurricanes don't piss me off," he said, more in character. "They make me mad because they screw things up for a few days." Bob took a long pull on his beer and then stuck the cigar in his mouth. "No, what pisses me off are these assholes who use drugs and think it's a victimless crime."

"They're too messed up to be concerned," I said and gulped beer. I didn't like talking about drugs.

"No, man, that's not what I mean." He sighed. "I knew guys in Oklahoma and Texas who considered themselves recreational drug users because they only did coke on the weekends. Fuck, they were stupid. I mean, think about it, recreational drug money is paying these assholes that are coming."

"You're preaching to the choir," I said and hoped that put an end to the conversation.

It stopped for the short while it took us to drain our first beer of the day. Well, in Bob's case the first legal beer of the day. Brian brought us a new round as we smoked the cigars.

I could tell Bob wanted to say more. We listened to Ken and Cuda warm up on stage. The honky-tonk piano sound and Cuda's voice as he spoke to the hungover audience streaked through the open bar. It was loud, but we could still carry on a conversation without yelling.

"You can count on my help," Bob said as he turned to face me. "Burt and Doug, too. We ain't gonna run like Pauly."

"Pauly is doing the smart thing. They'd want him to help."

"Because he used to smuggle their drugs," Bob sneered and I wasn't sure if it was a question or a statement of fact.

"He knew them in the day." I puffed on the cigar.

"How do you know he's really leaving for the D.R. and isn't meeting with them? Setting you up."

"I trust him. He's been out of that life awhile, but when they need you and you're around they expect loyalty."

"Shit, that's what I mean," Bob moaned. "You trust him, but he owes them. Maybe not going to the D.R. was a good move. Maybe the cartel isn't as threatening and powerful in the States as you think and they wanted to get you out of the country."

"Let's walk down to Schooner and eat." I paid for the beers. I needed to figure out a way to keep Tita and my friends safe and wasn't sure I could. Obviously, Bob had no idea how far the tentacles of Mexican cartels reached into the States, and it made me realize how unprepared all of us were.

CHAPTER 21

The afternoon collection of tourists filled the downtown streets as we left the Hog. It was easy to see that the Disney cruise ship had arrived because young kids followed mom and dad through the shops and along the crowded sidewalks, hand-in-hand and in strollers. They weren't all from the cruise ship; some were driven-downs from South Florida who usually stayed the weekend. In a few hours US1 northbound would be jammed with cars.

The tourists crossed streets where they wanted to, never concerned with traffic, ignored signal lights, were having a good time, often because of the drinks in their hands, and wished they lived in Key West. We were glad to have them and glad to see them go.

Bob decided to walk to a cigar shop on Duval. I continued to Schooner Wharf to escape the congestion on Duval Street. Bob's a guy who'd give you the proverbial shirt off his back without thinking twice, but when you did something for him, he felt he had to pay you back. He'd smoked one of my cigars, so he had to get me one to replace it. Neither of us wants to feel we're taking advantage of the other. Bob would cheat himself before he cheated a friend.

The tables in Schooner's P-rock patio were packed with a colorful variety of visitors in shapes and sizes that puzzle the mind. Michael McCloud was on stage with Carl Peachy singing original Key West songs he'd written, thrilling the alcohol-soaked audience as they bathed themselves in the harsh summer sun.

Locals took up most of the seats of the four-sided bar in the shade. Electric fans circulated water vapor in the air and that helped cool the bar as it dissipated.

Vickie handed me a Kalik and I watched the Weather Channel's hurricane report on the TV mounted over the T-shirt stand with the locals. It seemed Hurricane Fred had stalled off the Bahamas and it might, some forecasters predicted, turn north and head toward the Carolinas. Others, according to the various spaghetti-lines that indicated possible hurricane tracks, thought it would go across the Bahamas, skirt Puerto Rico and hit the Lower Keys or maybe Miami. And there was a chance, still others calculated, that it would move a degree or two south, hit Puerto Rico, the Dominican Republic, Haiti and Cuba, then fall apart.

Most of those sitting around the bar were quiet during the report. When a weather report for another part of the country began, the locals got back to dramatically arguing about saving the world or their part of it. Some sat silently and nursed their drinks.

I walked up the few steps to the empty poolroom, bright and airy inside because the large windows and doors were open, and looked out on the seaport. The noise subsided and it was cooler, so I sat down and wondered if Las Vegas bookmakers gave odds on those hurricane predictions. I avoided what I should have been thinking about.

I didn't have the room to myself long because Josh Bonilla and Woodrow Wentworth came up the steps, beers in hand, and stood over me. They reeked of marijuana and had silly grins pasted on their faces. It wasn't even two in the afternoon and they were stoned if not already drunk.

"You by yourself?" Josh asked, maybe seeing people around

that I didn't.

"I'm waiting for Bob and Burt." I took a swallow of beer and tried not to breathe in their sickly sweet stench.

"Man, I need you to forget what I told you yesterday." Josh stared at me and then looked to make sure no one was close enough to hear.

There was no one in the room with us and I hoped he was talking about the kidnapping, but there were no guarantees that he remembered what we had talked about yesterday.

"Forgotten," I assured him. I still wanted to ask Doug about it.

Josh and Woodrow looked around and then took long swigs from their beers.

"Doug said he had to rework the plan," Josh admitted. "So just forget it, man, okay?"

"Forgotten," I said again.

"They're fuckin' cops, man," Woodrow said loudly about Bob and Burt. "I don't trust 'em."

"They're my friends." I smiled at the thought of them being cops. "What they do in their off-hours I don't know."

"Let's go sit at the bar, dude," Woodrow whined to Josh and left.

"Sorry, man, but you know how he is about cops." Josh left, too.

I shook my head as he walked down the stairs and thought what a waste those two were. Sometimes they were amicable, other times they were on Pluto. They seemed to be traveling to the planets more often these days.

I looked at my wristwatch and saw it was almost two and I hadn't heard from Tita. Too busy to call me? I dialed her cell number.

"Hello, Mick," she said hurriedly when she answered.

"Hi yourself." I tried to keep my voice low. "Everything okay?"

"How sweet," she answered in a more relaxed tone. "Yes, of course everything is okay because I love twelve- and fourteen-hour days." She laughed, but I heard the frustration in her voice. "Where are you?"

"Schooner."

"Wish I was there."

"Me too."

"Bob and Burt with you?"

"Bob's on his way and I expect Burt will show up eventually."

"Sue and I lunched in the office so you and I eat out tonight." She almost sighed but caught herself. "I don't feel like cooking."

"My treat. I feel bad about you working on a Sunday."

"You should," she kidded. "I'll be home around six." After a pause, she added, "I hope. I'm going to need to cool off with a shower." There was silence on the phone. "A shower, then a good meal. Surprise me, but make it someplace with a choice of liquors."

"You got it." I said and knew if she was being social tonight it would be gin and tonic and if she was *drinking,* as she called it, it would be two rum and Cokes for the evening.

"See you then, *te amo,*" she said and hung up.

I looked at my cell phone, maybe hoping to see Tita's image. *I love you, too,* I thought to myself and then put the phone back in my cargo-shorts pocket. I needed to do something about the situation I'd fallen into, but I couldn't think of a damn thing that made sense. Running was on the top of the list, but that would put my friends in harm's way. No sense to that.

Burt Carroll walked upstairs, a cup of scotch on the rocks in his hand. He's spent his life delivering other peoples' boats around the Caribbean and Gulf Coast. His dirty blond hair was as shaggy as mine and his droopy mustache was stained nicotine-brown from years of chain-smoking.

"Bob's behind me," Burt said and sat down. "He's paying for his beer. Oh yeah," he gave his boyish grin, "don't start the story till he gets here."

"What story?" I sipped my beer.

"How many you got to tell?" He lit a cigarette.

Bob came up with two Kaliks in his hands and a pocket full of cigars. He handed me a beer and a cigar before he pulled up a chair.

"Now," he said, cutting his own cigar, "fill us in on what I don't know." He lit the cigar, a Churchill, with an old lighter I had given him when we first met.

While I prepared the cigar, I told them about the car wash shooting and how I was sure I was at the wrong place at the wrong time. I lit the cigar and brought them up to date on the rest of the events, including the car chase and shootout on US1 in Pauly's new Mustang.

Bob added his take on Pauly's breakfast talk about going to the D.R. By the time we'd finished our drinks, they knew everything I knew, even about my confusion with it all and my concern for Tita's safety.

Burt lit another cigarette between sips of watered-down scotch. The ice had mostly melted in his drink and our beers were gone. "Pauly's the smart one," Burt said, dragging on the cigarette. "And they ain't after him."

"I've got second thoughts on Pauly," Bob said, and put the cigar in his mouth. "I think he's workin' with them and wants to get Mick out of Key West because he's safe here."

"That doesn't hold water," Burt said as he waved at Gretchen downstairs. She came up, took our orders and left with a promise to return with a menu and drinks.

"If the Mexicans at the car wash and along US1 were from the cartel, they're here already and obviously not afraid to go after anyone, including the chief of police," Burt said and looked at me.

I nodded. "That's about it. Though I don't think they knew Richard was the chief. They wouldn't have cared if they did."

"What can we do to help?" Burt sucked on a sliver of ice.

I laughed out of frustration. "Go home and Google the 'Mexico in Crisis' series, read it and then tell me what you think the three of us can do. Hell, the Mexican government with all its resources can't stop them."

Gretchen brought our drinks and a menu. We ordered chicken wings to start and three fish sandwiches.

"You giving up?" Burt lit another cigarette. "Doesn't sound like you."

"Frustrated," I admitted and took a swallow of the cold beer. "I don't see a way out of this and that scares the shit out of me."

No one said anything. We drank and smoked, listened to the loud chatter from the bar and watched the people walk by outside as they gawked at the tarpon in the water and wondered what kind of fish they were.

"When your back's against the wall, you gotta surrender or fight," Bob said finally and blew thick smoke into the room. "You don't look like someone who surrenders."

"Or runs," Burt said.

"Running is on the top of my list." I finished my beer. "But it leaves Tita and my friends in danger. They'd torture you to find me and then kill you."

"No one has to know where you're going," Burt said.

"Then they'd torture you, believe you knew nothing and still kill you."

"All this trouble and you didn't do what they think you did?" Bob took the cigar out of his mouth and finished his beer.

My cell rang before I could answer him. I looked at the screen and saw Richard's name.

"How's the shoulder?" I said.

"What bar are you in?" Richard was in official mode and not interested in small talk.

"Schooner. There something wrong?"

He sighed. "Yeah, there's something very wrong. I'm sending a car for you. Be in the lane in three minutes."

"I just ordered lunch, afterward I can drive, where are you?"

"I'm at the hockey rink," he said. "The car will be there in two minutes. Go out and meet it and be thankful you haven't eaten." He hung up without waiting for my reply.

CHAPTER 22

"Richard is sending a car for me," I said and left thirty dollars on the table for the drinks and a lunch I wouldn't eat. "I'll call you when I'm on my way back."

"What's going on?" Bob asked. "You think they know about you and the US1 shootout?"

"Nope, that would be Sheriff Wagner and he'd send deputies to get me. He wouldn't bother to call."

Burt laughed. "He'd come for you himself."

I walked through the crowded bar and onto Lazy Way Lane as a Key West police car turned. No red lights, no siren, and I thought that was a good sign. When I'm wrong, I'm wrong.

Detective Billy Wardlow was driving and he didn't look happy.

"Billy," I said as a greeting and got into the front seat. "What's happening at the hockey rink?"

To avoid the tourists walking in the lane, staring at the small shops and gazing at Jimmy Buffett's recording studio—hoping he'd magically appear—Billy drove slowly. On Elizabeth Street he turned on the emergency lights and picked up speed. "Mick, the chief said to pick you up and keep my mouth shut." He turned left on Caroline Street, stopping at red lights, but then driving on through because the rotating lights on the roof of the police car allowed it. He didn't use the siren. "I've never seen him like this. He's pissed, so I'm not saying anything."

"He was shot yesterday, Billy," I said, thinking I could explain Richard's bad mood away. "You'd be a little upset the next day, too. Hell, he should probably be home resting."

"He was home," Billy growled, driving down White Street. "The shift commander called him in because of this." He turned left on Atlantic Avenue. "You'll know why in a minute."

Like the Buffett Christmas song states, we don't have snow in Key West, but his next version of the song should mention we do have a hockey rink. In-line hockey, it's called. The city built a large covered rink by the high school and the youth and adult leagues play there year round. Even on hot summer nights the adults use pick-up games as a way to practice. I don't play, hell, I don't even skate, and I doubted very much Richard did, so why was I headed there in a speeding police car?

There was no shortage of police vehicles at the hockey rink and yellow police tape encircled everything, including the mangroves.

"I hope no one robs a bank, Billy," I said as I lost the feeling this was a fluke call from Richard.

"Why?" He drove across Bertha Street and pulled to a stop in front of the yellow tape.

"Because all the cops in town are here." I got out of the car. "What do I do now?"

"You follow me," Detective Luis Morales said and held up a section of tape so I could follow him.

"What's going on, Luis?" I looked at the clusters of police. They were in the stands, on the floor of the rink, in the mangroves and I saw police cars and cops behind the high school, close to the soccer field. Some of them dressed in civilian clothing had to be Florida Department of Law Enforcement officers because Key West didn't have this many cops in total. I didn't see any sheriff cars, but there could be deputies here too.

"The chief will tell you."

I followed him to the gate of the rink's concrete floor and we stopped. A few of the cops I knew nodded to me, none spoke.

At the far end of the rink closest to the high school, half a dozen cops stood around talking.

I saw Sherlock Corcoran's crime scene van parked outside the rink near the soccer field with the back door open, but I didn't see him. I felt very uncomfortable because this gathering wasn't a Sunday prayer meeting—not for the living, anyway. Something had happened and from the look of it, it was something the local cops hadn't dealt with in a while or maybe ever.

"Mick," Richard said from behind me.

I turned. "Richard."

He had his left arm in a sling and he was dressed in casual clothing. His badge hung from a chain around his neck.

"I've got something to show you. Follow me," he said, business-like, no niceties, and walked onto the concrete rink.

I followed slowly and Luis walked behind us. The officers at the end stopped talking and watched as we headed in their direction.

"Santos from the car wash Friday, we found his partner," Richard said over his good shoulder. "Do you remember his name?"

"José Feliciano, something like that. Reminded me of the singer when you mentioned him," I said slowly, looking for the trick in the question.

"Caesar Felix Feliciano was his name," Richard said and waited for me to walk next to him.

"Was?"

"I suppose it's still his name, but he won't be answering to it."

We were only a few feet from a crowd of cops huddled together near the rink's inside wall. Richard used his good arm to wave them aside. They moved slowly and stared at us.

When they parted I saw they had gathered around what

looked like the remains of a scarecrow sitting on the concrete floor with its back against the rink's low wall. It didn't seem human. Blood covered the fancy shirt Caesar wore and had lost its bright red color. It now looked like a brownish stain. I knew it was blood from his neck, though, because his head was missing. Someone had hacked it off.

I had seen bodies cut up before in Central America but I had never expected to see something like this in Key West.

The shock of seeing a headless body wore off quickly as I kicked into my journalist mode. "How do you know it's Feliciano?" I asked Richard, and hoped my voice didn't hint at my queasiness.

"The killers made it easy," he said.

"Killers? How many? Did you catch them?" I pulled a small notebook and pencil from my cargo shorts.

"No notes, Mick," Richard said, a little louder than necessary. "You're not here as a journalist."

"What am I here as?"

"You're involved in all this," Luis answered as he walked up to us. "This connects to the car wash shooting."

"I didn't shoot Santos." I may have protested too loudly.

"No, but you were there, shot the shooter and now Santos' business partner is dead in Key West," Luis said. "Who else would you talk to?"

"How'd you ID him as Feliciano?" I looked at the body for any sign that could help and didn't see any.

"Follow me," Richard said and led the way out of the rink. We walked toward the soccer field with Luis right behind us. "We found his wallet in his pants. License, Social Security card, credit cards and money, too."

"So you're ruling out robbery." I wanted to take notes but didn't and hoped my memory would be good enough.

CHAPTER 23

There were fewer cops and vehicles near the sun-drenched soccer field. It was hot, probably in the high eighties, and a cloudless blue sky held the large sun as it beat down. The two-story high school stood to our left, and past the field on the right a large condo complex stole the ocean breeze that might have helped cool the open area. The cops were sweating and I was beginning to. The dirt road we followed ended where the grassy soccer field began. It was summer break, so its maintenance was periodic, not as well kept as it is during the school year when the students used it daily.

"Where we headed now?" I asked.

Richard was sweating noticeably. I wondered if he was on medication. They had called him at home, so he might have taken his pills before the call with breakfast or lunch and the heat wouldn't be good for him.

"When and how was the body discovered?" I was still curious.

Dorothy Parker said, "The cure for boredom is curiosity. There is no cure for curiosity." Curiosity is the cross I bear, according to Tita, but editors I've worked for say it's my genius. Go figure.

"Some kids called 911 early this morning but didn't stick around," Richard huffed finally. "No caller ID on the cell phone."

"What time?"

"What, are you writing a book?" Luis said.

"Trying to put a timeline to it."

"Why?"

"Luis, what do you have me here for? You know I didn't kill him. You're looking for my help, right? Well, the more I know, the more I can help."

"You ever see anything like this before?" Richard stopped just short of the field, cutting Luis and me off before our arguing became spiteful.

"When I was covering the civil wars in Central America I saw casualties from land mines, grenades, what you'd expect in a war zone," I said, leaving out death squad murders. "Decapitation wasn't something either side used."

"Who uses it?" Richard wiped his brow with a handkerchief. He watched me, waiting for an answer.

"Mexican drug cartels," a voice declared from behind us.

I turned because I recognized the drawl and couldn't believe my ears. Norm Burke stood there grinning, nasty as a nightmare in his worn cowboy boots and jeans. Richard turned too. Their last encounter had Richard giving Norm twenty-four hours to get off the island.

There was an even bigger surprise. Next to Norm stood an old friend from Tijuana, Alfonso Ruiz, a Mexican *agente federal* who worked with the American DEA long before it became fashionable. Seeing these two in Key West only added to my anxiety.

Norm smiled, Alfonso smiled, Richard sighed and I didn't know which way to go. I shook Norm's hand and then Alfonso's. I had to do something.

"What brings you here?" I finally asked.

Alfonso showed his Mexican Federal Police ID to Richard.

"We were flying to Miami," Alfonso said. "Our plan was to come to Key West tomorrow after checking in with the DEA bureau, but when we received word of the decapitated body we had to come here."

That the killing was already known outside of Keys law enforcement told me a lot.

Richard handed back the ID and looked at Norm. "And you?"

"I'm with him." He pointed to Alfonso.

"You're working for the Mexican government now?"

"No, no." Norm grinned. "I'm his American liaison."

"Liaison to what?"

Norm handed Richard a badge holder. "DEA," he said.

"You mean today it's the DEA." Richard handed it back.

"It is all over Tijuana that Mick was involved with a twenty-million-dollar heist from the cartel," Norm said. "There's a bounty on him, but they want him alive, and Santos and Feliciano were the money launderers, or so the cartel thinks. Rumor is that Santos was meeting Mick." Norm turned to me. "Why the hell did you shoot the Indian?"

"He was gonna shoot me," I said.

"Well, you should have shot 'em all. His partner recognized you from the good ole days in TJ."

"Wait a minute, wait a minute," Richard yelled and looked at me. "This is because of Mick?" He swept his arms around, encompassing the sweating cops and grounds.

"Oh, yeah. At first it was about Santos," Alfonso said. "But when Mick shot the Indian it became about him."

Richard continued to yell and pushed me with his good arm. "You got me shot, you asshole!"

Luis chirped in his two cents' worth. "I told you he was involved in all this."

"This is all news to me," I lied. "I haven't stolen twenty million dollars from anyone."

"Let's finish up what we started here and then you two can fill in all the blanks," Richard said to Norm and Alfonso and gave Luis a hard stare. "Quiet down."

"Fine with me." I frowned. "What are we doing here?"

Richard motioned us all to follow him and I got the feeling everyone knew what was going on but me. I wanted to talk with Norm and Alfonso, but when I tried to hold back, Norm shook his head so I caught up to Richard.

Sherlock was on the sidelines of the soccer field with his evidence bags.

"The coroner should be here any minute," Richard said. "He'll clean up, but I wanted you to see this. Right now I want to kick your ass, too, because you brought all this here."

"Let's not get too far ahead of ourselves," I said and felt the anger in my words. "If I'm the cause of this, it's news to me." It was a lie as I said it now, but it was the truth when I first said it on Friday. Things had changed since then and I wasn't happy with that. I liked seeing Norm and Alfonso; I only wished they hadn't needed to come to Key West.

"Well, your buddy is here and all he is, is bad news," Richard griped.

"I have nothing to do with him being here."

"Bullshit. He even said you were the cause."

"But I didn't do anything. Do I live like I've got twenty mil?"

We stopped close to Sherlock and when he saw Richard, he pointed toward the goal net. "Haven't touched it."

"Follow me," Richard said and walked onto the field.

"Where's he going?" I asked Norm.

"I think he has a surprise for you," Norm said.

"After they found the body, they did a wider search." Richard stopped in front of the goal net. "Eventually they found this." He looked into the soccer goal netting.

Inside I saw a dirty burlap ball held together by wide strips of gray tape wrapped tightly around it. The burlap was stained brown on some parts and grass stains covered the rest.

"It was used as a soccer ball," Richard said with disgust.
"What is it?" As I asked, I knew the answer.
"Feliciano's head."

Chapter 24

I looked at the burlap wrapping with antipathy and curiosity. What kind of person can cut the head off a body and then kick it around like a soccer ball?

I wasn't shocked at seeing the small, wrapped head because I have followed the drug cartel's war with each other and the Mexican government for years in the press. Decapitating a victim wasn't shocking news in Mexico, not since it became common practice for drug gangs to roll multiple heads into popular clubs to intimidate their enemies and the public.

Usually, authorities found the tortured bodies close by. Sometimes they belonged to journalists, police officers, soldiers, or federal prosecutors, mayors, and other elected officials that didn't go along with the cartel. Other times they were the heads of a competing cartel's gunmen.

What concerned me more than the grotesque burlap package was that I caused this horror to come to Key West. From the little information about the killers and their victims, I knew Feliciano would have died in Miami eventually; because I had wanted to make sure Tita's SUV was clean, I got mixed up in the murder of his partner Santos. If I had waited a day or not wanted to clean the vehicle, this wouldn't be happening.

"Over there." Richard's voice broke my thoughts. He pointed toward a small storage shed that cast a deep shadow.

We followed him. He leaned against the shack for its shade, stared at each one of us and then settled on Luis.

"I want you to listen," he barked. "If I want a comment from you, I'll ask for it."

Luis nodded his understanding.

"Which one of you has the official status on this?" He pointed toward Norm and Alfonso. "Who am I supposed to listen to?"

"I work with the DEA in Tijuana," Alfonso said. "I deal with this kind of situation almost daily, unfortunately. I am here to offer my experience and knowledge of how the cartels function, and why they do what they do, to the local DEA."

"That's you?" Richard turned his stare toward Norm.

"Yeah, for the time being."

"What the hell does that mean?" Richard wiped his brow. His mood wasn't getting any better.

Even in the shade of the building, we were sweating.

"If this continues . . ."

Richard cut him off. "We're talking about the decapitation?"

"Yeah, we are, but also we're talking about any cartel-associated violence. If it continues, if it gets beyond your control, you'll have Washington bureaucrats to deal with because D.C. doesn't want this shit happening in the States. For now, for good or bad, the cartel is focusing on Mick as the man they want. For that, you've got me to deal with," Norm said and frowned. "They've cut their ties to Miami with the killing of Santos and Feliciano, so they're putting it all on Mick because your victims were their link to the thieves. This is their form of intimidation. Don't help Mick is what they are saying."

"This is all bad," Richard grumbled. "When it hits the news . . ." he stared hard at me and stopped talking. "Do you expect more of this?"

"They want Murphy. If they cannot find him right away, they will go searching," Alfonso said. "The two dead hit men and the other two arrested by the sheriffs yesterday on US1, they were from the Arellano-Felix cartel in Tijuana."

All eyes turned to me.

"You did that, too?" Richard asked.

"What do you mean, too?" I said angrily. "I shot a guy who killed someone and then turned his gun on me. Otherwise, I haven't done a damn thing. You should be treating me like a victim if what these two are saying has any validity."

"You don't believe them?" Richard challenged me.

"I find it hard to believe some hired gun remembers me from fifteen years ago in Tijuana," I lied and tried to look stern. "I don't know when this cartel robbery happened, but you know as well as anyone the only time I've left this island has been to sail to Cuba or a day drive to Miami. When did I have time to steal twenty mil? Tell me."

"I don't know the answers right now. I am going to find out what they are," Richard said coarsely. He pointed to Luis. "You keep this investigation going. We're going to my office," he said to Norm and Alfonso. He turned to me. "You are coming with me."

Norm and Alfonso nodded, accepting his comment as a command.

"You're riding with me," Richard said again and wiped his brow. "I don't want you talking to them when I can't hear."

Richard was angry and not trusting as he pushed me to start moving. I couldn't blame him. We walked the sun-drenched road toward the hockey rink without talking.

CHAPTER 25

Richard had the air-conditioning on high in his city car and the cold air chilled my sweaty body. The ride to the police station took us ten minutes because we stopped at the two red lights.

"You lied to me," Richard yelled as we got in the car.

"No. What I told you Friday and Saturday was the truth then," I yelled back. "I am not connected to this. The cartel has it fucked up."

"A lot of good that's gonna do us." He sped onto First Street. "Who's the Mexican?"

"Alfonso Ruiz, I knew him in Tijuana," I said more calmly. "He's a *federale* just as he says."

"It's a strange bunch of friends you have," Richard said with mistrust in his tone. "And Norm's DEA?"

"He's never admitted to me what agency he's with," I said and took a deep breath to slow myself down. "We met a long time ago when there was trouble on a drug story I was working on in Panama, so, yeah, he could be DEA because he saved my ass that time. He was there and he was working."

"I don't believe it, he's too much of a rogue, a black-bag guy, to be DEA," he said and turned on Roosevelt. "One phone call and I'll find out about him and the *federale*."

The parking lot circling the police station was full; they had called every off-duty officer in because of the body at the hockey rink. Usually on a Sunday, there were less than a dozen cars in the lot. The stone fountain at the entrance to the police station

116

was turned off.

Richard skipped the elevator and punched in the code to enter the glass door on the first floor. We went in and stopped. The air-conditioned hallway was more comfortable and a lot less chilly than Richard's car. We turned and looked outside for Norm and Alfonso.

"I'd throw you in jail if it would do any good," Richard said unexpectedly.

"What?" I turned to him. "You don't think I'm the victim here?"

"Key West is the victim, Mick, not you. You'll probably skirt this like everything else you get involved in, except some won't and they're the true victims." He opened the door for Norm and Alfonso. "Upstairs," he said and took the stairs to his second-floor office. We followed.

The hallway was empty of civilian workers and cops, all the support offices closed for the weekend. Richard used a key to open the outer office, left the lights off, and walked into his interior office. He turned the lights on and stopped at his large desk.

"Sit down," he said and pointed toward the conference table. He checked his phone's message display. Either there weren't any or he wasn't going to listen to them. He came and sat down. "I've got some questions, so why doesn't one of you explain what's going on and maybe I'll get my answers."

Norm seemed relaxed as he stretched his legs out and pushed away from the table. Locked into his serious mode, his face was expressionless. Alfonso, always the professional, sat more rigidly.

"Explain how the cartel works," Norm said to Alfonso.

"I've just seen how they work," Richard said brusquely. "Why are they on my island and how do I deal with them? What has Mick done and how do we undo it?"

Alfonso looked at Norm, who shrugged.

"Okay," Norm drawled, and sat up. "We've known Mick for a long time, me and Alfonso. We've seen him be stupid and we've seen him be smart."

"I've known him for ten years, get to the point," Richard griped. "And I don't wanna hear any sweetness for his sake."

"My point is, Chief, I don't think anyone here believes he helped steal from the cartel," Norm said in a firm tone that surprised me. "If he did, he'd write about it, there'd be a story in it for him. I know that for a fact and the theft happened some time ago, and he hasn't written anything about it."

Norm and Alfonso were involved with me in the scheme to steal from the drug lord in Tijuana that got Mel killed and changed my life. Norm knew from my past that I wouldn't steal from the cartel again. He was sure of it.

"What theft? Tell me about that," Richard said, frustrated.

Norm looked to Alfonso.

"A few years back a cartel safehouse was robbed of twenty million American dollars," Alfonso began, as if reciting something he was well versed in. "I have an agent inside the Arellano-Felix cartel and in a debriefing he told us about it. Men protecting the house stole the money. Bodies started to show up on the streets of Tijuana, bodies of the supposed thieves.

"I've been told the money has not been found," he said and leaned on the table. "A few thousand here and there, yes, as they caught the thieves. We even looked for it. On your side of the border, you looked for it."

"No trace of it ever showed up," Norm cut in.

"Two of the smarter thieves were discovered living with new names in Miami," Alfonso continued. "They were followed and led the cartel to Santos and Feliciano. Accountants. Did you know that?"

"Yeah," Richard said. "Miami accountants, go on."

"This all happened a few months ago. Or at least that is when my man got word of what was going on." Alfonso pulled a pack of cigarettes from a shirt pocket.

"You can't smoke in here," Richard said.

"Land of the free." Alfonso smiled and put the pack back in his pocket. "Remember, he is deep cover, so he does not come and go with us at will. Sometimes the information he passes on is weeks old.

"Anyway, where was the money? Hundreds, fifties mostly. Twenty million dollars is a lot of paper and it's heavy. Is it in TJ or did it get to Miami, and if it did, how? The cartel asked these questions before they killed the thieves. They are very thorough but never found out who got the money out of TJ or how."

Richard listened intently. "And how did all this find its way to Key West?"

"Some of this is speculation and some of it came from my agent," Alfonso said. "They decided to kill Santos and hoped it would be an incentive for Feliciano to help them get the money back and answer some of their questions."

"Then they'd kill him?" Richard said.

"Yes, with a promise of doing it quickly. They are very good at slow." Alfonso sighed. "For whatever reason, Santos drove to Key West that day and the hit men followed him. The car wash was a perfect place for the hit because he had no escape. The two shooters were guns from the old cartel days. When Mick came out of nowhere and killed Osmel Garcia, the other shooter that got away, Duviel Gonzalez, recognized him from years ago in Tijuana. The assumption was that Santos came to Key West to meet Mick."

"Do I want to know why the shooter recognized him?"

"No." Alfonso half-smiled. "Someone else in the cartel remembered Mick was a sailor and that person was also familiar with the Friday afternoon keg race from a yacht club in San

Diego. These guys race to an island offshore and back to see who buys the first round of drinks at the club.

"The island in question is claimed by both Mexico and the United States," Alfonso went on. "It is uninhabited and boaters from both countries go there to picnic, and it is patrolled by our Navy and your Coast Guard. That person from the cartel put a lot of this together quickly and came up with the idea that Murphy got the duffel bags full of money. They know about the duffel bags because they got that information from one of the thieves. They assumed the bags were motored out during the race and switched to Murphy's sailboat. That is how they figure the money got into the States and then to Miami."

"Do they have any proof?"

"No." Alfonso laughed. "This whole scenario was put together in less than twelve hours after the car wash hit. They do not need hard evidence, speculation does fine. If the money was stolen by an outsider, that would explain why the thieves did not have much on them when they were caught. Whoever planned this was good because most of the thieves were caught and they could not identify the mastermind—and we know they were tortured."

Richard stared at Alfonso with hard cop eyes. "This isn't some bullshit story to protect your friend, is it?"

"I live with this *bullshit* everyday," Alfonso said impatiently. "You have no idea of the shit storm that is headed here. My job is to prepare you." He looked at Norm. "Right?"

"Prepare me," Richard said hesitantly. "What can we do to stop this?"

"Kill them all," Alfonso said without a smile. "And that is impossible."

CHAPTER 26

"What is it with your friends?" Richard said to me, but stared at Norm. "We try not to kill anyone, we like to arrest them, put 'em in jail and have a trial."

"That is our goal in Mexico as well." Alfonso smiled like a cat with a mouthful of lizard. "I am afraid you will learn that these men do not like to be arrested, they like to fight, to kill." He pushed away from the conference table and stood. "You will also learn that the men sent here for Murphy are better armed than your officers and your SWAT team. Your sidearms, nine-millimeter, right? What do you have in the cars? M-16s and shotguns? Vests?" He gave a shallow laugh and stopped behind Norm. "The cartel has automatic weapons and uses ammunition that penetrates vests, and they have grenades, RPGs and bombs and are not afraid to use them. Innocent casualties mean nothing. Are you ready for that? Because the Mexican army with all its weaponry is having a tough time fighting them."

"You think they'll get the weapons across the border?" Richard challenged with a curt smile.

"They don't have to." Alfonso shook his head and grinned at Norm. His slight accent didn't affect his English, but he said to Norm in Spanish, *"I thought Guatemala was a third-world country."*

"What does that mean?" Richard's tone stayed challenging.

"It means, Chief, that you've got your head up your ass," Norm said crudely. He remained stretched out in the chair.

"What scares the bureaucrats in Washington is that the cartel's tentacles reach into every major U.S. city and are still growing. We haven't been able to stop its growth or slow it down. It has bought politicians and cops we know about."

"The men coming do not have to bring weapons from Mexico," Alfonso said and paced between Norm and me. "They buy them here and smuggle them into Mexico like they do the American dollar from drug sales, so the weapons are available here and so are the shooters."

Norm smirked. "Welcome to the cartel's world. It's a dangerous place."

"The American news media focuses on the drug war in Mexico, but it is also an American war," Alfonso said. "Name a large North American city and I assure you that it has cartel members living there and selling drugs. The men could live in Atlanta or New Orleans, but their orders come from Mexico and their product is wanted by Americans."

"They may already be here," Norm said.

"Yes," Alfonso agreed and stood by my chair. "If they are not, they will be soon. They may send a kidnapping team from Tijuana." He looked seriously at me. "Mexicans have made an art of kidnapping." He slapped my shoulder.

"Okay," Richard sighed and gave me a look. "You've opened my eyes to the situation." He glared at Norm. "But you haven't told me what we can do. What are your suggestions?"

Norm smirked again. "The simple answer is to get rid of Mick."

"Though that would not make the trouble go away," Alfonso added. "The cartel's men would get to his friends, torture them to find out where he went and then kill them like the accountant, leaving the body in a public place. Eventually someone in Tijuana would believe he had left the island and then they would go away, but continue looking."

Richard kept his stare on me. "That's not much of a solution. Do you have anything else?"

I realized he was serious, that he thought there was a solution he could implement to what was coming.

"Call out the Marines," Norm suggested seriously.

"Never happen," Richard said when he understood Norm wasn't kidding. "We've got the sheriff and FDLE as backup." He watched Norm and Alfonso. "And the DEA if we need them, right?"

"You got me and Alfonso to start with," Norm said. "If you're figuring to go up against these guys, you've got more than a few problems."

"Outgunned, yeah, I get that," Richard said. "You're good at telling what I can't do; give me something I can do. Besides the Marines."

"Have the sheriff put up a roadblock north of the island and look for armed men traveling in SUVs," Norm answered calmly. "You can't do that," he said before Richard replied. "Or do ID checks without probable cause."

"So warn your officers to approach tinted-window SUVs with caution," Alfonso said, and sat. "And have officers travel in pairs."

Richard gave a short chuckle as he shook his head. "We have every available officer at the rink and field. If I put them in pairs, it would cut our force in half."

"Temporarily," Norm said. "Dead, the officer won't do you any good ever again."

Richard's cell chirped. He looked at the readout and stood. "I have to take this." He walked toward the large window behind his desk. "Talk to me."

We didn't speak; we tried to listen to Richard's end of the low conversation with whoever the caller was. Richard paced the length of his large desk. He looked out the window toward

Garrison Bight, nodding his head. "Are you sure?" he said, loud enough for us to hear. "Release the officers as you can and come see me when it's over."

He put his phone in his pocket and stood there staring at us as if we were from another planet. His expression turned to anger. He removed his sidearm and put it in the desk drawer before walking toward us. He took a couple of deep breaths and his expression softened a little. He sat down.

"When you showed up," he said to Norm, "I kind of hoped you were trying to help Mick out, free him from the cops." He laughed softly as if hearing a bad joke. "This whole meeting seemed to be you two trying to see who could tell the scariest story, get me to panic and send Mick to the mainland."

He ran his hands through his hair and pushed his glasses higher on his nose.

"Sadly," he griped, "you are who you say." He looked at me. "What the hell have you brought to my island?" he yelled, and pounded his fists on the table.

CHAPTER 27

"That went well, considering," Norm said with a terse laugh as we walked out of the police station.

I wasn't in the mood for his mind games and took deep breaths to control my irritation. From experience I knew Norm did and said things, no matter how bizarre, because he had a plan, a purpose, and I hoped that that was still true. I had to recall years of those experiences between us before I finally accepted his casualness toward the current situation. What wasn't he telling me and why?

Richard was fuming, to put it mildly. The blame for the grotesque killing at the hockey rink fell squarely on me, he told us without hesitation. Not that he thought I did it, he still assumed some news story I was involved in was responsible. He didn't care to hear about my feeling like a victim.

Norm and Alfonso showing up gave support to his assumptions, not to me. Finding out they were what they said only seemed to make him angrier and his doubts about Norm being a DEA agent remained.

I had never seen him this mad and feared the finale could be a messy end to our friendship. Norm and Alfonso's attitudes in dealing with him didn't help. They bruised his ego and surprised me by treating him like a hick cop on a TV show. Norm knew Richard better.

"You are going to leave him angry?" Alfonso stopped before we entered the sunny parking lot.

"Me? You gave me some help, *amigo.*"

"What are you two doing?" I finally said.

They looked at me as if I was speaking in tongues and didn't answer.

"I need a ride," I finally said to break their silence and stares.

"To where?" Norm took keys from his pocket and walked to his rental convertible. It seems that's all they keep at Florida airports.

"My Jeep's near Schooner Wharf." I got in the back seat.

"I could use a cold beer." Norm drove and headed straight to the waterfront.

"Things are happening very fast, Mick," Alfonso said, turning to look at me. "We need to talk."

"I couldn't agree more." I had questions for them that I didn't want to ask in Richard's office.

"We can't talk at Schooner, too many people," Norm said.

"I left Bob and Burt there. They might be gone, but I need to check, so I guess we talk softly, but we talk." I could show attitude, too.

Norm ignored my attitude. "How about we eat after the beer?"

"Good idea," Alfonso said.

"Are you going to tell me what's going on?" I had questions, but they were all rolled into that one. I was missing something and their blasé manner kept tripping my self-warning system that I have depended on for years as a journalist. Something wasn't right.

"Tell you what we know." Norm slowed down, looking for a parking space.

"What was it you told Richard?" Was there more to add to the horror story? It was a scary thought.

"We told him what he needed to know for the time being," Norm said.

"There's more?" I couldn't hide my anxiety.

Norm sighed. "Oh, yeah. You think I should care if a rental gets ticketed?"

"Care if it gets towed." Why was he being so aloof? What didn't I know?

"Yeah, I suppose you're right." He pulled into a legal residential spot on William Street, close to my Jeep and safe from a ticket.

"It is as if I never left Tijuana," Alfonso said of the heat as he got out of the car.

"Expect rain," Norm warned with a gloomy snort. "It always rains when I visit, but it has nothing to do with me."

I shook my head and shrugged when Alfonso looked at me and laughed. "I do not think Norm has good things to say about any place but Los Angeles."

"Hey," Norm said, getting out of the car, "at least in L.A. the bad guys wear black hats."

Alfonso had never been to Key West, so as we approached Schooner Wharf Bar he was in awe of the large boats docked in the bight. When he looked across the water toward the upscale marinas and saw the pricy yachts slipped there, he had to stop and stare.

"Is this the old part of town?" He looked at the anchored schooner and noticed the rustic bar with its knobby wood, weathered thatched roof and sun-drenched P-rock patio. He gave a stare at the modern two-story duplex rising by itself across the one-way street. "Condos going up like at the waterfront in Mexico?"

"Company went bankrupt." I led him into the bar's courtyard and we took the empty table near the kitchen. "No one knows what will happen to that property. We'll never look like Mexico's waterfront, too many building restrictions."

"Our condos are a sign of progress, modernization," he said

as he positioned his seat near the oscillating fan.

Bob and Burt were gone. I was glad I didn't have to come up with a story for them. They knew Norm from his previous trips to Key West so they would have hung around, swapped stories and made it difficult for us to talk, especially for me to ask my questions.

We ordered beers and waited for Gretchen to deliver them before we spoke. Norm took a long pull on his and smiled. "I can't find Kalik in California bars," he said and took another drink. "I'm beginning to like it."

"They should sell Bohemia here," Alfonso said, referring to the Mexican dark beer.

"I have it on my boat."

"Of course you do," he joked.

We both liked Bohemia and he remembered.

I checked the time and realized Tita would be home in little more than an hour. We were supposed to go to dinner and letting her know Norm was in town wasn't the way to end her day.

"Ah," I sipped my beer, "I have a problem, guys."

Norm sighed. "Don't we know it."

"Well, maybe I've got two problems, then."

"What's your other one?"

"Tita," I said. "She just got back from Boston and spent today at the office. We have dinner plans in a couple of hours."

"That's okay," Norm said as if there was nothing wrong and drained his beer. "We have to be in Miami and we're way late already. We'll grab something to eat at the airport."

"You can't go without talking to me." I knew I sounded anxious and I didn't want to.

"In a nutshell, Mick?" Alfonso finished his beer.

"Until you get back it'll have to do."

"You should have shot Duviel at the car wash because he is

the one that recognized you," Alfonso whispered, ignoring the noise that surrounded us. "He and Osmel were runners for the drug crowd fifteen years ago when you were in TJ for the bullfights. You were around with the chief of police back then, writing your Central American articles, and you hung out at Matteotti's with the PRI crowd. I do not have to remind you of your involvement with the drug lord."

"And in Mexico you stand out like Little Orphan Annie with your red hair and beard," Norm said and ordered us another round. "You make it easy to be remembered."

"El bastardo sabe tu nombre." Alfonso switched to Spanish and grinned. "He remembered someone saying anyone with red hair was an Irish Mick. Fifteen years and the cold-blooded ass remembered that."

"I did shoot him," I said quietly as our beers came. I let the comment about the drug lord go unanswered because Norm and Alfonso were there with me and knew it all.

"On US1 that was you." Norm grinned and tapped bottles with Alfonso. "Told you."

"We swap stories when you get back," I said.

Alfonso tried to smile, but his expression turned sour. I knew he had more to say and he was concerned about whatever it was. The afternoon's cheerfulness and music that filled the open space surrounding us didn't reach our table. The seriousness of the discoveries at the rink and soccer field kept the gaiety at bay.

"You understand what's coming?" Alfonso asked, and kept the bitter expression.

"I'm beginning to."

"Remnants of the cartel have been in the U.S. for a long time," he said and put his beer on the table. "We know Mexican kidnapping gangs exist in the States wherever there are major drug dealers. The Arellano-Felix cartel is well represented."

"That's who you think is coming?"

"We know they are coming." He looked at Norm, who nodded his agreement. "Because they are most likely in the country already, we do not know who to expect."

"It gets worse," Norm said.

"How can it get worse?"

"Everyone involved with the Tijuana cartel knows there is a bounty on you alive, not dead," Alfonso said and looked around to make sure no one was close enough to listen. He waited while Gretchen placed a food order at the kitchen. "Also, everyone in competition with the cartel knows. Recently in San Diego a kidnapping gang was broken up. We discovered they usually dressed like cops when they grabbed cartel associates off the street and held them for ransom because the cartel had killed the leader of the gang's brother in TJ."

"What he's trying to say, hoss," Norm wiped at his tired gray eyes, "is that one group wants to take you back to TJ before they kill you and the other wants you dead anywhere."

"They could care less about you," Alfonso went on to explain, "but your death inconveniences the cartel and that is what the one gang is all about."

"And there is every reason to believe they are on their way here," Norm said and drained his second beer.

"You two know how to brighten up a guy's afternoon." I sighed, finished my beer and wondered what Norm's plan was. What weren't they telling me?

CHAPTER 28

That was it, no mention of a plan. Our beers were finished and Norm and Alfonso left. Nothing about my trying to talk Tita into leaving with me or anything that involved our safety other than a *watch your back* comment and that they'd see me when they returned from Miami. Hopefully tomorrow.

The threat of cartel gang members coming to Key West scared me to the marrow even though I tried not to show it. I wanted to forget the past, but it was there, especially at night as I faced sleep. Norm knew that. He knew I was fighting that battle, but he also knew the war hadn't been won and wasn't close to being over.

There were things they should have done even though useless. Officially, they should have offered me protective custody. They should have tried to talk me into leaving. They remained nonchalant, but when talking to Richard they were very concerned about the cartel's men that were coming. It made no sense.

I know they saw I had the Glock, but made no comment. It was very confusing and troubling. Did Norm have a plan for my safety? For Tita's? I hoped so. Why not share the plan? I didn't stand much of a chance facing the cartel without his help. And even with his help my prospects for longevity were slim.

When I showed up at Tita's, I knew we would not be going out for dinner. When I walked into her house, she sat slumped

131

in a chair with half a rum-and-cola left in the tall glass she held in a death grip. Her weary smile was forced.

"Bad day?" I kissed her on the top of her head.

"The good parts of it were." She sipped her drink.

"We don't have to go out."

"Thank you." She took another sip. "I want to sit in the tub and let the hot water turn cold. A one-person office is hell when you come back from time off. Do you mind going to the Outback and picking us up something?" She handed me her glass. "One more, please."

I went into the kitchen and filled the glass with ice, then poured half rum and half cola with a large chunk of squeezed Key lime into it.

"Thank you." She smiled when I gave her the drink, though it wasn't her brightest.

"Wanna talk about it?"

"I've got ten DUI cases." She sipped the drink. "With the court overturning the Breathalyzer tests here in the Keys they're all hoping for acquittals. I can probably do it for most of them, anyway."

"There must be more." I smiled at her.

"Yeah," she said with a cheerless titter. "A few clients want me to go to foreclosure hearings and stop foreclosure on their homes. They want the court to have the banks renegotiate their loans. A little bit of knowledge is dangerous." She took another drink. "They've read in the paper about other people having success doing it. How do I take money they don't have for trying to save a house they can't afford but want to remain in? Then I turned down a child custody case because I don't think the mother is the right parent for the child's welfare. You want to hear more?"

"No. Anything special at the Outback?"

"A big steak, baked potato and salad." She closed her eyes

and held the drink. "You know how I like everything."

"You going to be awake when I get back?"

Even on a good night she wouldn't have eaten the whole meal. Her hunger came from frustration and I doubted she'd even finish the salad.

"Check the tub first." Her eyes remained closed.

"Can I suggest something?"

She nodded without opening her eyes.

"Give your clients to Nathan, close the office and sail with me around the Caribbean. We could both use the change." I tried to sound serious, hoping she would believe me.

"What?" She opened her eyes and sat up.

"You heard me," I said. "Let's get the hell out of Dodge. We could easily spend a year sailing the Caribbean visiting the small islands, and maybe even get to Puerto Rico on our way back."

"Do you think I can leave things behind that easily? And why would you leave Key West?"

"If you wanted to leave, you could."

She looked at me with an expression of sadness and shook her head. "I could have joined a law firm in Boston," she said. "They would have loved a Puerto Rican woman who was top of her class. The public relations alone would have been worth it to them. I didn't study law to become rich or famous. I wanted to help people, people who really need help but can't afford it. Sure, Nathan could handle it, but I'd be walking out on these people and as stupid as it sounds, I can't do that. I would be letting them down. More important, I'd be letting myself down.

"You want to plan on sailing in the future, I'm willing. But leave now, no way," she said and stood up. "I've got water running in the tub. I am going to soak while you get our steaks." She turned and walked to the bathroom door, holding tightly onto her drink. "When you get back, tell me why you decided to make me that offer."

I had a beer at the Outback while I waited for the food. The steaks smelled great when I got the to-go packages a half-hour later.

Tita was toweling her hair as I walked in. I put the takeout packages on the kitchen table.

"It smells wonderful," she said. She wore a beach towel wrapped around her damp body and walked into her bedroom.

When she came to the kitchen, she had on a large T-shirt and her damp hair hung down straight. She still looked tired and smelled of shampoo and soap. I didn't bother taking the food from its to-go container or setting the table for us.

"Which is mine?"

"They're both the same."

Tita opened the boxes and grinned because they were the same. Steam rose from the baked potato and the butter had melted.

"I'm too hungry to eat." Her expression was sad and she didn't try to smile. "Is that okay?"

"Why do you do this to yourself?" I closed the containers and put them in the refrigerator. "You'll eat in the morning."

She sighed. "It's just trying to catch up with a month's backlog. Tomorrow will be a regular day and I will eat a good breakfast."

"That would be nice," I said and decided not to tell her how I saw tomorrow.

CHAPTER 29

It was a restless night for Tita; she tossed and turned for most of it. I felt her leave the bed, go to the kitchen and open the refrigerator for bottled water more than once. Her radio alarm sounded at six-thirty. I got up too, heated last night's steak and potatoes and scrambled a few eggs while she showered.

Tita came out of her room wearing a sundress and a smile, her damp hair pulled into a ponytail. She smelled of soap and shampoo and looked delicious again.

"You've found your calling." She happily sat down and ate. "A *con leche*," she said with a laugh as she sipped her coffee. "You could live here if you'd cook full time."

We both laughed politely because living together was a subject we circled around like barefoot lovers on a floor full of broken glass.

She took small bites and smiled a thank you. "What are your plans?"

"Bob's boat is out of the shop and I told him I'd go on the shakedown run," I said, and ate.

"Catch a few fish for dinner." She left her breakfast half-uneaten. "My turn to cook." She finished the *con leche*.

"It should be a good day on the water," I said and tried to smile because I didn't want her to sense how anxious I was. "Maybe I'll take you to Abbondanza for dinner."

"It should be a less stressful day." Tita stood and kissed me. "I only scheduled four of the DUI clients. Unfortunately, they

135

are all barroom lawyers who think they understand the law."

"Let 'em go to someone else if they don't like what you tell them."

She sighed. "A couple of them were involved in accidents and won't understand why the Breathalyzer results being tossed won't settle their case. They'll probably look for someone else."

"What's the story on the body at the hockey rink?"

Bob drove his twenty-foot, center-console Seacraft through the shallow waters of Key West's backcountry. Its one-seventy-five engine purred. Thin white clouds swept through the dark-blue sky, casting shadows that floated randomly on the water as the Seacraft hydroplaned across the mangrove-dotted Gulf of Mexico. The mangrove islands pop up in the Gulf, their gnarled roots pushing out of the saltwater with unruly branches of small, thick green leaves, and offer a safe haven for fish below and birds above.

"He was the partner of the guy killed at the car wash."

"Which guy?"

The morning sun shimmered on the calm surface and played with the shadows. I didn't get to the backcountry often because the *Fenian Bastard* needed six-foot clearance for its keel and we were moving across less than a foot of water in some spots.

"The victim's partner."

I found Bob's ability to read the water's depth by its color impressive. Some sections showed dark blue—blue, blue cruise on through—other areas were the color of sand—white, white you might—and the shades of blues and greens—green, green nice and clean—were incredible. Each shade told him where it was safe to go or not go. Hidden sandbars crisscrossed the mangrove islands and were a danger to the inexperienced boater, and sea grass swayed under us in sections. Even the deep areas were not deep, maybe five-foot, but not more—

brown, brown run aground.

"Not the guy you shot."

We sped along at twenty knots toward Snipes Key, a popular sandy respite on the edge of the Gulf. To keep my baseball cap from blowing away I wore it backward like a teenager. The flat water made the trip enjoyable because the boat wasn't bouncing over choppy waves and I didn't have to navigate the impossible route.

"Nope. The other one."

The boat raced along, causing a welcome breeze as the summer sun dodged in and out of the Bimini-covered deck promising to burn our skin. In the clear, shallow waters I saw large stingrays sprint along the bottom, looking like prehistoric birds, mixing up the sediment. Mangrove snappers schooled unmolested and I thought I saw yellow tail snappers, but we moved too fast to be certain. Sharks were hiding somewhere.

"They're from Miami," Bob said without taking his eyes from the water. "Why here?"

"Drugs, money laundering."

"They didn't know much about Key West," Bob laughed into the wind. "There ain't any secrets here."

I pulled myself closer to the center console and told him what I had learned since leaving Schooner Wharf on Sunday. The beheading caught his attention.

He listened as we ran by mangrove islands, sometimes getting close because the channel was shallow or had other hazards beneath the water like sunken boats. Most of these dangers were not on charts. Smugglers may have had the channels marked, but not many regular Keys boaters bothered with them. Newcomers often ran aground with or without charts. Experience and patience got boaters safely through the backcountry.

Behind us, when mangroves didn't block the view, was the long, narrow concrete and asphalt stretch of US1, its bridges connecting the many island outcroppings. These two worlds existed next to each other and for the time being man and progress have not completely ruined the pristine water world.

"Well, the good news, I guess, is that Norm's here," Bob said after I had finished telling him what was happening. "What's his plan?"

Even Bob figured Norm had a plan. I wasn't alone in thinking it.

"He hasn't said."

"No shit?" He went by what passed for a marker in the back-country—a two-inch PVC pipe sticking out of the water and covered with a red cone—and turned left. I had no idea what the PVC marker indicated. The large red and green markers on the water when I sail were nowhere to be found. This really was a different boating world, fast and shallow, and required a lot of instinct.

"He'll have one when he gets back today."

Yesterday I had the same enthusiasm, but it had turned to doubt by the time I arrived at Tita's.

"That's a marker?" I wanted to change the subject.

He laughed. "You learn to recognize 'em. But I go by landmarks."

I looked around the mangroves for what I'd consider landmarks and couldn't tell one island from another accept that they varied in size. What was he looking at?

"What's Tita think?"

I didn't respond. Briefly, he turned away from the water and looked at me.

"You gotta be kidding." He turned back and moved to the center of the channel.

Mangrove islands were on both sides now, blocking the view of the highway and the Gulf. They formed a long channel that became narrower the farther we went.

"Bob, I have no idea what I'm going to do," I admitted, something I wouldn't have done on Sunday. "Norm's not too forthcoming and the cartel isn't going to stop because a few of their men are killed or jailed."

"Maybe Pauly wasn't wrong."

That was something for him to admit after his questioning of Pauly's reasons for wanting me to leave for the Dominican Republic.

"If Norm doesn't come up with something by tomorrow, I'm going to have to tell Tita," I said. "I already asked her to go sailing."

"What about her practice?"

"That's what she said, but maybe when she realizes the danger I've put her in, she'll change her mind."

We could hear the cries of birds on the islands we passed and the splashing of fish jumping out of the water to catch a mosquito. When we were close to a mangrove island, we heard the rustling of branches and the flapping of wings as birds took flight. It can be peaceful on the water if the weather is right and other boaters keep their distance.

"I don't envy you that conversation." Bob slowed the boat. "Listen," he said.

We could hear the straining engine of a boat. It seemed to be coming from behind us, but sound can fool you on the water.

"Another boat on its way to Snipes?"

"Listen to it," he said again and slowed our boat to idle.

The engine noise rumbled. I was sure it was somewhere behind us, between one of the many mangrove islands.

"That's a big engine," Bob said as the current pulled us along.

For someone who had spent the last fifteen years living on a boat, I didn't know a lot.

"And?" I was curious when I should have been anxious.

"The engine indicates a boat with too much draft for these

channels," he said.

"It could be an inexperienced boater."

"You're right, but why's he following us?"

"How do you know he's following us and not lost?"

"He's creeping along, forcing it." Bob notched up the speed and turned his boat into an inlet that was covered by mangrove branches. "If he was on the Gulf side of the mangroves, they'd be in six foot of water."

"Government boat?"

"No," Bob said as he slowed and moved us against entwined mangrove roots. "The government would use a chopper to follow us, at worst a Coastie on the deep side of the channel. And the marine patrol would know what boat to use in here."

Coastie is the locals' name for the Coast Guard crewmembers that came in and out of the base in Key West, and the old marine patrol is now the Florida Wildlife Conservation Department. No matter, locals still call it the marine patrol.

The unseen engine sputtered loudly as it maneuvered the boat through the shallow water.

Bob looked to the right, toward the noise. I pulled the Glock Pauly had loaned me from my backpack and Bob laughed. "If they get close enough to use that, I'll be in the water swimming away." He kept his eyes toward the approaching boat. "If it's Mexicans, they'll probably have Uzis or Gaili SARs. They like Israeli weapons, they're small and shoot a lot of bullets."

He was beginning to sound like Norm. I knew SAR stood for small assault rifle and I had experience with being shot at with the Gaili and the Uzi. I stuck the Glock into my waistband.

"It's all we've got," I said.

The white bow section of the mystery boat moved into view as it came around the outside of a mangrove island. It was a twenty-five-foot Bayliner with two men visible on deck, one steering while the other one kept an eye on the depth of the channel. It drew almost three feet of water, too much draft to travel safely through this section of the backcountry.

"How deep?" I asked.

"If they moved out about ten feet, they'd be in deep enough water," Bob said, his hand nervously on the throttle.

The Bayliner came with a two-twenty I/O engine and could do forty-five knots wide open. It would outrace us in open water, but in this section of mangrove-covered backcountry it poked along, getting hung up in the shallows. That told us the men were not experienced. The boat's beam made it almost nine feet wide. It should have been on the other side of the mangroves.

Bob pointed toward the Bayliner and handed me a pair of binoculars. I saw the two men aggressively pointing toward us and yelling. The passenger picked up the SAR and began shooting.

Bob pushed the throttle forward. The Seacraft shot out of the inlet with its bow high out of the water as we planed, and I fell back on my ass. Slowly, Bob lowered the speed and the boat settled. The Bayliner moved away from the mangroves and picked up speed.

"Take the wheel," Bob said as I stood. "Pass the next small channel and then at the second one cut a left turn and stay to the right in the channel."

"They're gonna gain on us at this speed," I shouted over the wind.

"Good," he yelled and moved forward.

CHAPTER 30

I'm comfortable at the controls of a boat on the open water and smart enough to realize I'm too inexperienced in backcountry boating to maneuver successfully through the tricky mangrove channels. I wanted to look behind me because I could hear the Bayliner, but was so concerned with the shallow depth and running aground that my eyes only wandered back and forth from the center console's depth finder to the water ahead. I was at the wheel in three feet of water and I was the only one who seemed concerned.

"He's gaining," I said and knew I was right even though I hadn't looked back.

Bob knelt at an open bow locker. "Watch for the second channel and make a left," he said with his back to me while he searched the locker. "And keep to the right as you turn."

"What are you gonna be doing?"

Bob got up, holding an M-16, and pushed extra magazines into his pockets. "Make that turn up ahead and there's a small cove to the right between mangroves," he said as he watched the Bayliner. "Go into the cove real slow and turn around."

I saw light from the break in the mangroves highlighted on the shadowy water ahead and knew the small channel was close. I prepared for the turn. The Bayliner would lose sight of us briefly and I wanted to slip into the cove without their seeing. I was witnessing a new side of Bob. Usually he was subdued and walked away from anything that looked like trouble. He was out of place with the M-16 and barking orders.

He walked to the transom as I made the turn. I heard shots from behind us, but no return fire. We were out of their sight.

"Slowly, Mick," Bob said calmly. "They can't see yet."

The small cove was where Bob said it would be. I slowed even more to snake the boat under overhanging branches. I idled the engine and then began to turn the boat around very slowly. It was a tight fit.

"Now what?" My hand stayed on the throttle.

"When I say, you're gonna run out fast at a right angle and go straight into the Gulf," he said. "I'll lay down cover so they shouldn't be shooting."

"Shouldn't?"

"Wouldn't want me to lie, would you?" He watched the Bayliner cautiously turn into the channel as it looked for us. "Ready?" And he nodded his head for me to go.

He brought the M-16 to firing position as my hand pushed down on the throttle. Branches scraped against the Bimini and the sides of the boat as it sped out of the protective cove. The shots I heard came from the Bayliner.

The throttle was all the way forward, the boat's bow out of the water, and we sped across the Gulf as fast as I could get the boat to go. The engine roared more than purred and I heard Bob shooting. It didn't take him long to empty the magazine.

"Slow down, Mick," he hollered and reloaded.

We headed toward the open Gulf. The depth finder indicated we were in eight feet of water and it would get deeper. I moved the throttle back a little, which made the bow splash down into the blue-green water; we didn't need to hydroplane at this depth.

"Slower," Bob yelled.

I slowed more to about ten knots. We were away from the mangroves and I turned to see the Bayliner with its engine wide open, bow high out of the water, heading toward us. The shooter was leaning over the side but I couldn't tell what weapon he held.

"They're coming." I don't know why I yelled it since Bob was looking at the boat, too.

"Yeah." He laughed and shot wildly toward them, hitting mostly water. "Watch them. Come on around."

I stared at him. Come around? I thought we should be back in the channel hiding from these bastards, but I slowed more and turned to face the Bayliner. The blue water was calm, the sun reflected off it and the boat, making the boat appear whiter than it was.

"What am I watching?" I stayed by the throttle, my hand ready to push it forward as Bob moved to the bow and emptied another magazine, shattering the quiet.

The Bayliner sped toward the open water where we were barely moving. They appeared unafraid. The shooter was firing blindly at us when their boat came to a sudden, violent stop. The bow rose and fell quickly back to the water, tossing the shooter overboard and sending up a large spray. The shooter stood up in the water next to the boat.

"What the hell?"

Bob laughed. "Sandbar. Move in. You feel okay driving?"

"Yeah, yeah," I said and watched the boat turn up the sand as the driver onboard tried to free it by forcing the engine into reverse. "Go in?"

"It's them or us, Mick, and I'm of the opinion it should be them," he said, more coldly than I'd ever heard him say anything.

"You have another one of those?" I pointed to his M-16 as I pushed the throttle.

"You won't need it," he said and pointed to the left. "Go that way."

I headed back toward the cove. Bob steadied himself as best he could against the center console. "Slow down," he said.

I slowed the boat and he let off a burst as the shooter tried pushing the Bayliner free of the sandbar. Then he raked the small isinglass-enclosed console and I saw the shooter try to climb into the boat, but he couldn't. He was hit and his rifle fell into the water.

"Move closer." Bob put in a new magazine and emptied it into the console.

I pointed as the shooter fell into the water and the current began to push him into the channel.

"Use the Glock if you have to." Bob dove into the water. He grabbed the chubby man by an arm and pulled him to the sand-bar.

I moved within a few feet of the Bayliner's engine, idled and held Pauly's Glock.

"Help me get him on board," Bob said, shaking the water from his head.

I tied off the Seacraft to one of the Bayliner's cleats and jumped in. The water was warm and the shooter dead cold. We pushed the pudgy body up the side and over onto the deck. Bob used saltwater to clear off blood smears from the side of the Bayliner.

He climbed onboard the Seacraft, picked up the M-16 and shot up the isinglass again. The loud report rattled the stillness of the mangroves. He jumped onto the transom, kept shooting, and when he stopped he put a new magazine in the M-16. I got back on our boat and he motioned for me to stay put with his raised arm, palm out telling me to stop.

Two short bursts from the M-16 scared the birds and seemed louder than they should have because we were on the water. Bob came back on the deck and threw me a stronger line to tie off to the Bayliner.

"Two of them," he said as I jumped onboard.

"Mexican?"

"No papers, lots of cash." He pulled bills from his pocket to show me and then put them back. "Latin male, so probably Mexican unless the Colombians are after you, too."

The shooter lay on the bloody deck, his wet body pockmarked with small holes.

"What's the plan?" I wanted to be off the boat and heading back to Key West.

"I'm going to tie off the wheel, put the boat in gear and head it due west," he said, and pointed at the Gulf. "There's almost a full tank of fuel, so it should go a hundred miles or more if it doesn't hit another boat."

"It's probably a rental." Then I thought about autopilot. "Why not use the autopilot?"

"A lot of work putting in settings and I don't want to touch too many surfaces. The rental company will report it missing and start a search for it at sundown."

"When they find it?"

"Not my concern," he said.

Bob moved into the isinglass-covered console and cut a piece of line for tying off the wheel. "You didn't touch anything, did you?"

"No," I said. "Just the line and I jumped over the transom."

"Okay, before you untie the line, tow her off the sandbar."

The Seacraft easily pulled the bigger boat free. Bob drove the Bayliner around the sandbar and into the Gulf. I pulled alongside. We were doing five knots side-by-side when he jumped onto the Seacraft. I pulled away and slowed down and the Bayliner kept going deep into the Gulf of Mexico. He took the M-16, broke it down and tossed the pieces into the water.

"Where'd all this come from?" I looked at him and saw someone new.

"Me?" he said innocently.

"Yeah, you. Norm I'd understand."

"I was in the SEALs years ago," he said and took over the wheel. "Back to Key West, right?"

"Yeah. I never knew you were in the military."

"I don't know what to say," he mumbled as the boat picked up speed and stayed outside the mangrove channels for a speedy trip back. "The Navy and I parted ways. Medical reasons."

"You were wounded?"

He laughed. "No. You need to know?"

"Want to, otherwise I'll spend too much time guessing."

"It stays with you? I don't want anyone to know. No reason to."

"Just between us. I wouldn't have expected you to be capable of what you just did."

"Yeah, well, that's it. I was good at this shit, enjoyed it too much, and it finally got to me." He looked straight ahead and then suddenly turned and looked at me. "I'm crazy, that's what the doctor said."

"Technical jargon, don't take it personal." I laughed and Bob laughed, so I knew he realized he wasn't being laughed at, but that I was laughing with him. "You fit in down here and I think we're all a little crazy for sticking around."

"Yeah, I agree." He continued to laugh as we headed back to Key West.

CHAPTER 31

Staying out of the mangrove channels made the trip back to Key West quick and easy. The seas were calm and Bob had his Seacraft's newly repaired engine wide open as I held onto one of the center console's T-top support poles to keep from falling overboard.

The Bob I've known for more than ten years, always taking charge of things on the water, was behind the wheel now, racing us toward Key West. I thought of him as a sailor but had never thought of him as someone with an M-16, on or off the water. He was quiet and friendly. That was now a changing image.

The lack of conversation allowed me to wonder what else I didn't know about him. In Key West, everyone has secrets and it was not politically correct to ask questions about one's past. You often didn't know the last name of a friend or their real name if they went by a nickname. No one in the Keys considers that unusual.

In some of the watering holes around the island, drinking acquaintances know me as Mad Mick or just Mick, however I was first introduced to them. They know I live on a boat but have no idea and don't care to know what I do outside the bar or what my full name is. This is an island full of writers and artists and sailors, and others escaping from life somewhere on the mainland, and while they are here they don't necessarily read newspapers or magazines or listen to the news or television. Less is more. Who's to say they're wrong?

I am a news junkie and miss the all-news radio stations. I am addicted to US1's Bill Becker and his "Morning Magazine" because of the local news coverage and I devour weekly news magazines and daily newspapers that I get through the mail. This addiction makes me not normal to most Key Westers.

The harbor came into view. We were getting back hours earlier than expected from what was supposed to be a stress-free day on the water. A cruise ship stood majestically at the Westin Resort's pier. We passed the stone seawall that kept heavy seas from the city's historic seaport businesses, and Bob took the cut between the Coast Guard Base and Fleming Key. We were headed toward the *Fenian Bastard*.

"You can't do this on your own," he said as he put the boat in its no-wake speed to pass Navy housing and the city's mooring field. He maneuvered easily through the manmade channel that turned into Garrison Bight. Clearly, he'd used the ride time back to think about his involvement in what was happening.

"Until I have one more talk with Norm, my plans are up in the air," I said and looked at my wristwatch. "He has until Tita gets home."

"You think he'd be here without a plan of some kind?"

The city's mooring field and Rat Island were to our left and Navy officer housing on our right. "No, I'm counting on him having a plan and sharing it. He seemed a little distant with me but concerned about the cartel coming."

"Maybe with the Mexican agent he has to be more careful." He kept the speed low as he turned the boat into Garrison Bight. "I don't read him as somebody that would let a friend down."

For only having met Norm on his two trips here, Bob had a good read of him. I've known Norm more than twenty years and should've had Bob's faith in him, but something was eating at me. Even when he lied to me, he never kept me at a distance as he was doing now. If things didn't change drastically when he came back, I was going to have to forget everything and everyone and get out of Key West with Tita. I wanted to bet on Norm and not run because dealing with Tita would be hell.

I jumped onto the finger dock, tied off the Seacraft and looked cautiously around the dock, fearful of cartel members hiding in the shadows. Of course there were no shadows because it was a little past noon and the sun was straight overhead. Plus, live-aboard boaters moved about on the dock and strangers wouldn't have been welcomed.

"I knew Alfonso in Tijuana," I said. "Norm has worked with him before, so I don't see the relationship causing this problem. I'm missing something."

"Let's not miss lunch." Bob pulled the ice-filled cooler from his boat and jumped onto the dock as I put another line on the boat.

We sat in the cockpit of the *Fenian Bastard* in the shade and ate cold chicken and coleslaw from paper plates. I had my Glock on the seat next to me.

"You like the Glock?" Bob said between bites.

"This isn't mine, it's one of Pauly's."

"The cops still have yours?"

"Yeah. Sherlock said I'd get it back in a day or two."

Bob put his plate down, went to the Seacraft and came back with an oilcloth-wrapped package.

"This is mine." He unwrapped an automatic and handed it to me. "It's not loaded."

"A Kimber?"

"Yeah, a Combat RLII."

Another surprise from Bob. I held one of the best 1911 replicas of the old .45-caliber automatics ever made. It wasn't the smallest of Kimber's models, but it was reported to be one of the best.

"It looks new," I said, and dropped the empty magazine out of it.

"The magazine holds eight."

"The Glock holds ten."

"I'm a better shot." He laughed and picked up my Glock. "Light." He dropped the loaded magazine into his hand. "I still like the .45." He put the magazine back and laid the Glock down.

The Kimber was metal and heavier than the Glock. "I'm sorry about the rifle."

"Plenty of 'em in Miami."

"I'll pay for it."

"No need," he said between bites of chicken. "The dealer owes me."

"I didn't mean for you to get involved." I tossed my paper plate in the trash.

"Well," he said and tossed his plate into the trash, too. "It's been a long time for me. I practice shooting sometimes out in the Gulf when I'm alone." He stared at the split of land that had the cut to the Gulf of Mexico. "At least I'm helping a friend this time."

"Let's hope Norm has this worked out when he gets here." I gave him a cigar and we both lit up.

"If he doesn't, we still have Burt and Doug on our side." Bob puffed to get the cigar burning evenly.

"I don't want it to come to that."

"When your choices are none and less than none, you don't get to be choosy." He smiled and sat back with the cigar locked in his mouth.

Before I could tell him that was the last thing I wanted, my cell chirped. I answered it when I saw Norm's name in the readout.

"Yeah."

"You okay?"

"I should be asking you how I'm doing." It came out sarcastically.

He chuckled. "Don't be a wise-ass. We're on our way back by car. We should be there around six and I need you to do something for me."

I decided not to mention our misadventure on the water until he was here. "What?"

"Don't say anything to Tita or anyone until we've talked. Keep everything to yourself."

"That's about the time she gets home. I'm concerned about her."

"I've taken care of that, so relax."

"Easy for you to say."

"Wait on your boat for us and put Tita off for a few hours. Can you do that?"

"You should get here sooner than that from Miami."

"We're in Boca, but need to stop in Miami. Just wait for us. We've got a lot to talk about, some of it good, some of it not so good."

That was Norm, always looking at the positive and never mentioning how bad things could get.

CHAPTER 32

I put a few bottles of Bohemia beer in the ice chest for Alfonso and gave Bob a cold one. We sat back with the beers and cigars and enjoyed the quiet. I was procrastinating because I had to call Tita and make some excuse about missing dinner with her and I knew after that, when Norm had said whatever it was he had to say, things were going to be worse.

"I didn't tell him about this morning." I bit down on the cigar.

"I noticed and you didn't tell him about me, either." Bob sipped the beer. "Whatever you decide to do, Mick, I'm with you. We're friends. You've got friends besides Pauly."

"I appreciate that," I said. "And I know who my friends are."

An inflatable ran by on its way to the mooring field and the small waves gently rocked the *Fenian Bastard*. Traffic ran in and out of Old Town on North Roosevelt Boulevard, with some of it turning on Palm Avenue to go to the Navy base. An ambulance siren sounded as it pulled away from the paramedics' office in what was once a Pizza Hut restaurant and headed toward downtown.

"I'm gonna take the boat back," Bob said and tossed the empty beer in the trash bag. "Should I be here?"

"Yeah." I stood. "You might as well be and we can find out what's what."

"Burt and Doug?" Bob untied the Seacraft.

"No," I said. "I don't want it to come to that."

"Okay." He started the boat. "I'll be back before six."

Bob went through the cut and out of view. I couldn't think of a story Tita would believe, so I didn't call. I left the half-smoked cigar on deck and went below. My stack of books to read rested on the counter. They were mostly Florida writers: Jim Born, Deb Sharp, Christine Kling, who was a sailing friend, Sandy Balzo, Sharon Potts, Tom Corcoran. Also Jerry Healy, Bob Morris and Don Bruns, who were cigar-smoking friends at signings, and Neil Plakcy. I enjoyed their books, had already started Sandy's new one, but didn't pick it up; I was too concerned with what was coming. Even though I didn't know what it was, I knew it was going to be nasty.

I changed out of my salty clothes, showered and put on clean cargo shorts and a short-sleeved fisherman's shirt I could wear untucked to hide the Glock. I slipped into boat shoes, grabbed my pre–World Series Red Sox hat and went back on deck for my cigar and my Glock. I cut the burnt end off and relit the cigar. A soft breeze brought the smell of seaweed from the Gulf and blew my cigar smoke toward the boulevard. It was hot and it made me smile.

Norm wouldn't be here for another four hours, so I had time to kill. A bar would have been easy, though I didn't think it was the time for afternoon drinking. I wanted to talk with Tita but knew I couldn't.

I smelled the seaweed, watched the cigar smoke blow away and felt the breeze as I stood on deck looking toward the Gulf. I realized I had nowhere to go and nothing to do because of the cartel and, indirectly, Norm. It made me angry. I bit down on the cigar stub, then decided to walk around the marina and try to find someone sane to talk to. Another impossible task, I thought, and stuck the Glock in my waistband.

CHAPTER 33

Bob's habit of being early for things is one of the reasons we get along. As a journalist, I showed up early for interviews and sometimes got to see interviewees out of character because they weren't expecting me. It often made for an interesting discussion and on occasion ended an interview before it began. Bob was back at the *Fenian Bastard* at five-thirty.

He handed me a Romeo and Juliet cigar as he came onboard. "I should have a couple M-4s, magazines and ammo before noon tomorrow," he said as a greeting. "I thought you could use one."

The M-4 is a short-barrel version of the M-16 he had used earlier and broken apart on the water.

"From Miami?" I cut the cigar and lit it.

"Unimportant." He did the same to his cigar. "But the price is right."

"Which is?"

"Settlement of an old debt." He laughed and sat down. "They're not gonna be early." He was talking about Norm and Alfonso.

"Driving down US1, no way."

We sat in the shade as a breeze blew in off the Gulf and the late-afternoon temperature settled in the mid-eighties. We decided on a beer and took two from the ice chest. Our fresh clothes were dry and we were no longer salty from the water.

The beer helped against the heat. We enjoyed our cigars and

didn't talk of earlier in the mangroves, or of what might be waiting in the shadows. Our feet rested on the rail and the cigars were almost gone when Norm and Alfonso walked down the dock.

Norm knew the boat and had sailed her from L.A. to Panama with me. When he was here a couple of years ago, we sailed to the Gulf Stream to spread the ashes of a friend. That was the trip when he met Bob and the others for the first time.

He took off his worn cowboy boots and left them on the finger dock. Alfonso slipped out of his shoes and they climbed aboard. Bob's presence surprised them, but Norm managed to smile, shake hands and introduce Alfonso.

"Mick's told me a lot about you," Bob said.

I got them beers and Alfonso smiled when he saw it was a Bohemia.

"Finally, a good beer," he said, and took a long swallow of the dark brew. "Now that's good."

I was too anxious to sit around and play head games with Norm because Bob was there. It would have been fun to see how long Norm could go with small talk, but I needed to know what he had to say, so I began by telling them about this morning.

"No names?" Alfonso asked as I finished.

"No papers at all," Bob said and failed to mention the money he had pocketed.

"And you think they wanted to take you out." Norm stared at Bob. He had to have the same questions I did about Bob's actions and where the ability to pull them off came from. I did not mention Bob's background with the SEALs, and wouldn't. If he wanted Norm to know, he would say something.

"They were shooting without caring who they hit." Bob got himself a fresh beer. "They came right at us, unconcerned, and that's why they hit the sandbar."

"The Arellano-Felix cartel wants you alive," Alfonso said. "It had to be Teodoro's men."

"They're moving fast." Norm spoke to Alfonso and seemed surprised.

"Faster than we gave them credit for." Alfonso turned his stare toward me and then back to Norm. "No better time than the present."

"Mick, I've got something to say and I need you to listen to it all with an open mind before saying anything." Norm stumbled nervously through the words. "When you were hanging around Mexico and Central America, you would've thought what I have to say was exciting and I could've brought it to you knowing you'd go along." He stood up and walked across the deck. "Things have changed since you've moved here, you've changed, but this needed to be done." He stopped at the rail and leaned against it. "I wouldn't involve you in something I didn't think you could handle. I wouldn't allow Tita to be put in harm's way without protecting her."

Norm's words made me so anxious that I hadn't noticed Padre Thomas standing on the finger dock facing Norm as they shared unfriendly stares. Norm's background check on Padre Thomas suggested he was an imposter, a con man who stole a dead Jesuit's identity. I didn't necessarily believe it. Too often the things Padre Thomas knew about, courtesy of his angels, were true and hard to explain if he was a phony. How was he profiting in being the Jesuit? A con man would do it with profit in mind. Norm and I hadn't talked about Padre Thomas since the Jesuit saved my life at the old Stock Island fish house.

"Has he told you what he's done?" Padre Thomas climbed onboard. He turned his attention to Norm, his voice loud and angry. "Are you telling him?"

After Padre Thomas' outburst, there was an eerie silence. Alfonso looked the most confused because he had no idea who

157

was speaking.

Padre Thomas is a skinny, balding man in cut-off shorts and a button-down collared dress shirt with the sleeves gone. Two packages of Camel cigarettes filled one pocket. In Mexico, he'd be a beggar.

"Padre Thomas," Norm said, composing himself. "Welcome aboard. Alfonso, this is the Jesuit I've told you about."

Alfonso smiled and nodded. *"Con mucho gusto, padre."*

"There is no pleasure here," Padre Thomas answered harshly. He turned to me and his eyes bulged with anger. "Mick." Then he pointed at Norm. "He is responsible."

"Thomas," Norm said callously.

"No, Norm, hold your sarcasm," Padre Thomas said in the same tone. "This isn't about what you think of me. This is about what you've involved Mick in. What you've brought to Key West."

CHAPTER 34

"Stop it," I yelled, and knew my words carried across the water. "Both of you."

Alfonso looked amused and I think Bob thought he'd be drawing the Kimber and shooting someone before sunset. I saw that expression on his face. Padre Thomas and Norm were angry, something I had never seen either of them express so forcefully. Norm controlled his emotions, I knew that from being with him in life-threatening situations in the past, and Padre Thomas was a turn-the-other-cheek man of the cloth. They were both out of character and it scared me.

"My life has turned to shit the past few days and listening to your bickering isn't helping." My voice moved down a notch. "I have no idea what you are talking about and I won't until someone tells me the truth about what's going on. Norm began, Padre, so let him continue with his epic. Then I'll listen to you."

"Thank you." Norm smiled and leaned back against the rail.

"Don't thank me," I said, frustrated and anxious. "Cut to the chase and leave the bullshit out. I don't want a long fairy tale."

Norm tried to look hurt but couldn't pull it off, so he smiled. Alfonso stared at Norm with an I-told-you-so smirk on his Latin mug. Bob still looked concerned about whom to shoot and Padre Thomas couldn't conceal that all this frightened him. None of it helped me relax.

My future rested on what was going to be said and I had very little faith in the speaker or any of my cronies.

"We are responsible for the Tijuana cartel connecting the theft of its money to you," Alfonso said as he lit a cigarette. He sat there as if he was making an official report, his tone bland. "Everything at the car wash went over their heads, but we need to catch them on this side of the border, so we used the shooting and you."

Alfonso's words caught me by surprise. Maybe they would have horrified me if I had had time to think about them. Why would he purposely send a bloodthirsty gang after me?

I took a deep breath and exhaled. "Why?"

Alfonso looked at Norm, but said nothing. Padre Thomas lit a cigarette and took a beer from the cooler. Norm stretched and his gray eyes turned cold.

"It was a gift from the gods, hoss," he began slowly. "I was in TJ with Alfonso when we heard of the Santos killing. The death of the shooter was secondary, then we heard about the redheaded *gringo* that did it. How many redheads are there in Key West who wouldn't run in that situation?" Norm looked at me, his cold eyes staring hard.

"We were meeting to discuss ways to infiltrate drug distribution on the U.S. side of the border," Norm went on and paced the deck, his gaze stopping on everyone in turn for a moment. "We got to talking about trying to isolate gang members and realized we don't know enough about who the honchos were."

"We were with my undercover agent," Alfonso said. "We do not get with him too often for his safety."

"It was my idea," Norm said flatly. "I figured if they thought you were involved, they'd come after you and we could catch them. I fed the agent the story about the sailboat race in San Diego and a lot of your background. He went back to *el jefe* with a story about the redheaded *gringo* from years ago."

"The idea of getting back some of the stolen twenty million was like a cocaine rush to them," Alfonso went on. "It surprised all of us how fast they set things in motion."

"What else has been set in motion?" The anger in my words surprised me.

"We've tried to remedy it," Norm said, sitting. "The DEA wants to keep the plan in play, but they don't know we're telling you. I didn't have time to run it by you up front, but I wouldn't put this on you without letting you know."

"Letting me know what?" It was my turn to be judgmental. "That two different gangs want me dead?"

"Actually, only one wants you dead. The other thinks you have their money," Norm said with a snide smile.

"And when they find out I don't know where their money is, what happens?" I was still angry.

"Your point's made," Norm said, sounding tired of the argument. "But it has nothing to do with the problem at hand. We help you and we catch some of them. If we don't help . . ." he stopped mid-sentence, raised his arms in surrender and hunched his shoulders.

"It's not only Mick." Bob's concern for what was happening was obvious. "I may not know the cartel like you do, but I've dealt with their kind. They'll go after Mick's friends if they can't get him." He took one last puff on his cigar and tossed it overboard. "The most vulnerable would be Tita. I'm guessing if Mick's not here, neither is she. That leaves Burt, Doug and me next in line."

Norm sighed and took a beer from the cooler. "Tita will have protection twenty-four-seven."

"You gonna tell her that?" I laughed. Not a funny laugh—it was a challenge.

"I'm going to explain the situation and I know she's rational enough to understand." Norm's stare chilled me.

"You don't know her at all," I shouted. "What about my friends? They know about Pauly and he's gone. A few questions around town and Bob and the others will be known, too. Are you gonna protect them twenty-four-seven?"

"You're missing the point, Mick." He took a long pull on the dark Mexican beer and smiled. "Tita won't leave because of a million senseless reasons. The most important one is, you're not leaving."

"How do you know that?" I was losing control and I knew a friendship had already been threatened.

"Because you're the bait. We want them to come after you."

I stared at Norm, not wanting to believe I'd heard him correctly. But I had, and I knew it.

CHAPTER 35

"Bait?" My abrasive tone carried across the bight. "Now I'm the bait in your scheme?" I stared at him because I couldn't believe he would do this without first discussing it with me. I knew it was something he was capable of, but I'm his friend and felt I deserved a call even after the fact. "Is this another one of your plans like the one in Tijuana that got people killed?"

"Bait." Norm sat down and chuckled, ignoring my comment. "Well-protected bait, I might add. I wouldn't risk Tita's life, especially," he said with a stern expression. "You know me better."

"I don't know you at all," I blurted out. "The Norm I knew would've picked up the phone at least because of what happened last time he had a scheme that involved me with drug dealers."

"The Mick I knew would trust me; he would understand that sometimes conditions don't allow discussion, only action." His face was as hard as his words. "There were a lot of circumstances responsible for what happened in Tijuana, so don't try and put it all on me. If I remember correctly, it began with a story you wanted to do."

Norm knew where my weak spots were and how to twist them.

"You had no right to bring this kind of madness here," Padre Thomas interrupted. He drained his beer and then lit another cigarette. "No right to involve innocent people."

163

"I am not interested in what you think," Norm exclaimed, turning his hard stare toward the priest. "I am not even sure who you are."

He challenged Norm's accusation. "I have proven myself to you."

When Bob stood, I thought he would start shooting. "You know, I am involved in this too, whether I like it or not or you like it or not," he said calmly, and pulled a cigar from his pocket. "We can sit here and argue responsibility, but it changes nothing." He cut the end off the cigar and tossed it in the water. "What we need is a plan, Norm, we need to be able to respond to these guys. What is the plan? What do we have to do? What can we do?" He lit the cigar and sat down. "Let's move forward and no more squabbling."

Bob was the only one making sense. His calm reprimand made us settle down.

Alfonso smiled, and Norm stood and leaned against the main cabin's hatch. Bob blew smoke into the breeze and checked the lit end of the cigar to make sure it was burning evenly. Padre Thomas looked frustrated. I don't know what I looked like, but I knew I was through with angry thoughts of the past and focused on angry thoughts of the present.

"You said you had a plan, let's hear it." I tried to control my impatience.

"The plan is simple," Norm said, losing his anger. "We catch 'em when they go after you."

"Oh, that's simple, all right," I agreed sarcastically. I stood, moved to the rail and sat away from him. "And I sit there maybe with Tita in a restaurant or with friends at a bar while this happens?"

"Can we cut to serious?" Bob tapped ashes off his cigar into the bight. The reprimands were getting shorter.

Norm turned and faced the dock. "That empty slip," he

pointed over my shoulder. "There'll be a sailboat in it soon. The couple onboard will watch the dock and your boat for anything unusual. Go about your normal activities. They have supplies for ten days, so they're not going anywhere."

"And how will they decide what's unusual on this dock?"

"They'll watch your boat. If anyone goes on her, hangs around her, does anything to her, they'll report to a crew on Marlin Pier and that crew will stop the intruders from leaving," he said. "These are the only people you need to know about, they'll be here when you're on the boat too, and there will be others around twenty-four-seven protecting you."

"That makes me feel real safe," I badgered him. "What do you have in mind for Tita—someone hiding in the cemetery's mausoleums?"

He sighed and looked frustrated because he wasn't used to explaining himself. "A female undercover agent will be Tita's new best friend. Her new roommate. There will be two agents keeping an eye on her . . ."

I cut him off. "Twenty-four-seven."

"Yeah," he said and forced a grin. "And there'll be at least two following you twenty-four-seven."

"What about my friends?"

"You're visible, easy to find, there's no reason for anyone to go after your friends," he said quickly and walked to the opposite rail. "What they've done so far has caught us off guard because they moved faster than we expected, you're right about that. However, everything's in place now. The accountants were doomed once they started laundering that money. They came to Key West, brought the trouble with them and I'm just taking advantage of it."

"And I go about life ignorant of what's happening around me? Is that it?"

"You continue like nothing is different. Alfonso and I are

here for a few days' vacation, and that's how you introduce us. Two friends from L.A. No mention of Mexico."

"And you're gonna explain all this to Tita and she's gonna be okay with it, why?"

"I'm not going to tell her the whole truth," Norm said and squirmed a little. "I don't think she'd accept being followed or protected like that."

"And her new roommate, how are you going to work that?"

"I'll explain that while Alfonso and I are protecting you, the young lady from the DEA will be protecting her."

"All that's fine," I said bitterly but didn't believe it. "What about the gang that wants me dead? They don't care about casualties as long as they get me. How do you protect all of us from them?"

"How do you protect Key Westers from them?" Padre Thomas demanded. "How do you protect the residents and tourists from these madmen?"

Norm looked perturbed as he rubbed his eyes. "You will be surrounded by undercover agents from the DEA and JIATF. They'll look like tourists or locals and fit in. If they see someone with a weapon, they'll react first and think about it later. That's my agreement. If you start looking around to find them, you'll give the whole operation away." He moved back to the cabin hatchway. "You and Tita are well protected."

"From what has already happened, it is obvious that both gangs are here," Alfonso said and lit another cigarette. "You have taken a few out and Bob has too, but others are a day away or less. We have everything and everyone in play. Norm made the decision, Mick, and I supported it. Using you was our easiest and quickest way to infiltrate the cartel's distribution network in this country."

"I still don't like it. One of you could've gotten to me before now," I said.

"You know better than that," Alfonso said. "If you were anyone else, and the same situation arose, we would be doing what we are doing, but would not be concerned if you lived or died, as long as we accomplished infiltrating the American side of the cartel. We know you. We like you." He tossed the cigarette butt into the water. "The situation we found ourselves in was not of our making, but it did play into what we wanted and will help us. There is no other way. We took advantage of the opportunity and we are trying to make it right."

"And what happens if I don't want to go along?" I said. "What if I get Tita and leave? What do you do then?"

"The cartel would still be looking for you, so you'd be on the run," Norm said. "I think I know you better than that. The one side of this I don't know about is how you will handle knowing you can't write about it."

"A story would tell the cartel what you did." I laughed, but it was at my own expense.

"Yeah," Norm agreed. "We talk with Tita and then Richard and it stops there."

"Maybe."

"To get your stories in Central America, you used sources, even me, and once the process was started you did what you needed to do to control the source," Norm said.

"You used me, too," I reminded him.

"Oh yeah, a few times, but I always worked with you, protected you."

"This time is different?" It was different in ways I didn't like, in ways that were going to affect our friendship.

"I'm still protecting you. You can't leave, Mick, we'll keep you here if that's what it takes because we need you. We've set the mouse trap and you're our piece of cheese."

CHAPTER 36

That I would stay was a foregone conclusion. Norm knew because he set up the scenario of my involvement in the theft from the cartel and there was nowhere safe for me to run and hide. We all grasped that the cartel wouldn't stop its search because I couldn't be found in Key West and I knew that not even Ireland would remain a safe haven forever. I might run, but eventually they'd find me and extract their pound of flesh, my flesh, my life. Is a question a question if you already know the answer, a John Prine song asks, and I wondered about the answer.

Alfonso assured me he was working on a plan using his undercover agent as a conduit, but nothing would happen until they met and no one knew when that would be safe to do. Not soon enough for me, that was for sure. If it worked, I would be off the cartel's radar, he promised. He wouldn't tell me the plan. I had to take him on faith, he said, and I wanted to tell him faith was something I was quickly running out of.

The only chance I had for survival was working with Norm and Alfonso; I knew it and they knew it. They counted on it. If I hadn't known it, they would have been happy to explain the facts of life to me again. I held out little hope that our friendships would survive, and that tugged at my conscience. Maybe Norm was right, fifteen or twenty years ago I might have been excited to go along, but today I wasn't and if given a choice I would have said *no thank you* to their proposition. Norm also knew this, so he waited until my name was so entrenched in the affair I couldn't walk away. How could I forget or forgive his deception?

Things change, I told myself when I was alone on the *Fenian Bastard*. Friendships don't really end, they just . . . I couldn't find a word for it. I was about to lose the last connection I had to my past, the only one I'd chosen to hold on to.

Norm gave in to my request not to approach Tita until breakfast. I promised to prepare her, maybe explain the whole truth or as much of it as he wanted her to be aware of. I drove to her house and beat her home. Of course, thanks to me she was walking from the office. I had forgotten. I doubted she'd been able to talk to Richard about her SUV. He was busy with a severed head and the corpse it belonged to.

She kissed me when she came in, her large purse resting heavily on her small shoulder. She looked less stressed than yesterday and I hoped I could still say that in a few hours.

"You look as if you've lost your best friend," she said gaily and went into the kitchen.

"I may have," I said without her jubilance. "Do you mind if we go to Finnegan's instead of Abbondanza?"

"You okay?" She stood in the kitchen doorway with her glass of wine. "Finnegan's? You usually go there . . ." she stopped herself and lost her gaiety. "Norm is here." She almost shouted it, and it wasn't because she was excited. "The shootings, somehow he's involved."

Her comments weren't meant as questions. She was stating facts and I gave her a half-hearted smile when I said, "Yeah."

"What's going on?" She came and sat next to me. Then she took my hand. "The truth."

She stared at me. Her green eyes had lost their twinkle and seemed scared. Her facial expression was neutral, waiting to see how it should change after I answered. I smiled as best I could and she imitated it.

"Norm's here with Alfonso, my friend from Mexico," I said, and wished I could continue with the truth.

"The Alfonso from your magazine articles? The guy you raced around Tijuana with looking for the actress?"

"Yeah, the same. He's a *federale* and working with Norm, not chasing an actress now."

"Norm is working for the Mexican government?" She let go of my hand and sat up.

"No, not for, but as a DEA liaison to the Mexican government."

"So the car wash shooting did have something to do with the cartels," she said, as if talking to herself. "Why is all this bothering you so much? Your being at the car wash was a coincidence. Right? Who are they chasing?"

"For me and the victims, it was a coincidence."

I explained the official version; Norm's version of the surviving shooter recognizing me and how Norm and Alfonso heard the cartel had connected me to the scheme and theft of the money. They came to Key West concerned with our safety, to protect us from the cartel. She listened quietly. I finished with the protection we were both going to receive.

"I understand your needing protection." She stood up and looked down at me as if I were on the witness stand, her wine gone. "Why me?"

"You've seen the binder I have, the one filled with stories for the *L.A. Times.*"

"Sure, big white binder," she said, and now her curiosity was piqued. "What about it?"

"It's filled with copies of articles the paper has done on the drug crisis in Mexico." I motioned for her to sit back down. She remained standing, the questioning attorney. "The series goes into detail about how the cartel works and punishes its enemies."

"I've heard the news accounts."

"They go after family and loved ones to set examples for others. You're the one person here that I am closest to, so you could be a target." I took a deep breath and tried to smile to indicate it was all only a precaution. "Most likely it's only me, but we do a lot of things together."

Tita looked at me with an expression I couldn't define. There was sadness in her eyes, and then she turned and walked to the kitchen. The quiet was murder.

"Finnegan's will be fine," she said, coming back to the living room with a fresh glass of wine. "Do you remember coming here Saturday?"

"Of course." What kind of question was that? I should have remembered her attorney background. "Why?"

"Who was with me?" Her face was blank.

"Padre Thomas." I was looking for the catch, but couldn't see it.

"We met at the airport in Miami."

"So you said."

"And we had time to talk. I found out the truth about the shooting of the commissioner and how Padre Thomas did save your life."

"I'm glad you found out."

"Do you remember our conversation on whether you believed in his angels or the report Norm and Jim Ashe had?"

She stood looking down at me and I felt uncomfortable because I knew she was testing me.

"Yeah," I said. "I told you I was holding off on a decision."

"And I said?"

"You believe him, you thought he was the real Padre Thomas and he saw angels." I was sure that was what she'd said. "I was kind of surprised."

"You never asked me what made me believe him." She sipped her wine.

I hadn't seen her in a month, she'd just returned from Boston and I was more interested in getting to know her biblically than I cared about her thoughts on Padre Thomas, a man I had doubts about. I kept it to myself.

"My personal opinion is that in your own way you've always believed him. It was your lawyer instincts, your thinking how he couldn't be called to the stand because of the way he knew what he knew, and that made you question him," I said with a smirk. "I wasn't surprised that you believed him. You surprised me because you finally admitted it."

She walked in a short circle, sipped her wine and stopped in front of me.

"After Padre Thomas told me about what happened with the commissioner, I asked why he was coming back," she said softly. "He hesitated and then went into the story about the cartel sending people for you. He wasn't sure why, but he knew they were after you. He assured me it had already begun because of the car wash and he said you wouldn't be at the airport to pick me up." She smiled sweetly. "Imagine my surprise when you didn't show."

"I tried to explain," I protested. Even with her innocent smile, her words were accusing. "You were with Padre Thomas and said we'd talk about it later."

"We had a lot of time before the flight to Key West," she continued. "We had a few beers and he told me a lot. He didn't know Norm was coming but he guessed it on his own without the angels, he said, because your friendship is strong.

"I remembered what he told me and thought about it when I read the paper at the office on Sunday. I read between the lines. You forgot to mention the car chase on US1." Her smile was an accusation. "At least the shooting at Harpoon Harry's we talked about."

"Everything that has happened has been a surprise to me," I said in my defense. "It's not of my doing, but I'm caught up in it now."

"Yes, I figured that." She paced again in small courtroom circles. "That's why I'm still talking to you. You need to tell me the truth, all of it. No holding back to protect me."

"I'm glad you understand," I said. "I don't know the whole plan. I guess we'll find out in the morning when Norm gets here."

"I'm going to let Norm talk, explain his plan, but I am pissed at him for doing this and he's going to know it," she said with more determination than necessary. "If he lies to me . . . well, you had better hope he doesn't, because I have a plan to solve that problem, too."

CHAPTER 37

There was little doubt that Tita and I would not become biblically connected tonight, so I spent a lot of time thinking of what
had happened since the car wash shooting, as I lay quietly
unmolested in her bed. What made no sense to me those first
few days did now because of Norm's explanation. I was the
unwilling pawn or bait, depending on one's opinion, in his and
Alfonso's deadly little game of infiltrating the cartel's distribution network on this side of the border. What they did made me
angry. If their deception had put only me in harm's way, I might
have understood, but their scam put Tita, my friends and countless innocent people within the lethal gun sights of cartel hit
men. The gang that wanted me dead would not hesitate to make
their move at a public place, killing and maiming others as they
often did in Mexico. It did not make for a restful night.

I awoke alone. Aromas of frying, spicy foods filled the
bedroom. At six-forty-five, Tita was busy cooking breakfast. I
dressed quickly and followed the scent to the kitchen. The table
was set for four, espresso hissed from the coffee maker and a
canister of milk waited to be heated.

Tita had almost finished frying a plate full of *tostones,* a
peeled, sliced green plantain. She removed about ten from the
frying pan and placed them on a paper towel-covered plate.
Then, using the bottom of a catsup bottle, she squashed the
thick-cut plantain and returned it squashed side down to the
heated oil. In a few minutes she scooped out the cooked banana

and drained the oil from it on another paper-covered plate. She repeated this until the last *tostones* were cooked a golden brown.

She saw me and smiled. "Hungry?" A night's rest had done wonders for her disposition.

"Starving. Can I help?" If I hadn't been hungry, the aroma would have changed that.

I looked at the table. It held a large covered dish of yellow rice with peas—*arroz con gandules*—fried eggs, *tostones*, and *bacalao fritos*, all under glass covers to keep them warm. The *bacalao*, a fried seasoned batter with small pieces of codfish in it, required a lot of preparation before cooking. Seeing all the food made me both hungry and curious. Did she get up in the middle of the night to de-bone the dried codfish? It required hours of soaking in cold water to help remove the saltiness. When did she do it?

I could smell the chicken that simmered on the stove. The last time I had seen this much Puerto Rican food was at her brother Paco's house when the family had visited from the island. The aroma made me think of Old San Juan and its many small restaurants.

"Steam the milk," she said, removing the last of the *tostones* from the pan. "And keep the salt away from my food." She chastised me with a smile.

I liked salty food and she always cringed when I salted a meal before tasting it. I also added hot sauce to most everything, to her dismay.

"All this for Norm?" I steamed the milk. When it was frothy I added it to strong cups of espresso and made us each a *café con leche*. I added two sugars to mine, but left hers so she could put the correct amount of sweetener in.

"Thank you." She took the coffee. "Fatten him up for the kill." She smiled—a big, dangerous smile that made me step back.

"What are you going to do?" I was concerned. "We need his help."

"Stick around," she taunted.

After placing the last of the food on the table, she went to get ready for work or battle, I wasn't sure. I found the hot sauce bottle and put it on the table.

When the doorbell chimed, I opened the door and was surprised to see Padre Thomas standing there alone with a scowl.

"Padre Thomas." He came in. "I didn't know you were coming."

"Do you think for a minute I would let Norm off the hook for what he's done?" He walked to the kitchen, looked at the setting for four and grinned. "I'll get the folding chair from the backyard. You need to set another place. Smells wonderful." He walked outside.

When he came back with the chair, I had pushed aside the settings and made room for him. He put the chair in the empty spot and then poured himself a *café con leche,* adding four sugars.

"I thought they would be here by seven." He sipped his coffee, snatched a *tostone* from the plate and ate it as he looked at the wall clock. "Still hot," he said and used his hand to fan his open mouth.

"She's been cooking all morning." I made another *con leche* for myself and poured cold milk into the container for frothing. "She could feed an army."

"A small army," Tita said as she walked into the kitchen. She was in a colorful summer dress and wore her hair in a tight ponytail. "Nice to see you, Padre Thomas."

"As I told Mick, I wouldn't miss Norm's talk for a minute." He sipped from his coffee. "I only hope that he is honest."

"You are familiar, Padre, with the Last Supper." She frothed the milk and made herself another *con leche.*

"Of course."

"Think of this as Norm's last breakfast." She laughed, mostly to herself, and then said more emphatically, "If he lies to me, that's what it will be."

"I cannot think of him at the Last Supper," he said seriously.

"That's okay, Padre, because I don't think we'd make good disciples, either."

"Let's hope there is no Judas among us." They both turned to me when I said it and frowned.

The doorbell rang and I recognized Norm's banging that followed.

CHAPTER 38

I answered the door while Tita heated more milk. Padre Thomas stood behind me, ready to confront a lie if he heard one. We were an army of three, Tita, Padre Thomas and me. Were we about to confront the enemy?

Norm's smile when he saw Padre Thomas didn't fool me. He wasn't expecting the priest. Alfonso pushed Norm through the door.

"Ah." Alfonso smiled. "I smell Latin cooking."

No one shook hands. We walked into the kitchen and Tita directed us to sit.

"*Café con leches?*" She poured the cups without waiting for an answer. "Alfonso, *yo deseo espresso tu?*"

"*Después del desayuno gracias.*"

"*Por nada.*" She gave out the coffees. "Orange juice?"

Everyone was happy with coffee and helped themselves to the food. Tita placed a bowl of hot chicken on a wooden disk on the table and sat down. I saw Alfonso eye the bottle of hot sauce as I splashed the red liquid onto my food. I held it up and he grabbed it. Puerto Rican cooking had to do with spices, while Mexican foods added hot peppers to the spicy mix. A good hot sauce was the equalizer when eating Tita's cooking.

"*Bacalao?*" Norm held up the pancake-sized *bacalao frito.*

"Yes," she said and filled her plate with small portions of food. "You've eaten them before?"

"Similar," he said, and took a bite. He smiled, nodded his approval and took a piece of buttered Cuban bread.

"I hope you will be as honest in everything you say." Tita added two sweeteners to her coffee and began picking at her food. "Mick told me what has been going on, Norm. Can you elaborate?" she said with a thin smile and a cold stare. "Of course, Mick may not have told me everything, though I expect you will."

"The food is delicious," Norm began with a grin.

"Thank you." Tita returned the smile. "Go on."

Norm quietly explained the official line of what happened from the time of the car wash shooting until he arrived. He ate as he spoke, stopping between bites as he explained why he thought we needed protection. Sometimes he looked toward Alfonso, who nodded his agreement. He did admit he had no information on the shootout along US1 and left out what he knew about the decapitated body at the school. Padre Thomas looked as though he was ready to interrupt, but a brief glance toward Tita kept him quiet.

"Pretty much what Mick said." She put her fork down and wiped her mouth. She picked up her purse from the floor and set it on her lap.

"Then you're up to date." Norm put the last of the *tostones* on his plate.

"There's one thing wrong."

"I'm sorry, say what?"

"I've known Mick a long time." She stressed the word *long* with her stare focused on Norm. "And you've known and worked with him, but it has been awhile. However, I know one thing about Mick that hasn't changed and I am sure we agree on it." She stopped and sipped her coffee.

The kitchen was quiet as we waited for Tita to continue or Norm to answer.

Norm blinked first. "I'm sure we agree on many things. What

one are you talking about?"

"Mick has never told the whole truth in his life." She spoke slowly while she continued to sip her coffee and kept a grin aimed at Norm. "So, since you and he told the same story, I have to assume you are not telling me the whole truth."

Norm smiled too broadly, which only added to his guilty look. Alfonso seemed uncomfortable and forced himself to continue eating. Padre Thomas laughed under his breath. I finished my coffee.

Tita opened her purse, removed a .38 caliber Saturday night special and laid it on the table. As Alfonso pushed back, Norm stretched his arm out and stopped him. I looked at the revolver and wondered where she got it.

"What's that for?" Norm finished his coffee without seeming concerned.

"I thought it might be an added incentive for you to tell the truth."

"Is it loaded?"

"There would be no incentive if it wasn't."

"Do you know how to use it?"

"Do you want to find out?"

Norm chuckled. "Good point. You plan on shooting me if you don't like my answers?"

"No." Tita smiled. "I know I'm not going to like your answers. I am going to shoot you if you lie. One lie, one shot."

"You're not gonna shoot anyone," I said, more surprised than I was concerned about her shooting Norm.

"Because he's your friend?" Tita challenged.

"I'm not sure he's my friend," I said. "But you won't shoot him because it's not in your nature."

"Mick's got a point, Tita. Especially if you're gonna shoot me in cold blood." Norm ate the last *tostone*. He looked at me, winked and offered a dim smirk. I hunched my shoulders. He wasn't sure what to do. Tell the truth, or part of the truth, or continue the lie. Tita's .38 revolver didn't intimidate Norm.

Padre Thomas' frightened stare focused on the revolver and I doubted he heard anything we said. Tita was not aware of the effect the gun had on the priest. I reached for the revolver and moved it toward Tita.

"Put it away," I whispered, with a nod toward Padre Thomas. "It isn't an incentive."

Tita saw the look of fear etched on Padre Thomas' face, turned to Norm and returned his smile as she picked up the gun and put it in her purse. "It is loaded and I know how to use it," she said in defense of her pride.

"I've no doubt," Norm said. "Your point was well made, Tita, and I believe you deserve the truth." He yawned. "It has been a rough twenty-four hours. What I left out was done to protect you, not to lie or to fool you."

"Mick calls it a white lie," she said. "A rose is a rose by any other name, or something like that." She looked at me.

"Something like that," I said.

"I don't know you, Tita, or Padre Thomas," Alfonso said, not hiding his irritation. "I have known Norm and Mick on a personal and business level, but what I am doing here has nothing to do with friendships. The violence in my country, especially my city, is caused by you." Alfonso's voice carried anger and frustration and it was easy to see he was tired. His battle had been long and he was weary and not interested in our squabble.

"I am fighting an enemy that is better armed than me and has financial backing larger than most Central American countries' annual budgets." He pushed his chair away from the table. "The guns and money for this war against Mexico comes from the United States. Your borders southward are wide open to such things. You keep Mexicans out that are looking for work, but drugs have no problem getting in. Americans' craving for cocaine and other drugs drives all this. It pays for it and that craving is responsible for the murders in Tijuana." Alfonso stood and walked to the espresso machine, poured the strong coffee into his cup and added sugar, no milk. "It is an American problem, but Mexico seems to have the worst end of the stick," he said from the coffee pot, with a look at Norm for assurances that his words were correct.

"The opportunity to infiltrate the cartel's distribution network in the States fell into our laps," he said hesitantly, and looked at Norm again to confirm the correctness of his state-ment. He was afraid of misusing his English in the angry rush to say what he had to say. At Norm's nod, he continued. "We did not have time to do more than a quick calculation. We re-alized we could take advantage of the opportunity and in some ways control it. Knowing Mick was an advantage for us. Within fifteen minutes the decision was made and in another hour the cartel's bosses thought they had set something in motion."

"Mick's involvement is made up," Norm said. "It made everything easy."

"Easy for who?" Tita shrieked. "You are going to have to explain how getting Mick almost killed helps you infiltrate the cartel." She got up and heated milk. If she didn't keep busy, maybe she would shoot Norm.

Padre Thomas walked to the back porch for a quick smoke and came back in when the hissing sound of the frothing stopped. Tita filled everyone but Alfonso's cup with hot espresso and milk.

"You want me to explain?" Alfonso asked Norm, who nod-ded. "Two things," he said, and sat down. "We arrest the shoot-ers, drivers, whoever we can and that lowers the ranks of the distributor. If we are lucky, we turn one of them and send him back, and we control him.

"By our cutting the rank and file, they need to recruit more men and we have undercover Mexican and American agents in low positions that can move up," Alfonso went on. "We will be creating a vacuum and with luck some of our men will get to fill it. If they send men from Mexico to fill the positions here, they also need to replace those people in Mexico. That gives our agents another chance to move up." He was in control of his voice again and kept eye contact with Tita.

"Intel," Norm said. "We can get firsthand intel from those we arrest. Some of the hard-asses will keep quiet, but with sentencing guidelines now it's not too difficult to turn someone and make a deal. The cartel reaches into the prison system here and anyone that has critical information seems to die in custody. These guys know that and if they have knowledge of routes, bribed officials and such, they don't have a long life expectancy in jail. They know about the witness protection program because some of their friends are in it."

Tita sat quietly, drank her coffee, and sent a quick glance toward Padre Thomas. Finally, she looked at me and then turned her stare on Norm. "So he didn't know about any of this until you told him."

"We came right away," Norm said. "Mick had no clue until we told him. Unfortunately, the cartel got here first. Which should indicate how well organized they are in the States."

"You two protect him, and some female agent and I become Siamese twins," Tita said, recalling the talk about protection. "It doesn't seem like enough." She reached into her purse and smiled. "Like I told you, this is loaded."

"As I said, I have no doubt." Norm grinned as Tita pulled her empty hand from the purse. "There will be DEA agents and JIATF agents all around waiting, and they will be responsible for capturing the cartel's men. We will personally protect Mick and the female DEA agent will be for your protection. Tita," Norm's voice became serious. "I don't believe you'll be a victim as long as you keep away from Mick for a few days."

Tita gave me a sideways look and a thin smirk that included a chuckle. "You want us to go about our normal routine, then you tell me to stay away from Mick. You can't have it both ways."

"She's right, Norm," I said. "She's been in Boston for a month and anyone with common sense knows I wouldn't keep away, just the opposite."

"Mick's right." She smiled. "I did miss some things about him. People know we're out for dinner at least twice a week and God only knows how many happy hours he gets to and I meet him at some."

"What would you do today, normally?"

"I'd go to work, eight-to-five, we might meet for lunch, maybe for a drink at five."

"Miss lunch today," Norm said, scratching his head. "It'll give us time to set things up. Where would happy hour be?"

"I don't make that decision until later," I said and picked at my rice and chicken. "I'd call before four and tell her."

"Your buddies?"

"If I don't have lunch with Tita, I'd meet Bob somewhere, maybe Burt, and if it's on the water maybe Doug too."

"Do you ever stay at the boat?" Alfonso said.

"We'll work it out," Norm said to quiet the confusion.

Tita looked at him. "You feel you can assure Mick's safety."

"We're doing everything humanly possible, Tita," Norm said. "Death and taxes can be guaranteed. All I can do is assure you we are doing our best and don't want anyone hurt."

"Apparently, you can add fucking with the cartel to death and taxes," she said with a scowl.

"We're gonna fix that," Norm promised.

Chapter 39

Padre Thomas commented on how disappointed he was in Norm and then went outside for a cigarette. Norm and Alfonso decided they'd drive Tita to work and stay until the female agent showed up, which they expected to be shortly. At ten o'clock they were meeting with Chief Richard Dowley and Sheriff Chance Wagner for an informative discussion on the situation.

"This is a federal action," Norm said as Tita got ready to leave. "We'll work with the local LEOs, but on a minimum. Because it involves the border, we can use national security as a reason to call in Homeland Security and that threat should keep the locals in line."

I drove to the marina. The sailboat they'd talked about earlier had already slipped across from me. A couple sat on deck reading the paper while they drank coffee. They waved and I waved back.

"You have a boat on the dock?" the man called to me.

This was a live-aboard dock, so transient rentals were not allowed. It had to be my twenty-four-hour security.

"Right here." I pointed to the *Fenian Bastard*.

"You're welcome to come aboard. We are hosting a happy hour later, a meet and greet," the woman said. "We want to meet our neighbors."

They were young, mid-thirties, tanned and athletic-looking. Maybe they really were sailors on their dream stakeout.

"I'm checking on a few things and then I'm gone for most of the day. Another time." I waved again and got onboard my boat.

Everything on deck looked in place. Down below was cool and dark. I turned on the CD player and listened to seventies Kristofferson and Waylon Jennings songs. I had forgotten what CDs were in the player. While I cleaned the Glock Pauly had loaned me, I called Bob and agreed to meet him at Kyushu for lunch. He would call Burt. I assured him that I'd fill in all the details on what was happening at lunch.

"Should I bring your gift?" He'd received the M-4.

"Leave it in your truck." I wasn't sure what I would do with it. It was smaller than the M-16, but not concealable.

I changed into a clean pair of cargo shorts and a tropical print shirt. The Glock fit snugly against my back and the shirt covered it. The extra magazines went into the pockets of my cargo shorts and I was ready to go. If I fell into the water, I'd sink like a rock. I grabbed my white Penn State ball cap. Twin sisters from New Jersey gave it to me one night at the Hog's Breath. They were regulars during the summer; then they got married and now it was only occasionally that they came to the island.

I locked up and looked around. The couple across the dock was still on deck reading the newspaper. Clouds covered the sky and a breeze that smelled of rain and seaweed wafted across the marina. Hurricane Fred was too far off for the coming rain to be outer bands; nonetheless, the rain was coming. Dark clouds filled the sky to the east and were moving this way.

"Rain?" the man yelled as I walked by.

"Within the hour," I shouted back and kept walking.

The parking lot looked as it usually did in the morning; half the spots were empty as live-aboard residents headed to work. I didn't see anyone hanging around to protect me. On the other hand, no one was waiting there to kill me.

Traffic was light from the marina to the Japanese restaurant. No one turned on Packard Street when I did or pulled into the small parking lot. So much for my security. I pulled in behind Bob's truck. I hoped I hid my nervousness as I slowly scanned the area looking for my protection or my killer. I saw no one.

A catering crew for the neighboring business loaded trucks on the street as I walked to the restaurant's entrance on Truman Avenue. Bob sat in the main dining room and Ken worked behind the sushi bar preparing for the lunch crowd.

"Burt is meeting us at Schooner later," Bob said as a greeting.

After the waitress took our order of various sushi rolls and the bento lunch box, I filled Bob in on what happened at Tita's. He was surprised at her acceptance of Norm's plan and thought the Saturday night special on the table was funny. "I knew she'd see through him. I wish I'd been there."

"It was a great breakfast, but I didn't eat much."

"Explains why we're here this early."

I had yet to meet anyone that left Kyushu hungry after ordering the bento lunch box.

"I have your M-4," he said after our soup and salad came. "You want it in the Jeep or on the boat?"

"Hold on to it for me." The small assault rifle would fit nicely on the boat, but it didn't belong in an open Jeep.

He grinned. "Burt and I are with you on this. Tell us what to do, what you need."

"I need this to be over," I said as our lunch arrived.

CHAPTER 40

I parked the Jeep in one of the two coveted parking spots behind Schooner Wharf Bar and hoped it was a sign my luck had changed. Bob went for Burt so they wouldn't need to search out two parking spots in the neighborhood. A small lunch crowd sat scattered around the P-rock patio, hoping to beat the rain by rushing their meal, while the covered bar was close to full. I looked the place over from the narrow employee side entrance and recognized some of the patrons. A few I knew well. Others I knew to talk to if we sat together. You get to be friends with people in Key West without knowing that much about them; you take people as they are. On one side of you could sit a wealthy TV producer hiding out from the extravagances of Hollywood and on the other a boater trying to scrape up enough money to make the next leg of his journey though the Caribbean. They usually all dress alike, so it's hard to tell who has the money and fame and who has the independence.

Hank Tester sat at the bar with the remote news crew from Miami. Maybe Hurricane Fred was closer than I thought if Hank was here. He sipped his favorite drink, a Bombay blue-sapphire gin martini from a real martini glass. I know his favorite drink because I was at the bar years ago when Hank was covering an approaching hurricane and convinced one of the bar's owners, Evalena Worthington, that martinis should never be served in plastic. She agreed with his arguments and found him a proper glass. Martinis, blue or otherwise, were not a common drink at the bar, but when a customer ordered one it arrived in a proper glass. Chalk one up for the power of the media.

Josh and Woodrow sat with their heads together as they worked on a new scheme. Bill and Karen ate hamburgers and drank beers at a small table for two by the T-shirt shop. Bill is an ad man with clients in D.C. and Karen is a local Realtor. Rob and Mandy ate fish tacos with margaritas by the magician's table. Rob hid out in Key West when not photographing celebrities in L.A. or New York. Everyone is someone in Key West and no one cares. Texas Rich leaned on the bar and tried to carry on a conversation with Vickie the busy bartender, and held tightly onto his can of Miller Lite. Becky from the sheriff's office and two uniformed deputies ate fish sandwiches and drank sodas at a large table on the patio. Had they met with Hank before lunch to discuss county hurricane preparations for a pre-hurricane story? Nadene sat on the patio with two women and I guessed she was discussing a bachelorette party since she planned weddings in the Keys. Meteorologist Matt sat waiting for the latest Weather Channel report and then he'd head back to his office. Michael MacLeod and Carl Peachy set up the stage for their afternoon music. Nadja watched the approaching rain from the bar with her Scotch on the rocks.

There were others I said hello to as I found an empty table. I accepted that I put these people in jeopardy by being here. What choice did I have? Somewhere at some time, someone was going to try to kill or kidnap me without concern for anyone else. It wasn't my doing. I was as much a victim as the accountants from Miami, but no one cared. I had no choice; I had to trust Norm, maybe for the last time.

"You back?" Alexis, the waitress from California, smiled at me.

"Alexis. What?" I lost my daytime nightmare.

She chuckled. "You looked like you were a million miles away. Kalik with lime?"

"Please," I replied as if it was a joke. "I'll try to stick around."

"At least until you pay the bill." She winked and walked away.

I wanted to get up and leave. What if the killers or kidnappers had arrived at that moment and Alexis had been hurt? I didn't want the responsibility on my conscience.

"Are you expecting someone?" Alexis asked and placed the beer in front of me.

"Yeah," I said, sneaking back from my dark thoughts. "Two, maybe four."

"Want menus? Or a bucket of Kalik?"

"I don't, but they might want menus."

She left two menus on the table and walked away.

After a little while, Norm greeted me with a slap on the back. "Tell him." He meant Alfonso, who was next to him.

"Tell him what?"

"About the damn rain," he hissed. "We should take a picnic basket to the cemetery."

Alfonso looked confused as he sat down. "There is a story behind his ranting, right?"

"Oh yeah, and I'm tired of hearing it."

They placed themselves at the table so Norm could see the patio and narrow Lazy Way, and Alfonso had a clear view of the waterfront. They both could see anyone walking from the bar toward the restrooms.

"Tita's roommate show up?" I sipped my beer while they looked for a server. "She'll be right back."

"Are you ordering?" Norm picked up the menu and scanned it.

"No." I sipped more beer. "A bucket of five Kaliks is the beer special."

"The Hog sells Negra Modelo." I finished my beer.

"We should go there." Alfonso said.

"Next stop." I waved for Alexis' attention. I introduced my guests and she promised to return with the bucket of beer.

"Nice girl," Norm said.

Men were moving the cigar roller's stand from the patio to under the old tin roof of the bar so it would be out of the rain. The sky to the east was dark and heavy with rain clouds; looking south over the water, the sky was still blue with a scattering of white clouds. If nothing else, Key West was capable of being contradictory on everything. The easterly breeze had picked up and it smelled damp from a mixture of rain, saltwater, deep-fried cooking from the kitchen and summer flora that blossomed around the Old Town neighborhood. The pungent scents attacked the senses.

"Did she show up?" I bit down my anger at Norm's ignoring me the first time I asked.

"Hoss, we wouldn't be here if she hadn't," he grunted.

"The agent's good?"

Alexis brought the bucket of beer while Norm shook his head and laughed.

"No," he said. "She's new and untrustworthy, so the DEA wouldn't even give her a weapon."

His reply was heavy with sarcasm and it kept me from worrying that what he said was true. I knew I was being foolish, but I couldn't avoid thoughts of Tijuana. They filled my mind, leaving me overly concerned. Something I should have been in Tijuana, and maybe I wouldn't have this personal hell to deal with, especially at night.

"Lighten up," Alfonso said. "Both of you."

"I don't want TJ all over again."

"Right now the only one that might get blown up is you." The coldness in Norm's words rushed across the table at me.

191

"Let us do our job and you do your part and we'll get this over with."

"If they use a bomb . . ." I kept my voice low and stretched out my arms, indicating all those that sat around us.

Norm looked at me and chuckled. "Look around, for Christ's sake, where would anyone hide a bomb? The size needed to take you out couldn't be hidden in a bathing suit, behind a T-shirt or in someone's shorts."

"A shopping bag," Alfonso said. He pointed to a portly woman walking a dog along the pier and carrying a Jimmy Buffett Margaritaville shopping bag.

"I could use some support here, *amigo.*"

"Keep an eye out for Bob and Burt." I stood up. "I'm going to the john."

"Can't you wait?" Norm said, and gave the patio a quick look. "JIATF guys aren't here yet."

"One way in, one way out." I pointed next to the kitchen's shelf of iced oysters and tapped my lower back. "I think I can protect myself at the urinal if you keep my back safe."

"I'll buy cigars." Norm went to the cigar table.

I walked up the narrow space between the kitchen and the lattice panels that served as a wall. Joe Bolter, a local writer I knew, was walking out and we nodded hellos. The bar used the space for its ice machine, freezer and other locked storage. Space is at a premium in Key West and none of it is wasted. A small plank lined the dirt path to keep patrons from walking in the soggy soil. The ramp turned left after the freezer and ended at a sink. The bathroom was off in a room to the left. I was alone.

I used the bathroom and when I turned to leave I was surprised to see a man wearing dress slacks and a shirt standing next to an opening cut in the lattice wall across from the bathroom door and next to the sink. He smiled. I smiled and turned to leave, but a rather large man, also dressed more for Miami than Key West, blocked the exit.

"Mr. Murphy, someone would like to talk to you. Please come with us." He spoke without an accent. As he stepped aside to show the freshly cut opening, I could see a black SUV waiting on Lazy Way. "Please don't be concerned. You can keep your weapon, but leave it under the shirt."

"Where to?" I mustered the courage to say.

"He's waiting at the airport. He wants to help with your problem." The man pointed to the gap in the wobbly fence. "We are unarmed, Mr. Murphy, and if we meant you harm, we wouldn't be."

I turned to look at the large man blocking the exit. "He's a weapon."

"That's Tiny and he's usually very gentle."

Tiny walked toward us. His bulk forced me toward the opening in an ungentle way. The polite one went ahead of me. He grabbed my arm as soon as I was on the other side of the lattice so I couldn't run, and we waited for Tiny to propel himself through the gap. The back door of the SUV opened for us.

CHAPTER 41

The polite one led me to the SUV, never letting go of my arm. The snorkeling catamarans were at the reef and only a trickle of people walked along the dock. Rain clouds darkened the sky. I hesitated at the SUV's door, but another nudge from Tiny directed me into the back seat. A man sat against the opposite door and smiled but said nothing. Tiny took up most of the front seat; my polite friend sat next to me and closed the door. The SUV moved slowly and turned on Elizabeth Street.

I finally mustered the nerve to speak. "Who wants to see me?"

"A man that wants to help," the polite one said. "We need your cell phone." He held out his hand.

I hesitated. I knew they could take it if they really wanted to.

"Alfonso and his friend should be wondering where you are by now," he said. "It's better you shut it off and we hold it. Removes the temptation to answer it, especially if the call is from Tita."

His knowing about Tita caught me off guard, but I understood he brought it up to show me how thorough they were. He made the right guess that Tita was my soft spot, my weakness. Letting me know he was familiar with Alfonso was another sign of their thoroughness. I wondered what kind of relationship they had.

Shutting off the cell phone stopped its GPS signal so I couldn't be located electronically. So far everyone had been polite, and if I wasn't thrown on a plane and taken to Tijuana, I was okay. Kind of okay, even if it only bought me time. The island was small and finding me, especially at the airport, wouldn't require brain surgery. By now I had surely been missed.

If these kidnappers wanted me dead, I'd be on the floor of the funky bathroom at Schooner Wharf. *What a place to die,* I thought, and shook my head.

Worst-case scenario, the kidnappers worked for the Tijuana cartel. I knew from my research that the cartel didn't bother with niceties when they kidnapped someone. More often than not, they put a bag over your head and tossed you in a car trunk. These men appeared unarmed and were polite, so I figured and hoped they were another mix in this crazy scheme. What did they want? What could this mystery man do to help me that Norm and Alfonso couldn't?

I sat back and watched the driver follow the vehicle's GPS directions to the airport. He kept within the posted speed limits and that meant even scooters passed us when we were on Flagler and South Roosevelt.

"Please," the kidnapper said, still holding out his hand.

I unsnapped my cell phone, shut it off and gave it to him. "I could've gone for the gun," I said, and grinned.

"Why?"

I looked at him and wondered if he was for real or trying to keep me under control. "Shoot my way out."

"Why?"

"To escape my kidnappers."

Even the driver joined in the laughter.

"We're offering you protection from kidnappers," the polite one said. "The man you are going to meet can fix your problem. Because it is the airport," he said while putting my cell into a small plastic zip bag, "I will need your gun too."

"I don't think that's up for discussion."

The man to my left moved so quickly, I didn't realize it until

I was bent over with my head on my knees. I didn't feel a thing until he stopped and held me there, head down with my arms useless. Just as quickly, he released his grip and helped me sit up.

"If we wanted to take the gun by force, we could have."

"I can see that." I rubbed the back of my head where he had gripped me. "Why didn't you take it?"

"We are not the enemy. You'll get the phone and gun back when we return you to the bar. Simple as that."

"How do you know Alfonso?" I reached for the Glock and no one flinched with expectation of my pulling it as a weapon.

I dropped the Glock into the opened bag and he sealed it. The SUV pulled into the airport road and made its way to the upper departure level. This level also held the airport restaurant, the Conch Flyer. No one offered any information on Alfonso.

When I first came to Key West, the airport terminal was a long, un-air-conditioned, one-story building. After a flight came in, luggage went into a long cut in the arrival lounge's concrete wall, and a canvas curtain on the outside protected it from sun and rain while it waited to be picked up. You could walk from the old Conch Flyer restaurant and bar, past the ticket stations to the arrivals. It was a fitting airport for America's one-and-only Caribbean island. It made you feel you were in the tropics and ready for an adventure. But that has all changed.

Today you look at the modern terminal and you could be at the airport in Anywhere USA. It's small, so you wouldn't mistake it for Los Angeles, but it has lost its personality and become a cold, escalator up-and-down, sanitary walkway, concrete-and-glass terminal that doesn't fit in the tropics.

The SUV stopped outside the terminal's automated glass doors.

"He is waiting for you in the restaurant." The polite one opened the door, got out as the rain began and waited for me.

"Who?"

"The man will recognize you."

CHAPTER 42

Monroe County, not the City of Key West, is responsible for the Key West International Airport. Its international status comes from the unscheduled flights of Cuban airliners and MIGs during the last fifty years. There are no scheduled international flights arriving or departing. The county built it, but I don't think anyone will come because of its modern design. Key West is a small tropical island and no fancy technological tricks will change that. People come because it is Key West; they always have and always will. Key West means different things to different people, but primarily it's Key West, known for its sun, pristine waters, coral reefs, bars, free-spirit attitude, artists and writers and good times. It doesn't need technology to bring people because most of them come to escape what technology has brought to their daily world.

There are hours between flight arrivals and departures, and when that happens the new terminal becomes a ghost town with empty ticket counters. There are no screens with readouts of flight information for passengers and no mass seating for them. The menu boards behind the ticket counters have daily flight information posted with push-on letters and they don't change even if a flight is delayed or canceled.

I walked out of the rain into the sterile terminal. It was devoid of employees and I walked the bright, empty hallway to the Conch Flyer. The new restaurant is a fine place, but has none of the character of the old one. Memorabilia showing the airport's history covers both walls as customers walk in. It makes arrivals wish they were at the old restaurant and reminds locals they miss it. The long mahogany bar on the right was deserted, not even a bartender. A waitress stood by the kitchen door. Large windows looked out over the street-level departure terminal and offered a glimpse of the tarmac and rain clouds.

Customers sat at three of the tables. One man was alone in a booth by the window. He looked up and nodded, so I walked toward him. He was an African American, his skin the color of coffee with a splash of milk. His hair was trimmed short and he wore expensive, well-fitting dress slacks and a shirt. He wasn't dressed for the tropics.

As I approached, he stood. He looked as if he could have been a basketball player, he was so tall. He grinned when we shook hands.

"Liam Murphy," he said, and took a seat. "But you prefer Mick?"

"Mick is fine."

His reading glasses were on the table with a Los Angeles paper and a cup of cold coffee. The waitress refilled his cup and placed one in front of me. She filled it and walked away. Sugar and cream were on the table.

"The coffee is good." He added two sugars to it. "I appreciate your coming and talking to me. I think I can help you."

"Do many people argue with Tiny?" I added sugar to my coffee.

He laughed. "Poor Tiny. He's a gentle giant and few realize it because of his size."

"Fooled me."

"Life and success is all about the bluff, isn't it?" He sipped from his cup. "Will it rain long?" He looked out the window as the rain became heavier.

"I haven't heard a weather report," I said. "This time of year we get afternoon storms and most are gone within an hour."

He reached into his shirt pocket and pulled out a business card. "I'm sorry. I should have introduced myself." He slid the card to me. "Jerome Smith, a pleasure to meet you."

"I knew a government agent named Smith." We weren't friends and I have no idea what Agent Smith's name really was, but I did know him. He almost got me killed in Cuba.

"I am sure we're not related." He looked at the rain and seemed concerned.

"Me, too."

"You may call me Jerome."

"Feel free to call me whatever you want." I looked around. None of the other customers appeared threatening and I'd seen the waitress here before. "The reason you requested my presence?"

"I'm sorry." He turned to me. "I do not like flying in stormy weather." He smiled nervously while admitting a weakness. "Do you fly much?"

"I used to all the time, but now not if I can avoid it."

"That's right, you like sailing."

"Yeah." I sighed. "Look, Jerome, you know all about me. I get that. What's going on?"

"I'm an attorney and I represent someone who can help you."

I read his card. *Jerome Smith, Esquire, attorney at law, San Diego, California.* Why do attorneys use esquire with their name if they are not a junior or a third or something with a lot of letters? I never remember to ask. "You're a long way from San Diego."

"Came all this way to talk to you."

"So talk." I sat back in the booth.

He pulled a manila envelope from the seat and withdrew a sheet of paper. "I need you to sign this." He handed me the paper and put on his glasses.

It was an attorney-client contract. It didn't indicate why I was hiring him, just that I was.

"Sign it and we have attorney-client privilege." He handed me a pen.

"No reason stated for why I am hiring you and no fee."

"One dollar retainer will do and then we can talk about anything and it's privileged. Do you have a dollar?"

I signed the document and wondered if I would get a copy. I returned the paper to him with a five-dollar bill. Now we were protected and could talk about anything, like who was trying to kill me. "Keep the difference."

He folded the document, put it back in the manila envelope and pocketed the money. With elbows on the table, Jerome removed his glasses, rested his chin on folded hands and stared at me. "I represent clients from Mexico that are interested in getting their property back. They tell me you have some of it." He folded his arms as he leaned back. "They are quite serious about it and they scare Tiny."

I sighed. "Let me make this easy. You know Alfonso, right?"

"My clients do, yes."

I recounted the concocted story of the car wash, Harpoon Harry's and US1. I explained that until Alfonso showed up and described how I'd been recognized, I had no idea any of these things were connected. I assured him that I did not steal twenty million dollars from anyone. He listened without changing expression.

"Very interesting," he said after I finished. "My clients were adamant about dealing harshly with you. Believe me, it took a lot on my part to convince them they could not use the same tactics in the States that they get away with in Mexico. To stress how serious these people are and how it concerns me, I should tell you I used to make visits to Mexico to talk with my clients and I would often spend a night or two there. I no longer cross the border. I fear for my safety, and I do not want to fear for my safety on this side. My clients now come to me."

"What is it you want from me? I've told you the truth."

"I believe you. However, that doesn't change much."

"It changes everything."

"Yes, for you and me, but not for them. I did convince them that you would not have all the money, only your share."

"I don't have a dime of the money."

"Yes, I realize that. I'm only telling you what I told my clients. They are missing most of the twenty million and will accept what is left of your share and leave you alone. I got them to promise."

"I can give them one hundred percent of my share."

Jerome sat up straight and looked surprised. "You can?"

"Yeah, I got no share and I can give them that."

He looked amused. "Journalists are killed too often in Mexico. I explained that the people here have a love-hate relationship with the press. They can hate them, but no one kills them. I eventually got them to agree." He grinned, still amused with the topic. "Reluctantly. But most other Americans don't have your protection."

"Are you threatening me?"

"No, no, no." He raised his hands in surrender. "I want to make sure you are fully aware of the situation. Can you raise any amount of money?"

"I couldn't raise fifty thousand if my life depended on it."

"It does," he said coldly.

I looked at him and there was no humor there.

Chapter 43

Jerome had suggested I buy my way out of the cartel's vengeance with his help. I wondered if that was even possible or if the whole thing could have been him wanting to get his hands on an ample amount of cash. Sounded like something a shady shyster would think up. The notorious cartel settling for a million or two million to reconcile a twenty-million dollar theft didn't seem logical. The money was gone; the cartel was out to make examples of the thieves, to discourage others from such acts and maybe get a little of the money back. I had nothing but Jerome's word that he was who he said, or that he really represented the cartel. By using Alfonso's name, he gave me a source to verify his credentials and that was his purpose in mentioning it. I decided out of desperation to believe him until I had a reason not to.

"My life or not," I said, and finished my cold coffee. "I can't give you what I don't have."

"It would have to be at least two million," he went on, ignoring my comment. "They will probably demand a minimum of five, but two will quiet them."

"You're not listening, Jerome. If I sold everything I owned, I'd be lucky to come up with a hundred thousand."

"No one you can borrow from?"

I laughed. "My mother wouldn't loan me two million dollars."

"She's dead," he said flatly.

What he must have known about me suddenly became frightening. It didn't take long to do background checks on people today thanks to the Internet. As a journalist, most of my writings were online; information about me is posted, sometimes by strangers, and available for search engines to find. This is only one downside of technology.

"I am leaving for Miami." He looked out the window. The rain had stopped and part of the sky was blue. "I can be reached at the number on my card anytime. Please think it over and call me."

"I have a question," I said before he got up.

"Yes?"

"You wanna loan me two million? I am good for it."

His laugh lacked humor and his look became cold and hard. "I am trying to help you for selfish reasons, but help nonetheless," he lectured. "I don't want the violence on this side of the border, and it's liable to come because of you. I don't know you and have no feelings of liking or disliking you. I have dealt with dangerous men in trying to save you and they have agreed to go along with me . . ." he paused as if to ridicule me. "To a point. I have until the end of the week." He stopped and continued his stare but said nothing more.

"Is that a yes or no about the loan?" I knew this would upset him, but said it anyway. I didn't like Jerome or his attitude and it had nothing to do with his skin color or height. I don't like drug dealers or attorneys on their payroll.

He looked at me as if I were a bug he wanted to squash. I wondered what kind.

"I can make one phone call and we wouldn't have to wait until Friday." The words came slow, precise and as a threat. "Remember." He stood. "Only you are safe until the end of the week. No one else around you is. They may want to do something that will help motivate you to return the money."

"That is the second time you've made a threat," I said through clenched teeth to keep from yelling. "I'm a hard man to kill and I believe in getting even. So I suggest you talk to your clients and turn this shit storm off before it goes any further."

"All I've read about you certainly indicates a charmed, adventurous life," he said calmly, and leaned against the table looking down at me. "Of course, that was during revolutions and the men were farmers, citizen soldiers and shopkeepers. It is not that way now, Mr. Murphy. The men coming are well-paid professionals who, I should say, enjoy their work. You are, forgive my crudeness, nothing but a pimple on their ass compared to what they do routinely in Mexico." He stopped for a breath and managed a shallow smile. "I have seen the address book taken from the car wash and you are nowhere in it, no mention at all in the appointment pages. That alone makes me believe you, but I suggest you beg or borrow or steal the money. Otherwise . . ." he crunched his face into an ugly expression. "My believing you doesn't change a thing."

The Conch Flyer was empty of customers. The waitress stood bored by the coffee station and kitchen entrance. Jerome held the envelope with our agreement and continued to look down at me. I was looking at him.

I sighed. "There is no money. And no chance in hell I can raise it, either. I can promise you this, if the shit begins to fly in Key West, you won't be safe from the violence no matter where you are."

Neither of us was smiling, but Jerome did force a short chuckle.

"The cavalry is here for you, Mr. Murphy." He grinned, but not because of my threat.

I turned to see Norm and three others standing at the entrance, automatic weapons aimed in our direction. Alfonso stood in the background.

"You okay?" Norm called.

"Never better." I looked at Jerome. "Right?"

"That's up to you. They come after you," he whispered sternly, "you would never make it to San Diego. So don't threaten me."

One of the armed men went with the waitress into the kitchen while Norm walked toward us.

"Anyone else here?" He scanned the empty restaurant and walked to the deserted bar. He stopped across from us.

"We were having coffee. Mr. Murphy is a client," Jerome said. "Is there a problem?"

"Jerome," Alfonso called out as he walked into the restaurant. "You are a long way from home."

"As are you, *Agente Ruiz*."

"I am working." Alfonso stopped in front of us.

Jerome grinned. "I am, too. Mr. Murphy is my client." He held out the envelope.

"And the four men in custody outside?"

"From my office in Miami."

"Tiny is in Miami now?"

"No, of course not. He goes wherever I do."

"There were weapons in the trunk."

"Oh yes, sadly it is an unsafe world. The men and weapons are licensed, but you notice they were in the trunk, not on the person."

"Except Mick's, it is in a bag on the back seat." He held out the bag.

"I don't believe a gun is allowed in the airport, security and all."

"What about the phone?"

"We didn't want any interruptions while we talked, but that comes under attorney-client privilege."

"Mick?" Norm walked up next to Alfonso. "This creep your attorney?"

"I have the contract right here." Jerome held out the envelope. No one reached for it.

"I asked Mick."

"Yeah," I said. "He's working on a problem I have. He may hold the solution."

Alfonso and Norm stared at me in amazement.

CHAPTER 44

Jerome walked out with an arrogant stride in his step like a tall black Moses parting the Red Sea of armed men. Alfonso handed me the bag with my Glock and phone. I slid the gun against my back and turned the phone on. The readout showed ten messages.

"Are the messages from you?"

Norm had me by the arm as we left the empty terminal and ignored my questions, especially when I asked who the armed men were.

"Why did you go with him?" he asked outside the terminal, anger in each word.

"You think I had a choice?"

When we got to their SUV, I told him how Jerome's men had escorted me from Schooner Wharf's bathroom and brought me to the airport.

"He would not be in the car," Alfonso agreed. "There was always the chance it could get stopped and Mick would scream."

"They followed the speed limit on Flagler and that should've made 'em suspicious," I said from the back seat.

Norm pulled the car in behind the fire station on Kennedy and Flagler between the various ball fields and the city's skateboard park. He wanted to know what Jerome said and what I agreed to. I told them.

"I have a question," I said when I was done with the explanation. I directed it to Alfonso. "Is he who he says he is? Can he fix it with the cartel?"

"Jerome's law firm has represented the interests of the cartel since long before the Arellano-Felix family ran it," he said, then lit a cigarette and turned to me in the back seat. "No one knows when or how it began, but he has invested for them, moved the money into Mexico and seen they had representation in your court system and many other services. They may be his only client. Your American system of law protects him and in its own way protects his cartel clients, too."

"It can't all be legal, even for an attorney."

"He's smart," Norm added. "You gotta give him that. The DEA and Justice have turned him upside down and shook him silly, but nothing falls out. I think it's interesting that he's here."

"Yeah." Alfonso lowered the window and tossed his cigarette. "We have not seen him in Mexico for more than a year. The safety concerns he mentioned to you could be the reason."

"Does that mean he wants to help me?"

Alfonso laughed. "For two million dollars. Where would you get that kind of money?"

I stabbed Norm on the shoulder with my finger. "You got me into this. You're DEA, get me the money."

He laughed. "You gotta be kidding me. They're not gonna pay two million for your sorry ass. Think of something else."

"I hate to lower myself to blackmail," I said and sat back. "But I could get a sweet story out of this. DEA sets up innocent journalists in drug cartel sting. I know a weekly newsmagazine that would pay me for it, especially since I can name names. Then every news agency would pick it up, I guarantee it. Even the cartel would read about it and realize their mistake."

"I told you before, we can't let you write about it."

"To stop me, you'll need to throw my ass into one of those secret CIA prisons or kill me yourself," I barked. "I didn't ask for this shit and now I've found a way out and you're gonna pay for it."

Norm turned and stared at me, then smiled. "I'll run it by the D.C. boys. I can't promise you anything."

"Don't shit a shitter," I said, got out, slammed the door and walked away.

Writing the story was a bluff and I wondered if Norm saw it. Jerome said life and success were all about the good bluff. Well, this was my life and I was bluffing. Could Norm and Alfonso risk it? I crossed Flagler and went into Grim's Grill. The TVs had either baseball or football on. I ordered a beer and called Bob. "Pick me up, will you? I'm down the street at Grim's."

"Be outside in five minutes," he said and hung up.

I watched Norm drive away from the fire station and turn on Kennedy Drive, and thought I was now without my twenty-four-seven protection.

CHAPTER 45

Bob took me to my Jeep and planned to meet me on the *Fenian Bastard* in the morning. He kept trying to give me the M-4, then finally agreed to bring it to the boat. He was more like his quiet self, but he was supportive in a demanding way and wanted to help.

The first thing I noticed at Tita's was a security light that lit up the porch and sidewalk as soon as I stopped out front. It wasn't there yesterday, so it must have been part of the security Norm promised. The second thing was that the front door was closed and locked. I knocked.

The door opened just enough for the person behind it to see me. I caught half a female's face, stern and pretty. I smiled. "I'm Mick Murphy."

The door opened and the woman smiled as I walked in. She held a Beretta by her side. "I know." She closed and locked the door. "What are you doing here?"

"My security detail and I parted ways." I looked around. "Tita?"

"Kitchen," she called back.

"Norm called, that was really stupid," the woman said as I walked to the kitchen.

"You've met Jenny?" Tita sat at the table with her glass of wine. "She's Puerto Rican."

Jenny nodded. "Juanita Mendez." She stretched out her arm and we shook hands. The Beretta stayed at her side. "People call me Jenny."

She could pass as Tita's cousin. They shared dark hair, olive skin and good looks, but she was taller. Neither had an accent.

"Pleasure," I said and took a beer from the refrigerator. "I didn't see anyone outside."

"If you were able to see them, they wouldn't be doing their job," Jenny lectured me. "You can't stay here."

"Yeah, I know." I sat down next to Tita. "You okay?"

"Tired," she said with a forced half-smile. "Hard to work with a security detail."

I looked at Jenny. "There are people outside?"

She nodded.

"I met with Jerome. Do you know him?"

"Not personally, but by reputation."

"He's given me a safe pass until Friday, but he threatened those around me twice."

"I'll be fine," Tita said. "They installed security lighting all around the house and, get this, I now have a kick-in generator so I'll always have electricity when the power fails."

"No one is going to get close to this house without our knowing it," Jenny said with a grimace. She didn't want me there. "But if the bad guys are following you, they now know where Tita lives."

I turned to look up at her and fought my anger. Things were not going well. "The plan explained to me was to capture these bad guys as they made attempts on me or my friends. Did they tell you that? Twenty-four-seven, more security than needed. Where is it?"

"It's out there." I could see the annoyance in her eyes. "And the plan didn't involve your friends, only you. You are supposed to be out there."

"Jerome changed that, at least until Friday."

"So go home or someplace and let us do our job." She took a

bottle of water from the refrigerator. "Norm will get you in the morning, but until then there are people outside protecting you both. Do your part."

Jenny walked to the front door and was ready to open it.

"Do all Puerto Ricans have a temper?" I kissed Tita. "If you need me, call and I'll be back in two minutes."

"I know you will." She kissed me and her eyes showed how tired she was. "I'm in good hands. I like her. When this is over, let's talk seriously about that sailing trip."

"You got it." I ran my hands along her ponytail. "I guess all we need to do now is keep low and let them do their job."

When did I start lying to myself?

The door closed behind me. The sound of the lock was like a knife twisting in my back. The gloomy cemetery darkened my mood. Tita's extra security must have been hidden somewhere by the shadowy crypts. I looked up and down the street. Where was mine?

CHAPTER 46

My drive to Garrison Bight from Tita's is through the Meadows and then Palm Avenue to the marina. At night it's a five-minute ride, but it seemed to take forever as I passed the sleeping neighborhood of one-family homes, dodging marauding cats, hungry raccoons and an occasional dog. The air was heavy with the fresh aroma of tropical plants that flourished in the yards around the expensive houses. The Jeep's tires sucked at the wet pavement as if I was driving in second gear on a jungle path in the Costa Rican rainforest.

I didn't like what was happening and found it hard to admit to myself, but I was nightmarishly scared for Tita and my friends and the innocent people who could be caught up in this, and it made me angry. Angry with Norm and Alfonso, angry with Jenny, angry with the couple slipped across from the *Fenian Bastard* and all the twenty-four-seven people.

As I parked I thought it strange how my anger seemed directed at the so-called good guys and not the cartel. A scornful laugh parted my lips because I have hated the cartel for a long time, but my anger now was directed toward those who selfishly brought the bastards to Key West to unleash their violence.

The parking lot lights were on, something the marina staff conveniently forgot to do each night. The halogen lights on poles at the end of each dock were also on and the marina was lit up like a movie set. Norm's work, I thought. No shadows to hide in.

Of course, the live-aboard boaters would eventually shoot out the dock lights, as they've done before because the brightness traveled through portholes, lit up the inside of most cabins and kept people from sleep. The marina finally gave up trying to keep the lights on because the expensive globes needed replacement twice a week sometimes and the staff never could find out who the shooters were. Leaving the lights off saved money in many areas.

The boat slipped across from me was dark. I wondered if the couple onboard had a night-vision camera aimed at the *Fenian Bastard*. Silly thoughts, I told myself, and climbed onto my boat.

Suspiciously, I glanced over the deck. Everything looked in place. I unlocked the main hatch and as I slid it open, my other hand went for the Glock. It was unlikely that anyone hid below, but it wasn't impossible.

The dock lighting splashed into the cabin. I couldn't see anyone hiding and everything looked normal. I walked the few steps down into the cabin and turned lights on. I closed the main hatch cover. Telling myself I was foolish, I checked the two heads and three cabins to make sure I was alone. Foolish be damned.

I took a Bohemia out of the refrigerator and removed the CDs from the player as I drank the beer. I was not in the mood to listen to Waylon and Kristofferson and Hank Jr. singing about lost love, lonely roads and barrooms. I chose CDs of Irish flute tunes and classical music. I had lost interest in songs and found music alone soothing. I turned it down low, finished my beer and headed to bed.

The bow cabin had more than enough room even with the double berth, but it was lonely. I pulled the curtains Tita had made for me over the portholes and the cabin was dark. Flute music wafted in and the darkness danced leisurely in my head.

I woke up startled from a dream I couldn't remember. It took a moment for me to realize that the yelling I heard was not taking place in a dream, but outside on the dock. I didn't recognize the voices as boaters I knew coming home too late or too drunk. The cabin lights stayed off as I slipped into my cargo shorts and took the Glock off the nightstand. Dock light filtered through the main cabin's portholes. I made my way to the hatch. A quick glance through a porthole showed half a dozen men surrounding three uniformed police officers, all with guns drawn. Since their backs were to me, I couldn't see if they were cops I knew. I did see the man and woman from across the dock.

When I started to open the hatch, I remembered Norm and Alfonso telling Richard during the interview at the police station how the cartel's kidnappers often dressed in police uniforms. If Jerome had told the truth, these could be the men who wanted me dead, not kidnappers. As if it mattered.

CHAPTER 47

I opened the hatch cover. It made enough noise to catch the attention of the armed men on the dock. The DEA man from the boat across the way looked up and nodded. The arguing had stopped and one of the uniformed cops had produced identification.

"Mick," the cop called without turning to see me.

I recognized the voice. Detective Donny Barroso. "Donny, you get demoted?"

"Funny." His voice indicated strain. "Will you tell these guys not to shoot us?"

"Who's with you?"

"Benkoczy and Woody."

Benkoczy and Woody raised their right arms in the air.

"They're friends of mine," I said and put the Glock away. I looked at my wristwatch. "What are you doing here at four in the morning and in uniform?"

The armed men lowered their weapons and began to walk away. The DEA couple from across the dock stayed. Surprisingly, none of the other dock residents were outside. Maybe it was seeing police that kept them uninvolved.

"We wanted to know that, too," the woman agent said. Her M-4 hung like a purse from her shoulder.

"Mick . . ." Donny turned and walked to the *Fenian Bastard*, putting his ID away. "The Chief woke me up, told me dress in blues and get you no matter where you were. He didn't mention DEA security."

"Get me and what?" I ignored his comment on the DEA.

"Something's going on at Smathers Beach."

Benkoczy and Woody joined him.

"We're supposed to find you and bring you there."

"Radio squawk says there's a body," Benkoczy added, and pointed at the armed men leaving. "DEA?"

Woody yawned. "You must know the vic."

"DEA." I nodded. "It's a long story. Can I meet you there, Donny?"

He laughed. "You want Luis to have a field day with me, don't you?"

"Let me get dressed."

Detective Luis Morales was Donny's boss and from what he said, Luis was at Smathers Beach along with Richard. Images of the soccer field filled my tired head. Three cops calling on me at four in the morning wasn't because I'd won the lottery.

"I don't suppose you can tell me what's really happening?" I got in the back seat of the police car with Woody.

"Can't tell you nothing," he said, shaking his head. "Haven't been there yet."

"Radio squawk?"

"Don't know what you mean."

"Can you tell us what's happening?" Donny looked at me in the rearview mirror; I smiled back, but said nothing. I can keep my mouth shut, too.

Donny drove along First Street with the emergency lights flashing and we were at Smathers Beach on South Roosevelt in a couple of minutes.

Police cars blocked the road where First Street turns and becomes South Roosevelt and travels along Smathers Beach. We were only a long block from the hockey rink and that fact was not lost on me. One police car moved aside to let us through.

The flashing lights went off and Donny stopped the car by the beach bathroom. A three-foot-high wall follows the wide sidewalk for most of the beach and the plants along the top keep the sand from blowing onto the street.

Key West beaches don't have sand. The city buys it, probably once a year, and spreads it along Smathers Beach for the swimmers. Hurricanes on the Atlantic side sweep the sand into dunes on the street and the city hires a company to clean it of debris and put what it can back on the beach.

Smathers Beach does have its share of coconut palms and a cluster of them grew around the circular, concrete bathroom building. A cold-water shower for swimmers to rinse off stood between the building and the sidewalk. Portable lights brightened an area close to the bathroom, so I knew that's where the body, if there was one, would be. I wasn't prepared for what waited for me.

Luis approached the car as we got out. "Wait there," he said to me, then waved the three officers to the front, where they spoke and then walked to the beach in separate directions. "Come here, Mick."

I didn't like the tone of the order, but smiled and walked to him.

"What do we have, Luis?" I used my journalist's approach. It was wasted on him.

"A murder mystery," he mocked. "You seem to bring a lot of mystery to my life these days."

"Luis, it's four o'clock in the morning, the sun ain't up and I'm barely awake, so cut the shit," I barked. "What am I here for?"

"To enlighten us like you do the Feds," he snapped back. "Follow me."

We took the steps up to the path that circled the shower and I saw pieces of a broken picnic table as we walked toward the beach. Lights were bright and reminded me of the marina. Cops roamed in groups of two or three along the darkness of the beach. Sherlock leaned against a palm and drank from a cup of coffee. Most of the cops had to be tired, but they weren't drinking coffee.

Richard leaned on a picnic table talking to a man I didn't recognize. We headed toward him and the stranger walked away.

"You alone?" Richard asked in a tired voice.

"Who did you expect?"

"Your Mexican and DEA friends."

I had no doubt the couple slipped across from me at the marina had called the incident in and Norm would be following close behind.

"I'm alone, but they'll be here," I said. "Do you want them or me?"

"Oh," he groaned with a shake of his head. "I want all of you. I want you to see what you've brought to the island." He stood up and stretched, his sore shoulder obvious. "You get the first look." He nodded to Luis and moved toward the cluster of palms.

Luis gave me a shove and I followed. Richard stopped and waited. When I got next to him, he was looking down at the sand.

"You're a piece of work, you and your friends," he blurted out and took a deep breath. He pointed into the middle of the palm trees and looked up.

The area was well lit and it wasn't long before I knew what he wanted me to see. A body hung on a makeshift cross, made from picnic table planks nailed to the palm tree. Crucified. The victim's head angled strangely from his naked torso. His arms were tied to the cross and his legs straddled the palm tree, bent at the knees and tied in back, making it look as if he was kneeling.

"Look down," Richard demanded.

I did and saw a car battery and cables. "Jesus."

"Lucky for Jesus, the Romans didn't have car batteries," Richard said, with gallows humor. "Come on." He grabbed my arm and led me closer. "Do you know him?"

I hesitated, because it had to be someone I knew. Richard tugged and Luis pushed.

"Know him?" Richard asked again.

I forced myself to look up and saw a gaping slash across the victim's throat. His head rested against the palm tree, barely attached to the body. A piece of cloth was stuck into his mouth, distorting his already macabre appearance. I looked away. Flies and other insects buzzed around the open wounds.

"Stifle his screams," Richard said about the gag as he watched me stare.

Traces of blood covered sections of the body, but most of it had pooled at the foot of the palm and been absorbed by the sand. A large hole where the bloody sand had been was all that Sherlock left behind. He had taken most of the evidence.

Black, blue and red welts spotted the body. I didn't know if the welts were from a beating and then the electric shocks, or electric shocks alone. The victim's penis and testicles had been crudely hacked off. The condition of the body was why most of the cops weren't drinking coffee.

"We're looking for them." Richard had watched me stare at the bloody groin and answered my unasked question.

I forced my gaze past the corpse's tortured chest. I recognized him and sighed heavily. "Woodrow Wentworth." Even to me, it sounded like four words slowly exhaled.

"Are you sure?" Luis asked.

"Yeah." I turned and walked to the pavement path.

Norm and Alfonso were waiting there, badges worn outside to identify them as LEOs. They must not have had any sleep because they looked dog-tired.

"You know him?" Norm asked as I got close.

"Twenty-four-seven and they won't go after my friends," I yelled into his face. "I told you Jerome changed the rules and what did you do?"

"We can't protect the world," Norm replied calmly. "We're doing what we can."

"Fuck you and the horse you rode in on," I shrieked, loud enough that it turned heads.

Richard grabbed my arm. I shook off his grip.

"What?" I yelled.

"You two stick around," he said to Norm and Alfonso. "Over there." He pointed me to the picnic table. "We need to talk."

CHAPTER 48

"Sit down," Richard snarled and pointed to the picnic table that was in the shadows.

I sat. Richard was angry and tired, not a good mixture for a cop even if he's a friend.

"Yeah." I looked into his enraged eyes.

"Yeah?" he growled, looking down at me. "Your friend is crucified, tortured, almost beheaded and castrated, and all you can say is yeah."

"What do you want from me?" I shouted. "What do you expect me to do, cry?"

"Some emotion would be nice," he barked. "You and your friends know what's going on and I don't think you've been honest with me. And I don't give a good goddamn about DEA cover or any of that shit. You understand?"

I nodded but kept my mouth shut because I thought anger was an emotion.

"I can't fight this unless I know what it is and what caused it," he roared. Then his expression changed and he looked like he was ready to fall down. "Mick, I know you care about the island and don't want this horror. What the hell is going on? I am tired; my men are being worked to death. I need to know the truth."

He sat opposite me, putting his elbows on the knife-scarred tabletop, rested his chin on folded hands and sighed loudly. "The truth?"

"I don't have much to add to what they told you in your office," I said after a moment's silence, sticking to the official story. If I told how it all began, I think he would have shot Norm and Alfonso and dealt with the circumstances later.

"Add something," he said with his eyes closed.

"The back-up is mostly JIATF." I kept my voice low because cops were paying attention to us and Norm wasn't that far away.

He looked up. "Jim Ashe's people?"

"I know there are two DEA agents on a boat across from mine," I said. "When Donny showed up, there were four more with them, but I'm not sure they're DEA. I haven't met Ashe yet."

"Tita?" he asked quietly.

"A woman DEA agent is with her. Staying at her house, goes to work with her too."

"What's her cover story?"

"An old friend from Boston. She says she's Puerto Rican, looks it."

"What are they really expecting?" He rubbed his chin. "What are they doin'?"

"Tita and I are supposed to have a lot of protection," I said and yawned. "The idea is to catch 'em when they make a move on me."

Richard turned toward Woodrow's crucified body. "What happened?"

"I think this was a warning, kind of an incentive to make me return the money they think I stole," I blubbered out. "I didn't steal the money."

"I realize that." He sat up. "The guys that did this took their time and needed at least three of them to do it. Sherlock said the blood indicates the vic was alive throughout. They may have wanted to send you a warning, but they enjoyed what they were doing."

"Sick."

"Beyond sick, and they're somewhere on my island, Mick," he snarled. "Someone, somewhere, and I don't have a clue. Give me something."

"I am told there are two groups after me."

"Jesus, you're making it worse."

"I know."

"What two groups?"

"Both Mexican cartels, but fighting each other," I said. "One wants me alive to find out what I did with their money."

"The other one?"

"Wants me dead so I can't give their competitor the money."

"And you don't have the money," he said with a sardonic laugh. "The first group do this?"

"Be my guess. Alfonso has an agent in the Arellano-Felix cartel." I stretched in my uncomfortable seat. "Eventually they can get him to pass along a story to end interest in me." I paused to see if it changed his morbid expression. It didn't. "They hope."

He stood up and banged his fist on the table. "They waiting for more innocent people to die?"

The cloudy sky in the east turned gray over the water and light from the horizon promised sunrise. The morning breeze picked up, cooling off the air but not Richard's temper. He left me sitting there and rushed to Norm and Alfonso. I wasn't excited to be part of that conversation.

CHAPTER 49

I watched Richard stab his fingers into Alfonso's chest, pushing him backward toward the shadowy concrete bathroom building. Norm grabbed Richard and moved him away. Everyone could hear the yelling, but the words were lost in the night. Arms flailed, but weapons remained holstered.

Seeing the three of them rhumba around each other in the shadows snapped me out of my dreariness. I remembered Josh and how he and Woodrow were joined at the hip. The cops continued to search the dark corners of the beach. Did they know another tortured victim might be out there?

"Richard," I called and darted across the sand. "There could be another victim here."

The arguing stopped and the men turned to me.

"Who?" Richard said with a panicky look.

"Josh, Josh Bonilla." I stopped next to them. "He and Woodrow were inseparable. Where one went, the other was."

"Jesus," he bellowed and rubbed his tired eyes. "Is there any end to this?" He turned to Norm and Alfonso. "We've checked the beach and the mangroves across the street. We wouldn't have missed another body."

"You have to go through the mangroves in daylight, maybe the hockey rink and soccer field, too."

"Tell me something I don't know," he griped. "Why do you think everyone looks so happy? We've checked it all twice. We're looking forward to doing it again at sunrise and that's because we were looking for his balls . . ." He stopped the sarcasm. Whatever he was thinking, he kept it to himself. "Now another victim. Wait till they find out."

"Ah . . ." Alfonso cleared his throat. "I think you will find them when you take the rag out of his mouth."

Richard looked at him in disbelief. "What?"

"When the cartel cuts off the penis and testicles, they usually stuff them in the victim's mouth," Alfonso explained calmly. "We find them like that."

"Jesus help me." Richard rested his head in his open hands and massaged his forehead. "Any more surprises?" He looked at us and waited for a reply. None came.

"The M.E. will be here soon and I'll have him check," he said, looking at his wristwatch. "Where does Josh live?"

"I don't know. I usually see him and Woodrow at a bar. I don't socialize with them."

"Do they live together?"

"No idea."

"Could they live on a boat off Christmas Tree Island?"

"What makes you think that?"

"We found clothes by the broken picnic table." He pointed at what was left of the dismantled table. "We think it's his clothes, no I.D., no cash, nothing, but the clothes were old and salty-looking."

"Sounds like his. Did you find a worn pair of sneakers?" His lucky sneakers, Woodrow called them, and planned to wear them until they fell apart. His luck fell apart first.

Richard gave one of his shallow, sardonic laughs. "You mean tennis shoes, right?"

"Yeah."

"We found a bloody one," he said. "Haven't found the second."

I looked hard at Norm and shook my head. "This guy

Woodrow, he wouldn't hurt anyone." I pointed in the direction of the body. "He and Josh are stoners. Always with a plan to make it big and then a toke or two and they're off in another direction. Maybe a little too much rum. But harmless, and now he's dead because of you." I ended with too much emphasis. "Maybe Josh, too."

Norm remained silent with a blank expression.

"How'd they live?" Richard was always the cop, something Tita often reminded me of.

"Woodrow was a decent boat-engine mechanic if you caught him early in the day," I said. "Josh, I have no idea."

"Take a guess."

A pink haze began to build on the horizon, threatening the shadows with the assurance that the sun was coming, but dimness remained. The breeze blew cool air from the Atlantic, though most of us kept sweating. We were tired from lack of sleep and angry for different reasons that were really opposite sides of the same coin.

"He's got two or three boats, pretty fast ones." I left the rest unsaid.

CHAPTER 50

"ICE might have some intel on him then," Richard said to himself. He understood that a couple of fast boats meant smuggling and Immigration and Customs Enforcement have intelligence on suspected local people of interest. He looked at his wristwatch and smiled. "I think I'll call and wake him."

"I need a ride back to the marina," I said before Richard walked away to make his call.

He looked from me to Norm. "I can't spare a car right now, they'll take you back."

"I'll call a cab."

"Meet it at the hotel," Richard said and walked away. "We're keeping the road closed."

"We'll drive you back," Norm said.

"Listen to me," I said harshly. "The next time I hear from you, you'd better have the two million for Jerome. If not, I will be working on a story for one of the weekly newsmagazines."

Alfonso yawned. "I have Jerome's contact numbers."

"Good. Call me when he's got the money. Whatever manpower you have watching me, put them on Tita. I'll take care of myself." I walked past the circular bathroom to the street and crossed between black-and-white police cars to Sheraton Suites. I called Five-Sixes Cab; Scott Saunders answered and promised a cab within half an hour. The shift change from nights to days was in process.

My next call was to Bob. It was almost six and I knew he'd

been awake for an hour. "Bob, you eat yet?"

"On my way to El Mocho now. You gonna join me?"

"No, but I need you to come to the marina and bring Burt."

"The M-4?"

"Yeah and your trusty sidearm, too."

"Should Burt bring something?"

"Smoke 'em if you got 'em."

"Are we going hunting?"

"For big game."

CHAPTER 51

The marina was still lit up like a Christmas tree when the cab dropped me off. A mixture of reds and purples settled on the horizon and the first stirrings had begun among the boaters. No one approached as I boarded the *Fenian Bastard*. Everything looked as it had when I left. A cool breeze crossed the deck, but it would go the way of the night when the sun rose. I went below cautiously. After a quick shower I changed into clean clothes and waited for Bob and Burt.

They had stopped at Sandy's for *café con leches*. I took mine and Bob laid the wrapped M-4 on the deck with a box of ammunition and extra magazines. We drank our Cuban coffee and I told them about Woodrow.

"Why Woodrow?" Bob brought up a good question. "Was he a friend?"

"I've talked with him and Josh at Schooner," I said. "Hell, I talk to a lot of people at bars."

"That means anyone you've talked to at Schooner or the Parrot or anyplace could end up a victim," Bob said. "Shit, Mick. You can't protect them all."

"Yeah, that's what Norm said."

Burt finished his coffee and finally spoke. "He was easy. Woodrow was an easy target, that's why they took him."

"What do you mean, easy?" I had never thought of Woodrow as being easy.

"I've had him work on engines for me," Burt began. "You ask

231

him a question about an engine problem and he'd go with you to fix it. It meant easy money, got him appreciation drinks and status around the docks."

"So they'd approach him with a question and he'd leave Josh and whatever else to go with them?"

"Yeah, and Josh wouldn't think twice about not going with him."

"We need to get Doug, too." We had focused on Woodrow enough and now it was time to watch out for the living. "He doesn't know about any of this."

"What about Tita and Josh?" Bob looked a little concerned that I had not brought her protection up.

"Tita has DEA protection and I told Norm to put everyone on the detail," I said with a dry mouth and sipped the last drops of coffee. "The cops are looking for Josh."

"Where?" Burt tossed his cup into the trash.

"I couldn't tell them where he lived."

"Conch Marina." Burt ran his tongue across his droopy mustache for the remnants of his coffee. "He's got a forty-foot trawler there. *Bliss*, I think it's called."

"You're full of surprises," I said. "Should we tell the cops?"

"Let's get Doug and check ourselves." Bob stood and tossed his cup in the trash.

"Wait a minute," I said as they began to leave. "You have the Kimber?"

Bob patted his waist.

I looked at Burt. He's tall and lanky. If he came back as a Schooner Wharf dog in his next life, as McCloud's song goes, he'd be a golden retriever or Irish setter, not a pit bull.

"Any more surprises from you?"

Burt pulled up his shirt and touched the handle of a revolver. He grinned. "Cavalry, single action .45."

"Colt?"

"Yeah, from the fifties when it first came back into production." He took the revolver out and handed it to me. "No safety, be careful."

It is a beautifully made single-action six-shooter with a seven-and-a-half-inch barrel. I handed it back. "Why do you have it?"

"Lot of blackhearts out there on the water, Mick," he teased. "Whenever I deliver a boat, I have this and my pump-action shotgun."

"Have you had to use them?"

"Forty years of delivering boats between New Orleans and South America and I'm still here. I think the Florida coast is the most dangerous."

"He's good with it," Bob translated.

Life is full of surprises—some good, some bad. Bob had surprised me, now Burt, but no one surprised me as much as Norm had.

We walked to the parking lot and drove off in my Jeep. We would steal Doug from the marina for his own safety and keep him with us. We didn't discuss finding Josh, but we hoped for the best.

CHAPTER 52

The orange-red rays of sunrise began to accentuate the clouds in the morning sky over the homes and businesses on the east side of the island by the time we arrived outside Conch Marina. The dawn's glimmer followed the moon into the Gulf of Mexico as I pulled the Jeep into the parking lot. First we had to get Doug and then we expected to find the worst at Josh's trawler. The silence between us on the ride was nerve-wracking.

"Will he be in the dockmaster's office this early?" I looked at the boats bobbing on the water as the breeze began to die. Most of the expensive vessels were dark, but lights glowed from Doug's office.

"Doug's been up for hours," Bob said.

Bob and Burt were quiet and followed me. Unlike my marina, those that lived here didn't get up early because of work. Traffic sped along Caroline Street and the city parking lot had just opened. Looking through one of the large windows, I saw Doug reading from a clipboard. I rapped on the glass. He looked up, waved and walked to unlock the door.

"I don't suppose you brought coffee," he greeted us and smiled.

Doug is the oldest of us and he has spent most of his life on the water. Living outdoors all these years has given him a tan the color of burnt walnuts. His lively brown eyes take in everything, missing nothing, and he keeps his thinning hair hidden under a wide-brim straw hat or a ball cap; even this early in the morning he had the disheveled look of someone that has been working for hours.

"We'll go get some," I said and locked the door behind us.

I sat down in front of his cluttered desk. Doug sat across from me while Bob and Burt stood at the counter. He studied us as he stacked papers.

"Who died?" he asked after an awkward silence.

I knew I had to tell the story, but waited and moved around anxiously in the seat.

"Woodrow," I finally said, unable to get comfortable.

Doug looked at each of us and sat back in his chair, making its springs squeak.

"There's more," he said. It was a statement, not a question.

I gave him a capsulized version of the past five days, slowing down and adding more detail when I got to Woodrow.

"You know, he and Josh were talking about your plan to kidnap the oil executives," I said as the beginning to the end of the story. "Is there any truth to it?"

"You think oil executive bodyguards did that?" Surprise came with each word.

"You tell me."

"Mick, we were having a beer and I was bitching about the price I had to charge boaters at the pump." He pointed outside toward the fuel dock. "The *Citizen* had a story on a couple of oil executives that were vacationing on Harbor Key." He gestured toward the west and the exclusive island hotel. "I said something about how they should be held as hostages until gas prices came down." He spoke as if he didn't believe his own words. "Hell, you know them, they took the idea and the next thing I know they're recruiting help. I cut them off, told them to stop it. To get them to listen, I said I needed time to rework the plan. I assumed they had another drink and forgot about it."

"Yes and no." I took a deep breath. "I think they did, or tried to. They told me you had someone in the kitchen who'd drug the bodyguards, and a plan to hide the hostages."

"We were in a bar bitching. I probably said that's what we needed," he grumbled. "Woodrow was a mechanic, Mick, who'd do that to him?" He sighed as the brutality sank in. "Who?"

"I haven't talked with you since Bob and I came back from Miami."

"I've read about you," he tried to joke. "I've been busy, that's why I didn't call after the car wash incident or what happened at Harpoon Harry's."

"We've both been busy . . ." I paused, looking for the right words, but couldn't find them. "Woodrow may have been a victim of the drug cartel because of me," I blurted out. "That's how the cops are thinking."

"They're after Mick's friends, any of them," Bob said. "Now we need to check on Josh."

Get-to-the-point, don't-waste-words Bob. I was seeing that new side of him again.

"And we need you to stick with us the rest of the day," I added.

"Let's go wake up Josh, then we'll talk about the rest of the day." He got up and we followed him to the dock where Josh's forty-one-foot Defever trawler *Bliss* was. "I didn't see him yesterday," he said as a warning when we climbed aboard.

The sweet smell of marijuana reeked from the aft deck.

"Someone's been here," he said and banged on the cabin's door.

"I'll be stoned all day." Burt grinned as he smoothed his mustache.

Josh slid the cabin door open. He stood there stoned in his jockey shorts, exposing his bony physique and trying to focus his bloodshot eyes. Marijuana smoke escaped through the open door. I was relieved to see him even if he was a mess.

"We need to talk, Josh." I pushed him aside and we entered the cabin.

Bob quickly opened the other cabin door and the two large windows that looked forward. The crosswind from the last remnants of a morning breeze helped lessen the marijuana stench.

"What time is it?" Josh sat on a galley barstool, confused.

"Go put on some pants."

"Huh?" He still hadn't focused.

"Go below and put on your pants," I said, standing over him. "*Now.*"

Bob helped Josh up and walked him below. Judging from the noise coming from the aft cabin, Josh was having a difficult time dressing. The main cabin's teak walls and floor were in good condition. A small but functional galley took up a section of the cabin. A large flat-screen TV hung on one wall. Two comfortable-looking chairs and one settee faced the TV. Off to the side was a small desk with an opened laptop on it. The interior was cleaner than I expected.

"Anyone hungry?" Josh squinted, trying to get his guests in focus. "I've got sandwiches." He opened the refrigerator and peered inside. "Potato and curry chicken salad from Fausto's, too."

"You got coffee?" Doug asked.

"I think so." He took a beer for himself, opened it and slugged the first drink.

"What a mess," Bob groaned after he came up from the bow cabin.

Doug went through the cupboard, found a bag of Baby's Coffee and prepared the coffee maker on the counter. Josh sat down on the barstool, beer in hand.

"What do you want?" He lit a cigarette he found on the counter.

"Where's Woodrow?" I saw a package of Kools and knew he wasn't smoking a joint. "Do you know?"

"Man, Woodrow was right, you guys are cops," he said bitterly and took another swig. "Fuck."

"No, Woodrow wasn't right. He should have spent more time worrying about the bad guys and less about the cops." It sounded like a lecture.

"Huh?" He stubbed out the cigarette.

Coffee aroma began to fill the cabin.

"Where's Woodrow? Simple question."

"Last night he went to work on someone's engine."

"Someone who?"

"I don't know. A guy showed up and talked to him about an engine problem or something," he muttered. "What do you care for?"

"Where were you?"

"Everywhere, man. We met two girls at the Tree Bar, took 'em to Sloppy Joe's, Schooner . . ." He stopped and shook his head. Maybe he thought that would clear it of cobwebs. "I think at Schooner someone talked to him about engine problems."

"He left the two girls and you for work?"

"Man, it's too early for me to think clearly . . ." He stared out the open doorway.

I grabbed him by the belt, above his crotch, and pulled him up. He dropped the bottle and beer spilled onto the teak floor. "Woodrow is dead, you asshole," I yelled and forced him across the cabin to the settee and made him sit. He looked confused at first and then frightened. "Do you understand that? Your friend died violently while you got stoned."

My anger boiled over. Angry with Norm and Alfonso, angry at myself, but I was taking it out on Josh because he had wasted his life with drugs. I felt like I had exploded and the ugliness I'd seen at Smathers Beach drove me and I became part of it.

"Huh? Woodrow?" Reality resided outside the trawler for him.

"Yeah, Woodrow. He was tortured, his pecker was cut off and his throat was slit, you wanna go see him?" I screamed.

Bob pulled me back, his arm around my chest. "Slow down," he whispered into my ear. "We need to find out what he knows."

CHAPTER 53

I accepted a cup of sweetened black coffee from Doug because there was no milk and sat on a barstool staring at Josh, who looked more confused than frightened now. He refused coffee.

"What right do you have comin' in here and fuckin' with me?" he said from the settee. "I've got rights and cops can't do this shit."

"Josh," I said, too loudly for the confined space we were in. "Listen carefully. We are not cops, but they will be here soon. If you have a brain cell left in your head, you'll know there's some serious trouble coming down and it affects you."

"Fuck man, I ain't involved in nothing," he muttered. "You got nothin' on me."

He was focused on our being cops and wasn't listening to me. He was still stoned and paranoid.

"Bob, you and Burt check below and see if you can find his stash." I stood up and walked to Josh. He cringed. "Where is your stash?" I opened my cell phone. "I'll call the dogs in and they'll tear your boat apart looking for it."

"Man, I thought we were friends," he whined. "Below in the head, under the sink." He sulked after he spoke. "In a shoebox."

Bob and Burt went below, came back with a shoebox and put it on the countertop. Inside were nickel baggies of grass and small jewelry packets of white powder.

"You dealing?" I dumped everything from the box onto the countertop.

"No," he said softly. "The coke is Woodrow's."

"Convenient for you." I opened one package of coke and dumped it in the sink. "Woodrow won't be needing it, not where he is." I ran the water to wash the coke away.

"What's that mean?" He stood up. "Hey, don't fuck with my shit."

"Sit down," I ordered, and he did. "Woodrow's dead. Do you understand that?"

Josh closed his eyes and nodded. A tear appeared and he wiped it away. I wasn't sure if the tear was for Woodrow or for the lost coke.

"The man with the engine trouble probably killed him, so you need to remember last night." I lowered my voice, kept my distance and held a second package of coke over the sink.

Bob moved behind Josh and was ready to stop him if he charged.

"What do you want me to remember?" he sobbed.

"Describe the guy."

"Can I have a beer?" His nervous eyes looked toward the spilled beer on the floor.

I nodded to Doug, who got a beer from the refrigerator and handed it to Josh. He took a long swallow.

"A big guy, shaved head," he said with his eyes closed. "We were at one of the big tables . . . at Schooner . . . I think . . . with the two girls."

"Did he have an accent?"

"Man, how would I know? I was tryin' to talk the broad into comin' to the *Bliss*." He took another drink. "Next thing I remember is Woodrow tellin' me he'd be right back and he left us there. I remember thinking I'd score with both broads if he didn't." He tipped the bottle back and then stopped and looked excited. "Yeah, yeah, I remember, Woodrow walked to the bar with the big guy and two other guys joined them and they left after buyin' him a beer."

"What did the other two look like?"

Vicki and Sissy were probably working behind the bar and I could ask if they remembered the three men later today. But I wanted Josh to remember some things.

"Smaller."

"Smaller than who?"

"The big guy," he moaned, his eyes open. "They walked out and I went back to the girls."

"What time was it?"

"You gotta be fuckin' kiddin' me," he said and finished the beer. "I don't even know what day it is, who owns a watch?" He raised his two arms in the air to show he had no wristwatch. "It was dark and the bar was crowded."

"Lot of help there," Bob muttered. Josh turned to look at him.

"I didn't care what time it was," he griped and turned back to me. "Would you, with two good-lookin' broads ready to go to your boat?"

I put the drugs into the shoebox and covered it. "Where are the girls now?"

"I don't remember, man, that was last night," Josh mumbled.

On my way to the aft deck, I handed the shoebox to Bob. "Trash it on the way out of here."

Josh look devastated and was about to protest.

"The cops will be here shortly, they'll find it and you'll go to jail." It was a warning. "You want that?"

He sat down, his devastated expression hiding the fact that he was stoned.

Outside I noticed that daylight had arrived and the marina was getting busy. I called Richard Dowley. "You still at Smathers?"

"Yeah, Mick," he said quietly into his phone. "I just left the

M.E. Your Mexican friend was right about what we'd find in the mouth. Where are you?"

"With Josh."

"He breathing?" Richard and his gallows humor.

"Wasted, but otherwise okay."

"You gonna make me beg? Because if you are, I am too tired and probably shouldn't care anyway."

"Conch Marina," I said. "His boat's name is *Bliss* and it's right down from the dockmaster's office. I'll wait here."

"And why should I care? Tell me again."

"Josh and Woodrow were together last night. He doesn't remember much, but it might help."

"Me or you?"

"It helps you, it helps me."

"Wait there."

"I wouldn't think otherwise," I said and hung up.

CHAPTER 54

I sat outside on the aft deck, on one of four canvas director's chairs, and watched the sky full of brightly backlit clouds that hid the sun and promised rain. I finished my coffee. Bob and Burt joined me, leaving Doug to deal with Josh.

"Richard is on his way," I said.

"Doug is trying to talk sense into Josh," Bob grunted. "Impossible."

"Gotta try something," I murmured. "I'm glad he's alive."

"Josh?" Bob seemed surprised.

"Yeah, if he wasn't, it would be because of me."

Burt scoffed. "Bullshit. You didn't dump this crap on Key West."

Their defense of me did little to lessen my guilt or anger. They knew more of what was really going on than Richard did and they still offered support because of our friendships.

"That doesn't help Woodrow. No one on the island is safe. Me? One group wants me dead, we haven't even begun to deal with them, I have until Friday to settle up with the other cartel, and they've killed someone I knew to give me incentive to pay. Like it or not, it's about me."

"You had the chance to run, but that wouldn't have protected your friends," Bob said as a reminder of Pauly's offer. "We can do what we can do, Mick. No reason to dwell on our failures, so let's work on doing our best. Hell, they'll probably end up killing us just because they know who they're looking for and we don't know who they are."

There was something sardonic in my chuckle. "I don't want anyone to die for me."

"Nobody asked you," Bob grunted. "You'd do it for us and we know it."

"Well then, Bob, I guess we'll have to keep them from killing us." My sarcastic mood lightened.

"Screw that," Burt said seriously. "Let's kill them first."

I laughed. "Sounds like a plan."

Bob laughed along. "I can live with it."

"Someone tell a joke?" Richard asked as he and Detective Luis Morales walked down the dock.

"Nervous laughter, Chief," Burt said and stood. "Hell of a way to begin the morning."

"We began before morning," he asserted and climbed aboard. He sniffed at the marijuana stench. "Like your perfume."

I pointed inside and realized Bob had set the shoebox with the drugs by his chair.

"Doug is with Josh inside," I said, and stood. "He's already drinking."

Luis finally spoke. "Did he say anything?"

"Yeah, he and Woodrow picked up two women and then someone asked Woodrow to help with a boat engine," I said.

"Why would someone ask a drunken stoner to help with an engine problem at night? And why'd he go?" Richard shook his head. "Gives another meaning to drugs kill, don't it?"

No one answered. Maybe we weren't supposed to.

"It's why they call it dope," Bob called out as I led Richard and Luis toward the cabin.

I couldn't smell the marijuana anymore, I was used to it, but they did. I could see it in their expressions as they walked into the cabin. They didn't ask Josh for permission to enter. Maybe the stench of marijuana gave them probable cause.

Doug stood up. Josh sat on the settee, looking no better.

"He's still stoned," Doug said.

"Thanks for keeping him safe," Richard said, barely keeping his eyes open. "Wait outside with the others and don't leave. Please stick around," he added as an afterthought.

Doug and I walked outside and took the last two director's chairs. Bob picked up the shoebox and smiled. "I'll meet you at the Jeep."

"Me, too." Burt got up.

They walked down the dock and I think I saw them stick a few small baggies in their pockets before they dropped the shoebox in the Dumpster.

"Why do you want me hanging with you?" Doug wiped his brow.

"You three are the best friends I've got and they're gonna find that out." I turned to face him. "Stick together and we've got a chance to survive this."

"Or end up like Woodrow?"

"Probably worse, if there's a way."

"Let me get to the office for some stuff and then I'll turn the day over to Bill." He got up and looked toward the cabin. "I'm going with you so I can help, not because I need your protection."

"I probably need yours," I said as he got to the dock.

"I'll find Bill and grab some things." Doug walked away slowly. Bill Murphy was his assistant dockmaster. When the city fired Bill, Doug gladly hired him.

The morning sky was miraculous, with the sun hidden behind clouds that reflected its reds and purples while darker clouds threatened to burst with rain. Richard sank down onto the chair next to me. He took a small red bottle from his pocket and drank its contents.

"A little hair of the dog." I knew better.

"We are living on this energy drink." He showed me the small bottle. "At least, I am. I hope that's what my officers are using." He put the bottle back in his pocket. "Your friends don't take police requests seriously?"

"Doug had business to take care of. Bob and Burt just needed to stretch their legs."

"Tell them about the energy drink." Richard had closed his eyes. "Luis is dealing with Josh. He's been to training and is good at it."

"I'm sure." He knew how I felt about Luis and his enthusiastic approach to police work.

"Mick," he screeched like an alley cat. "Give me some slack."

The marina slowly came to life. Coffee aromas eddied about and from somewhere I could almost taste the frying bacon and eggs.

"Where are the other ones?"

"I left them with you."

Richard laughed softly. "Did you see the guy at the table with me when you first got to Smathers?"

"Yeah." He wasn't looking for my thoughts or questions, only answers.

"Ed Scales, my CIA contact." He sat forward and rubbed his eyes. "Norm has DEA cover, but he's no agent. Ed warned me they were coming."

"DEA cover would've been my first guess."

"Alfonso, he's who he says. A good man, the DEA claims."

"I believe it. We've been friends for years. We hung out in Tijuana."

"Doesn't make him honest, not with drug cartel money."

"No, it doesn't, but I've worked with him and so has Norm," I said. "If he's dirty, he's damn good at it."

"I am told he's clean and dedicated."

"So?" What was he working up to?

"What they told me about your past and the cartel, is there any truth to it?"

"Depends on what they said."

Richard stopped rubbing his eyes. He smiled briefly, more to himself than at me, and kept whatever made him smile a secret. "Alfonso's agent is in deep cover, and he wants to keep him that way, so he can't pull him out."

"I know that."

"He has sent word, but the agent decides when and even if he will come in for a meet." He looked at me with bloodshot eyes. "This could go on for awhile."

This was what bothered Richard; my one chance of ending this rested in the hands of a Mexican agent deep undercover within the Tijuana cartel and it took precautions to keep the agent safe. My life and the lives of people in Key West were secondary and they needed me to understand that.

"Don't any of us have good news to share?" I griped. I understood the problem, I just didn't like it.

"Tita's safe. That's good."

"Ed tell you the DEA is protecting her?"

"Yeah," he said. "Some of Jim Ashe's people, too."

"I've been told he's involved, but I haven't seen him."

Richard snorted. "I guess if you see them, they aren't doing their job."

"So I've been told."

Richard was quiet and I thought he might have fallen asleep. The medication for his shoulder had to make him tired, but then again, maybe he stopped taking it and the pain helped keep him awake.

"How's the shoulder?" I asked.

"Hurts." He looked toward the sky. "Fred's gonna come too close." He spoke about the hurricane out by the Bahamas.

"I haven't heard any reports."

"The two killed on US1," he said, changing subjects suddenly.

"I read about it."

He looked at me and squinted his eyes shut. "Their weapons matched the ones used at the car wash. The two in the rental car had weapons too, but they hadn't been fired."

"What's that tell you?"

"There was a third car, another shooter." He moved uncomfortably in the canvas chair.

"There are two cartels here and they fight wherever they are. Maybe they ran into each other on the road?" I lied and watched him squirm in the chair.

"Wrong type of ammo for the cartel," he said slowly. "They like Israeli weapons. A .357 killed these two." He stared at me with tired eyes barely open. "Just wanted you to know there was another shooter. Let me get some sleep and maybe I'll dream about someone who would want to shoot them and why. Suppose it was someone protecting you?"

He was half-asleep, so I didn't answer him with another lie, and wondered about the energy drink.

Chapter 55

We waited for Doug outside the dockmaster's office as the morning cloudiness gradually moved across the island. He walked out slowly as he always walked, wearing a large-brimmed straw hat, a clean T-shirt and a bulky fanny pack strapped to his waist.

"Where are we going?" He climbed in back with Burt.

We drove less than a football field along the waterfront to the next parking lot. "Turtle Kraals for breakfast."

"We couldn't walk?" He got out of the Jeep.

Bob pointed to the floor by the front seat. Doug saw the M-4 and nodded. Bob slid the rifle under the seat.

"I brought this." Doug tapped the fanny pack.

"What is that?" I was sorry I asked as I spoke.

"Same as Burt's." Doug smiled at me and slapped Burt on the back.

We were a walking arsenal now. Only the bad guys were going to be better prepared.

At Turtle Kraals, we sat on the outside patio and ordered our breakfasts. The server left a pot of coffee. I started the story and Bob and Burt added their color to what was happening. Doug's eyes showed surprise a couple of times, but he listened quietly.

People chose the patio seating for breakfast because the clouds kept the hot sun at bay, so we talked softly of the horrors since Friday. Tourists were already on the boardwalk, staring at the wide variety of dinghies and charter boats. The dinghies got those that lived illegally on the hook into town and they paid the city a monthly fee for the use of the dock. The Turtle Museum was closed, but people tried the doors instead of reading the posted schedule for the hours it was open.

I called Tita as breakfast arrived. She was leaving for the office. "Jenny insists on driving me," she said in a tired voice. "Are you okay?"

"Yeah." I kept my voice upbeat. "This will be over soon."

"I hope so, Mick. I can do without so many people looking over my shoulder. A lot of my work is confidential, so it's difficult."

"It's for your own good."

"You dealing with them all around you?" There was doubt in her voice as she ignored my comment.

"Mine's a little different," I said. "I'm not supposed to see them."

"Lucky you," she chuckled. "Will I see you soon?"

"I hope so." Probably the most honest thing I'd said to her recently.

She sighed. "Jenny's rushing me. I'll talk to you after lunch?"

"You got it." She hung up.

"Not a happy camper?" Bob said.

I shook my head and began to eat.

"For her own good."

"I told her that."

My cell chirped again. I looked at the screen and saw Pauly's name. It surprised me, but I answered, hoping the call delivered good news from Mexico. *"Qué tal hombre?"*

"What's that noise?" he asked in a serious voice.

"Breakfast."

"Can you talk?"

"If there's something to talk about."

"Privately. I'm gonna surprise you."

I stood up, nodded at the guys who were still eating, walked over to the boardwalk railing and sat at an empty table.

"I'm alone now, what's the news?" I was nervous because I knew Pauly wouldn't call to chat.

"Are you sitting down?" Now there was levity in his voice.

"Yeah, what've you got for me?"

"I think I know who stole the money."

I couldn't believe his words. "What?"

"You heard me."

"Who . . . how?"

"No 'Thank you, Pauly'?"

"You said you think, and that's not definite."

"Okay, you're a little uptight . . ."

I quickly told him about Woodrow.

He sighed. "Every one's gotta be more gruesome than the last. Okay, listen to how I got it first, then I'll tell you who and I guarantee you'll be surprised."

He dated a Dominican woman executive who worked in the shadowy banking world that specialized in offshore accounts. She had business contacts in the Bahamian and Cayman banks. Her position allowed her entry into the banking files, though she wasn't supposed to abuse the privilege by going into the private, offshore accounts. Her computer-hacking ability allowed her to find information from the private files.

Twenty million dollars had to go to an offshore bank. It would be impossible to deposit in an American bank without a lot of paperwork and questions. Thinking this, Pauly had the woman check for a deposit of between fifteen to twenty million dollars around the time of the theft.

"I assumed whoever did the job had to pay bribes," he said. "Did you know that twenty million dollars is not a major deposit in these banks? What's the world coming to?"

"It's going to hell in a hand basket," I said.

"She got a few hits within the time frame and deposit guidelines I gave her. Lucky guess on my part that paid off. I went through the names. Amazing how many Americans have these accounts."

"Pauly," I said anxiously.

"Okay, okay. Like the fifth name I recognize, and then I remembered why. So, we isolated it and saw the account had two offshoots. You ain't gonna believe this."

"What is it?" I said rudely.

"Mick, you're taking the fun out of this for me."

"Pauly, I'm not having a fun week."

"You should've come with me."

"Tell me who the fuck stole the money," I said cruelly with clenched teeth. I wanted to scream it.

"I've got three suspects. You want them all?" He returned to being serious.

"Yeah, please."

"The initial deposit was made by Norm Burke." He stopped.

I couldn't believe it. Something was wrong. Norm wouldn't use his real name. "Go on."

"That's your buddy, right? I remembered him."

"Who else?"

"A Melanie Flores Trust Fund."

The words hit me hard, harder than Norm's name.

"And guess who my third suspect is."

"I don't wanna guess. Tell me."

"Liam Michael Murphy."

"Pauly, this is not funny," I said angrily. "Why are you doing it?"

"Mick, it's the truth. Norm has eight million in his account, the trust fund has five, and you've got one." I could hear the smile in his voice. "Interestingly, Norm has account activity now and then, a few thousand taken out, no deposits since the first one. The trust fund has regular withdrawals each month and you, you're just leaving it there and accruing interest."

"Pauly, if this is some kind of joke . . ."

"No joke."

"Can you send me copies?"

He laughed. "You think I was allowed to make copies, get real. I'm telling you what I saw on the computer screen."

A week ago I wouldn't have believed him, friend or not. I had the highest respect for Norm and to shake that faith would have been impossible. But today, because of what I'd learned about being used by him, I had my doubts. I knew Norm was smart and sneaky, but that didn't eliminate the idea Pauly had planted.

"He's here."

"Norm?"

"Yeah. Supposed to be here to help me . . ." I left it at that because if I told him about the set-up of the deep cover agent in Tijuana, Pauly might be tempted to warn his old cohorts.

"I can come back, be there tonight."

"I don't know what good it would do, maybe even get you hurt."

"One more person watching your back. One you can trust."

I looked at the table with my friends. Did I need another person to be concerned about? Pauly wasn't really another person, he was someone with years of experience dealing with the smugglers.

"You want to wait a day? We're going to meet in a few hours and I'll confront Norm about this and find out what's what. Afterward I might need your help."

"I'm coming back, Mick, no use waiting to the last minute," he said. "I know what I saw on the computer screen, but you still have your doubts. After all, he's been your friend for a long time."

"I have doubts because it's in his name. I can't see him being so careless. He did leave me a million, my old friend did," I said, but couldn't get the cheeriness I wanted in my voice. "Pauly, a question for you."

"Shoot."

"You know an attorney named Jerome Smith?"

"From a long time ago. San Diego. If you got in trouble, you were supposed to call him. Why?"

"He was here. He said two million would buy my way out of this. He could get it all to stop."

"He's got their ear, but two out of twenty. Sounds like wishful thinking."

"He said it's a gesture and after all this time they'd take it."

"Get it from Norm. They like gestures that show they're respected."

"That's what I was thinking."

"See you later. Be careful." He hung up before I could say anything.

It was nine o'clock and my breakfast was cold. So was the coffee. I called Norm.

"Where are you?" he wanted to know.

"I got some errands to do. See you at the Schooner around noon."

"Jim Ashe's people are watching Tita and there's a few going to be with Alfonso and me."

"I need to talk to you. I have some interesting info."

"About what?"

"Who I can get the two million dollars from that Jerome needs to stop this."

"You got someone to loan you that kind of money?" He seemed surprised. "You have to be kidding me."

"No, not a loan, a two million dollar gift." I hung up before he could ask me who.

CHAPTER 56

At Sandy's kiosk on White Street we ordered large *café con leches* and finetuned our plans for the day. I hadn't shared Pauly's information. We merged on the corner of White and Virginia with our *con leches* and knew our plans were based on wild speculations, but we needed to deal with the overabundance of nervous energy that excited us, so we discussed possible scenarios. None of us could've foreseen the afternoon's events.

Bob and I walked into Schooner Wharf with Styrofoam cups and asked Alexis for a menu as we sat at one of the large patio tables. Gretchen came by to say hello.

Our plan called for Doug and Burt to come in later and sit at the bar to keep an eye on our backs. Looking for discarded bags and backpacks was a critical piece of the plan and it was part of their responsibilities. A bomb was not out of the question.

Dark clouds continued to threaten rain as they slowly wandered across the sky. A breeze came in off the water, nothing like the early tropical storm winds the weather indicated were due. A hurricane-like humidity engulfed us.

It was a little before noon and the bar was already buzzing with activity. Jack Dey and Carl Avila sat nursing beers, talking business. Tracy and Phil Tenney huddled together at a small patio table, oblivious to those around them while they ate. I was surprised to see Joe and Judy Hart because they usually came to go sailing after hurricane season, but they sat at the bar. A few stools down from them were Dick and Marylou Walsh, a couple from Boston that visited often. Mark Howell stood at the railing writing in his notebook as he interviewed radio host Bill Hoebee. Vicki, Sissy and Bob were busy behind the bar. Rob Murdock was on the boardwalk talking on his cell. Wayne and Gina Bruehl laughed at something the tourist next to them at the bar said.

No one talked of Woodrow's murder, so the news hadn't leaked. He and Josh wouldn't be missed until the afternoon and then they'd quickly be forgotten. I wondered how long before the coconut telegraph's rumor mill discovered the murder and started reporting it. Woodrow would make one more splash before oblivion.

I was doing everything but focusing on the present, so when Norm and Alfonso walked in from Lazy Way, I was surprised. If I had been paying attention to the surroundings and the people, I would have seen them walking along the narrow road. I smiled, but I was upset at my lack of concentration.

"Just you two?" Norm looked around the busy bar and sat down. "Jim's people are filtering in and I think Richard has a few people keeping an eye on Tita."

He knew Tita was my priority.

Alexis took our beer order and when she came back we ordered lunch.

"Have you thought about a bomb?" I left the beer on the table and sipped my *con leche*.

"We have an agent working as a barback and that's his concern," Norm said, sounding piqued. "He's checking everywhere. Let us do our job, Mick."

"I'd love to, Norm." I took a cigar from Bob, cut and lit it, while I bit down on my anger. "But I'm not sure I understand what your job here is." I blew thick smoke into the humid air.

Alfonso spoke for the first time since sitting. "You know why we are here."

"Maybe we should talk over there?" I pointed to an empty table for two by the boardwalk. "I need you to straighten out a couple of things."

Norm took a short pull on his beer and put it down. He rubbed his chin and his gray eyes looked right through me as he nodded, smiled and stood up. "Let me enlighten you, hoss." He walked across the patio to the table.

"He's looking out for you both," Alfonso said. He meant Tita and me. "Whatever your problem is, you have it wrong."

"We'll see," I muttered and walked to Norm.

"You don't want them to know who's giving you the money?"

He guessed at what I wanted and must have had a good belly laugh at my expense. I wanted to tell him *he who laughs last . . .* but kept quiet. I sat down, biting on the cigar, and looked at him. I saw the Norm from twenty years ago. He helped me out of jams, life-threatening in some cases, more than I ever helped him; he was my story source many times. I wanted to tell him what Pauly had said and then both of us share a laugh at the absurdity, but a twisting in my gut said sharing anything between us had come to an end.

"I don't really give a fuck what they know," I scoffed. "But I do care about what I don't know." I left it at that.

"If looks could kill," he finally said and sat back in the bar-stool. "What's causing this? What aren't you tellin' me?"

"Me?" I wailed through clenched teeth, shaking the small table. "What aren't you telling me? Why did you bring this here when I had nothing to do with it and you did?"

He looked at me, amused. He must have flashed on the offshore accounts, but it didn't compute, it couldn't have because it was his secret and how would I have known? I knew he'd dismissed the idea because he tried to go back to the old story line. "Alfonso and I told you how it was . . ."

"Bullshit." The word came out harshly and I held onto the

table so tight, my fingers turned white. "Cut the shit, you stole the money."

I let go of the table and sat back.

I've known Norm for twenty-something years and this was the first time I'd ever seen a glint of surprise in his eyes. He was always prepared because his survival depended on it. His confusion was brief, but for that moment I had him and he knew it.

"By money you mean . . ." he began in a controlled voice. Still depending on the bluff.

"Cut the bullshit." I pulled myself up straight in the chair. "I know."

Norm squirmed as I enjoyed the last of the cigar. He looked around the bar but didn't stop his stare on anyone. He was trying to figure out how I knew and what it meant to his scheme.

"I can explain," he said with a guilty smirk.

"Explain."

"Here?"

"Fuck you, Norm." I kept my voice low, but I wanted to scream and pound him in the face. "You stole the money and then set me up as a scapegoat and people are dying."

"These are two different problems."

"Damn you, they are not different problems," I banged the table. "Your setting me up got these people killed. You know what really pisses me off? I've killed people in the last couple of days and almost got myself and another friend killed, and all because of you. It didn't have to happen."

"Yes it did," he said with a sneer. "It was gonna happen somewhere, hoss, and here we could have a little control."

"You've really been in control, haven't you?"

"It's not scripted, Mick. We are doing the best we can."

"What . . . what were you thinking?" I had a hard time finding the words. "You stole the money and deposited it using your own name. Then you added mine and Mel's. Why?"

Michael Haskins

"An opportunity presented itself that was too good to pass up." He ordered a beer and waited for it before going on. "A friend of a friend, too much tequila and the next thing I know I've got a trunk with duffel bags of money."

I knew he was lying. Situations didn't present themselves to Norm unless he wanted them to, but I let him go on.

"Next morning I'm still in TJ with the cartel's money." He laughed softly, shaking his head. "I even thought of giving it back. When I realized there was no way, I began to work on a plan."

"The sailboat race from San Diego?"

"That's how I got it out. Cost me a million, but it went off without a hook."

"Why not just keep it all?"

"Mick, what would I do with that kind of money?" He shook his head and grunted. "Retire to the tropics with you? Naw, not for me. I like my life in California and get all the traveling I want."

"Five million in bribes?" I wanted him to know I knew how much he had.

"Cash to some people who needed it or could use it," he said, and looked hard at me. "I put some in a safety deposit box for an emergency. How'd you figure this out?"

"Answer my questions, and how I know what I know is none of your business."

"I didn't think anyone would ever check an offshore bank for me, I'm not that kind of guy. But you were smart enough to," he said with a smirk. "I wanted to help Mel's family and had an accountant friend set up the trust fund. She had sisters and brothers and her parents are getting on. Now they get a check each month."

"Sentimentalist." It was my turn to smirk and I still didn't believe him. "Doesn't sound like you."

260

"Maybe there are things you don't know about me." He finished the beer.

"I'm beginning to realize that. Why me?"

"Hell, I don't know. It seemed like a good idea at the time." He shrugged his shoulders.

"I only get a million?"

"You weren't supposed to find out for another ten years and by then it would've been a lot more."

"You know that all this is gonna change our friendship?"

"Yeah, I got that feeling from you." He almost sounded sad. "In the last ten years our lives have changed anyway. What we had back in Central America, Mick, it's gone like the guerrilla wars. Change is a constant. Friendships grow old and move apart."

I ignored his sentimentality. "Let me tell you what you're gonna do."

"You telling or asking?"

"Think whatever you want, but you're gonna get the two million Jerome wants to end this. Take my million and add one from your eight million. I don't care how you do it."

"He could be lying and . . ."

"I don't care," I said harshly. "If he's lying I'll kill him, but right now it's the only viable option on the table. We can't fight two cartels and if we try to, more innocent people die."

"Do you really think he can settle a twenty-million debt for two million?" He tore at the label on the beer bottle.

"I think he's brokering the deal for selfish reasons," I said. "Selfish counts for a lot."

"How do you want the money delivered?"

"I'll have to call and ask him." I looked at my wristwatch. It was twelve-fifteen, nine-fifteen in San Diego. "He might still be in Miami."

"He's staying close, I can assure you of that."

261

"He's arranged to give me until Friday, but he told me that wouldn't include anyone else's safety."

"That's why the DEA and everyone I could gather up are with Tita."

My phone chirped. I had a call from the local area code, but the number displayed was unfamiliar.

"Answer it." Norm stood up and walked back to the large table.

"Yeah," I said and waited to see if I recognized the voice.

"Don't shoot the messenger, Mick." I didn't recognize it.

"What?"

"I'm the messenger, not the culprit."

"Who is this?"

"Jerome Smith."

"We were just talking about you."

"You know already?"

"I don't know what you're talking about, but I've got the money, so tell me what's next."

"They have raised the ante to five million, Mick."

"I thought two."

"They have a trump card, so they want more."

"That's a lot more."

"You will think it is worth it."

"How much time do I have?"

"Friday, six P.M., at Mallory Square during the sunset show."

"You want cash?"

"They want cash before they will make the trade."

"What do they have to trade?"

"Tita," he said matter-of-factly. "They just grabbed her and they'll trade for the money."

I almost dropped the phone as I shivered uncontrollably.

CHAPTER 57

"I'll call you back," I said to Jerome. I disconnected the call and tried to control my tremors. Then I speed-dialed Tita's office. Sue answered. "Let me talk to Tita, Sue." I was abrupt.

"She's gone to lunch with Jenny, Mick," Sue said politely.

"Where'd she go?" I was in a hurry for answers.

"I'm not sure, but I think they were talking about the Half Shell."

I speed-dialed Tita's cell. It rang and rang and then her voice mail picked up. I listened impatiently to the message. "Call me as soon as you get this, it's important." I closed the cell phone, but kept it in my hand.

Tita never had her phone off and even at lunch she'd answer my call.

I stood next to Norm at the table and he realized something troubled me. He turned and grabbed my arm. "What's wrong?"

"Jerome called and said they've got Tita."

"No way." Norm looked at Alfonso, who nodded his agreement. "Did you call her?"

"She's at lunch with Jenny, but she's not answering her cell."

"So Jenny and a half dozen agents are with her," Norm said. "They wouldn't have gotten Tita without a fight."

"Sue said they were going to the Half Shell." I pointed toward the boardwalk. "Two blocks." I started to walk.

Norm was on his cell as we walked hastily toward the restaurant. Bob and Alfonso followed us. Norm stopped me outside the turtle museum.

"Jenny drove Tita to lunch and the agents staggered following her," he said, his voice full of unease. "They lost her somewhere off of Virginia. It could be Jenny being evasive, what she's trained to do."

"Where was the backup?" I pushed his hand away and walked toward the restaurant's parking lot. "Bob and I will check the Half Shell."

Two government sedans drove in off Caroline Street. Norm went to them a little too quickly while I searched the small parking area for Jenny's sedan. I didn't see it. Bob and I went into the restaurant and told them we were meeting someone. We walked through the busy dining area and back to the bar. They weren't there.

I called Tita's cell again and left the same message. I called her office next.

"Sue, if you hear from Tita, please tell her to call me right away. It's important."

"Is everything all right?" My calls were worrying her.

"Yeah," I lied. "I just have something important to ask her."

"As soon as she gets in, you'll be her first call."

"Thanks." I hung up. "Jenny was taking her to lunch here." I pointed to the Half Shell.

"Relax, because they probably lost these guys so Tita could chill. It made her nervous having everyone hanging outside." Norm's words didn't match the distress I saw on his face.

"How would Jerome know?"

"I don't know. What else did he say?"

We stood in the parking lot. Bob and Alfonso were out in front of the restaurant and the government cars had pulled off to the side.

"They want five million in exchange for Tita."

"Did he say how they'd make the exchange?"

"Friday at Mallory Square during the sunset celebration."

"Money won't be a problem."

"This whole thing's a fucking problem, Norm," I said heatedly. "If they've got Tita . . . if anything happens to her . . ."

"We've got the money and that's what they're after," he said calmly. "You don't know they've got her. We need to find Jenny. She wouldn't give her up without a fight."

"They got her, Norm, just like they had Mel." I couldn't keep my voice from trembling as I remembered Tijuana. "It's my nightmare come to life again."

"The money will be here in the morning, earlier if needed," he said. "There's no bomb this time and the exchange will take place in a crowded area. They get the money, they get away and you get Tita. Jerome will make them keep their word."

"Now you trust him?" I looked for a sign he was lying. "You think they've got her?"

"He wants to keep the violence on the Mexican side of the border," Norm said. "They need him on this side, so they'll listen. He's probably afraid of you, too. He knows you'll kill him if it goes bad."

"Jesus, Norm," I grumbled, holding in my anger. He didn't answer my question about Tita, which was an answer in itself. "Why? Why me, why here? Why now?"

"Mick," he grabbed my shoulder. "You gotta keep it together. This ain't TJ. We all want Tita back and we'll give them the money. They'll hold the violence down because there's already been too much. The cartel doesn't want to be connected to this, believe me."

"There's no belief left," I said coldly. "We've got to let Richard know."

CHAPTER 58

Richard was asleep on his office couch when I called but woke up, answered the phone, and agreed to meet me at Tita's. He was bringing along Luis Morales. I didn't care and closed the cell. Bob called Burt and Doug as we walked to the Jeep and told them where to meet us. The drive to the house took less than ten minutes, but it was a long, anxious ten minutes. Norm and Alfonso pulled in behind me as I parked in the red zone at the corner. Tita hid her extra house key under a flowerpot; I got it and opened the front door. Norm pushed me aside, gun in hand, and went first.

It took him less than three minutes to check the small house. It was empty, but I knew it would be. My anxiety was fed by being right. Norm was cautious while I was being a morbid fatalist.

Richard parked on the sidewalk across the street by the cemetery and Burt and Doug parked right behind him.

"Tell me it all," Richard demanded as he walked in with Luis trailing behind. Burt and Doug came in without saying anything.

I told Richard about the phone call from Jerome.

"I'm gonna be pissed about how you know this Jerome, right?" he growled. "Let's focus on getting Tita back first." He ran his hands through his uncombed hair. "How long have they had her?"

I checked the kitchen wall clock. It was one-fifteen. "Less than an hour." Forty-five minutes since I received the call. "She

266

left the office a little after twelve."

"The DEA agent with her, have you found her car?"

"Yeah," Norm answered, surprising me. "It's in the city parking lot close to the Half Shell."

"When did you find this out?" I shouted.

"On the ride here the agents called me," Norm replied harshly. "They're doing their job."

Luis spoke up. "Any sign of a fight?"

"Nothing. No blood, no mess at all. Whatever happened, both women seem to have gotten out of the car on their own."

"Shit, how do you know that?" I opened the refrigerator, looking for what, I don't know. It gave me something to do. "There's not much they could do against someone with a gun."

Norm and Richard ignored me. "They had to be grabbed between the parking lot and restaurant."

"If they're heading north," Richard looked at his wristwatch, "they've been on the road for about an hour. You agree?"

"They're not going to Miami," I said. "Too far from the money."

"I can't imagine the agent being surprised," Norm said, not listening to me. "We're missing something."

"We're covering all the bases, Mick." Richard looked at Luis. "Call Chance and see if he'll have the deputies set up a roadblock at the drawbridge north of Islamorada, and when you mention Tita's abduction, try to keep Mick's name out of it." Luis walked to the porch to make the call. "They wouldn't be speeding with two kidnap victims, so the drawbridge is more than an hour-and-a-half ride."

"You should tell the sheriff that the men they are looking for are armed and dangerous," Alfonso said. "Very dangerous."

"They'll kill the hostages," I hollered. "These guys will fight."

"He's right," Alfonso said.

"What would you have us do?"

"I'd have you undo all this," I bellowed. "But you can't."

Richard turned to Norm. "What have you done?"

"I've told you," Norm snapped. "What we need to do now is find the women."

"They're not going to Miami," I said. "If he wants the money, he's gotta have her close or he would've chosen Miami for the exchange."

"Okay," Norm said quietly. "What else? Where would he have taken them?"

"Doug, what did you tell Josh about holding the oil executives?"

Doug stood by the living room window, staring outside.

"Jesus, do I want to hear this?" Richard sighed and rubbed his tired eyes.

"They wanted to lock these guys in a hotel somewhere and I suggested a boat, keep them off the coast and away from curious eyes," he said without turning to us. "It was to give Josh and Woodrow something to think about besides the kidnapping."

"We need to talk," Richard moaned. "When this is over, we really need to talk."

"Suppose they had a boat at the dinghy dock," I thought aloud. "Take her out to another boat, keep her away from prying eyes and it would be easy to get her back for the exchange."

"Christmas Tree Island," Doug said, still looking out the window. "They could keep her there, too."

Norm looked at me. "Christmas Tree Island?"

"In the middle of the harbor, next to the island with all the pricy homes," I said. "Kind of a no-man's land for the homeless that can get there."

"How dangerous are the kidnappers?" Richard sat on the couch and yawned.

"You have seen what they are capable of." Alfonso paced the

living room. "They are not afraid to kill and they are not afraid to die."

"Suggestions?"

He smirked. "Caution. Shoot to kill them first. Mick is right about one thing, they will kill the hostages if they see a rescue attempt."

"That's a suggestion?" Richard grumbled.

"My suggestion would be to proceed quietly." Alfonso stopped by the window across from Richard. "I would put someone that looked homeless on the island to search. Find out what if anything is there before you send in SWAT. Go in quietly at night to see if they are there."

Luis came in off the porch. "The sheriff will okay the roadblock," he said, putting away his cell phone. "But he wants to hear from you as soon as possible."

Richard yawned again. "Okay."

I sat on a chair in the kitchen doorway and buried my head in my hands. I had lived through another version of the same conversation in a safehouse in Tijuana fifteen years ago and the outcome is the cause of my repetitive nightmare. I took a deep breath and fought back the desire to strike out at everyone. I walked into the living room.

"They've got 'em on a boat out there," I said, more calmly than I thought I was capable of. "Two guys watching them and one of them can handle the boat, so they're moving. Maybe to the reef or the backcountry, maybe fishing."

Everyone looked at me.

"Why?" Luis asked.

"Because that's what I'd do." I opened the front door and saw Padre Thomas walking toward the house. A light rain had begun. "They're movable and not drawing anyone's attention. I think at this point Jerome has a say in this, and he wants to play it safe, get the money and put an end to it."

"I think Mick is right," Alfonso said. "In Mexico the hostages would already be dead, and Jerome does not want that to happen. Not that he cares about them, but he does not want the attention. For his own reasons, he wants this over."

Padre Thomas walked in and looked hesitantly at Richard and Luis. He spoke softly. "Tita is okay."

I put my arm around his shoulder and led him toward the kitchen. Norm followed, but wouldn't allow Alfonso to. Neither of us wanted Padre Thomas to spout off about the angels like an eccentric in front of the others. I hoped he had some good news from them.

"Padre Thomas, what are you doing here?" This always sounded like a useless, redundant question when I asked it.

He looked into the living room and then at Norm and me as we moved toward the back door. "Tita is okay but scared," he said.

"Where is she?" Norm blurted out like a believer.

"I don't know for sure." He looked at me. "But she is unhurt."

"Did you see the boat?" Norm seemed anxious as he paced the small kitchen. "Can you describe it?"

"A motorboat, white . . ."

"Christ, Padre, they're all white," Norm grumbled. "Something distinctive, please."

"Anything you can remember. Was it a dream or did the angels tell you about it?" I pleaded.

"I saw them in the dream," he said in hushed words. "Two men and a woman took her out on a small boat to a bigger one."

"Wait," I interrupted. "Wait a minute. You said two men and a woman. The woman was abducted with Tita, she's a DEA agent."

"No." He shook his head. "She led Tita to the men in the boat."

"You gotta be wrong, Padre," Norm said, but there was little conviction in his tone.

Chapter 59

I looked at Norm as Padre Thomas took a beer from the refrigerator. "That didn't sound very convincing."

"No." He sat down at the kitchen table with a frustrated look on his face. "When I talked to the agents outside the Half Shell, they seemed to think Jenny misled them."

"How?" I stood next to his chair.

"Told them she was going to El Siboney," he grumbled. "They staggered following her, which is SOP, and it allowed them to see if anyone was tailing her."

"They lost her?"

"They staggered the routes to Siboney and when the first car arrived, she wasn't there." He looked up at me and frowned. "Two, three minutes, that's all it took and she was gone. She didn't answer her radio. They put out an alert and started their search. This ain't a big island. They thought they'd find her."

I sat down next to Norm and rubbed my forehead. "She trusted this agent." It was a feeble comment, but it was what I thought. Trust is important to Tita.

"Mick," Norm put his hand on my shoulder. "Jenny's received commendations for her undercover work in Atlanta, San Juan and Miami. She was more than qualified and she shared a Puerto Rican background with Tita. Maybe we're missing something?"

"You still think she isn't involved?"

"It doesn't compute." He shook his head. "She's responsible

for putting a lot of them in jail and the DEA had to move her out of Atlanta because there was a price on her head. She's good."

I sighed. "Maybe she's better at lying."

Padre Thomas leaned against the back door and drank his beer. "You cannot be thinking of Tijuana now, Mick."

I looked up at him and wondered what he really knew or understood about that time in my life. "Why's that, Padre?"

"You cannot change the past," he said with a sly grin. "But you can forge the future from what you have learned."

"You're a wise man, Padre," Norm said and got up.

"No," Padre Thomas said. "I will take luck like you and Mick have and give wise to anyone that wants it."

"Luck?" Norm protested. "I think of it as skill."

Their conversation made no sense to me and then there was commotion from the living room that caught our attention. I got up and followed Norm and Padre Thomas. Jim Ashe and Bryan Blankenship were at the doorway talking to Richard. It was raining harder now.

Richard turned and I don't know if he was looking at Norm or me. "More help?" He held the door open.

Jim Ashe had a large envelope in his hands and nodded to us. His eyes moved quickly to his left toward Richard, and then he smiled while tapping his fingers on the envelope.

"What do you have?" Norm answered Jim's unasked question on whether or not he could talk freely.

"I don't have this." He smirked and glanced toward Richard. "Right?"

Richard grabbed Luis' arm. "You want to stay for this? It never happened."

Luis looked at me. He thinks of me as manipulating and sneaky, so maybe he thought I'd compromised the police chief.

I didn't trust Luis' word. "It might be better if he waited outside."

Richard stared at Luis while Jim Ashe waited. "You want to wait outside?"

"I want to catch these guys," he said.

I wondered if by "these guys" he meant the cartel or us.

"Go ahead," Richard said to Jim.

Jim Ashe is a captain in Navy Intelligence working out of the Joint Inter-Agency Task Force, JIATF, in Key West. Part of his responsibilities concerns drug smuggling. JIATF has representatives of many law enforcement agencies including the CIA, DEA, Navy Intelligence and some foreign police agencies. The head of JIATF is a Coast Guard admiral, which makes it part of Homeland Security.

Jim opened the envelope and removed five eight-by-ten, black-and-white photos. "I just downloaded these off the satellite." He spread the photos across the table.

I looked at them and realized instantly that they showed Tita with Jenny and two men. Norm did, too.

"That's at the parking lot." Norm pointed at one photo. He organized the photos in what he thought the order should be. "They're walking toward the water." He looked at me.

The last photo ended at the dinghy dock and one of the things that caught my attention was that Jenny walked behind them while Tita walked between the two men. I pointed to the last photo and looked at Norm.

He groaned. "Shit."

Jim looked at him. "What?"

Norm pointed to the last photo. "That's the DEA agent that's supposed to be protecting Tita. She's working with the kidnappers."

Richard turned to Luis. "Cancel the roadblock and tell Chance I said thank you, but don't tell him about this."

"He'll want to know why we're canceling it."

"You're following orders."

Luis nodded and walked to the front porch. I wondered if he'd obey the orders.

Richard looked with concern at Padre Thomas, Bob, Burt and Doug, and then turned to us. "Who's in charge here?"

"I'm working with you, Chief," Norm said. "Alfonso is a liaison officer from Mexico."

"I'm not here," Jim said quickly. "I'm visiting friends."

"Me too," Bryan Blankenship said.

"Let's cut the bullshit," Richard said and stood straight. "Between us we have a lot of ability and resources, so let's pool it and get Tita back and put these bad guys down."

We were all quiet.

"I will work officially with the DEA." He pointed to Norm. "How you get your information doesn't concern me." He looked around at the rest of us. "I'll listen to you," he pointed to Alfonso, "because you have experience in situations like this. Can we agree on that?"

We nodded almost in unison.

Richard then pointed to Padre Thomas. "What are you doing here, Padre?"

Padre Thomas looked sheepishly back at him. "I am praying."

"Have your prayers been answered?"

"He believes Tita is on a boat off the dinghy dock," Norm said. "I believe it to be true."

"Tell me about the ransom and how it gets here and who delivers it." Richard stood by the couch, ready to hear a long story. "And why do you trust this Jerome? Tita's life is in his hands."

Outside the sky was dark gray and the rain beat down steadily. Norm pulled the curtain aside and sighed. "Didn't I tell you about the rain?" He pointed outside for Alfonso to look.

"It's not rain," Jim Ashe said. "We're getting the effects of the outer edges of Hurricane Fred."

Norm shook his head and walked across the room. "It's always something in this damn place. It never rains in Southern California," he sang off-key.

"Who's going to answer me?" Richard rubbed his eyes before looking at me.

CHAPTER 60

Richard slumped down in the large overstuffed chair while Norm sat opposite him in the living room; Bob and Alfonso claimed the couch, leaving room for a third between them, but there were no takers. Padre Thomas stood outside the kitchen impatiently holding his empty bottle of beer; Doug stayed by the window, paying more attention to the rain than to us. Burt leaned against the wall close to the front door and Luis paced slowly a few feet behind Richard. I looked out onto the porch and listened as the heavy downpour beat on the house's tin roof. The edges of the cemetery were visible but the headstones and crypts were swallowed by the weather. Mid-afternoon grayness blanketed the island. Jim Ashe and Bryan Blankenship lingered off to the side.

I began by telling Richard about Tiny and friends spiriting me away from the men's room at Schooner and meeting Jerome at the airport. Richard listened quietly, turning to stop Luis as he tried to ask a question. When I finished, Richard rubbed his brow and frowned.

"And everyone knows this guy is the cartel's attorney and no one kept him under surveillance. He comes and goes as he pleases? What's wrong . . . why is that weird, or am I the only one that thinks so?" Richard sighed.

"No one here is in the pay grade to know that," Norm said stoically. "We don't make policy."

"Bullshit, Norm," Richard snarled. "We know what you are,

so don't play the DEA card with me. You two who ain't here," he said sharply and pointed to Jim Ashe and Bryan Blankenship, "isn't he with you working in the shadows?"

Jim Ashe shook his head. "We're working with the DEA agent from JIATF, not Miami."

"Why did I expect anything different?" He almost looked disappointed. "What do you think of Mick's assessment of Jerome?" Richard looked at Alfonso as he fought a yawn, and left Norm behind. "You know this guy from the Mexican side of the border, right?"

"I think Mick is right about Jerome not wanting the violence coming to his side of the border." Alfonso smoothed his mustache. "He has not, to the best of our knowledge, crossed into Mexico in two years. He meets his clients in San Diego, Las Vegas or Los Angeles because the cartel wars scare him. He no longer feels safe in Mexico."

"So he's not dealing with the drug lords directly because they wouldn't dare cross the border."

"They use men and women who cross regularly," Alfonso said. "The cartels have businessmen and government employees on the payroll and they take messages to Jerome as well as contacts in other cities. They give him secure phone numbers to call. He handles their business on this side of the border and he is influential. And remember, the cartel also bribes officials on your side too, so he knows a lot."

"We know all this and it's allowed to go on?" Richard barked. "Who runs this chicken-shit outfit? Where are the wiretaps?"

"I think you're missing the big picture," Norm said as he leaned forward in the chair. "If we do away with Jerome, the cartel gets another lawyer and we've gotta find out who. We keep an eye on Jerome, we know who he sees, who comes from Mexico or Colombia, and work from there. It leads us to bigger fish."

"So why wasn't anyone watching him when he took Mick?"

"Don't know." Norm held his hands up in surrender and sat back. "Like Jerome or not, he's the one we have to deal with now."

"I've got something you all seem to be overlookin'." Jim Ashe moved forward and pulled a curtain aside so we could see out. "We've got outer bands of a hurricane throughout tomorrow, lots of rain and wind, and the kidnappers have Tita on a boat."

"I haven't watched an update since yesterday," I said. "What's happening?"

"Fred's going to hit south of Miami as a Cat Three," Bryan Blankenship said. "It grew in size off the Bahamas and the outer bands are starting in the Lower Keys."

"What can we expect here?" I was thinking of Tita in a small boat in the unprotected harbor.

"Tropical storm winds, some stronger gusts," he said. "Clearing between bands. The worst should be around five and six tomorrow morning and then it will taper off, but you can expect rain and wind gusts for the rest of today."

"If they're smart, they'll move her to land," Bob said.

"Can we send Robert's crew out?" I looked to Richard. I knew the police marine patrol often checked on boats in the harbor.

"I doubt anyone's going out in this weather." Richard stood up. "But I'll ask him and when he knows why, maybe he'll do something."

"We've got guys who will go out," Jim Ashe said. "Probably glad to have an excuse to do so."

"Of course you do," Richard grumbled. "The more the merrier." He opened his cell to make the call.

Jim Ashe made his call and the room became so quiet we could hear the heavy rain as it pelted on the tin roof. Bushes swayed in the yard and off in the distance we heard thunder.

This was a prelude to what would come in the next twelve hours.

"Robert is already with the Coast Guard checking on the boats moored in and around the harbor," Richard said and sat back down.

"My guys are with the Coasties too," Jim Ashe said.

"Where is the ransom money coming from?" Richard changed the subject back to the kidnapping. He looked at me and saw my edginess. "Mick, right now we've done all we can do about the boat. Let's move on."

"We're supplying the ransom," Norm said hesitantly. "Unofficially."

Richard sighed. "Of course. Five million dollars. How are you going to transport that much money?"

"It'll fit into a large gym bag."

"You want it back?"

"No," I spoke up. "They get the money and Tita is set free and it's over."

"Where is the FBI?" Richard glanced at Norm, ignoring my comment. "Since when does the DEA handle kidnappers?"

"This is a DEA operation and your involvement is a courtesy," Norm said with a sly smile. "If it was someone other than Mick involved, we would handle it without you."

"Ain't I the lucky one." Richard scratched at his beard stubble. "You said the exchange would take place at the sunset celebration on Mallory Square on Friday, how will this weather affect that?"

"If they wanted a crowd for protection . . ." Norm said.

I cut Norm off. "Jerome is calling the shots. If he wants Mallory Square, we go there. We go wherever he wants."

"Will the money be here tomorrow or Friday?" Richard asked.

"The plan was for tomorrow." Norm looked at Jim Ashe. "The weather may change that."

"It will be here late tomorrow," Jim Ashe volunteered.

"And you know that why?" Richard said.

"We have a plane picking it up in the Bahamas."

"Of course you do. Why in this age of electronic transfers are you dealing with cash? Especially that much cash?"

CHAPTER 61

"What does any of that have to do with getting Tita back?" I yelled, unable to control my frustration. "Who gives a good goddamn where the money comes from or how it gets here?" I opened the front door, letting in the humidity while I stared at the downpour and swaying tree branches. I hated the helplessness that overwhelmed me. "No one should be on a boat in the harbor during this storm and that's where Tita is." I turned to Norm. "You had no right to bring this here." I closed the door.

"We've beaten that horse already," he said quietly, but his expression showed anger. Was he mad at himself for what he'd done or at me for constantly reminding him? "Mick, none of us can change the past, so stop dwelling on it. The harbor is being checked."

I knew he meant Tijuana as much as he meant what was now happening in Key West and it made me want to scream.

"And my men are watching from shore. If any of the boats in the harbor tries to dock anywhere, we'll be on them," Jim Ashe said from across the room. "There's a chance the kidnappers will leave her alone and head to land."

"Will not happen," Alfonso said. "If they come ashore, she will come with them. These men follow orders. They will not leave her."

"That's good to know." Richard stood. "Anyone on a boat in this weather is anxious, so let's hope these guys are a little off their game and the Coast Guard will do its job and Tita . . ."

"They'll kill her first," I shrieked as images of Tijuana clouded my mind. "You don't know what you're up against."

"You want us to do nothing?" Richard growled at me. "Is that what you want?"

"I want to pay the ransom and get Tita back." I looked around the room as they stared at me.

"What do you want us to do?" Bob stood and walked to me. "You name it, we'll do it."

"Damn right," Burt agreed.

"While you're waiting, I'd be thinking about the *Bastard*," Doug said, talking about my sailboat. "Is she prepared for this weather?"

Padre Thomas sighed. "Waiting is what hell is all about, Mick. I hate waiting. It only adds to my anxiety, so if you can go to your boat and do something, it might be good therapy."

"Patience is supposed to be a virtue, Padre," Jim Ashe said.

"Virtues are often overrated and sometimes they become vices," Padre Thomas answered. "We should check your boat, Mick, and let these men practice patience." His gaze was an inspection of those standing around. "They need to try righteousness for a change."

I was in a private hell and needed to get out. Norm understood not being able to change the past. If I dwelled on what should've happened, I would be of no help to Tita. Norm knew that, too.

Outside, the hot wind kept up but the rain turned to drizzle. I looked at Bryan Blankenship. "Is there a break coming?"

"You could have an hour or a little more." He looked out the window. "I'd need a computer to be exact."

"An hour is enough time to secure my boat."

I received nods from Bob, Burt and Doug. I looked at Richard. "I need to know."

"If we get any news, I'll call," Richard promised. "If Luis gets it, he will call." He turned to look at my nemesis. "You understand that, right?"

"You get some rest, Chief, and if we get any news I'll call Murphy before I wake you," Luis said. "Is that good enough?" Was he asking Richard or me?

"Yes," Richard said.

"Where is everyone going?" I fought the separation angst of leaving.

"I'm staying here," Norm said.

"Me too," Jim Ashe said. "It's a good base of operation and it's dry."

"With a kitchen and bathroom," Bryan Blankenship said. "I'm having my laptop delivered here."

"We've got the phone numbers, Mick, take advantage of the break." Richard yawned and headed out the door. "I'll be in my office waiting to hear from Robert."

Richard and Luis were gone before I could reply.

"If there's a problem with the ransom because of the weather . . ."

"The money will make it here tomorrow." Jim Ashe sounded sure of himself.

"Call me." I stared at Norm and he nodded as we left the house.

My Jeep has a bikini top that gave no protection against the windswept rain, so the interior was soaked as we piled in. Bob pulled the M-4 from under the seat and wiped it down using his shirt.

It's a short ride through the Meadows to the marina. The skies were gray and we knew the rain was on hold, not over. Small patches of blue sky flashed through, but held no promise.

Most of the vehicles were gone from the parking lot. A few live-aboard boaters had no place to go, so they rode out the storm. Some might have sought shelter at the Green Parrot Bar or Schooner Wharf. They may even have found the Tree Bar on Duval open; of course, it was also open to the weather.

Padre Thomas pulled me aside as we got out of the Jeep. "I haven't seen the angels and I am concerned," he whispered.

"You knew about Tita."

"Yes, but I usually see more and I've seen nothing since noon." He sounded as anxious as I felt. "I have a bad feeling."

"About what?" I asked as we walked toward the dock.

Padre Thomas shook his head. "I don't know."

CHAPTER 62

The Jeep offered no shelter from the wind and rain and we were drenched, so the flooded parking lot was not an obstacle. A thick humidity swirled in the oscillating wind and helped my wet clothes stick to me. My phone chirped as we sloshed forward toward the dock. The readout flashed Pauly's name, so I answered.

"Yeah." I covered the phone with my hand to keep the wind from whistling into the speaker. "Where are you?"

"New Orleans," he said. "No flights to Miami and none to Key West right now."

"Hurricane Fred is hitting Miami and we're getting the outer bands here."

"Yeah, I know. You okay?"

"For the time being," I lied. I didn't say anything about Tita.

"I'll be there as soon as I can get a flight. I've got a couple of calls out lookin' for a plane."

"You be careful."

"Watch your back till I get there." He hung up.

"Pauly's stuck in New Orleans," I told them as we approached the dock.

"He won't be able to get here for a couple of days," Bob said.

"I wouldn't bet on it." Pauly had a way of getting what he wanted.

Debris had washed out of the mangroves and some of it was scattered on the dock while other pieces of trash floated in the bight. Storms often clean out the shoreline, leaving the harbor filthy. We should be allowed to shoot those that use our waterways as their personal dump, but we're not.

"What do we need to do?" Bob asked as he headed down the ramp.

"The roller furling is wound tight," I said. "We'll wrap the new mainsail on the boom with line and store the things that haven't blown out of the cockpit. That should do it."

"There enough lines on her?" Doug asked. His marina didn't have floating docks.

"All the mooring lines are tight and should hold." The wind swayed the dock as we walked along it.

A floating dock goes with the tide flow, up and down. In storms no special lines are required for tying off a boat because the boat floats with the dock. Unless hurricane surge raises the tide higher than the dock's pilings, the boats ride out the ups and downs of storm surge.

Chop from the bight splashed us and two-foot whitecaps pushed through the marina's harbor. None of the live-aboard boaters were taking advantage of the break in the weather, which indicated they had gone to dry land. Boaters checked lines as often as possible during a storm, and a break from the rain was a gift.

Bob moved up and pushed Padre Thomas from my side. "Do you think the DEA crew left the boat?"

"Good question." Looking down the dock, I could see no one. "There's also agents on Marlin Pier watching from behind. They might've all left."

Padre Thomas grabbed my arm and forced me to stop. He looked worried. Bob moved forward a few steps and then turned toward us. The wind whistled between the boats, lines screeched as the blustery weather strained them, and halyards snapped against masts, sending a repetitive metal-on-metal clanging throughout the marina.

Bob staggered forward with a surprised look and then fell to the dock. A small patch of blood showed below his right shoulder and began to spread. I hadn't heard the shot, but the second shot was followed by a third and then multiple shots that ricocheted off the dock.

Bob rolled into the choppy water. "I'm okay," he said, holding onto a mooring line. Doug and Burt split up, taking cover behind boats on opposite finger docks. I grabbed Padre Thomas as shots punctured the cacophony of sounds from the wind and pulled him along, seeking shelter behind a boat. He cried out and I saw blood above his knee.

He sat up and held his leg. He touched the trickle of blood above his knee and forced a grim smile. He licked his fingers. "Blood. Are you okay?"

"Quiet," I whispered in his ear as I wrapped my handkerchief around his wound.

"Okay?" Bob startled me as he called out from the water.

"Yeah, how about you?"

"I've been shot worse. There are two on the boat across from you."

"That's the DEA boat." I looked above the sailboat that protected us from the shooters. "They must have mistaken us."

"No mistake," he said. "They waited till we were close."

"It must be the other cartel. That's a DEA boat," I whispered, repeating myself.

"Not anymore. Where's Doug and Burt?"

I pointed at the opposite finger dock and then at the boat beside us.

Bob nodded. "They'll come looking for you, so be prepared."

He sank underwater and swam away. It was hard for me to think of this good-natured friend as a hardened Navy SEAL, but his recent actions indicated he really had been one.

I pulled my Glock. "Padre, if anyone comes, you go into the water and hide under the dock. You understand?"

"I will be okay," he said softly.

I used the hull of the boat as cover and crawled toward its bow until I could see the two men on the sailboat across from the *Fenian Bastard*. Two men, not a man and a woman. If the agents hadn't evacuated, I didn't hold out much hope for them being alive. Where was the DEA backup from Marlin Pier?

What were the shooters waiting for? None of us had returned fire, so they had to consider we were unarmed. I hoped they thought so.

The wind filled the night with wailing marina noise as it made water splash on the teetering dock.

"Mick," Burt called quietly from the deck of the boat on my right.

I looked up and saw him lying flat, holding his peacemaker revolver.

"There's two more coming down the dock real slow, carrying M-16s." He pointed at the DEA boat. "We focus on these two. Bob and Doug got the new ones. Okay?"

I nodded my understanding.

I watched as the two men climbed from the boat to the dock. One spoke into something in his hand, a phone or radio. I couldn't see the others, so I kept watch on the two from the boat. They waited quietly and changed out magazines for their M-16s. I hoped that when they stepped forward, I would have a clear shot. They'd waited for backup and were now ready to catch us in crossfire.

The shooters knew one of us had been shot and was out of commission. We hadn't returned fire and that had to give them confidence, too. No matter, we were outgunned. Handguns against M-16s, probably fully automatic, wasn't a fair fight. We could use surprise once and then it would be over for them or for us.

The loud reports from Bob's and Doug's .45s carried on the howling wind. The return fire, rapid pop-pop-pops, of the M-16s were almost lost in the same wind. I wanted to look, but knew it would make me an easy target, so I lay on the finger dock and let the saltwater splash me as I watched the two gunmen cautiously move forward. They ignored the gun battle as they looked for us.

Now they knew we were armed, so surprise was gone. I didn't know where Burt was and decided not to wait for him to shoot even though he had the high ground. I watched the two men and almost had a clear shot of the gunman furthest from me. The second gunman was out of my sight, hidden behind the same boat that hid me.

The .45s exploded again, followed quickly by the M-16s and then the .45s for a third time. I couldn't tell if one gun was doing the shooting or if both Bob and Doug were firing. It was impossible to tell exactly where the sounds originated from or how many were shooting.

The gunman was less than twenty feet away. I took my shot, hitting him high on the chest. I'd aimed lower, but all things considered, I was glad to have hit him anywhere. His M-16 fired wildly; flashes from the barrel circled in the shadows as he went down hard and then slid into the choppy water. Stray bullets hit the boat closest to him.

Suddenly bullets tore into the dock from above me and then I heard the loud report of Burt's .45 twice. I skirted away from the bullets, unable to stand. When I turned to look up, prepared to shoot back, the second shooter was caught on the rail of the boat, the strap of his rifle wrapped around his arm. He was dead.

"You okay?" Burt jumped down to the dock. He grabbed the

M-16 with a yank and when the rifle was free, the shooter toppled into the water. "You okay, Padre?"

"Scared," Padre Thomas said softly as he blessed himself. "Very scared."

Burt touched Padre Thomas' shoulder and nodded. "We all are. Wait here and you'll be fine." His concern for Padre Thomas surprised me.

Burt ejected the rifle's magazine, then looked into the water. "I should've checked him for extra magazines," he said. "This one's almost empty."

The .45s fired again. Bob and Doug were only two boats up from us, but the wind carried the sound of the gunfire toward the parking lot and it was difficult to hear the return fire from the M-16s.

Burt darted from the finger dock to the safety of the next boat. I checked Padre Thomas' leg. The bleeding had slowed. That was all I could do. He was soaked from the ride in the Jeep and his leg must have hurt like hell, but he would have to wait until this was over for medical help.

I moved slowly to the bow of the boat as the rain began. A light drizzle at first, but I knew the clouds would open soon and another downpour was due. Burt hid one finger slip up from me and I could see Doug on the same side of the pier as Burt crouched at the bow of a trawler. I couldn't see Bob.

The two gunmen were behind boats three slips up. One on each side of the dock. A third gunman stood at the parking lot entrance next to the shadows of the mangrove bushes. He raised his M-16 and carefully aimed toward us. He leaned against the railing for support. I fired in his direction, but I was too far away to hit anything. Did he see Bob in the water? I saw the barrel flash, but didn't hear the shot. Doug stayed where he was; Burt too. Where was Bob?

"Bob," I yelled, but didn't know if anyone heard me because

291

of the wind.

Burt pointed across from Doug and gave me the okay sign.

A second barrel flash came from the shooter's rifle. The gunman I could see on the dock fell. The shooter stood up straight and walked into the shadows of the parking lot.

CHAPTER 63

The rain came down steadily, not heavy, not light. The wind stretched mooring lines until they screeched and the halyards continued to slap against masts, sending out a pinging chant. The gunman by the parking lot had killed the two shooters that had us pinned down. No one was sure he'd left or who he was, so we stayed where we were and waited. The abrasive weather continued to blanket the dock. The place held an evening eeriness in its shadows because of the bodies and the shootout, as the rain sloshed around us driven by the humid wind.

"He's gone," Padre Thomas said from behind me. He couldn't have seen the shooter from where he was.

"Who?" I turned to him.

"The man who fired the last shots."

I looked at him. Even in the grayness of the storm, I could see the pain on his troubled face as he tried to smile. "I stopped you because it didn't feel right," he said slowly. "A man killed the shooters. You understand how hard it is for me to explain what I know."

I stood up and could see the body of the man Burt shot trapped in the water between the boat and the slip. I caught Burt's attention as I walked from the finger slip to the dock. "It's over," I shouted, trusting Padre Thomas. "Where's Bob?"

"Over here," Bob yelled. "Someone give me a hand."

Burt beat me across the dock and helped Bob out of the water. His .45 automatic lay on the dock. I picked it up and handed it to him. "Did you hit anything?"

"Just a boat, apparently," Bob laughed and looked toward the parking lot ramp. "Who the hell was that?"

"No idea," I said. "How's the shoulder?"

"The saltwater is good for it." He kept looking toward the parking lot. "We sure he's gone?"

"I'm not even sure it's raining." I turned and walked to Padre Thomas. I helped him up. "Can you walk?"

He winced. "Not very well." He put his arm around my shoulder and hobbled to the *Fenian Bastard*.

Burt and Doug were already wrapping line around the mainsail and boom. Bob looked at the body I'd shot as it floated in the water. Then he climbed onboard the DEA boat and disappeared.

I sat Padre Thomas on the dockside step unit. Most everything was still in the cockpit. I tossed the wet cushions below, dumped the water from two ashtrays, put them in a storage locker, and ignored the rain.

After I locked the cabin hatch, I saw Bob lean over Padre Thomas. I'd say they were laughing, but I know how Bob feels about the priest.

"We need to get you two to the hospital," I said when I got on the dock.

"I was just telling the padre that Jim Ashe's people will fix us up," Bob said. "He should be able to walk with a cane. Make him look distinguished."

Bob was full of surprises. Maybe he should get shot more often.

"He says I took this for you." Bob turned to me, rubbing the hole in his shirt. "Thanks."

"Shouldn't I be the one saying thanks?" I kidded.

"Yeah, there's that," he joked back. "What are we gonna do with the bodies?" he said more seriously.

"The storm will blow them into the mangroves."

"I don't dislike the mangroves that much."

"Mexicans?"

"Do you think?" Bob said with sarcasm. "Latin males. So Mexican or Cuban, what difference does it make?"

"Remind you of the two on the water?"

"Yup." Bob moved me away from Padre Thomas. "The man and woman," he nodded to the boat across from me. "Their throats are slit."

"Shit."

"We gotta let someone know. Richard?"

"We go back to Tita's so Jim Ashe can look at you and Padre Thomas, we gotta tell them something. Then we'll decide." The bodies were not going anywhere, so that gave us time.

"Tell them the truth?"

"It will set you free." I sighed because I couldn't find a reason to laugh.

CHAPTER 64

Padre Thomas looked on in despair while we stumbled along, trying to keep our balance on the wind-pitched dock as dark water splashed around our feet and a cool rain gave a brief respite from the humidity. He draped an arm over my shoulder, clinging to me like my clothing, and we hobbled quietly behind the others who walked so we'd all stay together. I wasn't sure if the despair came from the bullet wound in his leg or the deaths of the four men who tried to kill us. Or maybe he'd flashed back to when he used my Glock to take a life, to save his and mine?

Bob cautioned us to wait on the dock ramp as he checked out the marina parking lot. I don't know what he hoped to see, since visibility was minimal with the rain and grayness of the evening. Maybe ex-Navy SEALs can see better in those conditions than I can.

We sloshed through the parking lot when Bob called us. The Jeep was so wet it offered no protection from the weather. I drove the long way around the lot because I wanted to go under the Palm Avenue Bridge. I stopped and got out, using the bridge embankment as shelter from the rain and wind, and called Norm.

I told him what had happened and that we needed Jim Ashe's medical help. I mentioned the two dead DEA agents; when he asked about the backup group on Marlin Pier, I told him we hadn't checked on them. I didn't need to see more dead bodies, especially with their throats cut.

The ride to Tita's house was short, but with the flooded road conditions it took a while. When I parked in the red zone, Burt took Bob's keys and drove Doug back to his marina. They were getting dry clothes and foul weather gear and promised to bring Bob his.

I helped Padre Thomas up the porch stairs. Norm opened the door and we entered the comfortable coolness of Tita's. We dripped water through the living room on our way to the kitchen. Norm, Alfonso and Bryan Blankenship were in the living room watching the Weather Channel. Jim Ashe waited in the kitchen.

"Look at him first," Bob said to Jim and pointed to Padre Thomas.

A small medical bag sat on the kitchen table. I got Padre Thomas to sit and he winced in pain as his leg bent.

Jim Ashe removed the bandanna I'd used on Padre Thomas' leg and then cleaned the area around the wound with a wet kitchen towel. I thought how mad Tita would be. I'd forgotten for a moment what trouble she was in.

I got a look of surprise from Jim Ashe. "It's not bad," he said. "Probably a ricochet. You're lucky, Padre, it's only a flesh wound."

"It hurts," he said. "It hurts when I walk."

"It's gonna for a while," Jim Ashe said as he took a liquid from a bottle and used the towel to spread it across the leg. The bleeding had stopped as he wrapped white gauze around the wound. "You'll be fine in a day or two," he said.

He pointed to an empty chair for Bob to sit in. "Take the shirt off." He examined Bob's shoulder. "You're luckier than the priest."

"Will he need to lose the arm?" I joked and helped Padre Thomas up. I left him in the bathroom, where he tried to towel himself dry.

Jim smiled. "He'll be playing basketball next week."

I don't know where Jim Ashe received medical training or if his ability came from on-the-job experience, but he went about an examination of Bob's wound, poked around in it and then cleaned it. Bob winced quietly once or twice. Otherwise, he sat still and let Jim do his thing. When he finished poking, probing and wiping, Jim put a bandage on Bob's chest where the bullet exited and then another one on his back where the bullet entered. When all that was done, he added one more bandage that went over Bob's shoulder and covered both wounds.

Somehow, Padre Thomas had gotten a beer and was leaning against the wall.

"I have dry clothes that should fit you," I said.

He smiled and took a drink of beer. Maybe the beer was his medication, since he hadn't received a pain pill.

In Tita's bedroom I toweled off and dressed in dry shorts and a T-shirt. I grabbed a pair for Padre Thomas and gave them to him. Slowly, he limped to the bathroom to change.

It was dark now, the wind was blowing harder, the rain was heavier and we expected it to keep up until morning.

"No one on Marlin Pier." Norm stood in the kitchen doorway after hanging up his cell. "You should've checked on them." His words came out harsh.

"No, I shouldn't have," I answered callously. I walked to him and pushed him into the living room. "I shouldn't have had to deal with any of this shit," I hollered. "Six more people are dead because of you, and only because of luck the five of us are okay. Those two DEA agents shouldn't have died like they did and it's your fault." I pushed my hand against his chest. "I had nothing to do with this before you threw me to the dogs."

Norm slapped my hand away. "Get over it, Mick."

"Get over it?" I yelled.

Alfonso and Bryan Blankenship watched us from the couch while Jim Ashe, Padre Thomas and Bob stared from the kitchen.

"How many has your plan killed? Two at the car wash." I raised my hand in front of him, fingers spread wide, and bent two down. "Three at Harpoon Harry's." I turned my hand into a fist. "That's five. Then there are the two goons on the water." I raised two fingers. "The headless corpse at the hockey rink." Three fingers up. "A hapless pothead tortured to death as he hung on a tree at the beach." Four fingers. "Just now, another six." I held both hands up with my fingers spread apart. "What's that make? Fifteen? Ah," I said, "your lucky number."

Norm looked at me and I saw a glint of disappointment mixed with the anger on his face. Probably disappointed in me, not for what he'd set upon Key West.

"What do you need? Five more?" I shouted.

Norm moved away, shaking his head.

"Five more and there'll be twenty dead bodies," I yelled after him. "A million dollars apiece. Price used to be thirty pieces of silver."

Norm turned to face me. "Your mouth works well. Too bad your brain is dead." He walked outside and closed the door behind him.

CHAPTER 65

Everyone stayed still when I exploded at Norm and the house was deadly quiet after he closed the door. Even the Weather Channel had been muted. I had lost it. The shootout at the pier and getting Padre Thomas and Bob medical help had kept me from thinking of Tita and rescuing her. Now, in her house with mementos everywhere, all I could think about was her, and I felt guilty for having had other priorities. Seeing Jim Ashe use one of her good kitchen towels kick-started my anxieties and I forgot about the pier and injuries. Black-ass helplessness engulfed me, leaving me feeling useless. Inept. A failure again, like in Tijuana.

I could hear the rain and wind as I stared at the closed door. My first thought was I had been too hard, but that changed as I recalled Woodrow's mutilated and tortured body hanging on a tree. My stomach twisted because there wasn't a guarantee anywhere that Tita wouldn't end up tortured and crucified. I counted on a fixated cartel attorney for her safe return and distanced myself from someone who had proven his friendship countless times when the chips were down. I reminded myself that he had also deceived me and set this disaster in motion.

Alfonso draped his arm over my shoulder and with a devious smile moved me toward the kitchen. Bob and Jim Ashe left us alone.

Alfonso opened the refrigerator. "No Mexican beer." He had been in the house for hours, so he knew that already.

I kept my mouth shut because I wasn't sure if my frustration had run its course. The feeling of ineptness hadn't.

"You blame Norm for this," Alfonso began.

"Damn right," I barked.

He took a cigarette from a pack in his pocket and I wanted to tell him Tita didn't allow smoking in the house. If I had a cigar, I would've smoked it. He lit the cigarette and opened the back door. He stood close to the doorway, and the howling wind blew dampness and humidity into the room.

"Do you know what happened after Norm left you at the Panama Canal?" He tossed the cigarette outside and closed the door. "He really got into the boxing game." He chuckled because Norm had used the scheme as his cover in Mexico and Central America. "He had two middle welterweight Mexican fighters and one Salvadoran."

He was quiet, maybe expecting me to say something. I didn't.

"I am not sure what agency he really works for. Do you know?" He waited a few seconds and went on. "Does anyone? I ran into him at a hotel in Mexico City and we went to the fights. His boxer actually won a six-round bout. I was impressed. Met the boxer in the dressing room. Norm and I went out for dinner. It was late for him, but dinnertime in Mexico.

"I asked a few questions about his fighters. I expected him to be thrilled with the win." He looked to make sure I was listening and swept his fingers through his hair. "He kept switching the talk from boxing to you. He wanted to know if I had heard from you. He told me stories about some of your adventures. Not assignments, he used the word "adventures" as if he was telling a story, not recounting facts. I learned things I did not know." He lit another cigarette but didn't bother with the door this time. He pulled over the wastebasket instead and used it as an ashtray.

"Talk is cheap, right?" He shook ash into the wastebasket.

"In Mexico, we were all friends. You wrote about civil wars, revolutionaries and drug smuggling. Norm chased both around Mexico and Central America. Me, I only cared about the cartel." He took a long drag on the cigarette, stubbed it out and trashed it. "You used Norm and me for sources and leads. Norm used you. He would put a tail on you, I know because I helped."

"Tell me something I don't know," I said impatiently.

"We all knew the rules of the game," Alfonso said. "We lived within the rules and we were friends. Recently, Norm talked about you as if you still played the game. He missed you, in his strange sort of way.

"I do not know how he got the DEA cover or why he did. I walked into the office in TJ one day and I was introduced to him. My superiors did not know we knew each other. After that, we worked together and he did report to the DEA office in San Diego. I know because I went with him to meetings."

Padre Thomas limped into the room and took a beer from the refrigerator. He smiled and left.

"Timing is everything in what we do. At least in my part of what we do, it is." He gave me a short grin. "Norm was with me when I met my operative. The agent told of the hit at the car wash in Key West because Norm was American, otherwise I do not think it would have come up." He gave me another thin smile and ran his hands through his hair. "Mention of the unknown red-headed shooter caught Norm's attention. We talked about the chances of there being two redheads in Key West with the ability to act so quickly. You know the rest."

"Why are you telling me this?" I looked at him and tried to see if I had missed something. "I don't know and I don't give a good goddamn what agency Norm works for. I care about Tita and he's responsible for the trouble right now and that's not forgivable."

"You need to understand that Norm made the decision as if

you were still a player and he expected you to walk in the door. It was as if the years you were gone had vanished, we were back in the nineties, and he was excited about working with you again," Alfonso said seriously. "Fifteen years and things change. We are older and slower, but not Norm. He honestly thought you would still be excited."

"If he was fifteen years back in time, he should have thought about Mel," I grumbled. "He should have called first."

Alfonso rubbed his hands together and frowned. "I was thinking of that and said so."

"And he didn't care," I said.

"No, no, he cared but said he could protect you. He told me a little about Tita. He knew she was in Boston, so she was safe," he said. "When he was done explaining his idea, I supported him, Mick."

"He was wrong, his plan backfired and others are paying for it," I shouted. "I'm not excited, I am pissed."

"Obviously," Alfonso said. "Rightfully so, I guess."

"Guess?" I continued to raise my voice. "You guess? Fifteen dead and Tita could be number sixteen . . ."

"Fifteen dead," he mocked me. "How many do you think have died in Mexico this year?"

"I don't care."

"Yes, well, you are among the majority of Americans," he snapped. "You want the drugs, it's your money and guns, but it is a few thousand Mexican lives that have been lost. Some of them were innocent, too. Mexicans, we are tired of hearing Americans cry because of us. The problems we cause. Fuck you," he yelled, angry enough to be out of character. "Clean up your own problem and Mexicans would have to find something else to do. Americans have the drug demand, have the money for it, billions of dollars, and all we do is service your addiction just like we clean your houses and pick your fruit. We deliver the drugs you demand."

CHAPTER 66

We were fighting two different battles. Alfonso fought to save his country, and it was a battlefield with thousands of combatants and many casualties. Mine was a personal battle to save Tita; it involved a handful of combatants in Key West and had more than its share of casualties. Alfonso's argument had truth to it, but it was one side of a two-sided coin. Corruption was at the root of the problem, beginning in Mexico and creeping into the States. The drug business made men tremendously wealthy and that wealth bribed people on both sides of the border. American immigrations and border officials had accepted bribes; so had American law enforcement. Some were caught, but no one knew how many remained on the hidden payroll or how many had sought out the money.

"Your argument reminds me of two men deciding which came first, the chicken or the egg," Padre Thomas said from the doorway. He took a cigarette from his pack of Camels and offered one to Alfonso, who took it and lit it with a lighter and offered the flame to Padre Thomas. "If two men are eating a breakfast of scrambled eggs and chicken fried steak, it doesn't really matter which came first." He inhaled smoke and then slowly released it. "How things happened isn't as important as how you are going to save Tita," he said to me while he pulled out a chair and sat down. "You can't do it without their help." He pointed to Alfonso, but meant Norm too. "You need them, you need Richard too, and your friends. Focus on that." He stubbed out the cigarette and dropped it in the wastebasket. "Put the bickering aside."

"You don't understand the whole situation, Padre," I said quietly. "It's more than just using me. Norm put us all in danger for something we had nothing to do with. Something he was responsible for."

They both stared and waited for me to go on.

"You don't know about that, do you?" I said harshly to Alfonso. "You looked for who might have stolen the twenty million, right?"

"We never found out who ended up with most of it." He stubbed out his cigarette and put it in the trash. "The men the cartel tortured and killed might have been involved, but they were not the mastermind."

I smiled wickedly. "The *we*, did that include Norm?"

"Sometimes, when we shared information with the Americans. They looked for the money, too."

"I guarantee you that Norm didn't share pertinent information." I couldn't get the silly smirk off my face. "I obviously know something you don't."

"Tell me," Alfonso said with an anxious smile.

"I know who stole the money and it wasn't me."

"I know you did not take the money." His smile died. "Who did?"

I looked out the kitchen window and watched the rain blow sideways as tree limbs and bushes shook. Somewhere an undeserved loyalty to Norm told me to keep the secret. Did Alfonso really not know? Did he think the DEA would supply the five-million-dollar ransom for Tita? Maybe Norm received unquestionable loyalty from Alfonso as he once did from me.

"You should ask Norm," I said, slowly, because I wanted to yell the truth. "He has the answers."

CHAPTER 67

Ask me why I didn't scream that it was Norm who stole the twenty million dollars that caused this nightmare and I couldn't give you an answer. Telling the truth would have explained my erratic behavior and frustration. It might even have made my friends side with me. But my friendship with Norm still had me in its grasp. When the moment of anger brought me to the point of betrayal, I hesitated and, with a brief glimmer of the past, I chose not to betray an old friend. Alfonso knew or he didn't. Had Norm grudgingly trusted me with his secret? Trust didn't come easy to him.

Had Norm kept his secret so well that not even the angels knew?

When I turned away from Padre Thomas and Alfonso, Burt and Doug were standing there decked out in wet foul-weather gear. Bob had changed into dry clothes and had his yellow rain jacket and pants in his hands.

"This might fit you." Burt held out a set of extra rain gear. "We decided to stay away from your marina."

"Thanks." As soon as I said it, my cell phone chirped. Pauly's name flashed on the readout screen. I walked to one of the living-room windows and answered. "It's still stormy here."

"Yeah, I heard a recent NOAA weather report," Pauly answered. "I'm sitting in an airport restaurant outside New Orleans. A place called Slidell. Know it?"

"No. Should I?"

"No reason to," he said casually. "But you might be interested in who just got off his plane and is coming into the restaurant."

At that moment I couldn't have cared less who was in Slidell. "Pauly, you want to tell me something, tell me." It came out colder than I meant it to.

"The storm giving you cabin fever?" he said lightly. "You lose your sense of humor, Mick, you're on the downslide."

"Sorry, Pauly. I'm wet, tired and hungry. What's happening at the airport?"

"You said Jerome was in Miami, right?"

"Yeah." Now he had my attention.

"Well, he just got off his plane with an entourage . . ."

I cut him off. "Did you see Tita?"

"Tita? Why would she be with him?"

"Pauly, did you see her?" I demanded.

"No, Mick," he said hesitantly. "Did he grab Tita?"

"Yeah."

"Son-of-a-bitch." He garbled the words in anger. "What the fuck for?"

"For what he thinks is my share of the stolen money."

"How much?"

"Five million."

He whistled. "And?"

"And I am going to pay it Friday at the sunset celebration."

"Miami to Slidell isn't the route to Key West."

I was thinking the same thing. Was Jerome leaving or evacuating?

"Maybe the hurricane scared him? Maybe he had to move the plane?"

"Maybe," he said without much enthusiasm. "I can see the plane from my seat. The rear door is open, lights are off and the pilot is coming out, too. Tiny isn't with Jerome."

"Do you think the plane's empty?"

"Yeah, it looks empty. Tell me what's going on."

I told him the whole story, including Woodrow's death, the kidnapping of Tita and how I hoped to get her back. He listened quietly.

"Do you need help getting the money?" he asked after I'd finished.

"It's coming by plane," I said.

"I don't mean getting it to you, I mean raising the funds. If you need it, I can help."

Pauly surprised me with his offer. I never would have thought to ask him. Of course, I never would have thought to go to Norm, either.

"No, Pauly, I'm okay there. Norm is putting up the ransom," I said.

"If he wants it back, it won't work," he said bleakly. "They take Jerome with the ransom, this won't be over."

"I've thought of that," I said and watched everyone looking at me as I talked. "It's taken care of."

"I guess you'll have to tell me the whole story when I get there." He almost laughed, knowing I was holding something back. "I might have a flight late tonight, if there's another break in your weather. He just came in the restaurant," Pauly whispered. "I'll tell you what he's wearing and who's with him. If I were you, I'd call as a reminder that you're keeping an eye on him. He'll believe you. He just landed and you know where he's at, what tie he has on." He laughed. "I think I'll stick around and watch his reaction."

"Doesn't he know you?"

"I met him a long time ago, but it was a friend who needed his services, not me."

Pauly told me everything he could about Jerome and his entourage, the weather and the restaurant. I thanked him and hung up. All eyes were on me. I smiled and dialed Jerome.

"To what do I owe the pleasure?" he said cheerfully. "We don't have a problem, do we, Mick?"

I tried mimicking his cheerfulness. "No, Jerome, we don't. I was curious about your flight. I thought you wouldn't fly in bad weather."

He was used to being in control. I could tell by the silence that he was trying to interpret what I'd said.

"You there, Jerome?"

"Yes, I'm here." He tried to put authority back in his words. "What do you want? I'm busy."

"I wanted you to realize I know where you are," I hesitated, "and always will until Tita is safely back with me. Do we understand each other?"

"Are you threatening me?" He was losing his attitude and trying to hide behind bravado.

"No, Jerome. I'm not threatening you. I'm reminding you of my promise. I get Tita back, you get the money and all's well with the world," I said slowly and waited a moment to finish. "If Tita has a scratch on her or something screws up, I am gonna kill you. You can't hide. I wanted to remind you of that, and that I'm a man of my word." I hoped I sounded as threatening as I wanted to.

"And where do you think I am?" he said quietly.

"You just got off your plane in Slidell and you're in the airport's small restaurant with a few others, but without Tiny." I forced a cruel laugh. "The lights are off in the plane and the door is open and you have an ugly paisley tie on."

The information was so specific, I could almost feel his momentary anxiety. It took a long minute for him to compose himself.

"I am impressed, Mick," he said, controlling his voice. "But this is a waste of our time, believe me. I left Miami, as you seem to know, because of the hurricane. New Orleans is one of my favorite cities, so we stopped here and will go to the city for a hotel and some gumbo."

"I love a good gumbo."

"Yes, I am sure," he said, sounding annoyed. "I am a man of my word, too. Tita will be back with you unharmed Friday at, what did we decide? Six at Mallory Square? Of course, there won't be a sunset celebration, will there?"

"Not on Friday. No tourists, no crowds on the square because of Fred."

"No problem, right? You'll have the money and Tita will be at the square. The exchange will take place and, as you so elegantly put it, all will be right with the world." His blustering words were wound tight and couldn't hide his anger and concern.

"All this will end? That's what you promised," I reminded him with a cold challenge in my words. It surprised me that Mallory Square was still acceptable since there would be no throngs of tourists.

"I have been given assurances by the men in Tijuana, but I should add that if you ever return to Mexico, all assurances are off," he said lightly, almost like his old self. "They would take it as a personal insult if you came to a bullfight and so would I."

"I understand. So you'll not be in Key West Friday."

"No, but people will be there to take care of business. I hope to be in New Orleans, maybe having a second bowl of gumbo while I wait on the phone call from my associates."

Bob's cell phone rang, causing me to turn as Jerome spoke. I smiled and turned back to look outside. I saw Bob's reflection in the window as he approached. He put his cell phone against my free ear and I heard Pauly.

"They're fueling his plane right now and you've fuckin' spooked him, man." Pauly laughed and the line went dead.

"Jerome," I said forcefully. "How much does it cost to fuel that plane? It's gotta be cheaper in Slidell than Miami. Right?"

"You are wasting my time," he said again, nervously. "We should never need to have contact again. You understand? Never. This will be over and you stay out of Mexico and away from me." He cut the connection.

Seemed Pauly was right again, I had definitely spooked Jerome. When someone loses the feeling of safety in his surroundings, he loses the edge. Jerome thought he'd lost the edge he had against me, but I didn't want to panic him into doing something stupid. I played the bluff card and hoped he didn't call me on it.

CHAPTER 68

Norm must have watched through the window from out on the porch. When I put the cell phone away, he came inside. The rain had stopped but the wind swirled the humid air like sand in a dust storm, so there was no way to escape it if you were outside. Everyone's eyes turned to me because of the one-sided phone conversation.

"Jerome is at an airport outside New Orleans," I said.

"Afraid of the hurricane?" Norm joked, and then got serious. "Or is he running?"

"No, not running," Alfonso corrected him. "Jerome distances himself from things. He will have Tiny do the exchange, and if it goes badly, he handles the legal aspects."

"That the way he works?" Jim Ashe asked.

"Always," Alfonso said. "He keeps his distance from anything illegal."

"He told me about the same when I asked why he was leaving." I looked at Doug and Burt in their foul-weather gear. "You two look like Big Bird."

They quietly slipped out of the wet yellow suits.

"There's a break in the rain, hoss," Norm drawled quietly. "Might be a good time to stretch our legs."

It wasn't a peace offering, but it was as close to normal as we would get, so I nodded and looked out the window. Then I turned to Bryan Blankenship. "How much time do we have?"

He looked at his laptop screen. "Could be a couple of hours, maybe less."

"We're staying," Jim Ashe said, and in his authority spoke for Blankenship. "I need to monitor our men out there."

"Thank you," I said. "You'll call."

"Of course." He forced a smile. "You should think about checking in with the locals."

"Richard would call if he heard something."

"Think about it," Jim grumbled and glanced at Norm. "Richard's given a lot of responsibility to Morales." He paused and turned to me. "I gather you two don't get along, so think twice before leaving it in his hands."

"Would Morales keep Richard out of the loop?" Norm asked.

"If it was about me, maybe, but I think his cop instinct has kicked in. Like it or not, he knows we have to share information. He wants to catch these guys . . ."

Jim cut me off. "And free Tita?"

"I hope he doesn't cowboy the exchange," I said, shaking my head. "That's where Norm and Alfonso pull rank to make sure he knows it's a DEA operation . . ."

"Done already," Norm said before I finished. "Let's check out Mallory Square."

Norm, Alfonso and Padre Thomas left without rain gear. The rest of us carried yellow jackets.

"Mick," Jim Ashe said before I closed the door. "You won't see our boats."

"That's fine, just so you call if you hear anything."

"Give Richard a call," he said as I closed the door.

The wind shook the trees and bushes behind the cemetery fence and dim streetlights helped them cast ghostly shadows that danced atop the crypts and old tombstones. Black clouds filled the sky, ready to burst, and hid the stars and moon.

Norm knew the way and turned toward the waterfront. We walked along quietly, passing old shotgun houses with muted light spilling out of windows onto porches and worn sidewalks. The humidity was thick and my clothes became damp before we passed Southard Street. Bob handed me a cigar. I cut and lit it as he gave one to Norm and Alfonso. Burt and Padre Thomas lit cigarettes and Doug went smokeless.

We walked the deserted streets, trying to ignore the humidity, and followed Norm into Sloppy Joe's bar. The crowds had thinned because of the hour and probably the storm, or maybe the tourists weren't in town mid-week. We ordered beers. The cold brew was a temporary relief from the heat as powerful air conditioners filled the room with chilled air.

Poster-sized black-and-white prints of Ernest Hemingway hung high on the bar's walls. His ghost roams the bar, maybe sitting on one of the barstools; all you have to do is ask the tourists who often fill the place. The writing icon has been dead almost as long as he lived, but his reputation remains larger than life and still brings people to the island. Tourists pack the Hemingway House and Museum on Whitehead Street and Sloppy Joe's because of the man. He left a legend behind wherever he went and no one will let it die in Key West, not as long as people can visit his home where he created and drink where he drank. Wannabe Papas drink themselves silly as Papa did without realizing that the heavy drinking was a major cause of his suicide and kept us from reading all the unwritten stories that died with the lonely shotgun blast.

"To Papa." I raised my beer toward one of the posters.

It was close to two A.M., the stage was empty and the six or eight people who sat around looked as if they had nowhere to rush off to. We raised our beers and smiled.

"They revere him in Cuba," Alfonso said. "I've visited *la Finca* a few times."

"Me, too." I drained my beer as I finished the cigar.

"Another round," Norm called to the bartender and put

money down.

A few cars and tinny scooters rushed up and down Duval while the wind swept plastic cups and food wrappers along the partially flooded street. The second beer went down almost as fast as the first one.

Norm didn't say anything as he stood and walked outside. We followed. He chose Greene Street, walked toward the Custom House Museum and cut through its grounds toward the Westin Hotel's pier. A few couples leaned against the railing, holding hands while looking out at the blackness of Key West Harbor.

"Those the million-dollar homes?" Norm stopped before the footbridge to Mallory Square and pointed at the dim lights that twinkled on the manmade island in the harbor.

"Yeah. Homes on this side and hotel suites on the other side," I said.

A few small white anchor lights bobbed on the black water. Most boats anchored on the backside of Christmas Tree Island and that officially kept them out of city jurisdiction. The lights were probably on the boats of people cruising toward or from Cuba and Mexico who had stopped in Key West for supplies, repairs or to party.

Some of the sailors would lose a girlfriend or crewmember in port for as many reasons as there are mosquitoes. Cruising is a wonderful adventurous dream that quickly turns to cold reality when you are miles off shore. Fortunately, not everyone is cut out for the life.

Doug looked toward the harbor. "Not many lights on the water."

"Good or bad?" Norm asked.

"By maritime law, when a boat is anchored at night it has to show a white light on its aft section or from the mast if it's a sailboat," he said. "I know there's a hell of lot more boats out there than lights right now."

"They evacuated to land?" Norm wondered.

"Some," Doug grunted. "Most of 'em are derelict boats and don't have electricity anyway. They pump their shit right into the harbor."

Norm gave a sardonic laugh. "They live on the water, you'd think they'd show some respect."

Doug sighed. "Yeah, you would."

Padre Thomas put his hand on my shoulder and I followed him to the pier railing. Norm and Alfonso walked slowly in circles, checking out the hotel windows and the footpath.

"Tita is not out there," Padre Thomas said quietly as he looked into the blackness.

"Where is she?" I followed his stare.

"I don't know, Mick," he said in a sad voice. "But she is safe." He perked up a little. "And she's not on a boat."

"Is she in Key West or on Stock Island?" I said, holding in my excitement.

"She isn't close," he whimpered. "I'm sorry."

"But you said she's safe."

"Yes," he answered. "She's not scared. Maybe mad, but not scared."

"Yeah, well, we know it takes a lot to scare Tita." I took it as good news and didn't ask how he knew. Maybe I believed him because I wanted to. Maybe the angels were real. I wanted to believe that, too.

CHAPTER 69

Lightning flashed intermittently far out in the Atlantic, highlighting menacing cloud formations, followed by the rumblings of thunder. The outer edges of Hurricane Fred were passing and we received tropical storm winds and rain from it. Humidity, too. Miami, more than a hundred and fifty miles northeast, would get the gale force of the hurricane in a few hours.

Small groups of homeless people clustered around burning cigarettes watched as we walked slowly across Mallory Square, battered by the winds. Where did the men and women go in the rain?

Norm and Alfonso scanned the large plaza looking for places a gunman could hide. Without the tourists to fill the concrete square during the sunset celebration, there were few hiding places. Would the shooters disguise themselves as homeless?

"Did Jerome give you a precise location?" Norm waited for me to catch up with him and Alfonso because the wind swept away words yelled into it.

"Mallory Square is all he said." I looked at the empty, wide-open space. "He thought it would be crowded for sunset," I said loudly to overcome the howling sound.

"But now he knows it won't be," Norm said, his curiosity piqued. "And he still wants the exchange here."

"Tiny cannot be missed," Alfonso hollered. "Not even in a crowd. You will recognize him, Mick?"

"He isn't easy to forget," I said. "Gentle giant, Jerome called him."

"Do not let the gentleness fool you," Alfonso said seriously. "He is a killer. To him it is business, not personal. When he kills, the victim is just as dead and that is why Jerome keeps him close."

"Nowhere in the plaza to hide or for protection." Norm turned full circle. "Peripheral spots." He pointed toward the distant public restrooms, the Waterfront Playhouse and the historic brick building that housed shops and a Cuban restaurant. "They're all locked at night, but this will be an afternoon exchange." Norm stared at the many possible entry locations. "Will anything be open Friday afternoon?"

"Depends on the city," I said. "The chamber of commerce will want the city open for business. But if you can't get through Miami, you can't drive to the Keys."

"Can the road be closed up north of the Keys?"

"It can flood or wash out in a few places north of here and that would close it."

We huddled like football players so our words were not lost in the wind.

"What is their escape plan?" Norm spoke more to himself than us as he scanned the surroundings again.

No one answered him.

The city's large parking lot was part of Mallory Square and sat empty. Only a scattering of lights shone from the Ocean Key Resort's windows on the other side of the desolate lot.

Norm stared at the building. "Can you access that hotel from here?"

"The footpath continues along the railing, then it leads to the hotel's Sunset Pier and to Duval Street," I said. "The pier's crowded during sunset."

"Snipers on the roofs of both hotels and you'd control the

plaza, especially if it's crowded," Norm said to Alfonso.

"And around those outer buildings." Alfonso scanned Mallory Square's entry points from Front Street. "What will be open is the question."

"The restrooms." I pointed toward the shadowy block building. "If the shops and restaurant are open, there will be a band playing outside." I turned toward the other section of the square and pointed.

"Lot of commotion, lot of noise," Alfonso said.

"Oh yeah, each sunset act is trying to attract people." I indicated the empty space. "They work for tips, it's like having circus barkers all over the place."

"How many?" Norm asked.

"A dozen acts spread out and then there's artists selling their goods," I said.

"Sniper with a silencer and you wouldn't hear a thing or know where it came from." Norm looked at the Westin Hotel's roof and then turned to the Ocean Key Resort's roof. "Without the commotion, without the sunset crowds, what?"

"They would have to use the outer buildings," Alfonso said and turned to the theater. "If that is closed, they could use it as a staging area."

"Nothing's scheduled, so it's closed," I said. "Could they come from the water?"

"Unlikely." Norm turned toward the dark harbor. "Too unstable for getting people on and off the pier."

"Who's coming?" I began to wonder what all the concern was. What wasn't I seeing? "I hand over the money, they release Tita."

"Mick, are you forgetting the guys we ran into on the water?" Bob said and joined the huddle. He must have been listening. "There's a whole other side to this."

Bob was joined by Burt, Doug and Padre Thomas.

Norm sighed. "Bob's right. Jerome only speaks for one cartel. Did he promise the other one would go away?"

"Once the deal is done, they don't have a reason to be here," I said.

"How many of them have you killed?" Norm grumbled. "Maybe they want the money for themselves. Five million ain't chump change even to these guys."

"That might not be important," Alfonso interrupted. "We are a long way from Mexico and if the Arellano-Felix cartel gets what it wants, then Teodoro's men may walk away and cut their losses. It is business for them to hassle a competitor, not a grudge match with some *gringos.*"

I hoped Alfonso was right. The past few days had been hell; I wanted it over with and Tita back. I also remembered if it hadn't been for Norm and Alfonso, none of this would be happening. That only made my disposition darker.

"They wouldn't try one last time for the money?" Norm grinned at me. "I would."

"If they know where the exchange is going to be, they might," Alfonso frowned.

"What?" Norm growled at Alfonso's sour expression.

"If they know where Tita is, they may not wait for the exchange and decide to go after her. That would get them the ransom and really jerk off the cartel in TJ. Or they might kill her and keep the money from changing hands."

"I didn't need to hear that," I shouted. "How would they know?"

"Each cartel has spies inside the other," Alfonso said. "You cannot dismiss the possibility that they know where she was taken." He turned to look at the blackness of the harbor. "It may also be why things have been so quiet."

"They would contact me about the ransom, right?" I asked nervously. "If they had her."

Alfonso stared at Norm before answering. "Or watch and see what you do when they come for the money without her."

"This ain't Mexico, hoss," Norm said hurriedly. "They don't have the bosses here to do the thinking, so I wouldn't worry too much. Jerome's people have Tita and you'll get her back." He sounded sure of himself. "It's unlikely the cartel has spies in this operation because it was put in motion too quickly, believe me."

Padre Thomas put his hand on my shoulder and smiled when I turned to him. The thunder and lightning was getting closer.

"I'm going home, Mick," Padre Thomas said softly. "I will see you in the morning." Then he whispered, "Tita feels safe, wherever she is." He said his good-byes and walked across the deserted square toward Front Street, minutes ahead of the rain.

"I hate the rain down here," Norm bellowed and started walking toward Sunset Pier. "It's all it does," he said to Alfonso. "I told you that. I think this sunset celebration is a farce."

How could Tita feel safe? I wondered as I walked away in the drizzle trying to deal with Alfonso's comments and Padre Thomas' whisper.

CHAPTER 70

We stopped in front of the Glass Bottom Boat, docked where Duval Street meets the harbor between the Ocean Key and Pier House resorts. The rain became heavy and steady within minutes of our leaving Mallory Square and the wind continued to blow it sideways. Muted light from the resorts' security lamps perforated the darkness and cast shadowy illusions on the roadway. We moved under the Ocean Key's lobby overhang to briefly escape the downpour.

Norm looked at his watch. "We're going back to our hotel," he said. "I have calls to make. We'll see you at Tita's in the morning, around nine."

I nodded, but didn't say anything. Who would he call at two in the morning?

"Jim Ashe's people will fly the money in as soon as it's safe for a plane to take off," Norm said. "It's downtime until Friday. They're using it to prepare and we'd better be doing the same thing."

"I know the exchange can be dangerous." I tried to hide my concern. "But what has you and Alfonso so worried?"

Norm's laugh was forced. "I prepare for the worst whenever I do anything, you should remember that. This is no different. I'm looking for what could go wrong so that if it does, I'm ready. I don't like surprises."

It was his way of telling me he was treating Tita's kidnapping as he did all his black ops. I knew he was good at what he did;

not always successful, but dedicated.

"What could go wrong?" I stared at Norm, hoping for the truth.

"Beginning with your buddy Morales and the Key West cops, a lot," he grumbled. "They could screw this up by trying to arrest people at the exchange. They have a couple of gruesome murders to solve. You throw the second cartel into the mix and things could get real dicey a dozen times over. Then there's Jerome. You want more?"

I shook my head. "No. I understand . . ."

"Yeah, but you're involved this time, right?" he said before I finished. "It makes everything different. In your stories in Mexico and Central America, you were an observer. Now you're a participant and the outcome affects you."

"Reluctantly," I said, and our eyes locked.

"What do you want me to say?" Norm hissed as the rain beat against the pavement. "I made a quick decision, I've told you that, and when I made it I thought it was the right thing to do." He looked out into the rain. "If I'd known it would turn to shit so fast and involve Tita, I might have made a different decision. Okay?"

"Might have?" He didn't answer. "You've always told me to deal with the now first because I can't undo yesterday," I said, loud enough to be heard over the wind. "You and I are yesterday. The now is getting Tita back and the cartel out of my life."

"We're gonna do that," he assured me. "I promise."

"Afterward we'll deal with us." I did not return his grin.

"We'll talk." Norm grabbed Alfonso's arm and they walked away in the rain.

Bob, Burt, Doug and I had already slipped into our yellow rain jackets, so we prepared ourselves to be soaked as we headed back to Tita's. The windswept rain made our jackets useless.

When we arrived at the house, we were wet to the bone. They decided to head home and return when weather was better and everyone dry.

I found Jim Ashe asleep on the couch as I entered the house.

"Nothing?" I asked Bryan Blankenship.

"Nothing," he said. "The pilot thinks he can fly the money out of the Bahamas by mid-morning and that would put him here no later than noon."

"Well, that's something," I said. "There's a guest room."

He yawned. "Get some sleep. I'll stay by the phone, catch forty winks on the floor. Just in case."

"Thanks. Wake me . . ." I didn't finish. He nodded.

I stripped down, dried off and lay in Tita's bed. I stared into the darkness more than I slept, listening to the rain pound against the tin roof while the wind rattled the bushes and trees. I feared going to sleep because I didn't know how Tita would fit into my Tijuana nightmare. Maybe this was the beginning of a new nightmare. If something went wrong at the exchange . . . I forced the thought out of my head by focusing on Padre Thomas' whispered words that Tita was safe. Tita said she believed in his angels. At the moment, I wanted to believe too. I wanted to believe Padre Thomas wasn't insane or a con man.

The pillows held Tita's scent and the more I tossed and turned, the more it attacked me. When I closed my eyes, I could see her in every corner of the room. I heard the brush strokes as she combed her hair and the soft tinkle of perfume jars that she played with each morning before leaving the house; the mysteries of the fertile imagination.

I must have fallen asleep or into a trance of some kind because the strong aromas of brewing coffee and sizzling bacon startled me awake like smelling salts. I couldn't remember a dream and that was good. Maybe I hadn't dreamt. Light shone through the bedroom window, and for that brief moment between sleep and waking I tried to hear Tita as she moved about. Then reality shook the cobwebs away. I dressed in yesterday's clothes and splashed cold water on my face. Everything in the bathroom looked like it was supposed to. I reminded myself that nothing was normal and it wouldn't be until Tita was back yelling at me for letting the cold air into the bathroom as she showered. I smiled at the thought and headed toward the coffee and bacon.

Sunshine made it past the trees and filtered into the living room. The television had a Miami station on, with the reporter's voice over footage of Hurricane Fred as it slammed into the city in the early hours. Crashing surf along South Florida's beaches and marinas, along with damaged roofing, seemed to be the prevalent scenes for the camera person.

I headed toward the aromas in the kitchen. Bryan Blankenship was scrambling up a large order of eggs. A plate full of bacon sat on the table next to a stack of buttered toast. Jim Ashe, Norm and Alfonso drank coffee. I poured a mug full for myself and sat down.

"Has anything changed?" I added sugar to the coffee.

"The plane will leave the Bahamas at ten and should be here around noon." Jim Ashe looked at Norm. "I'll meet the plane at Boca Chica and pick up the money."

"What's it take to carry five million?" I sipped my coffee and took a piece of toast.

"Shrink-wrapped hundreds should fit into a large gym bag," Norm said. "Heavy but less noticeable than a duffel bag."

"I'm gonna make the delivery." I ate the toast as Bryan Blankenship delivered plates of scrambled eggs to us.

"If you want." Norm added pieces of bacon to his plate and began to eat without arguing.

"I want," I said and wondered why he agreed so quickly.

Alfonso reached for the hot sauce, splashed it on his eggs and handed me the bottle. The five of us squeezed around the table and ate without talking.

"What are we doing next?" I took my plate to the sink and refilled my coffee mug.

Norm smiled. "Hurry up and wait. I have to get with Richard. He should be feeling better this morning."

"Are you giving him details on the exchange?" I sat back down.

"We need to see if Morales has gotten anywhere with the murder investigation," Norm said.

"Unlikely." Alfonso went for more coffee.

"So what do we need Richard for?"

"We don't need him for anything, we need him to keep his distance," Norm said. "He needs to solve the murders and won't like letting the perps walk away with all the money and disappear."

"Can you keep him away?"

"Oh, yeah." Norm grinned. "It won't be easy because he's a good cop. And it won't be pretty, either."

CHAPTER 71

Outside the sky was robin's-egg blue with puffy white clouds skimming across it. The wind had turned into a breeze, but the humidity lingered like a nagging in-law. After a tropical storm or hurricane, everything hastily returns to normal; if you hadn't experienced the storm, the destruction left behind would be the only indicator of how frightening the weather had been hours before.

Sun filled Tita's front porch, forcing itself through the closed window blinds, and across the street in the cemetery it reflected off the old mausoleums. The neighborhood was bright, birds chirped and I realized I hadn't heard a bird in two days.

After breakfast Matthew Pearce came to give Bryan Blankenship a break. Pearce monitored the JIATF crews while Blankenship went home to get some rest. Norm and Jim Ashe left and said they'd get in touch by noon.

"Waiting is the hardest thing to do," Norm said. "It doubles the time and the anxiety, so don't do anything foolish. Read a book, watch a TV movie, but stay home because no one's protecting you on the street."

"Do you think they're still looking for me?" The thought of the next thirty-plus hours gave me an anxiety attack; that and the fact that Norm didn't want me to tag along only heightened it. What were they up to?

"Teodoro's men have orders to kill you," he said without a smile. "Or they might be interested in the money now, so they may want to grab you instead. Either way, you're not safe on the street."

"Thanks for nothing." I closed the door and they walked away.

By ten I had showered and changed clothing but didn't feel any better. The clock ticked loudly in the quiet house, yet the second hand barely moved. I called Bob and Burt and they agreed to meet me for lunch. There was minor damage at the marina, so Doug didn't know how his day was going to be. We would all meet in a few hours.

At ten-thirty my cell chirped. Pauly's name showed on the screen.

"It's a beautiful day here," I said and was happy to have someone to talk to.

He laughed. "Don't I know it. I'm leaving my house. Where are you?"

"You're here?"

"In the flesh, *amigo.*"

"How? It stormed most of the night."

"I know a guy who'll fly in anything."

"I'm at Tita's."

"She back?" He seemed surprised.

"No."

He sighed. "Sorry. See you in about fifteen."

"You got the Mustang?"

"Nope, not yet. I'm in the Jeep." He cut the connection.

I went into Tita's bedroom and grabbed my Glock and extra magazines.

"You leaving?" Pearce asked as I came into the living room.

"Yeah." I opened the door and looked outside. "A friend is picking me up and I'm meeting the others for lunch."

"It's not safe out there."

"My sanity's not safe in here." I smiled as I said it.

I closed the door and waited on the porch. The humidity hit me like a blast furnace. The air-conditioner had cooled the small house and kept the lurking mugginess outside; kind of out of sight, out of mind. As I stood there sweating I thought maybe I should have stayed inside and waited the thirty hours out.

Pauly drove down Frances Street on the cemetery side. His Jeep was shiny blue with a tight bikini top, and unlike mine out front, was dry and clean.

"Welcome back." I climbed in. "Where to?"

"Bayview Park is a mess, tree limbs all over the place." He began driving toward Truman Avenue. "I wish I had good news for you."

I stiffened in the seat. "What do you have?"

Uncharacteristically, Truman had little traffic flow. Pauly turned right. "Let's check out the water at the end of Simonton." He turned left and followed the empty street toward the water.

"What do you have, Pauly?"

"Maybe you can make something of it?" He drove slowly as the humidity continued to attack us.

"What is it?" I asked again.

"My friend in the D.R., the banker babe, got bored and did some deeper checking on Norm's offshore account." He kept his eyes on the road. "She discovered something."

"I'm listening." I prepared for more bad news. Where was this going to lead?

"Seems," he said, and hesitated. "When she checked for past interest payments, there weren't any. Six months ago the bank shows it paid interest on the three accounts for the first time."

"Fifteen million and no interest payments, doesn't make sense."

"Just what she said." He pulled over and parked at Simonton and South streets. "I'm no banker or hacker, so I'm in the dark about all the shit she did. She went back further than the initial deposit, moved forward and found nothing. No account name change, nothing that would explain where payments could have gone or why the account had none."

Pauly handed me a cigar and prepared one for himself. I borrowed his cutter and lighter, prepared mine and lit it.

"Cuban," he said about the cigar, trying to keep his tone light.

"Did she come up with anything? Any idea?" I blew thick smoke at the humid air.

"Yeah," he grunted and rolled the cigar between his fingers. "She says it ain't possible, but the deposit must have been backdated."

"Why?"

"You tell me. She estimates that a million or more in interest is missing. It wasn't paid and withdrawn; it was never paid."

"It's a good account," I said, thinking of the ransom, and remembered it hadn't arrived yet. "The ransom is coming out of it." I wanted to believe it. I had to believe it.

"You're right, it's a good account, but only in the last six months. Where's the money been for five or six years?"

We got out of the Jeep, walked the short block to the concrete seawall and, along with a dozen others, watched the large waves roll in off the Atlantic and crash, sending high walls of water onto the flooded street. Cold spray came far enough over the wall to wet everyone and I enjoyed the temporary coolness.

Pauly and I walked quietly back to the Jeep. I was focused on getting Tita back and couldn't fathom what difference Pauly's information meant to the situation. The money was in the bank and it would be in Key West within hours. The new information bothered me, though, because it meant Norm had lied again. Or was it still? Was this operation, Norm, Alfonso, the DEA, all an elaborate hoax that was beyond my comprehension? Hell, I couldn't sleep and I couldn't think straight, which meant I was useless.

We leaned against the Jeep and finished our cigars. The humidity was part of our lives and we lived with it.

"Pauly, I need to get my head straight," I finally said and crushed the cigar. "There's too much happening."

"Yeah." He sounded surprised. "You're focusing on Tita and you should be."

"Right. I agree." I pushed away from the Jeep. "What if that's what they want me to do?"

"Who?"

"I don't know." I thought about it for a minute. "Can't be the cartels."

"Why?" He crushed his cigar on the curb.

"They want to kill me or scare me into giving them the money back," I said. "One of them killed Woodrow to intimidate me."

"Did it?"

"Yes," I admitted. "I don't want people I know being killed because of me. And that's the reason they did it. He was the easiest one to get."

"But he wasn't a friend. You talked to him at a bar every so often."

"They're working on the run in unknown territory. They see me talking to Woodrow a few times at Schooner. We sit and drink and smoke."

"To them, that's friendship," Pauly agreed.

"Good enough for what they want."

"Okay," he said and pushed away from the Jeep. "Your buddy Norm and his team want you to focus on Tita. Why? What are they doing that they need you for but don't want you to know about?"

I laughed. "That's a mouthful. But you're right. What are they doing? Norm took off this morning and said nothing."

"Didn't ask you along?"

"No. And I thought that odd."

"You're the principal in this whole thing."

"What am I missing? What is the whole thing about?"

CHAPTER 72

Pauly and I got back in the Jeep and drove to Sandy's Café for *café con leches*.

"What could they be doing, Mick?" We sat in the Jeep with our Cuban coffee.

I told Pauly everything that had happened since he left for the Dominican Republic. He listened quietly and sipped his coffee.

"They set you up for this." It wasn't a question, it was something he found hard to believe. "They made up your involvement in the theft because they wanted to put you in the cartel's sights. For what? Why you?" More disbelief crept into his words. "With friends like these guys, you really don't need enemies."

He didn't believe the story I was told about wanting to catch cartel soldiers on this side of the border. Even the theory about turning them on the cartel he found hard to swallow.

"I'm beginning to see that." I finished my coffee. "What I don't see is the truth. In a little more than a day, I'm supposed to turn over five million dollars in exchange for Tita and I don't want to jeopardize that. I don't believe they'd put Tita in harm's way, but too many things don't add up and my trust is just about gone."

"I can get you the five million," he said with a smile. "As a backup plan. It might be tight to meet tomorrow's deadline."

I didn't know how to answer him. Five million dollars is a lot of money and I don't care who you are.

"Why?" It was an honest question I didn't know the answer to.

Pauly laughed. "Mick, I can count my friends on one hand. Friends I can depend on, and you're one of them. I know we're not bosom buddies like you and Bob, but I consider you a friend. You haven't judged me. I appreciate that. And I always have a good time with you." He kept his boyish grin as he spoke.

"You know there's no way I can pay back that kind of money, and good times with me ain't worth that much."

"You're honest, Mick," he said with a grin. "That's worth a lot in my book. I don't know, maybe I'll get free legal service from Tita for awhile."

"I hope you're not in that kind of trouble." I was trying to keep it light, but we both knew a storm cloud hung overhead. "You can really get that kind of money here tomorrow afternoon?"

"Might be tight, but I think I can. It's backup just in case your *friends*," he said it sardonically, "don't come through."

"Yeah, okay." I felt a pang of guilt for doubting Norm, but his recent actions left me wondering about his motives. "I've gotta think of Tita and what would happen if things screwed up."

"Let me make a call." He climbed out of the Jeep and walked away, dialing on his cell phone.

Pauly paced along next to the sand sculpture studio on Virginia Street, his cell to his ear. Twice I saw him shake his head. Another time he looked toward the Jeep and smiled. He kept pacing and talking. Finally, he closed the cell and headed back.

"With a little bit of luck, Mick, the money will be here by three in the morning." He got in the Jeep, closed the door and smiled.

I stared at him in wonderment. "How are you getting it into the country?"

"My lady friend will bring it to my backyard."

"Your backyard is the Gulf of Mexico."

He grinned wider. "She has a friend who's a pilot. I'm beginning to think I know too many people with seaplanes."

"You're certifiable. If you get caught, you're out five million, if I need it to pay the ransom you're out five million."

"I'm rich," he shouted and slapped my shoulder. "That makes me eccentric, not crazy."

"I thought making the exchange deadline would be a problem."

"This is a bright woman even if she hangs around with me," he joked. "She'll get the money this afternoon and fly it here. We have to avoid Customs, so she'll fly in early in the morning when it's dark. The plane will drop her at my place and take right off."

Pauly lived in Key Haven, an upscale neighborhood of expensive single-family homes on canals and open water.

"Done this before?" I began to relax.

"Once or twice." He started the Jeep. "Hard to hit a moving target," he said, grinning, and drove toward Old Town. "I'm serious about being friends." He lost the casualness of his earlier conversation. "I know a lot of people, hell, I know too many people, except they're not friends."

"I know what you mean." I nodded and watched the empty street as he turned on Duval. "Knowing people for however long doesn't make them friends."

"Do you know if they reconned the square?" He smiled because now we were friends.

"Last night when there was a break in the weather, we took a walk. Went through the Westin to Mallory to the Ocean Key and Duval. We spent most of the time at Mallory."

"Do you know their plans?"

"Snipers on the roofs. They can't decide how the exchange will go, and they've ruled out the water."

"I'd use the water." Paul turned on Front Street and drove illegally up a one-way street to the city's parking lot on Mallory Square. There were half a dozen cars parked and no one at the attendant's booth.

He looked at the roof of the Ocean Key and got out. I followed him.

"Wide open," he said, looking at the empty square.

"Outer buildings." I pointed to the large brick building next to the parking lot. "The bathrooms and the theater."

Pauly turned to the water. "Snipers on the roof would give them control of the square, especially with no sunset celebration."

"Yeah, that was discussed."

"Okay, Mick, I'll tell you what I'm gonna do," he said with a toothy grin. "If it's okay with you, I mean."

"I'm open to anything," I admitted.

"I have a couple of guys that owe me." His grin got bigger. "Not friends, but I trust them. Two SEALs and two jarheads. We're gonna have your back, so fuckin' forget about these other guys."

"What are you going to do?" I worried that Pauly would end up being the cowboy in the mix, and not Luis and the Key West cops.

"The SEALs will be on the water because it is an option. A good one as far as I'm concerned, and the jarheads at the outer buildings will be with me. If it all goes to hell, we'll pull you out of here."

"Tita too?"

"If you've got her. We'll get out of here using the water."

"Do you think both cartels will show up?"

"Oh yeah, for the money, and they won't care who's in their way." He thought about it for a minute. "Actually, the more of you they kill the better for them."

"Norm and Jim Ashe will have DEA and JIATF agents here," I said.

"Yeah, that's what they tell you, but you haven't been to the base or the federal building, right?"

"You're right." I was angry at my lack of insight into what was going on around me.

"A rogue operation maybe, maybe not," he griped. "Go along with them and when you make the exchange I'll get you and Tita to the water and out of here. Let everyone else shoot themselves."

CHAPTER 73

Pauly couldn't have lunch because he had people to see and arrangements to make. The SEALs would use one of his boats and be in place off Christmas Tree Island late tomorrow morning. The jarheads and he would be somewhere on the outskirts of Mallory Square by tomorrow afternoon.

"Bob and your friends want to help, right?" he said as we drove away from the square.

"Yeah, but I don't like it."

Pauly laughed. "Didn't they prove themselves on the dock?"

"Yeah, they did, but we'd still be pinned down if it wasn't for that shooter. He took out the two gunmen and I have no idea who he was. Probably one of Norm's people."

"From what I can see, Norm hasn't done much to protect you or Tita." Pauly lit a cigarette. He smiled sheepishly and then gave a short chuckle. "Okay, the shooter was one of my jarheads."

"What?" I turned in surprise.

"I had him staking out the marina just on the off chance . . ." His boyish grin widened. "He told me you took good care of yourselves."

"Great care of ourselves," I grumbled. "Bob got shot, Padre Thomas got hit with a ricochet and the two DEA agents got their throats cut."

"You're vertical," he said bluntly, stressing that survival was the name of the game. "Have Bob call me and I'll find something for them to do on the periphery. Backup because if it goes to shit, three extra guns coming in can only help."

Who the shooter had been bothered me, but I had assumed it was part of the twenty-four-seven protection Norm promised. Finding out the truth didn't make me feel any better about my old friend.

"One other thing, Mick." Pauly spoke without a smile as he stopped the Jeep across from B.O's Fish Wagon on Caroline Street. "Norm and the JIATF guys don't need to know about our plan. Understand?"

I got out of the Jeep. Sunshine filled the old street and it felt good. "Yeah, but I don't like it."

"Think of it this way, Mick, it ain't really about what you like or don't," he muttered and stubbed out the cigarette. "It's the safest thing for Tita and unless you have *total* confidence in Norm and his team, you need an alternative plan and that's me."

"You're right."

"Okay. I'll call later today. Go back to Tita's and sit tight." He lit another cigarette. "Send Bob and the others to the high ground until I get with them. Hang out at the house, be natural." He looked at his wristwatch. "They should have your money now." He said it with a wicked grin. "See what they say when you get back."

"If Jim Ashe has it?" I leaned against the side of the Jeep and stared through the open window.

"Make sure it's all there. Tell 'em you wanna see it."

"It's in shrink wrap."

"Look it over. Tell 'em you've never seen that much money."

"I haven't."

He laughed. "So you're not lying. Let me know if the money arrives and I'll have the backup cash if you need it. Keep your cool, it's almost over." He drove away smiling.

Locals filled B.O.'s. I ordered the special fish sandwich that includes a free half order of fries and found Bob and the others at a table in back. Doug told of his minor problems at the marina. Mostly it was people not knowing how to tie off a boat in a storm.

Our food came and I told them of Pauly's plan.

"You trust him?" Bob wondered aloud.

I thought about it as I chewed on pieces of mahi and pushed a few French fries into my mouth. I couldn't decide, not definitely.

"Yeah," I said finally, not sure I did. "I trust him, I trust Norm and Alfonso and I trust Richard, too."

"But." Bob pushed away from the table.

"Something ain't right. Where's the twenty-four-seven? How can the DEA agent so trusted for her anti-drug actions be the one that kidnaps Tita? I am not missing something, they're covering something up. Pauly's offering me an alternative, one I'm involved in, and while I want Norm's plan to work, Pauly's my backup." I finished my food and chewed on pieces of ice from the empty glass of tea.

Doug promised to check in with Bob first thing tomorrow morning and left. Burt stood, lit a cigarette and moved to the sidewalk. Bob and I joined him. "So what do we do now?" he asked.

"Go to the high ground," I joked. "Pauly will call you as soon as his plan begins to take shape."

"We'll probably end up shooting each other," Bob griped. "How are we supposed to tell the good guys from the bad guys?"

"Let's hope the exchange goes without a hitch and no one has to shoot anyone." My tone didn't have much conviction in it.

Bob and Burt drove off to the higher ground, I assumed, and I walked in the humid breeze to Tita's. I had a little more than

341

twenty-four hours to do nothing in, and it was going to be hard if not impossible. The road to hell may be paved with good intentions, but when you get there hell is waiting around and doing nothing, just like Padre Thomas said. I was chained to my private hell.

CHAPTER 74

Padre Thomas sat in Tita's living room while Bryan Blankenship and Matt Pearce ate pizza in the kitchen. The television had a cable news channel on showing hurricane damage at marinas in the greater Miami area. I switched to the local NBC station to see if Hank Tester went back to Miami or reported storm coverage from Key West. He was probably trapped in Key West, wishing he were in Miami or maybe wishing the hurricane had hit here so he'd have a real story to report. Hank wasn't in Miami, so he had to be stuck somewhere on the island. I'd see him at Schooner or on Duval Street with his camera crew.

I stopped by Padre Thomas. "How's the leg?"

"Too sore to ride my bike, but feels a lot better now that I've walked." He rubbed the bandage Jim Ashe had put on yesterday.

"You should change the dressing."

"I hoped Jim had some extra."

"Why aren't you eating pizza?" It smelled tempting.

"I ate a sandwich at Sandy's."

"We got enough if you want some," Bryan Blankenship yelled while he chewed.

"Just ate, thanks," I called back. "Norm or Jim call in?"

"Nope." He continued eating.

"What are you going to do?" Padre Thomas scratched his leg.

"Wait. I need to talk with Norm."

"I'll wait with you. Maybe we can play gin later?"

"Poker, Padre, not gin," I said and bent closer. "No news on Tita?" I whispered. I wanted him to have had a vision or whatever he experienced.

"You're still in danger." He leaned forward. "Staying here is probably a good idea, but I have nothing on Tita." He frowned and shook his head slowly. "Maybe it means nothing has changed."

"Maybe." I forced a smile. "Watch TV, I'm going to grab a nap. Maybe some cards later." I walked to the kitchen door. "If you hear from Norm or Jim, let them know I'm waiting here."

Bryan Blankenship nodded as he chewed on a slice of pizza.

I closed the bedroom door and lowered the blinds in an attempt to make the room darker. Tita's scents attacked me as soon as I lay on her bed. I closed my eyes and welcomed the darkness, but sleep was elusive. I fought negative thoughts by forcing myself to remember the good times Tita and I had shared. It didn't work.

I went back in my head to the afternoon of the car wash shooting and then ran forward, scrutinizing each situation that led to where I now found myself. I looked for the link I was missing, the something that would explain why I wasn't in the loop, why things I couldn't understand were happening. I found nothing and went through it all again.

What was Norm hiding? Why was he keeping me in the dark? Did it have to do with Alfonso? I questioned everyone's loyalty, including Richard's. Was the money real? Why did I believe the theft of cartel money happened? Was Jerome who he said he was? Why did I believe everyone when all this started to unravel?

Five million dollars is a lot of money, but I didn't have a problem raising it because Norm had it. But did he? Pauly came through as a backup because we were friends. Five-million-dollar friends. Hard to believe. Why did I believe?

All the dead were real, though, that was for sure. The ones I killed were real; Woodrow, all the others that someone else killed were real. I knew that. What about the living? Who was being honest, who was lying and why? Who to bless and who to blame?

I woke with a start. The room was darker than before. I looked at the bright readout from the bureau clock. It was six-fifteen. I had been asleep for three hours. Outside the room, the TV still broadcast the news and I could feel people walking around. I must have slept the sleep of the dead because I had no recall of anything. When I sat up, I felt more rested than I had all week. Dead tired had been what I was. At least I could recover from the tired part.

A few men slouched around the living room watching the news. I heard Norm's voice from the kitchen and followed it. He was there with Jim Ashe, Alfonso and a couple of others with a map of Mallory Square spread out on the table. The close-cropped haircuts told volumes about who the men were.

"Where's Padre Thomas?" I looked at the empty coffee pot.

"I changed his bandage and he went for a walk," Jim Ashe said. "You okay?"

"Slept for three hours." I sounded surprised and they smiled.

"You looked like death warmed over last night," Norm drawled. "You want in on what's happening tomorrow?"

"I'm delivering the money," I said as a reminder. I turned to Jim Ashe. "It's here, right?"

He smiled. "Like clockwork." He pointed toward the living room. "That's why they're here."

"I've never seen that much money," I said with a silly grin to cover the distrust in my comment.

"Let's get done with this and then you can see it," Norm said with a smile almost as silly as mine.

I looked over their shoulders as he pointed to the two hotels and the sniper spots. Two men to each roof. A full-scale search of the roofs by noon to make sure the cartels didn't have their own snipers.

"If they do?" I was curious.

"We take 'em out and work from there," Norm said without a smile.

There would be a surveillance van from JIATF in the parking lot up against the Ocean Key Resort and it would be in place before going to the hotel roofs. More men would be in and around Mallory Square, beginning in mid-afternoon. All locked buildings would be secured by the Key West police.

Another surprise. "When did you meet with Richard?"

"At lunch," Norm said.

"You didn't call me."

"Didn't have time."

My insecurity came back quickly.

Chapter 75

Norm turned to me. "Did Jerome say where on the square he wants the exchange to take place?"

"No." He waited for me to say more. I didn't.

"Okay." He turned back to the chart and pointed. "This is the four columns and small roof area. You'll be there with the money and let them come to you."

"Why there?" I was curious.

"The snipers on both roofs have clear shots to protect you," he said, pointing at the sniper positions. "It's out of the sun and has columns for cover, if you need it."

"Over here past the restrooms," I pushed up to the table's edge, "is a tower that goes with the Wreckers' Museum. It's high with a good view of the square. What if they have someone there?"

"We'll have people there first."

"I didn't know," I mumbled. "I wasn't in the loop."

Norm gave me a hard stare. "You were never a planner, Mick. I didn't think it was your kind of thing."

"When it involves Tita's safety, it's my kind of thing," I snapped.

"Okay, you're here now," he said tersely. "There's something you gotta be prepared for."

"What?"

"Jerome is likely to call and change the meeting spot."

"Why?"

"Because there's no crowd for cover. Why else would he choose the sunset celebration if he didn't want crowds?"

"What do I do?"

"Refuse or go along. We'll follow your lead."

I looked at Norm. He wasn't smiling. I nodded my understanding. He had put the burden on me if that happened.

"Let's assume it goes as planned," he said. "You and Tita want to exit through the Ocean Key Resort. It fronts the closest street and we want to move you out of there as quickly as possible."

"If the money goes that way, what do I do?"

"We'll have a golf cart on the other side of the footbridge waiting to take you to a vehicle at the Custom House Museum."

"Where are we rushing off to?"

"The police station to debrief Tita."

"If it turns bad?"

"We've got a small army surrounding the square, so hope for the best."

"If there's shooting?"

"It'll be like the Wild West," Norm groused. "You go to ground and cover Tita, and let us do our thing until someone can get to you."

"What if the cartel gets to us first?"

"They'll go after the money. Jerome's people will be protecting the money and we'll be protecting you. The snipers will."

I looked at the chart and saw how far from the hotels and peripheral buildings the area was. Pauly's plan to escape on water only feet away sounded very good, especially if a gun battle broke out.

"You got it?" Norm tapped the chart. "There's no place to run and hide if it goes south, so drop and cover Tita and let us do our job."

"Sounds like a plan." I slapped his shoulder and thought

again of how close the water was. "You always were the plan-ner."

He stared at me questioningly. "Yeah," he said without too much conviction.

"Show me the money." I smiled and we walked into the liv-ing room.

He didn't bother to introduce me to the others.

Jim Ashe pulled a large gym bag along the floor and unzipped it. Inside I saw packages of hundred-dollar bills compressed in what appeared to be Saran Wrap. I reached in and took a pack-age of bills. I didn't open the thin package, but the top and bot-tom bills looked real.

"Counterfeit?" I put the pack back.

"A good idea, but too late, Mick. It's real," Norm said. "Lift it."

I pulled the shoulder strap and barely moved the bag. I gave it an extra yank and lifted it onto my shoulder. It was too heavy for me to carry across Mallory Square.

Everyone in the room seemed to get a good chuckle out of my dilemma.

"We'll deliver you and the money on the golf cart." Norm took the bag from me and easily handled it. "No one's expect-ing you to be alone."

CHAPTER 76

Funny word, *alone*. Have you ever been at a crowded party, department store or restaurant and felt alone? How does that happen? Are you alone if you're in a crowd? I felt alone and I was with people I considered friends. An army with the purpose of protecting me waited outside and I felt stranded, alone on a desert island surround by a sea of people.

The damn second hand on my wristwatch ticked along so slowly I wasn't aging. Time didn't stand still; it moved in eerie slow motion. I watched Hank Tester on TV reporting about Duval Street flooding and other minor damage because of the tropical storm. I realized on the third airing that I was watching a rerun. By the time of the ransom exchange, he and the camera crew would be on their way back to Miami.

Jim Ashe made and received phone calls regarding his team's preparation. A surveillance crew reported hourly on what was happening at Mallory Square: nothing. By midnight the crew made its last report. M-16 and M-4 rifles were everywhere and so were boxes of ammunition and extra magazines.

I learned that the police had closed Mallory Square to any sunset celebration because of possible flood damage to the area. It was a ruse to keep the square unoccupied. They also closed the surrounding buildings. The restaurant and shops in the historic building stayed open, but not the parking lot or the public restrooms. I never found out why that was.

All this happened while I was experiencing an out-of-body

occurrence like those reported by people who come back from the dead. I observed everything even though I was part of it. I ate chicken wings and pizza from Finnegan's Wake. Norm talked to me about Richard controlling the buildings off Front Street with backup from JIATF and the DEA, but his crew would control the hotel entrances and exits to Mallory Square. I watched all this happen. Strange.

My mind raced with thoughts I couldn't stop. It was as if I'd heard an old song and couldn't stop whistling the tune and repeating the words in my head. In fact, the harder I tried, the worse it became. I thought of Tita because everything in the house reminded me of her. I kept going over the past few days, trying to find something I'd missed; I thought about when Norm, Alfonso and I were close; most of all, I saw Mel die in Tijuana. All these thoughts ran through my head at the same time and I knew I would go insane if I didn't take control.

Padre Thomas made it through security and told me he'd be back in the morning. "Nothing has changed," he whispered, looking very uncomfortable with all the weapons out in the open.

I lost my pocket change at the nickel-dime poker game in the kitchen and when the players tried to explain Texas Hold 'Em to me, I left. The crowd thinned before the late news came on and I slunk off toward the bedroom.

"Are you okay?" Norm asked as I walked away from the kitchen.

"Anxious," I said and hoped there was a smile with it.

He yawned. "We're gonna pack it in and call it a night too. A couple of people will stay here and there's others outside. Try to get some sleep. We'll see you before nine." He slapped my shoulder and walked away with Jim Ashe.

Sleep was another thing I feared.

CHAPTER 77

Fear. It's an interesting condition. Conquering fear makes you stronger. Unfortunately, surrendering to fear keeps you ignorant. Fear of the unknown is the most dangerous because it tyrannizes people. My fear of sleep was due to dreams of Mel dying in Tijuana. Vivid dreams. Now I was experiencing the fear of losing Tita and that would add to my nightmares. In a week I had gone from a self-assured individual to an insecure snot. It had to stop.

My mind continued to race with uncontrollable thoughts while I lay in bed. It was a fitful night, but I didn't dream. My mind didn't have room for dreams because it was full of desperation.

My cell phone chirped at six-thirty. I must have fallen asleep sometime during the night, but I didn't feel rested. Pauly's name appeared on the screen.

"Yeah." I sat up and tried to shake the sleep from my head. "Pauly."

"Wake you?"

"Yeah. Thanks. I didn't mean to sleep this late." My words dragged out because I wasn't fully awake. "Everything okay?"

"I wanted you to know the money arrived."

"Here, too. I saw it. Bundles of shrink-wrapped bills."

"That's a positive step. We're still a go?"

"It's the only thing keeping me from losing it." I was fully awake now.

"The boat will be in place in a few hours. Late this afternoon for the rest of it so we don't look out of place."

"How will I know them? I mean the guys on the water."

He chuckled. "Easy, Mick. They'll be the two guys not shooting at you."

"That's good to know." I tried but couldn't match his jocularity.

"Hey, if the money's there maybe Norm's legit and everything will go off without a hitch."

"Think so?"

"I hope so," Pauly said. "But having a backup plan is always good. From experience I can tell you that having more than one way out is the only way to go."

"I'll call you around noon. After that I might not be able to phone."

"Anything changes, you call me. I've got a good feeling about this, Mick. Hang loose." He cut the connection.

Pauly's positive mood rarely seemed to change. In the direst situations he smiled and laughed. When we were being chased along US1, our lives were in danger and he joked the whole way. I wanted that devil-may-care attitude and thought about how to get it while I showered and readied myself for the stressful day ahead.

The cable company's country music radio channel played as I walked into the living room. Half a dozen men moved about. The rifles and ammunition were gone or well hidden. Coffee aroma seeped from the kitchen. Matt Pearce stood at the open door, looking toward the backyard.

"I made coffee," he said without turning.

"Thanks." I poured a cup and wished it was a *con leche*, but happy to get anything.

Norm and Alfonso showed up a little after seven and brought *café con leches*, thank God. Jim Ashe and Richard Dowley came soon after. Everyone else in the house seemed to find their way outside.

"Tell us what you've got, Chief." Norm sat down on the couch. Alfonso took a chair and Jim, Richard and I stood.

"Today's *Citizen* has a small piece on Mallory Square being closed for the sunset celebration," he said with a hardened stare toward me. "Public Works will close Front Street to vehicle traffic beginning at noon from Simonton to the hotels. We will reroute whatever traffic there is on the one-way section of Greene Street. By three we will have men in the outer buildings that touch on the square."

Padre Thomas walked in. Norm looked at me. I didn't react.

Norm ignored Padre Thomas. "Jim, what've you got?"

"The surveillance van command post will be in the parking lot corner against the hotel this morning. At noon we'll sweep the roofs, close all entrances to them and have our snipers in place. Along with DEA, we'll have men at both piers by five." He glanced at each of us to see if there were any questions. "The threat of Fred hitting here has kept the hotel's occupancy low, so we haven't run into any problems there."

"Mick," Norm said and everyone turned to me.

"Unless I hear differently from Jerome, I'll be on the square with the money at six and wait," I said.

"There's always the possibility of change of location, and then we'll go mobile," Norm reminded us.

"Jerome chose the square for a reason," Alfonso said.

"Yeah, the crowds. He expected sunset celebration crowds for cover," Jim Ashe said. "He knew it would keep us from shooting."

"That is what the cartel would do and they would shoot, but Jerome is trying to avoid violence on this side of the border, it is why he brokered this deal," Alfonso said. "There is a reason for the location, but we do not see it."

Norm spoke up. "Any suggestions?" No one answered. "Chief, will you be at the command center?"

"I'll be on Front Street," Richard said.

"We'll keep in touch." Norm's words dismissed him.

"We need to talk when this is over," Richard said to me as he left. "We really need to talk."

"When the command center is in place, there'll be DEA and JIATF staff there, the rest of us will be out, but we need to be reachable, so no unnecessary chatter on the cell phones." Norm got a nod from each of us. "I'll be with you and the money, hoss, until the golf cart drops you at the hut."

It was nine o'clock. That left hours for my anxiety to wind up tight. I felt a little giddy because I knew about Pauly's plan and no one else did. Maybe Pauly's personality was catching. I could think of worse things to catch.

CHAPTER 78

"The high tide," Pauly yelled through the phone.

I pulled the cell away to protect my ear from his excited voice. "What about the high tide?" It must have meant something or Pauly wouldn't be so hyper.

"Jerome needs the high tide, not the crowds at Mallory," he said more calmly. "He knows there won't be a sunset celebration, so if he wanted crowds he'd change the meet to Duval Street." He paused but wasn't through talking. "He could've chosen the Hotel La Concha, where all the TV news crews are, and that would've kept the DEA and cops from shooting, but he didn't."

"He stayed with the original location," I agreed.

"Yeah, because he needs the high tide."

"Why?" But I had a good idea.

"He's using a boat. You said the kidnappers took Tita to the dinghy docks and out. They took her to a bigger boat anchored offshore." He got quiet and cleared his throat. "Mick, you have to consider that they stayed out there during the storm and that wouldn't have been good."

"I'm trying not to think of that."

"You have to," he said. "If they show up without her and want the money first . . ." He didn't finish his thought.

"I thought of that, I'm just not thinking of it right now."

"He's bringing Tita in by boat. I don't know from where, but I'll bet my five million on it." He went back to being supportive.

"When the shooting starts and you have Tita, don't listen to what they're telling you."

"Who's telling me?"

"Anyone. Follow the money and I'm betting it heads toward the water."

"Tiny trying to drop down the seawall onto a boat would be impossible. He'd capsize it."

"All Tiny has to do is get the money there, he won't leave."

"Then what?"

"You go with the SEALs and get the hell out of there with Tita."

"I like that plan, Pauly."

He laughed. "Me, too. I don't understand why no one else sees it. Hell, man, we're on an island, why is everyone looking the other way?"

CHAPTER 79

Late morning, and everyone had their *café con leches* from Sandy's and an egg and cheese sandwich on warm Cuban bread, too. Padre Thomas stayed close and seemed to know I had other plans than those discussed.

"Nice shirt," Norm said, holding a Kevlar vest. "Put this on."

"Kind of muggy out." I unbuttoned my loose-fitting shirt.

The vest was standard issue in Israel, weighed five pounds and was called the executive vest because it fit under a suit. Comfortable I wouldn't call it.

"Muggy isn't as good at stopping bullets as this is."

"You expect me to need this?" I put my shirt on over the snug vest.

He grinned. "I hope not, but if it does, the shooting won't stop for you to dress properly. So wear it."

"You have one?"

"Everyone around the square or transporting the money has one." That didn't answer my question.

"It's early to head out."

"Yeah, we're getting a head start," Norm griped. "We're gonna drive around your little island paradise and see if we pick up a tail. Or maybe it'll rain again and we can stop at the cemetery," he joked. He had a thing about the Key West cemetery and needed to get over it.

Padre Thomas looked worried because no one had included him in the plans.

"What about Padre Thomas?" We were getting ready to leave.

"He stays put." It was a no-nonsense reply.

Padre Thomas understood and nodded slowly without smiling.

Alfonso took the front seat of a four-door, hardtop Jeep; I sat in the back as Norm spoke to a group of men on the sidewalk. Finally, he got in.

"We'll get lunch around two at El Siboney." He drove toward Truman Avenue and made a left when traffic allowed. The island had forgotten yesterday's storm and noon traffic had returned to normal.

Alfonso made calls to Mexico as Norm drove around in no special route I could determine. The ransom would stay at Tita's until delivered to the hotel, when Norm and I would take it to Mallory Pier. He ran the plan by me twice, making sure I understood what to do if gunfire broke out. If? I nodded, said I understood and wondered if he could tell I was lying.

We ate at El Siboney. Even at two in the afternoon, the restaurant was busy. I looked around for the other vehicles but didn't see them. It was a long, stressful afternoon with little conversation other than shoptalk. I'd been on operations with Norm before and had forgotten how focused he became. Back then it was impressive, now it was irritating.

After lunch we stopped at Higgs Beach. I saw two Jeeps drive by, but they kept going. Norm and I smoked cigars and walked to the White Street Pier. Alfonso stayed at the Jeep doing whatever he was supposed to. The humidity was high and the Kevlar vest made me sweat. Norm stopped to read the names on the AIDS Memorial mural at the foot of the pier.

The shallow water was calm and blue, the sky was clear and the sun hung high as it sloped toward its late-afternoon descent into the Gulf of Mexico, a little west of Mallory Square where we'd meet in a few hours.

"Do we have a tail?" I bit down on the cigar.

"Looks like Jerome kept his word so far." Norm tossed the stub of his cigar into the groundcover plants. "This might turn out all right."

"I hope so."

"When this is over, we'll talk and I can explain things to you." He looked out toward the horizon. "Maybe you'll understand."

"Understand what?"

"When it's over," he said and headed back to the Jeep.

Norm drove one more zigzag route through Old Town before we arrived outside the Custom House, a little after five. The museum had closed for the night and we parked in the back. A section of the hotel began at the museum's parking lot and went to the water. More Jeeps pulled in.

A small command center had been set up on the back deck of the historic building for this side of Mallory Square, and Norm talked to the men there before carrying the gym bag to me. He dropped it at my feet.

"You ready?" he said.

"I'd like to see the money again."

He stared at me with disbelief. "You've seen it once."

I knelt down and opened the bag. "Yeah, but all these bags look alike and I want to make sure this is the right one."

The bag was full of the shrink-wrapped packages of money. I dug in and took one from the middle. I used my pocketknife to cut the shrink-wrapping away and made sure there were no blank papers between the hundred-dollar bills. I did the same to two more packages.

"Satisfied?" Norm growled.

"You taught me to be careful, not trusting." I put the money back and zipped the bag closed.

"You still don't trust me?" He lifted the bag. "Maybe you

should carry this."

"Norm, right now the only person that hasn't lied to me is Jerome. How do you expect me to act?"

"I wouldn't do anything that would harm you or Tita."

"It's already been done, and for what? So you can grab some drug gunmen. Has it worked?" Ridicule filled the comments, my anxiety taking over. "How many people have to die before you're satisfied?"

"You'll never know." He dropped the bag on a golf cart.

We sat on the back and the driver took us through the tiny gathering of sunset watchers on the hotel's pier, across the footbridge to Mallory Square. We stopped at the small hut. Norm dropped the bag on the ground. He handed me a small earpiece so he could talk to me. I fitted it in place.

"Don't let your guard down," he said and got back on the golf cart. "And listen to me and we'll get you out safely."

I nodded and sat down on the gym bag. I looked around at the empty square and wondered how long a wait I had.

CHAPTER 80

"Tiny is leaving the hotel with two *gringos*," Alfonso's voice screeched in my ear. "Big guys, loose shirts."

I couldn't reply. Only on TV do they talk into hidden microphones. I wasn't supposed to give input, just follow orders; this wasn't a *Burn Notice* episode.

I wondered how big these men were, if they looked large next to Tiny. I sat on the gym bag with my back to the water and tried to keep the hotel entrances to the square in view.

"Which hotel?" I heard someone ask through the earpiece.

"Ocean Key," Alfonso answered.

I saw them. Tiny is a big man because he's wide. About five-ten and his weight had to be three hundred pounds or more. I would call him fat, but he didn't move like a fat man. Maybe he was on steroids. The *gringos* with him were six-something, lean and no doubt mean. Even from a distance I could see the bulk hidden under their shirts. I touched Pauly's Glock resting at my back and felt underdressed.

They stopped about fifty feet away and looked around the deserted square. Tiny smiled, a know-it-all grin. I stood up and smiled back. He walked forward. The *gringos* separated and walked on different sides of the pillars.

Tiny pointed to the gym bag. "If that's the five million, it has to be shrink-wrapped," he said with the strange grin.

"All but three bundles," I said. "I cut them open to make sure they were all hundreds."

"You had doubts?" He didn't move, keeping his distance and the grin.

"No trust among thieves."

"You're a thief?" He seemed surprised.

"One way or another we all are."

Tiny coughed a shallow laugh as if he'd swallowed something and it went down wrong and caught him by surprise. "Yes, I suppose you could look at it that way. May I?" He pointed to the bag again.

"You don't trust me?"

"No trust among thieves," he mimicked without the grin.

"Where's Tita?" I didn't move, but the *gringos* now held menacing-looking MAC 10s. Did the snipers have them in their scopes?

"If I brought Tita with me, your snipers could've eliminated us." He pointed toward the two men with him. "I didn't want to chance that."

"You made your point," I said as firmly as I could. "Where's Tita?" It was more a demand than a question.

"If the money is in the gym bag, she'll be here within ten minutes. You didn't really expect me to trust you, did you?" He walked to me. "May I?" He leaned down.

I took the Glock from my back. "Look, but don't be grabby."

Tiny glanced up as he unzipped the bag and grinned like the Cheshire cat again. He pushed aside the opened bundles, took one wrapped package from the center and cracked it open. He checked the bills. He put the money back and zipped the bag closed.

"It looks good." He stood up. From his pocket he took a cell phone and dialed. "Come in," he said and put the phone away. "You know, we're going to have a problem."

His words surprised me. "What problem?"

"Your DEA isn't the only one keeping watch over us." He

moved within a few feet of me. "I am sure Teodoro's men are somewhere out there. Five million is not much to the bosses, but to these men it will be extra payment and they get to kill us too, especially you."

"Sounds hopeless." I silently thanked Pauly for his insight.

"The DEA expect this?"

"I'm a pawn and Tiny, you're the knight. I know nothing of their plans."

"When I pick up the bag, they'll know it's the money and come for it."

"What are your plans?"

"First I want to tell you that Tita was not harmed. She was more a guest than a prisoner."

"If you say so."

"I say so." He looked puzzled at my slow reply. "And I'm to remind you that Jerome has kept his word and he expects you to keep yours."

"When I'm with Tita and no one is trying to kill me, the deal is done."

"When the money is out of here, the deal is done. We won't have much time." He looked toward the water. "You follow me to the seawall when I go."

"She's on a boat?"

"No, not in that storm. A boat would have been dangerous last night." He shook his head. "Seaplane. She'll need you to help her off the pontoon as the pilot takes the money." He looked toward the sunset and squinted. "He'll fly in with the sun at his back, so listen."

"What about you?"

"I'm here for the fight." He looked at my Glock. "You should be glad you won't need that."

"I'm leaving as soon as I have Tita. This isn't my battle any longer."

I heard the drone as the yellow single-engine plane came out of the sun and began its approach.

"Let him land and turn toward the seawall, then we'll go." Tiny pointed for the *gringos* to spread out a little more.

"How much time do you think we've got?"

"Depends on your snipers. If they can keep Teodoro's men away, shoot some of them, we've got a few minutes," he said matter-of-factly.

"There's a small army out there. They'll stop them."

"The local cops? They ready for grenades, automatic weapons? These guys are ruthless. That's why Jerome doesn't want this crossing the border. He's trying to help you and help himself."

"It's more than the cops. The DEA and JIATF have men out there too."

"Might give us a minute or two more." He turned to the water. "Ready?"

"Does it matter?"

Chapter 81

The thunderous explosion on Front Street drew our attention as we moved. A cloud of dirty smoke rose over the Waterfront Playhouse and the sculpture garden.

"What the hell was that?" I glanced around. Too many people spoke at once for the earpiece to be useful.

"If you had a surveillance van out there, my guess is they blew it up." He spoke calmly and hefted the gym bag onto his shoulders. He did not have a weapon. "Follow me."

Small arms fire and more explosions came from the street hidden by the peripheral buildings of the square. It seemed to go on for a long time and then two men appeared between the playhouse and public bathrooms. They were running and carrying M-16s. The *gringos* used the arch for cover and shot toward the runners to slow them down. They shot back but didn't stop moving.

Tiny went to the seawall as the plane taxied in on the water. He turned once to see what was going on and then returned his attention to the aircraft.

The plane rode high on the water and its wings cleared the seawall as it maneuvered into place with its prop spinning loudly. That's why Jerome needed this time, this place. Pauly was right. The seaplane's wings had to clear the seawall so it was close enough to get the money, and could only do it safely during high tide.

"I have a boat out there," I said to Tiny.

"DEA?" He turned to me as the pilot and Tita stepped onto a pontoon.

"No, the men are with me. The DEA didn't think you'd use the water. I did."

Tiny smiled and scanned the water. "Where are they?"

I couldn't take my eyes off Tita. She was dressed neatly in slacks and blouse and smiling. Her hair was in its normal ponytail. She was beautiful. The pilot helped her along the pontoon. He was a tall, thin man with long salt-and-pepper hair that tossed about in the wind from the propeller. They arrived together, no one else.

I waved my arms over my head like a wild man and hoped the two SEALs would respond. The pilot held onto Tita and turned so he could see the harbor.

"It's okay," Tiny yelled over the engine noise. "Take the money." He turned to me. "Help Tita."

I put the Glock in my waistband and reached for Tita. She gave me her hand and made the short jump to the seawall. The pilot took the heavy gym bag from Tiny without saying anything and carefully walked the pontoon. He tossed the money into the plane and climbed aboard. Tiny waved and the plane taxied out.

Gunfire still came from behind us. I hugged Tita and turned. Two gunmen lay dead outside the playhouse. They hadn't run far. Three more used the building as cover and fired toward the street. It was too far for a MAC 10 to be accurate, so the *gringos* watched the gunfight from the pillars.

I hugged Tita. "Are you okay?"

She hugged me back. "Yes. What is going on?"

An open speedboat raced from behind Christmas Tree Island toward the seawall. Two more explosions went off out on the street where the automatic gunfire continued without letup. Smoke rose above the buildings and the chatter in my earpiece spiked. I removed it and dropped it in the harbor. Sirens wailed in the background.

Everything seemed to be coming from the direction of Front Street, not the hotels. The snipers kept the gunmen pinned down at the playhouse, but a large tree kept the shooters out of the Westin sniper's kill vision. The shape of the building protected them from the Ocean Key sniper. The open square would be kill ground.

The speedboat pulled alongside the seawall. The haircut and the fact that they weren't shooting at me gave the two SEALs away.

"We have to go," I whispered in Tita's ear and pointed at the boat.

She looked confused, but nodded and one of the SEALs helped her aboard.

"Tiny," I yelled over the gunfire and boat's loud engine.

He was armed now. Where he'd gotten it, I have no idea. He turned.

"There's room," I called to him.

He laughed. "And miss the fun?"

"The snipers," I said. "I can't vouch for them, this is all out of my hands."

"Once you had Tita, they could've got us," he said. "Sometimes you gotta trust the thieves. Go. Get her out of here. We're all good, right?"

"Yeah. Thanks."

"See you at the bullfights." He laughed again and turned away.

I climbed into the boat and it sped off.

"Where to?" the driver asked.

"Garrison Bight." I pointed toward the Coast Guard base.

"I know the way," he said, gave the engine full throttle and called Pauly to tell him we were aboard. "Pauly said to tell you he and your friends are pulling back and will see you later."

CHAPTER 82

It had turned into a goat-fuck, a bloodbath on Front Street at the entrance to Mallory Square between the cartels and the law enforcement SWAT teams. The fighting had gone on inside the buildings as well as on the square, and included hand grenades and automatic weapons. The death toll rose for days as people died from their wounds at the trauma center in Miami. Those with minor injuries were treated in Key West and arrested if they were from the cartel. The good guys took losses, too.

For one sunset celebration, Mallory Square looked more like hell than paradise.

There was no mention of Tiny and the two *gringos,* so I assumed they walked away.

Homeland Security took over because of the foreigners involved and Richard lost whatever control he thought he had. He was able to clear the murders from the books when it all settled. Norm and Alfonso worked easily with the agency and kept Tita and me out of it. The *Key West Citizen,* Bill Becker, Bill Hoebee, the *Miami Herald* and Reuters reported only what Homeland Security gave out at its one press conference.

The official story was that members of two Mexican drug cartels were vacationing in the Keys at the same time and when they met they continued the war being fought in Mexico. All were killed or captured, they reported at the press conference.

Wednesday, Tita and I came in from a sail to nowhere and found Norm, Alfonso and Padre Thomas at the dock. We'd talked on the phone, but this was the first time I'd seen them since Friday.

I tossed Norm a line. He pulled the *Fenian Bastard* into her slip and tied off.

"Not much wind," he said and came aboard.

Alfonso and Padre Thomas joined us in the cockpit.

"Weren't going far." I handed out Mexican Bohemia beers to everyone.

"I promised you an explanation." He sat on the cabin roof.

"Yes, you did." I took a long swallow of beer.

"If you'd listened to me and stayed on the square, you would've been okay, the both of you." He drank from the beer.

"I did what I had to do."

Norm looked at Alfonso and he nodded. They both looked at Padre Thomas.

"Padre, think of this as a confession. You can never repeat what you're told," Norm said and waited for a reply.

"A little unusual," he said. "But these days call for rule adjustments and the unusual, so if you'll indulge me, I agree."

Padre Thomas mumbled the words that went along with confession and then nodded as a sign to begin.

"I didn't steal the twenty million," Norm began. But the Mexican and American DEA knew the cartel had been ripped off and never recovered the money. They also knew the cartel would not miss a chance to get the money back or punish those that stole it.

They worked out the plan in advance and only needed the opportunity to implement it. The DEA's money was chemically marked and would be traceable when spent, so they needed to get it into the cartel's hands.

"We need to know where the money's being spent, on what and by whom," Norm explained. "If they got some of the twenty million back, it was likely they'd use it for payoffs."

The DEA placed the money in a Bahamian bank with Norm's help and the bank's cooperation, and let it sit there. When the car wash hit went down, they saw a chance to put their plan in motion and had the bank back-date the deposit but forgot the interest payments. Tiny was on their payroll and knew he could get Jerome to involve the TJ cartel.

"How'd you get Tiny?" I asked.

Norm grinned. "Working with us beats twenty-five to life for manslaughter. It wasn't a difficult choice."

Tiny and DEA agents faked Tita's kidnapping and took her to Cuba using an old smuggler named Crazy Paul. He was a whiz with seaplanes, a legend among smugglers and trusted by the cartel. He worked for Tiny and never knew he was a pawn. I wondered if he was Pauly's friend too, but didn't ask.

"What about Jenny?" I needed to know.

"She's with the cartel in TJ," Alfonso said. "They understand greed and believe they have bought her loyalty. They will use her for her knowledge of DEA operations, but she's a double agent and we will get her out as soon as we can."

Why didn't I believe him? She'd probably be killed first. That was the life of a double agent, the life she chose.

"Very brave and dedicated," Tita added.

Crazy Paul flew the money to New Orleans. Once Jerome was satisfied all the money was there, he moved it to Tijuana and the hit on me was called off.

"Tiny and the two men with him were for your protection," Norm said. "We never expected the cartel's men to make it across the square. I thought you'd pick up on that when he mentioned the shrink-wrapped money. How would he know how it was wrapped if I hadn't told him?"

His words surprised me. "I had my own plans."

"Tell me about them. Who helped you?" Norm said.

"Can you keep a secret?"

"Yeah, sure I can."

"So can I," I teased.

"Now we sit and wait," Alfonso said, so we'd get back to the real discussion. "We expect it to show up in the accounts of officials on both sides of the border and it will help us stop the bribery and corruption. Once we can stop it, the drug war will be on its last legs."

No one had a corner on corruption and it took dishonesty to make the cartels successful. I didn't believe catching a few devious officials on either side of the border would do much.

"What about Woodrow? Why?" I asked.

"One innocent person," Alfonso said. "How innocent was he, really? He used drugs and he consorted with drug dealers. He put himself in a position to be a victim. We couldn't protect him."

I didn't agree with Norm or Alfonso. It seemed that there were many arguments defending what they did and why they did it. The end justifies the means. Maybe that's what it takes to fight the drug war. I don't know. But I didn't like them bringing their war to my island or the toll it took on the residents and businesses.

I don't like the selling of drugs either, but if there wasn't a demand, there wouldn't be a need. Capitalism at its purest.

Tita sat close to me. I felt her warmth from being in the sun, and I was glad she was there. She wanted to sail to Cuba now that she'd had a small taste of the forbidden island and its people, and that was exciting.

I listened to Norm and Alfonso go on about the drug war and tried to remember our adventures in Mexico. That was a long time ago, but it held better memories than their time in Key West.

When they were done, we agreed to dinner the next night. They still had paperwork and people to report to, and Padre

Thomas silently gave us absolution.

Tita and I were alone to watch the sunset from the stern of the *Fenian Bastard.*

"Norm did protect us like he promised," she said.

"He didn't tell me the truth. He could have."

"If you'd known the truth, you wouldn't have been as worried about me and he needed that." She kissed me hard. "Jenny told me that. They need to make you angry to be believable and if you knew it was a setup, you couldn't pull it off."

"It's good to know he has faith in me," I griped.

She pushed back and stared at me. "How did you know about the seaplane?"

"I didn't at first, but something Pauly said about living on an island and everyone looking at the land got me to thinking," I said. "I figured Norm kept me preoccupied with your safety and everyone away from the water. He needed the money to go. I don't think even Jim Ashe knew the real plan or its purpose."

"But you figured it out."

"With help and a lot of luck."

"Norm kept his word because you're his friend. It's what he does, who he is."

"Yeah, he's my friend, but I can't trust him."

We both laughed and hugged as the sun set over the Navy housing. It wasn't as pretty as watching the sunset from Mallory Square, but it was private and we needed that.

"You're lucky to have the friends you do," Tita said after the sunset.

"Padre Thomas said he wished he had Norm's and my luck," I told her. "I need to appreciate my luck more. Norm's lie made me realize how much you mean to me."

Tita pushed away again. She was smiling. "I like knowing you were worried about me. Kind of romantic. Norm told me that if you were let in on what was happening, you wouldn't have been as anxious."

"Well, it worked," I said, and hugged her. "I missed all the signs of what was really happening because of my concern for you. Don't let it happen again," I pouted and then smiled.

She hugged and kissed me. "All I want to be is part of your life, a special friend." She laughed. *"Te amo."*

ABOUT THE AUTHOR

Michael Haskins lives in Key West, Florida. He has been the business editor/writer for the daily *Key West Citizen* and the public information officer for the city. He now freelances for Reuters News Service and the biweekly *Keynoter* newspaper. He has continued his Mick Murphy series in a few short stories that have appeared in *Ellery Queen Mystery Magazine* and the *Saturday Evening Post.* He has finished the fourth book in his series, *Stairway to the Bottom,* and is waiting out the end of hurricane season. He has lived in Boston, San Juan, Puerto Rico, Los Angeles and occasionally in Tijuana, Mexico, before moving to Key West more than fifteen years ago.

Find out more about Michael Haskins by going to his website: www.michaelhaskins.net.